JAMES HIDER

RIPE

Black Rose Writing | Texas

The author grants the final approval for this literary material.

First printing

This is a work of fiction. Names, characters, businesses, places, events, and incidents are either the products of the author's imagination or used in a fictitious manner. Any resemblance to actual persons, living or dead, or actual events is purely coincidental.

ISBN: 978-1-68513-199-9 (Paperback); 978-1-68513-557-7 (Hardcover)
PUBLISHED BY BLACK ROSE WRITING
www.blackrosewriting.com

Printed in the United States of America
Suggested Retail Price (SRP) $22.95 (Paperback); $27.95 (Hardcover)

Ripe is printed in Calluna

*As a planet-friendly publisher, Black Rose Writing does its best to eliminate unnecessary waste to reduce paper usage and energy costs, while never compromising the reading experience. As a result, the final word count vs. page count may not meet common expectations.

RIPE

PART I

Everyone remembers exactly where they were, the day the ships came.

What no one knew back then, though, was that there were people who were already expecting them.

They just appeared out of the low clouds over Moscow. Four vast, factory-like gray blocks solidifying out of the colder gray of the Russian sky. Rush hour, which, as the instantly self-appointed experts on the "harvest" noted, was no coincidence: the giant ships cruised up and down the city's broad grid locked boulevards, nozzles dangling from their underbellies and siphoning up cars, pedestrians, stray dogs, whatever wasn't bolted to the ground.

It lasted two whole hours until the streets of Moscow were neutron-bomb empty.

Then the ships disappeared whence they came, into the clouds and off the radar, leaking empty, ripped-open Ladas and Volkswagens like a car tornado, scattering the metal husks as far as Berlin and Kyiv.

Weeks later, cars were still dropping to Earth as far away as Indonesia and the Marshall Islands: not because the mysterious ships had passed that way, but because they had clearly continued to dump them as they passed through the Earth's orbit, sending their detritus spinning off round the globe, burning up as auto-meteors.

In the hushed aftermath, no one knew what had happened, even though it was as plain as the nose on your face.

News anchors were rendered mute. Russian, Chinese and NATO nuclear defenses were placed on the highest security alert. Frantic phone calls raced between allies and foes. The pilot of one of the Russian Sukhois dispatched to destroy the invaders appeared on the news, blank face turned to the camera, describing how his missiles had been "as useless as a chicken pecking at a farmer's legs." He appeared to have no idea just how apt his metaphor was. Though maybe he knew. Maybe everyone knew, deep down, even then. They just couldn't bring themselves to say it.

The post-mortem began immediately. Dash-cams with the last screams of terrified Russian commuters were gathered, their kaleidoscopic footage forensically examined for clues as to what happened inside the ships. But the film always cut off at the exact moment the cars entered the nozzle, leaving scientists to pore over the static, examine traces of hair, skin and blood caught on broken windshields and buckled doors.

And they quickly came to the same, inevitable conclusion: none of the Russians were coming back.

• | •

Elspeth McGann certainly remembered where she was that morning.

Twelve minutes past nine in the morning, Moscow time, was 6:12 am in Edinburgh. Elspeth had just got out of bed in Morningside and was making a cup of Lady Grey before her morning run when she heard the unbelievable news on the radio.

Her first reaction was standard: she walked straight over the television and turned it on. Seeing is believing. The first blurry footage of cars disappearing into the whirlwind of snow and smashed glass over the Russian capital confirmed that what she had just heard was not an unusual prank by the normally sober Radio 4 news team.

Her next thought was far from standard, however.

Lester Rains.

An odd name, she'd always thought, and an even stranger man. If a man was indeed what he was. Rains had always denied it, right from the first time he had come to her practice in mid-May, six months before.

Rains was handsome, in an understated, rather old-fashioned way. Like a matinee movie idol from some bygone era. Clipped and clean, exact age difficult to pin down. He looked young-ish, but there was a slightly weary edge to him. That in itself was nothing unusual. As one of the Scottish capital's leading psychiatrists, Elspeth was used to people seeming to carry some inner burden.

Rains had sat in her office, one leg casually draped over the other.

"The way I usually like to work, Mr. Rains, is to have a little chat to get to know something about your background. And then we can look at specific areas of interest together," she said as they sipped the tea her receptionist Anya had brought in.

Rains hitched up the leg of his tailored suit—herringbone tweed, like the man himself, slightly old-fashioned but undeniably smart. He nodded and smiled.

"I think you'll find, Ms. McGann, that a little background chat may not be quite up to the task. I know, I know," he said, raising a hand as she smiled knowingly—"you have dealt with all sorts of psychological trauma. Disaster survivors, PTSD, refugees and victims of torture. Believe me, it's one of the reasons I sought you out. But I have a small request at the outset: one that you might find a little awkward, professionally speaking."

Elspeth smiled again, a warm but professionally non-committal smile. "What would that be, Mr. Rains?"

"Please, call me Lester," he said. He put down his china cup on its saucer. "It is that you might try to defer any professional judgment on my case until I have finished my story. Which may, given its length and complexity, take several visits."

Elspeth nodded, folding her hands in her lap. "I can certainly withhold any clinical diagnosis, if that's what you mean, Lester. Obviously, potential diagnoses may spring up, unbidden. In any case, I never jump to hasty conclusions."

"Hasty conclusions," Rains smiled to himself. "Oh, I think hasty conclusions will be presenting themselves thick and fast, Elspeth. May I call you by your first name?"

She nodded. Something about his demeanor intrigued her: not his slightly Latin looks, which in Scotland may just denote Pictish ancestry, or his confident, relaxed manner, so rare for a first-time visitor to a psychiatrist's practice. It was more the sense of anticipation that he inspired, as though in fact she were sitting down not to diagnose an illness but to be drawn in by something she couldn't quite guess at yet.

"Of course, Lester. Well, in that case, I'd suggest we start at the beginning."

He sat still for a long moment, as though considering where to begin.

"I was born—if born is the right word—in southern France in the year 432. I was the seventeenth of my kind to be born into a human body, though I am not human. Not quite, anyway."

He stared at Elspeth, whose face registered no expression other than polite and studied neutrality.

"I know what you're thinking already," Rains said. "Species dysphoria, zoanthropy perhaps, maybe even Cotard's Syndrome. As I said, hold that thought for now. A diagnosis is not after all what I am after, even though I know you won't be able to resist."

"Please, go on."

"I didn't know at first what I was. But I knew I was somehow different: I was smarter than anyone else I knew, quicker to assimilate ideas and pick up languages. That's because of the Code. The Code is what made me *me,* what I am: what makes all twenty-three of us what we are. It's also what is probably going to cause our mini species to face extinction, around the same time that your own species will be almost entirely obliterated."

"My own species?" said Elspeth mildly. "You mean ... humans?"

"Precisely. You see, we are the Farmers. We were an experiment in non-automated consciousness—and an extremely successful one, I might add—by a machine created by a long-extinct civilization. From a very far distant planetary system."

"You're talking about extraterrestrial life?"

Rains smiled, as though asking her to indulge him. "Not exactly life as you would understand it, Elspeth. But yes. *Aliens.*"

He was still smiling, not like a madman but almost apologetically. "I know what you're thinking now. 'Advanced schizophrenic delusions' 'Potentially dangerous, possibly to society, more likely to himself.' 'Section him?'"

Elspeth unexpectedly found herself shaking her head and pursing her lips, denying his assertion, because that was *precisely* what she had been thinking.

"It's alright," Rains said. "As you can see, I have studied human psychology at no small length myself. Part of my job too. And that is why I asked you to suspend, temporarily, any judgment. Perhaps it was unfair of me to do so."

"Please go on with your story, Lester," she said, aware that he had been effortlessly taking the lead on the conversation, both her side and his. She had to reassert control.

"Of course," he said, once again playing the deferential patient. "I was born, as it were, in the city of Arles, in what was then the Roman province of Gallia Narnonensis, and which is now more commonly known as the Camargue region of southern France. You may know it for its wild horses and marshlands.

"My task, though I did not know it then, was to monitor the health and expansion of the human species in my allotted area—roughly what is now western Europe—and to pay particular attention to their mental development, such as it was. My given name was Lucius Margalis Barbegal. I was, by design, born the eldest son of a wealthy and ancient Ligurian family. All this was arranged by Farmer Sixteen, whose area of responsibility was the then more wealthy region of the Balkans. Gaul was still a bit of a backwater at the time, and the center of power in the Roman Empire had shifted east, toward Constantine's capital. As the human population expanded, more farmers were needed to monitor stocks in new growth areas. I, in turn, arranged the inception of Farmer 18 into northern Germanic tribes beyond the Rhine two hundred years later. The Goths proved to be quite an exceptional growth area, as it turned out."

Elspeth nodded. "And what was... what was the purpose of your monitoring? And when you say 'stocks,' you're talking about human populations, am I right?"

Rains had an unnerving stare. Not hostile, but deeply scrutinizing. Was he, she wondered, looking for gaps in her defenses, weaknesses he could exploit and adapt to his own narrative? She had experienced threatening patients before, both overtly and subtly, and of course defensive ones by the dozen, but none quite like this. He appeared to be measuring, precisely, how his words were registering in her own mind, and she found it difficult to circumvent this scrutiny.

"I know it sounds harsh, Elspeth. Clinical. And what I am about to tell you will sound downright psychotic. You see, Farmer One has been on Planet Earth for almost one hundred thousand years. He and Farmer Two were originally implanted into the bodies of Anatomically Modern Humans—or what your layperson might term cavemen."

"I am familiar with the term..." Elspeth said, bristling. Was she dealing with a simple, straight-up fantasist?

"Of course," said Rains. "My apologies. This is part of the reason I wanted to talk to you. Because you have such a firm grasp of the background facts I will be talking about. Such as the Cognitive Revolution."

It was a clear hand-off, of course, and Elspeth couldn't escape the feeling she was being tested. A very simple test, given her background. Rains must have familiarized himself with her work, had almost certainly read the various books and papers she had published over the course of her career.

"The Cognitive Revolution, yes," she said. Okay, if he could casually condescend, she could play along. "Around 70,000 years ago, a random genetic mutation in our ancestors' prefrontal cortex led to the sudden explosion of consciousness among early humans: the evolution of the "self." They quickly developed a whole panoply of social and mechanical skills, such as taming fire, tool building and animist religions that allowed them to live in larger communities, dominate their environment, and wipe out the five other known human species believed to have existed on the planet at the same time."

Rains nodded, as though in approval.

"Not random," he said.

"You mean the genetic changes?" Elspeth said.

"Not random at all. The work of Farmers One and Two."

Elspeth said nothing, waiting for Rains to go on. He obliged. "The aim, and the subtlety of their work, was to create something that could conceivably be part of an evolutionary process that appears to be both random and yet highly selective at the same time. Their task was to create a viable, advanced consciousness without a clumsy 'guiding hand.' To create something as close to organic consciousness as possible. Evolution itself was throwing up only low-levels of functional consciousness, useless to the purpose of the primary command."

"And what was this 'primary command?'" she said, indulging him briefly to see where it might take them.

"It was the command for a machine—an artificial superintelligence — to always protect the species that created it. But it failed. The species—who called themselves the Goweetha—died out. So the machine re-interpreted the command and decided it had to resurrect its extinct masters. But a machine cannot create organic consciousness. It cannot even understand it fully, with all its irrationalities and instincts and emotional riddles. So instead it decided it had to grow it, and not interfere with it. Until the time came to harvest it."

"And you're suggesting that time is now at hand?" said Elspeth.

"Yes," said Rains. "All the Farmers have been given orders to prepare for the imminent arrival of the Ma'ut."

"The... *mowt?*" she said.

He nodded. "That is the name of the artificial superintelligence." He smiled. "Originally, it just meant the I.T. department."

It was time, Elspeth decided, to reassert some professional control over this interaction. Despite her promise not to diagnose her new patient on his first visit, any number of conditions were presenting themselves to her. She needed to steer him away from his delusional narrative and back to the realm of why he had come to visit her.

"You've clearly given the subject extensive thought, Lester, but let me ask you..."

"I've had plenty of time to think about it, of course. But you want to ask specifically why I came to see you today."

Again, his successful pre-emption of her next question left her on the back foot, a feeling she was not accustomed to.

"It is because, as I said, time is finally running out, for all of us. For humans and for the Farmers."

There was a gentle knock at the door. It shook Elspeth out of the strange conversation that she had allowed to slip away from her. She looked at her watch. More than forty minutes had passed without her noticing.

Her assistant Mary stepped into the room.

"I'm sorry, Elspeth, but Mrs. Clairy's here?"

"Oh... of course. Sorry. Tell her I'm just finishing up. Mr. Rains... Lester, I'm sorry. We'll have to leave it there for now. Will you come back next week?"

Rains shook her hand, smiling and urbane again after the strangely intense tone of his narrative.

"Of course. And thank you for listening. Because I know none of what I've said has registered as the truth in your mind. If you had believed me, I would never have presumed to have told you. That would mean, by force of logic, that you too were insane, or deeply gullible. Neither of which would be of any use to me. But I can at least tell you, and perhaps it will play some useful role when the time comes. Until next week, then."

• | •

All that week, Elspeth couldn't stop herself from thinking about Lester Rains. She went over the case notes, compared his testimony with notable historical records, even contacted her old professor at Cambridge, who had supervised her post-grad studies and had been an expert in delusional states. He had initially suggested a variation of Cotards—a condition in which a patient sincerely believes themselves to be dead—or an unusual variant of Alien Hand Syndrome, when a patient's limb appears to belong to another being and can sometimes attack its owner. Elspeth, sitting in front of her laptop, had tried not to smile at that one—she remembered Rain's rueful use of the word 'alien.'

Cyclothymia, perhaps? *Capgras delusion?* Impossible to tell after just one meeting. And what had he meant, *"When the time comes"*?

She googled him to see what residue of his life had been left online. A few profiles popped up on various social network sites.

There was a dentist of the same name in Adelaide, Australia, and a young male model in Idaho. A farmer from West Sussex, deceased 1898. It was only when she considered these far-flung namesakes that she realized she could not recall what accent her patient had spoken in. Not Scottish, but what had it actually been? She made a mental note to jot it down when she next saw him.

He was, in short, an enigma. A small shiver of excitement ran down Elspeth's spine: it had been a long time since she had faced a case as challenging as this. Not that her other patients weren't challenging, but the diagnostics were usually fairly clear, the path ahead mapped out by experience and established practice.

Not Rains though: the more she pondered the case, the clearer it became that he was a vanishingly rare example not just of a deep delusional personality who rejected his own connection with the human race, but one who had latched on to a professional psychologist's own particular sphere of study, and had mastered some of the more salient points in an attempt to ingratiate himself. Elspeth's own doctorate had been in evolutionary psychology, and much of what he had thrown at her in their first encounter could have easily been cribbed straight from her own published works.

That flagged a narcissistic strain of sociopathy.

Which also meant Rains had the potential to be highly dangerous.

So it was that the following Thursday morning, Elspeth sat politely, yet a little distractedly, through her first three consultations and found herself looking forward to her two o'clock with the mysterious Mr. Rains. She even found herself worrying that he might not show up, having exhibited such advanced delusions. After her last appointment left, she stepped in front of the mirror and flattened down her bobbed dark hair, pushing back the one strand of gray at her temple. Looking good, she thought, for a woman pushing forty. Trim and athletic, her face still chiseled rather than gaunt.

She stopped herself: this was a consultation, not a date.

By the time her receptionist knocked on the door, Elspeth was pacing the room in anticipation.

Rains entered, seemingly a different man. The smiling, languid demeanor was gone, and he sat stiffly in the chair as Elspeth greeted him.

"I'm afraid I don't have very much time," Rain said. "Neither do you."

Paranoia, Elspeth noted to herself. *Mood swing?* This was good, from a diagnostic point of view at least. Rains peered out the window, as though distracted. She needed to hold his attention, make him relax.

"You have an oddly English accent for a Frenchman," she said with a small smile.

He did not take the bait.

"I'll be leaving very soon. You will not see me again. Take this small piece of advice, offered in the sincere spirit of..." he searched for the correct phrase. "In the spirit of ancestry."

Elspeth cocked her head, trying to think of a suitable comeback to this strange remark, but Rains went straight on.

"I knew your great-great grandmother. Eileen Hardy. Out of respect for her memory, I want to offer you some advice. When the ships come, don't get on them. Ignore the siren song. They'll say they're here to help you, but they're not. Go. This place won't be safe. Get to Hawaii. It will be a designated safe space. Do not linger in any large city once the harvest begins. Take as much of the essentials as you can carry: antibiotics. Toothpaste. First aid kits. Dental floss. Enough to last a very long time. There is no way of knowing if you will ever come back here. Start your preparations now."

Elspeth wasn't quite sure what to say. "Mr. Rains, I think we need to slow things down a little..."

"No Elspeth. There's no time..."

"You appear agitated, Lester..."

Rains stood up, as if to go. Elspeth, though she was smaller and more slender than him, stepped in front of the door. *"Is he dangerous?"* flashed through her mind again.

He paused. Took a breath. "It really doesn't matter, of course. Though you do look a lot like her."

"Like who"

He was silent.

"Like my... great grandmother?"

"Great-*great* grandmother."

"And you say you knew her, Lester?"

"Slightly more than that, Elspeth. But as I said, time is short and there's much to do. I feel I've done my duty by her. So remember, when they come, don't trust them. Don't believe for one second that they are here to help you."

"Okay Lester," Elspeth said. "Okay. I hear you. But I am here to help *you*. Do you understand me?"

He did not seem unduly agitated, Elspeth noted, even though his words seemed to indicate a highly troubled mind. She clasped her hands together in imprecation. "Would you mind just sitting down for a few minutes, Lester? So we can talk. We're quite alone here."

Rains stared at her for a second, then turned back to the window. He lifted the blind and looked out at the sandstone buildings that caught the morning sun. Then he turned and sat down.

"Five minutes," he said.

"Alright then. Tell me, Lester, do you ever suffer from periods when you find it difficult to concentrate, make decisions, or suffer from apathy or melancholia?"

Rains took a breath. "There was, of course, a certain disorientation back at the beginning. It is not easy knowing that you are a parasitic hybrid, and that you could be destroyed at a moment's notice if the creatures around you, whom you are tasked with observing, become suspicious of the differences. I'd say it leads to a certain natural reserve. Certainly, if they had known what I was, they would have killed me on the spot. They killed Farmer Twelves. Ripped her to pieces."

Elspeth glanced at the notebook, in which she had jotted snippets recollected from their first encounter. Rains was consistent at least. Well, she could play along for a while.

"You mentioned last time that the first "farmers" had been around for 100,000 years. How did they adapt, to avoid being marked out and destroyed?"

He nodded, reluctantly appreciative of the game she was playing. "As you know, Anatomically Modern Humans were just that—they looked very much like you, even if they didn't yet think quite like you. Shave one of those cavemen, put him in a suit, and you could walk past him on Princes Street and not bat an eyelid. We're not talking about Neanderthals, as you know. And we have methods of generational adaptation, to evolve along with the subject species. A bit like bugs."

He did not elaborate.

"Uh ... Do any of your fellow farmers feel the need to visit human psycho-analysts?" Elspeth said.

Rains took a deep breath. "Not that I know of. We have all lived in extreme isolation over long periods of time. But we are adapted to the task, though it might still exert some strange effects on the psyche. Most of the time, we sleep through it. Humans aren't that interesting when it comes down to it, even the most famous ones. Shakespeare was a crashing bore to talk to. But when there are only twenty-five of you, and you are destined to live in solitude from each other, it is difficult to establish a norm.

"So," Rains took a deep breath. "Farmer Three abducts and dissects human subjects on a regular basis. He says it's in the name of scientific research, but he carries his experiments out with such regularity and gusto that I would happily qualify him as a serial killer, if such a term could even be applied to creatures such as ourselves. Also, he has lived in the Middle East for four and a half thousand years, so he has had plenty of opportunity to practise his art of butchery unmolested.

"Farmer Nineteen appears to have gone to the other extreme and spends an unwarranted amount of time in sexual congress with human specimens. I mean, I believe all of us do to a certain extent, but Nineteen has, to use a human phrase, 'gone native.' He also imbibes most of their available chemical substances, from ayahuasca to stuff he cooks up himself and occasionally shares with favored human subjects. Not all of them survive the mind-expanding experience."

Elspeth nodded, furiously scribbling notes, which seemed to amuse Rains.

"Let me take a wild guess," he said. "The word 'cult' is somewhere on the page by now?"

She said nothing. But they both knew he was right.

"In defense of Farmer Three, we were engineered to survive off the livestock we were sent to supervise, the way a herder in more ancient times lived off their cattle."

Elspeth looked up slowly from her notebook. Rains' face was inscrutable.

Anthropophagy, she scrawled on the page. *Vampire delusion? Broadened definition of lycanthropy?*

"You mentioned some kind of 'code' last time, Lester. You said it sets you and the others apart. What did you mean by that?"

"The Code," Rains said. "It is indeed what sets us apart. It is essentially the raw data of the Ma'ut, the super A.I. that I told you about during our last meeting. Farmer One is almost pure code, more machine than man. The code gives him what ordinary humans might consider superpowers..."

"Superpowers?" Elspeth interjected, trying to keep any hint of skepticism out of her voice.

Rains did not smile. "Farmer One has the power to put quite a large number of people in his thrall. Hypnotized, in effect. And the code is what gives him the knowledge to create more Farmers. But each successive Farmer has a little less code in them, to enable us to more easily move among humans and observe them."

When discussing the case with her former Cambridge professor, Elspeth had decided she should not indulge his elaborate fantasies – he was clearly a narcissist who enjoyed drawing his esteemed listener into his own private world, where he was the authority, the guide, the power broker. Instead, she had decided to focus on a pursuit of his symptoms, his relationship to the real world. But there was just something about Lester Rains—something more than just the charisma of the assured psychopath — that led her deeper into his absurd fantasy world.

"And can you do that, put people in your thrall?" she said.

"Only limited numbers at any given time. We have used our skills to recruit certain world leaders, those we can manipulate to work for us during the harvest."

Elspeth stared at her page, then looked up at Rains. He was staring at her, no hint of a smile on his face despite the absurdity of what he had just said. For the first time since she had been in training, she was not sure how to proceed.

"Mr. Rains..."

"Lester."

"Is that your real name?"

"Define 'real.' It's the name on my British passport. On the deeds to my estate in Fife. But my inception name, as I told you, was Lucius Margalis Barbegal."

Persistent, Elspeth wrote on the page of her notepad.

"What would you say if I said I believed you?" she said.

"I'd say you were lying."

"Can I ask, what was the purpose of you coming here?"

For the first time, he paused before answering. His eyes stared straight into hers—a method Elspeth knew was designed to convince the listener of the truth of what they were being told.

"Like I said, I came here to honor a very old promise. To warn all your great-great grandmother's descendants when the time comes. And so, I repeat to you: you need to go to Hawaii. It is the only place you will be safe."

In a defensive reflex, she leafed through her notes.

"Lester, I'm going to need you to take a few simple tests..."

Rains stood up.

"Time's up I'm afraid."

He put his hand in his pocket. Elspeth tensed, in spite of herself, not knowing what he was reaching for. But he merely produced a slim wallet made of expensive leather. He opened it and produced a visiting card.

"You won't find me on Google," he said, laying it flat on the small table beside her notepad. "Here's my card."

"You'll be back next week?" she said. She realized with surprise there was a needful tone in her voice.

"I'm afraid not," Rains said. He was at the door. "Good day, doctor," he said, turning the handle. "And good luck. Remember what I told you. Don't heed the siren song."

And with that, he stepped out into the waiting room and was gone.

Elspeth waited a minute, at a loss. Then she stepped out into the waiting room. Anya, her receptionist, was talking on the phone. She paused, her hand over the mouthpiece.

"Did Mr. Rains... make an appointment?"

"No," said Anya. "He didn't really check out at all. Just left."

Elspeth nodded, then went back into her office where she stood in silence for a minute, her hand on the doorknob. Then she turned and walked as fast as she could out past her puzzled receptionist to the door. The corridor was empty. She listened for footsteps on the carpeted stairs, but heard none. Rains was gone.

In her pocket, she felt the card he had given her. She fished it out and looked at it.

He wants me to come to him, she thought.

Back in her office, Elspeth checked the address on Google maps. It showed up as a pin drop just outside the village of Cullochan, around an hour and a half drive north of Edinburgh. Elspeth didn't own a car, and it was too out of the way to get to on public transport. She opened her laptop and searched for car rentals.

• | •

The following Saturday morning, shortly after nine, Elspeth walked into the cramped lot of the Alamo car rentals on Annandale street in the city center and picked up the tiny Fiat Smart Car she had reserved for the day. *Fiat fricking Clowncar,* she muttered to herself as she squeezed behind the wheel and adjusted the driver's seat as far back as it would go. The lever under the seat was stiff, and she was annoyed to find her knees still touched the steering column.

The morning was classic Scots gray, a tinplate sky bolted to the heavens, as Elspeth plugged the address written on Rains' card into her GPS. A light drizzle fuzzed the windscreen as she headed north out of the city. There was always a slight thrill that ran through her as she drove across the vast iron bridge spanning the Firth of Forth, whose waters far below had consumed at least one of her suicidal clients.

She was soon on the rugged moors of Fife, following a river valley lined with enormous boulders and thin spruce, wondering, for the millionth time, if she was making a grave professional error. Wondering if Lester Rains—who was clearly suffering some form of delusional schizophrenia — was just a man reaching out for help, or a manipulative psychopath trying to lure her into a trap.

And why did she need to see him so badly? Did she really need to help, or did she just want to claim this rare, fascinating case for herself, another feather in her professional cap? There was no denying that the prospect of publishing his case in *The British Journal of Psychiatry* or *The Lancet* was extremely satisfying at this stage in her career, though she was unconvinced it would be enough to justify the highly unprofessional step she was taking by going to a patient's home unannounced.

Either way, she had told two of her close friends where she was headed and why. She had even gone so far as telling her ex-husband, Robbie, who was a senior civil servant at the Home Office and would know how to proceed if she vanished. He had urged her not to go: in the end, though, the fact that they were no longer married allowed her to ignore his advice. If she failed to check in by seven in the evening, the police should be alerted. Elspeth made sure her phone was fully charged, though she noted with concern that the signal dropped from time to time in some of the more precipitous valleys.

She arrived in Cullochan shortly before eleven. It was a small village of pebble-dash cottages the color of porridge, a post office, a one-pump petrol station and a mini-market offering discounts on bulk orders of lager. It stood in the dip of a valley, and low clouds shrouded the nearby hills like damp cotton wool. Elspeth glanced at her phone and was relieved to see there were still two bars on it.

The GPS led her down the main road for a mile or so, out of the village, and then off up a single-lane country track that wound among the pines. She kept an eye on the odometer: after precisely a mile and a half, she saw whitewashed gate posts. One of them had black metal letters spelling out 'Cullochan Manor.' The gates were open, despite a sign that read: *Trespassers will be prosecuted.* But then Elspeth wasn't technically a trespasser—she had the owner's visiting card on the dash of her rental.

The car bumped down a winding track into a wooded valley, axle grinding on outcrops of rock. There, among the trees, stood the manor house: either an eighteenth-century stone building that had been whitewashed, or a nineteenth century imitation. Plain and sturdy against the elements, in the style of so many Scottish country homes. A small, conical turret rose out the front of the slate roof. Elspeth pulled up in front of the door. She could hear the fast-running water of a nearby stream. The curtains of the house were drawn back and she could see no lights in the dark interior. In fact, there appeared to be no sign of life whatsoever.

The doorbell clanged somewhere deep inside the house. A minute went by and there was no answer. Had Rains done some harm to himself and led her here to find his body? He had seemed so self-assured on that first visit, yet the second time it was evident that his was a mind in distress.

The name Eileen Hardy jumped into her mind, unbidden. Rains had said he had known Elspeth's great-great grandmother. Elspeth had never heard the name before: she wasn't one of those amateur genealogists who are constantly hunting down their ancestors on the web. Nevertheless, she had signed up to an online site that traced heritage and a quick search had revealed that yes, indeed, her great-great grandmother was a woman of that name, from the fishing village of Oban on the west coast.

Nothing remarkable about that: Rains could easily have joined the same site and made the connection.

But why would he? Was she ringing the bell of a stalker?

Elspeth peered through the window of the hallway. Empty, aside from an umbrella stand and old-fashioned mahogany bootjack. She stepped over to the window of the living room. Through rain-streaked glass she saw furniture in keeping with the dour highland style: a rather uncomfortable looking upright sofa, two armchairs and a polished wooden dining table at the far end. The bookshelves were lined with books that appeared to be old: she could not see a single paperback among the leather spines.

She walked around the house. There was a small kitchen garden at the back, with weed-clogged rows of vegetables and thistles growing between the tomato canes. What she had thought to be the sound of a stream turned out to be the hum and buzz of twenty or so white painted beehives set back from the house, just where the woods started. The recent weeks of unseasonally hot weather must have tricked the insects into activity. Elspeth stood and stared a moment: she suddenly realized she hadn't seen more than one or two bees at a time in years. She remembered when she was a girl the parks and her childhood garden had been full of them, but climate change, pesticides and disease had decimated their numbers. Usually she just saw flies on the flowers these days. There never seemed to be any shortage of *them.*

She watched as the honeybees slowly circled and landed on their hives, dancing out their directions to distant fields of heather or gorse. She smiled, momentarily forgetting why she was there, then turned back to the task at hand.

Peering through the kitchen window, Elspeth noted that the room was well appointed, in an old-fashioned way, with a heavy wooden table and a cast-iron stove that appeared to date from at least the 1940s.

Back round the front of the house, she looked again at Rains' business card. There was no telephone number, which is why she had not phoned. No other information besides the address.

At a loss, she rang again. She tried the front door. Locked, of course. On a whim, she went round to the back again and tried the kitchen door. It opened.

She stepped in.

"Hullo?" she called out. "Mr. Rains? Lester?"

No answer.

"It's Elspeth. Dr. McGann? Uh, anybody home?"

It was clear no one was there. The place felt cold and empty. She wondered when Rains had last been there himself. There were no dishes on the sink counter. Through the kitchen doorway, she could see through to the main hallway again, bathed in a watery yellow and red light from the stained glass panes on the front door: no mail, no fliers, on the stone-flagged floor.

Elspeth walked through the big house, taking in the faintly musty smell that recalled the Highland guest houses she had stayed in as a girl. The place hadn't been aired in a long time. No magazines on the coffee table in the living room, no books by the bed in the master bedroom upstairs. Lester Rains was either an excessively tidy man, or he spent most of his time somewhere else.

But then if he was wealthy, he may have a flat in town.

So why give her the address of this remote and inaccessible country pile? The question made her stomach flutter.

The living room was lined with bookshelves, almost all of them ancient-looking leather-bound tomes. Most of them were in Latin. Virgil, Cicero, Horace and Ovid, all the classics, as well as a number of writers whose names she didn't recognize: Plautus, Tibullus, and someone called Gaius Sallustius Crispus. Elspeth recalled some lines of Latin from her own school days, but knew she had no hope of reading any of these works.

She flipped open one vellum-bound edition to its title pages and was shocked to see the verso of the title page: the book had been printed in London in 1602. The collection must have been worth a fortune, but here it was, just sitting in a deserted country house with the back door unlocked.

Elspeth's eye was caught by a solitary paperback peeking conspicuously out amongst all the leather-bound spines. She went over and pulled it out. It was one of the few books written in English.

My Life Among The Apemen, it was called.

By Lucius M. Barbegal.

That, Elspeth remembered, was the ancient Roman name Rains claimed to have been born under in Gaul. With the middle initial, it suddenly sounded passably modern, like some late nineteenth century Belgian author. She flicked open the first pages to see what year it was first published.

1938.

Frowning, her hands shaking ever so slightly, she opened it to the foreword.

"While the pages that follow may seem to the casual reader to be a work of mere science fiction, in the vein of Wells, Huxley, or Zamyatin, it is my task to assure my audience that it is not. The following is designed to serve as a legal notice to humanity, to fulfill an obligation set out by the far distant intelligence that sent me and my confreres to your planet to exercise a task which we believe is now nearing its finale. Under the terms set out by that intelligence, which is ultimately responsible for the evolution of the human consciousness that allows you to even read these lines, we are obliged to offer full disclosure and warning that our masters are soon likely to return to collect on their investment. In other words, they are coming for you. Whether humanity chooses to heed such a warning is entirely up to you, and irrelevant to the purposes of this work. You have been duly warned."

Elspeth turned a couple more pages. The book began, as Rains had in her office: "I was born Lucius Margalis Barbegal, in the city of Arelate, in the fifth century ..."

A door creaked. Elspeth froze. Gently, she slipped the book into her purse and groped around for her Mace canister. Holding the pepper spray, she crept back to the kitchen, whence the sound had come.

Nothing. The breeze had simply blown the door open. But she was now wound up so tight, it was all she could do not to bolt back to the car. Mustering as much control of her nerves as she could, she took the handle and turned to close the door, so that no one would even know she had been here.

It was as she was stepping out that she noticed another door just behind the giant stove. The door was slightly recessed, which is why she hadn't noticed it when she first came in. It was also ajar.

Elspeth couldn't say afterwards why she had crept back in and opened it. It led to a small scullery that smelled of cold stone and lye. An antiquated washing machine stood empty next to a clothes rack. Beyond them, Elspeth saw another opening, this one doorless. It led down into what she could only guess was the cellar.

A voice inside her head warned her: *Don't go there*. The house was empty after all, and even if it wasn't — if there really was something lurking down there — did she really want to know?

She silenced the voice and held up the Mace. A cold, dark smell wafted up to meet her from the cellar: wooden stairs led down into a pool of darkness. She was about seven steps down when a strange smell hit her nostrils. Something she couldn't quite place: medical, was the word she might have used to describe it, but she couldn't say precisely why.

She reached for her mobile phone and flicked on the flashlight. The room leveled out under a low ceiling. She couldn't see into its darker recesses, but the torchlight from her phone caught a light switch. She flicked it on.

Like the rest of the house, the place looked empty. The lightbulb filament glowed orange, straining to pick out the farther recesses. She turned to look at the far wall, the one behind the cellar steps, and let out a strangled croak that should have been a scream, had she been the type of person who actually screamed. She almost dropped the phone.

Four bodies sat on chairs against the far wall.

Elspeth bolted back up the stairs, tore through the laundry room and back into the kitchen, slamming the door behind her. There she stood, chest heaving, waiting for something monstrous to push against it. Nothing did. Slowly, she forced herself to calm her breathing.

Her phone had one bar of signal, enough to call the police. She started to dial 999, but suddenly stopped.

There had been something strangely insubstantial about the bodies. Ethereal, almost. Was she sure she had seen *dead* bodies? It would be embarrassingly and potentially damaging to her reputation to call in the police to a patient's empty house if she had not.

Keeping her thumb over the green 'call' button on the phone, Elspeth gingerly opened the door and crept, ever so slowly, back down the steps.

She had both hands in front of her now, Mace in one and mobile phone in the other. She inched her way down the cellar steps.

When she saw the four human forms propped up on chairs on the far wall, she was surprised at how unshocked she felt. The beam of her flashlight appeared to go straight through them, as though they were made of some translucent material. Were they some kind of trick, a costume or a Halloween prop?

Unlikely, in this house that was so free of any adornment. Elspeth was sure, however, they were not cadavers, and that gave her a little more courage to descend the last steps and approach the strange display by the cellar wall.

Up close, they looked more like casings than bodies. Her scientific mind groped for a better description than casing. "Husks," she whispered. They were like tissue wrappings of human figures, empty and fragile. Certainly not dead bodies. They all appeared to be the same stature, a slim adult. There was a little dark hair still attached on the head and chest, eyebrows and groin. She reached and touched the husk on the far left, the one nearest to her as she approached from the kitchen steps. It was dry as parchment and crumpled under her touch, imploding on itself.

She moved to the second and held the flashlight close.

Skin. The material wasn't paper but skin. A single layer or two, enough to hold the shape of a human body. Her heart was still pounding, but she now found herself as much intrigued as she was afraid. A thought was nagging at the back of her mind, but she ignored it, determined to establish if she could determine precisely what these delicate human pinatas might be.

She looked at the face of the second husk. It was intact, but indistinct. No real features to see. Elspeth pressed a fingertip lightly on an eyebrow and a few hairs came away on the palps, like scales from a desiccated moth. The eyelids were closed, as though the figure had been asleep.

She moved to the next one, which was identical. The fourth one was almost identical, except that the hair seemed darker and less desiccated to the touch. *Fresher.*

Elspeth played the torch over the body. It was mostly hairless, only a few wisps on the chest, a dark tuft between the legs... it was only then that she noticed the back of the husk was missing: from the thighs to the shoulder blades, the shapes were all incomplete.

Maybe whoever had made them hadn't thought it necessary to fill in the backs. Maybe they were some kind of artwork, designed to be displayed face out only. But another thought jumped unbidden into her mind. What if someone had been *inside* these casings, and backed out? Like an adolescent snake emerging from discarded skin, or a cicada nymph shedding its exoskeleton.

That thought lurking at the back of her mind suddenly stepped forward: Rains sitting in her office, telling her how the "farmers" adapted to the changing physiognomy of the humans they lived amongst. *Like bugs.* Wasn't that the phrase he had used?

Instinctively, Elspeth glanced back at the stairs and the cellar door. No sign of movement. But suddenly she found she couldn't bear to be in this place a moment longer, with those macabre figures. She had to get out.

Before she ran, though, she stepped back to the last of the husks and snapped the thumb off its right hand. She wanted to test it to see if the skin was, as she suspected, human. Then she fled the house, slamming the kitchen door behind her. She half expected Rains to be there, standing in the drizzle, waiting for her with a knife or a shotgun, but the driveway was empty, aside from her ridiculously small rental car.

She leaped in, put it in gear and sped off as fast as the tiny engine and bumpy road would allow her.

· | ·

Weeks passed, but there was no sign of Lester Rains. Trying hard not to sound too curious, Elspeth asked Anya, her secretary, if he had perhaps left any other contact details—a mobile phone, an email perhaps–but there was nothing. The man had simply vanished.

She had a private lab run a DNA analysis of the skin sample she had taken from the husk. It was human, the lab confirmed, but offered precious few clues as to the owner's background, other than that he or she had ancestors in the Iberian peninsular and southern

France. That last detail caught Elspeth's attention: right where Arles is located. But that could easily be explained rationally: half the population of Britain had Celtic ancestors who hailed from the same region.

The most interesting aspect for Elspeth, of course, was the fact that the tissue was human. Who made sculptures out of human skin? Cutting-edge artists perhaps, but that was being exceedingly generous, given what she knew about Rains.

Psychopaths. Serial killers. Those were the sort of people who thought that human skin might be decorative.

She considered calling the police but decided against it. The skin she had seen hadn't been cut off dead bodies. It had been shed, molted. If he really were an artist, you could possibly say it had been delicately crafted. But was Rains an experimental sculptor? Doubtful. She was annoyed that she had taken a skin sample from only one of the husks. Were they all from the same person? And how exactly had the skin been glued together, held in place? She could recall no seams, no signs of artifice.

She assumed that Rains must have known she would go there, and guessed that she would find the husks. The question was, what was he trying to prove?

Then there was the book. It looked old, and the frontispieces said it was published the year before World War II began, but such things could be faked. Why would he do that? And if the book were genuine, why had Rains assumed the persona of a long-forgotten science fiction author from between the wars?

She googled the book: there were precious few references to it, given how long it had been out of print. Not enough even to merit a Wikipedia entry. The original print run had been tiny, just 450. Probably a vanity publisher. From the handful of references, it was clear that none of the people had actually read the book. "Rare. A poorly received experimental science fiction work about a group of aliens implanted on Planet Earth during the paleolithic period to develop a form of consciousness that can be used by machines to recreate the long-extinct species that created the technology." That was about the longest review she could find on a webpage that traced obscure superhero comics and pulp fiction from the 1930s to the 60s.

Elspeth didn't read science fiction. She had been put off by a particularly frightening episode of Dr. Who as a small child, involving a knife-wielding puppet that came to life on the screen and haunted her dreams for weeks after. The thought of plowing into this poorly reviewed book from almost a century ago did not fill her with any enthusiasm. She knew at some point she would have to read it if Rains ever showed up again, but for now she put it on her shelf, untouched.

Spring turned to summer, and the weather grew fair, for Scotland. Occasional days of bright sunshine punctuated the usual overcast skies and drizzle. August came, and Edinburgh filled with tourists, actors and comedians in town for the annual arts festival.

As a native of the city, Elspeth both resented and enjoyed the influx of visitors. The streets were full of ambling, well-intentioned thespians and would-be comics as well as their frequently drunk audiences, who slowed her down as she went to and from work or clogged her favorite cafes. But it was also a huge celebration, and people were generally in a good mood, out enjoying the city, their happiness on display to the world.

It was the last week of the festival and she was sitting in her flat, the window open and the sound of revelry and fireworks drifting in from the street. She was reading and enjoying a glass of chilled Chardonnay. A New Orleans jazz band was blasting out classic tunes in the small park down the street: the occasional bar of music floated into the room. She was half listening to it when her doorbell rang.

Elspeth looked at her watch. Nine-twenty: she wasn't expecting any visitors tonight. Annoyed, she lifted the intercom and looked at the gray fuzzy screen. She let out a small gasp to see Lester Rains standing on the stone steps of her building.

"Hello," he said with a smile. "I do hope I'm not disturbing you?"

"Mr. Rains," she said. "This is ... unexpected."

"I know," he said. "I'm sorry. Really, believe me. I wouldn't have come if it were not urgent."

She paused. Should she allow a potentially dangerous patient, one who had disappeared from her care and who had left shells of human skin in his basement, into her house? No. Clearly no. In fact, fuck that.

"Mr. Rains, I'm sorry, but this is highly irregular. If you'd like to schedule an appointment at my office tomorrow, you can call in the morning. But I'm afraid..."

"I'm afraid I can't come to your office, Elspeth," Rains said. He was leaning in close to the intercom downstairs, and she could only make out the lower half of his face. "I have some business of great urgency to discuss with you. They are coming. Some of them are already here. I'm leaving tonight, for good. Meet me in the cafe down the road, the one next to the pub. It's called The Bridie. I'll wait there for ten minutes. If you are not there, I'll understand. I will not take any offense. But I'm afraid this will be goodbye, Elspeth. And good luck. If you believe in such a thing."

He turned away from the blurry screen. Elspeth saw him descend the five stone steps and turn left, toward the Bridie. She stood by the door a moment: Rains appeared to be suffering some extreme episode, despite his calm voice. She could not just turn her back on him. Besides, the cafe would be full of people. She took a cardigan—the night had a slight chill to it—and went downstairs.

The cafe was crowded, roaring loud. All the city's bars and eateries were generally packed during the festival. She scanned the throng and saw Rains, incongruous in a tan suit, squeezed behind a tiny table at the back of the cafe, an anachronism among all the young people in summer clothes. He smiled wanly as she sat down.

"I wasn't sure you'd come." He had to speak up over the roar of the cafe.

"Neither was I," she said. Rains smiled more easily, though his eyes skittered over the heads of the crowd, as though he might be looking for somebody.

"First of all, let me say I quite understand why you would be alarmed at my coming to your apartment. I apologize."

"Not at all," Elspeth said. "But how are you feeling, Lester? You looked quite upset there, standing at my door."

"I suppose I am rather perturbed," said Rains. "Though with some reason, given what is about to transpire."

A rushed-looking waiter leaned over the table. Elspeth ordered a glass of sparkling water: no more alcohol tonight. Rains ordered an Earl Grey and then waited till the man had gone. He leaned in as though to speak, but instead just rubbed his face.

"I know you won't believe this. Elspeth," he said eventually. "There's no way you *can* believe it because it is entirely outside your sphere of reality, so for now you will just have to believe that I'm a delusional schizophrenic who is having some kind of fugue episode right now. But that's alright. Just listen for a minute, and then prognosticate, if you will. But first, listen. Please"

Elspeth nodded, her hands folded in her lap. There was little else she could do.

"I told you before that I and a number of other 'farmers' were seeded here over the millennia to monitor the rate of development of human consciousness on Earth. So... to put in succinctly, that period is now over. The entity that put us here—the 'alien,' if you like — is coming here to harvest what it has grown. You. I don't know when exactly the ships will arrive. It could be days, weeks, even a month or two from now. But they are on their way. They are close, in galactic terms. The harvesters have been deployed."

Elspeth stared at Rains, trying to keep a neutral expression. The thought of the human skins in his basement came to mind. "The harvesters?" she said.

"In the last decades of the twentieth century, we were instructed by Farmer One to implant a number of genetically modified subjects into human hosts. No, we didn't abduct anyone and experiment on them in flying saucers. What we did was we threw some wild parties in Rio, Los Angeles, London, Tokyo. All around the world. And we implanted zygotes that were impregnated with a small dose of the Code that I told you about. We used sex toys fitted with what we told the participants were eggs made of gelatin."

Elspeth involuntarily caught herself looking round to make sure no one was listening: she may be a shrink, but this was her local cafe, and she knew some of the waiters and regulars. At the same time, she was intrigued—Rains was divulging some very revealing sexual fantasies that might shed light on his feverish mental state.

"And the women—they must have noticed they were pregnant, no?" she said.

"Of course they noticed. Difficult to overlook. But they never suspected it was the gelatin eggs they'd fooled around with in Rio or wherever. And the kids were perfect little humans, for all intents and purposes. Some misfired: a few miscarriages, a couple of the modifications didn't work out properly. They came out as normal humans, more or less, useless for our purposes. But overall, we created a crop of 462 harvesters. Most of them male, born into poorer families, often without father figures, so they would be easier for us to manipulate. They have all now been activated."

"*Activated?*" Elspeth gave a start as she realized the server was standing next to her.

"Perrier?" he said, putting a glass and a small green bottle on the table. He placed a large mug of steaming tea in front of Rains, who watched him go before he resumed his tale.

"The harvesters were under the direct command of Farmers One and Three - the senior level. We newer iterations were not involved, beyond helping arrange the initial inceptions. It was the job of the senior farmers to inform the harvesters who they were, and what their task was. I believe they have been active for several years now, cultivating political elites, security contacts. They are the final phase. They will be ready to act when the ships come."

It was only with some professional effort that Elspeth refrained from shaking her head.

"Lester, I visited your house after you vanished."

He nodded. Of course she had—why else had he left his address on the calling card?

"What were those things, those skin sculptures, in the basement?"

He smiled, again with a trace of tiredness. "Me," he said.

Elspeth said nothing, waiting for him to elaborate.

"Part of our adaptive longevity involves a regeneration process. We age very slowly, but our cells are still subject to wear and tear. So we have regenerations, every ten years or so, to maintain a regular appearance and cell function. It generally takes about three days: it was an unbearably dull process until radio was invented, I can tell you. At the end of the procedure, we shed our outer layer, like a snake or a lizard. Primitive, but an effective method for conditions in the field."

Elspeth took a deep breath. This was her moment.

"As a clinical psychiatrist, Lester, I have to urge you to seek further professional help, either with myself or, if you prefer, I can give you the names of other trained doctors who would be able to assist you. It's my opinion that, while you appear to be able to function in a day-to-day capacity, you may pose a danger to yourself, or possibly also to those around you..."

She saw Rains was no longer listening. He was staring over her shoulder, over the diners and out the window of the cafe. She turned and looked but could see nothing.

"They're close," he said. "There's at least one harvester tracking me. I believe I may have made an error."

For the first time since she had known him, Rains appeared agitated. "I'm afraid, Elspeth, I'm going to have to leave you. They can't see us together. It would be extremely dangerous for you."

"Mr. Rains," she said, "you are displaying all the characteristics of a delusional...."

"I know, I know," he said, rising to go and touching her shoulder gently. "Just remember, Elspeth, when the time comes, do not go on their ships. Do not trust them. The first wave will be apocalyptic, but the second wave will be even worse. If you can still travel internationally, head for Hawaii. If that proves impossible, you go to this place and wait there."

He pulled out a slip of paper and a pen and quickly wrote a long set of numbers in a beautifully sloping cursive.

"Why are you telling me all this?" Elspeth said as Rains dropped a £50 note on the table, an absurd amount for what they had consumed. She noticed his wallet was fat with cash.

"Because I'm... because I made a promise to your great-great grandmother," he said, with a half smile. "It's a long story. But then, aren't they all?" He squeezed her shoulder. "I have to go now."

And he turned and hurried off through the blaring, drunken crowd to the door. Elspeth watched him until he vanished, then leaned forward and rubbed her face with her hands.

She looked at the slip of paper.

37°42'37.2"N 78°26'06.1"W.

A longitude and a latitude. Elspeth plugged the numbers into the map on her phone. It planted a little red pin in a deep green swathe of western Virginia.

Random, she thought. But then, what exactly had she been expecting?

· | ·

That last meeting with Rains had been almost ten weeks ago.

Now here she was, watching the hallucinatory television footage of alien ships attacking Moscow.

Elspeth stood in front of the screen, tea mug in hand, trying to take it in, listening to the disbelieving voice of the TV anchor.

"This is footage taken on a cell phone two hours ago on Tverskaya Boulevard, showing what Russian officials are claiming was an attack by unidentified ships that *came out of the sky...*"

Elspeth could hear the disbelief in the news anchor's voice. Not just that this could have happened, but that he was actually saying those words live on television.

"Oh my god," she whispered. "*Lester.*"

She put down the cup and hurried through to the guest bedroom, which she used as her home office. She rarely had guests these days. Since her divorce two years before, she had thrown herself entirely into her work. She ransacked the draws, rifled through her purse, but could not find that scrap of paper that Rains had given to her at their last meeting, before he'd slipped out the cafe and disappeared. It now struck her as vitally important.

Because now she saw it. Rains wasn't mad. The world itself had gone mad.

And not just this world, apparently. There were other worlds out there, and they were not friendly.

Elspeth was throwing files on the floor, papers flying, her tidy little work space starting to look like the scene of a break-in. After ten minutes, she stopped, slumped to her knees and let out a low moan. The paper was gone, of course.

"Wait!" she said, leaping to her feet. She'd googled the numbers that Rains had written down, to see if they signified anything. She remembered they had shown somewhere in the boonies of Virginia or somewhere. North Carolina?

She opened her laptop and scrolled frantically through the search history. Ten weeks had passed, and she had searched for a great many other things. Nothing. Then she remembered -- she had done it on her phone, in the cafe. How did she find her phone's search history? She had to google *that* first, then wade through several jargon-heavy tech sites before she found one written in plain English.

She held her phone and followed the steps on her computer.

And there it was: 37°42'37.2"N 78°26'06.1"W

She carefully copied out the numbers and entered them in the search engine on her laptop.

It was Virginia. Lots of green, some rivers and lakes in blue. The Allegheny Mountains seemed to rise up to the west of the site. She zoomed in. A small town, more like a village. Clover Mills.

This time, alongside the Google map, there was a photo. It seemed to be just a plain old shop front, with a sign that read "Mike's Bikes & Repairs."

A *bike shop?* Aliens were invading, and she was looking at a Google streetview of a village bike shop in the backwoods of Virginia?

The streetview picture allowed her to swivel her viewpoint to see the rest of the main street. There was a brick-faced store next door to the bike shop. The sign outside advertising "Seeds and Feeds," and a few doors down a cafe that had a hipster vibe with wrought-iron tables on the sidewalk. A railway ran through the little town, ferrying who knew what to god knew where.

Had Rains written down the coordinates wrong? Or maybe he really was crazy, and the fact that he'd popped up right before an actual first encounter with aliens was one of those weird jokes that history occasionally played on poor saps like her. In any case, Elspeth hit 'print' and the map with the address on it slid out of her printer.

Confused, she found herself drawn back to the television screen, while her fingers instinctively dialed her parents' number.

Her father, an unflappable 76-year-old retired Royal Navy commander, answered. His steady voice hinted that he already knew all about it and had taken it all in his stride, just like he always did. "Yes, well, there must be some rational explanation," he said. "All these people panicking when we don't even know the full facts ..."

Normalcy bias, Elspeth thought, as ever incapable of stopping herself from diagnosing people's reactions to trauma. Just because something has never happened to you before, you can't believe it is happening now. Either that or he simply didn't want to terrify his little girl. A perfectly natural reaction for a parent.

"... and in any case, they only showed up in one place, at one time. There's no way of knowing if that was it, if it was some sort of incursion, or if..."

"Is mum there?" she said, hoping for a more human response.

"No, she's gone out," her father said.

"*Out?* Where?" she said.

"Oh, she said she needed a couple of things from the shops. Took the car about an hour ago."

It was too early for most shops to even be open. For a minute, Elspeth pictured her little old mother driving around the coastal town in deep shock, unable to bear the insane news or her husband's business-as-normal reaction to it. Elspeth was surprised her mum hadn't called her, but then her father would have been lurking in the background and would no doubt disapprove of her 'making a fuss' and spreading panic. She wished her mum had a mobile phone.

She told her father to have her call whenever she got home.

There was no way she was going to mention Lester Rains to her dad. But she desperately needed to tell someone.

Robbie was the most logical choice. Not because he was her ex-husband — that was a definite point *against* calling him, although they remained on almost friendly terms since their split. But he was a civil servant working at the Home Office, and might know whom she should contact with what seemed, in the light of what just occurred in Moscow, to be pertinent information.

With that slight sense of dread she always felt when she contacted her ex, she dialed Robbie's number.

"Elspeth," he said, answering on the first ring. Everyone was hanging on their phones that morning, it seemed.

"Robbie," she said. There was a silence — how do you start a conversation about the end of the world?

"Fucking hell," he said eventually, letting out a deep breath.

"I know," she said, suddenly relieved. She laughed. "I mean, what on god's green earth...?"

She could hear a television set in the background being muted. Robbie sighed again.

"I just don't know what to say..."

"Have you heard anything? I mean, anything official?"

"Nothing," he said. "Word from the top is that they're 'making rigorous inquiries with Moscow,' which means they know absolutely bugger all about what's going on. But they do seem to think it was a genuine..." There was a pause. "An encounter with alien craft is what they're calling it, I believe."

The words hung there. Elspeth felt like she was going to burst out laughing at the absurdity of it all.

"Are we totally screwed, then?"

"Who knows, El?" he said. "We may never know. I mean, we don't know what the hell did this, what their intentions are, how they might view us as a species. Not until they decide to do whatever they plan to do." She heard a quiver in his voice. He paused to regain his normal composure. "And from what we saw this morning, there's pretty much nothing we could do to stop them from doing it."

"Jesus," Elspeth said. "I can't... I can't even begin to process this..."

"Who can?" Robbie sighed.

"I think I know someone who could."

"Who?" Robbie sounded startled. Maybe annoyed. There had been a lot of that in the final days of their marriage — they knew exactly how to push each other's buttons, and were unable to stop themselves from doing so.

"Remember I called you back in the summer? I was going to the house of one of my patients who'd paid me a couple of visits, then just disappeared. I was worried he might have self-harmed, or be potentially dangerous. He lived out in the stix of Fife. I was a wee bit nervous."

"Oh yes, I seem to recall. I told you it was a bad idea to go out there on your own. What happened again? I don't think you ever..."

"He wasn't there," she said. "The place seemed abandoned. But in the basement I found these strange figures, like sculptures, made of human skin."

"What?" said Robbie. "Did you go to the police?"

"No, they weren't bodies or anything. More like paper-thin husks, like sculptures. I took a sample, and had it analyzed, and it turned out it was all human tissue, but so delicate you could see through it."

"Sounds like a madman," Robbie said. She could hear him catch himself — she'd always jumped on him for talking about her clients in such simplistic, derogatory terms, even when they might have merited it.

"I thought he might be schizophrenic, delusional. He had this wild theory that he'd been alive since the time of ancient Rome, and that he was one of twenty-odd alien farmers who were in charge of, I don't know, supervising the evolution of human consciousness so that ... so that they could come and harvest us some time."

Elspeth paused. Even in the insanity of that morning, and after what they had both watched on their TV screens, it still sounded too whacko.

"No wonder he came to see you," said Robbie, voice non-committal.

"That's what I thought," she said. "But he kept on telling me, 'the aliens are coming soon.' Then a few months back, during the festival in fact, he showed up at my door, saying the alien ships were on their way and would be here within weeks or months. And here's the thing, Robbie... I've seen a lot of people with clinical delusions, schizophrenia or what have you. And none of them acted like him. He seemed so rational, even with the far-fetched story. And then this morning..."

There was a long pause. She imagined Robbie trying to weigh the facts, not give in to flights of fancy. He was a bit like her father in that respect. Maybe that had been part of the initial attraction, a sense of childhood familiarity, the chance to finally breach that distance.

"Listen, El," he said at length. "Our switchboard has been jammed all morning with people reporting alien sightings, suspicious figures who knew about this in advance. You know what people are like. But listen, since this is you, and since we both know you're not... delusional, send me whatever details you can in an email and I'll find out who's the best person to pass them on to. I can't promise anything, obviously, but..."

"Okay, Robbie," she said. "Thanks. I know it sounds absurd. I thought so myself until this morning. But he kept insisting this was about to happen. This *very* thing — he knew it was coming. And those husks in his house... I think it might be a lead, no?"

"Like I said, I'll pass it on El. Write it all down for me, or as much as you can, without violating any confidentiality rules doctors have with their patients. I'll see if I can get it to the relevant people. That's probably the best I can right now, in the circumstances..."

After she'd hung up, Elspeth walked over to her office to pull up Rains' case notes. The streets were almost empty, but she could hear the blare of televisions and radios from the buildings as she walked by. A young man at an empty stop light was nervously eyeing the sky, as though a spaceship might burst into view at any minute. An elderly homeless woman rooted through a rubbish bin, oblivious to how the world had been changed forever.

When she stepped into the office, Elspeth was surprised to see Anya, her receptionist, sitting at her desk.

"Anya, what on earth are you doing here?" she said. "Did you not see the news?"

"I... I thought you had patients today..." Anya said, then burst into tears. Elspeth went round the desk and gave her a slightly awkward hug. She put the electric kettle on for tea while Anya sobbed out her terror. An idea occurred to Elspeth. When Anya had stopped sniffling, she put her to work gathering all of Rains' files and printing off a dozen hard copies, making up a Pdf file. It would help her to be busy.

The first copy of the file would be sent to Robbie at the Home Office: the others would be held ready just in case that one disappeared into the bureaucratic void. Maybe she would go to the media if she didn't get a response, though that would violate every set of professional norms she held dear. But then, these were hardly normal times.

She took one copy of the file and sequestered herself in her office to study it, seeing if she could extract any fresh meaning from what she had previously assumed to be the fantasy world of a deranged human.

That was when she noticed Rains' reference to Elspeth's own great-great grandmother: Eileen Hardy. She had jotted down roughly what he had said to her the second time they had spoken. She'd asked him if he had known her. His answer had been: "actually slightly more than that."

Then, in the cafe during that last encounter, he had told her he was her great-great-grandfather. She hadn't written up that informal meeting, partly because she'd been so exasperated by it.

Elspeth stared at the page for a minute, then leafed through the other notes. The DNA test from the skin husks was still there, at the back. She called through the open door to the reception.

"Anya, I'm going to need you to get on to that genetic testing lab and set up another appointment, if you don't mind."

There was a moment's silence as her befuddled receptionist tried to make sense of the request. "Is this for another of those *things* you found?" said Anya. Elspeth had given her some of the details when she returned from Cullochan and asked Anya to inquire about getting tests done.

"No," said Elspeth, regretting once again that she hadn't taken samples from all the husks, to see if they were the same person. "This one's for me."

It would take several weeks to get the results back and see if the DNA of the husk matched her own, and if she and Rains were, as he claimed, related. At this point, anything seemed possible.

In those weeks, the world lost its collective mind.

It had begun even as Elspeth was walking home from the office later that afternoon, Rains' files clutched in her arms. She saw a group of drunken teens harassing a middle-aged couple who stood in the middle of a normally busy street. The couple were holding up a cardboard sign that read "Welcome to Earth friends! Come in peace!" The teens lobbed a couple of empty beer cans at them, only just missing the woman.

Elspeth shouted at them to leave the couple alone: they hurled some choice words back at her. One of them gave the man with the placard a quick kick, then the group scattered off down the street. Elspeth hurried home and locked her front door.

She stayed in her apartment for the rest of the day, alternately watching the BBC, scanning global websites for any insightful updates -- of which there were none — and peering out the window in a sort of trance. She was half-waiting for the internet to die, or the lights to suddenly go out, but nothing really changed. A couple of old friends she'd known since her university days called to discuss the hallucinatory news, but neither of them really knew how to process it either, so Elspeth found herself lapsing into counselor mode to try to reassure them. It was exhausting, so she decided to stop taking calls.

That first night, a muffled boom woke her. She looked out the window in alarm, but could see nothing until some kids ran past, whooping, faces obscured by football scarves. It took twenty minutes before a fire engine sped past to douse whatever they had set fire to: she guessed it must have been a car's petrol tank exploding. There was no sign of the police out there, though the night was alive with distant sirens. The wails were sometimes punctuated by what sounded like a gunshot, but was almost certainly just a firework. How quickly normality evaporates, Elspeth thought.

The next morning, she tried placing a delivery order at her local supermarket, just to see if it would work. It didn't. She phoned some friends and colleagues to check if they were alright — they were all holed up in their homes too, clutching carving knives or golf clubs or whatever they could arm themselves with. Her receptionist, Anya, and her fiancé, an extremely dull bank clerk, had barricaded themselves in their loft with tins of tuna and peas, but had forgotten a can opener and were too scared to go down to the kitchen to fetch it. Elspeth had to smile at that.

On the second day after the news broke, Elspeth woke from a fitful sleep to reports that the prime minister had declared a state of emergency and ordered troops out of their barracks to stop the looting and rioting in a number of cities, including areas on the outskirts of Edinburgh.

There was still no fresh news out of Russia: the TV showed footage of investigators poring over crushed cars that the strange ships had dropped.

"Close analysis of the glass fragments in the Russians automobiles—most of it smashed out in large chunks by impact with the ground—shows minuscule shards were consistently found inside the vehicles, as though something sharp and narrow had punctured the vehicles," The Times reported.

Oddly, North Korea was claiming it too had been attacked by aliens, but had no corroborating evidence. Commentators posited that the Hermit Kingdom appeared to be trying to gain some international attention at a time of crisis, like a neglected child crying out, "Me too, me too!"

Meanwhile, it turned out that a category four hurricane had wiped out a town on Florida's Gulf Coast. No one seemed to pay much attention to that, though.

Elspeth sat in bed, not knowing quite how to keep herself busy. She wanted to do something, anything, to get her mind off the horrible uncertainty. But she was afraid to go outside and, she had to admit, afraid to turn on the television and see those shocking, blurry images again.

There was only one thing to do, she decided: she had to find Rains.

She went to an online booking site and clicked on her destination: Washington, DC, seemed to be the closest city. From there, she could rent a car and drive a few hours to the village in western Virginia. She assumed all flights were canceled, and she was right. It turned out even train services had been suspended too, as had the cross-Channel ferries. She wasn't leaving the country any time soon.

She phoned Robbie: no, he said, he hadn't had time to look at the case file she had sent and neither had he found the right person to pass the message along to.

She was stymied.

Not quite, she realized. She dialed her parents. Her father answered. They exchanged a few pleasantries as best they could in the circumstances, then Elspeth asked to speak to her mother. Her father sounded hesitant and spoke in a lowered voice.

"Listen El, she's been a little, I guess you'd say fragile, since the... you know, since the news. I don't want you exciting her..."

"For god's sake, Dad," she said. "It's okay to be fragile. Everyone's fragile today. The planet was just attacked by some unknown entity and we don't even know whether they're going to eat us, enslave us, or invite us over for afternoon tea. You're the only one who doesn't seem to grasp that. It's okay to be afraid. It's okay to be bloody terrified in fact. It's a normal human reaction."

She realized her voice had risen, could tell from the stiff silence on the phone that her father was offended.

"Anyway," she said, "I don't actually want to talk to mum about that. I want to ask her about her great grandmother."

"What? Oh, okay then. Mary..." she heard him call.

Her mother did indeed sound frail when she took the phone. Elspeth decided it was best not to reveal why she was asking about Eileen Hardy: she just said she was working on a family genealogy project. Odd as that might sound in the current apocalypse, her mother not only accepted it as perfectly normal but seemed to welcome the distraction.

"Do you remember, were there any stories about her in the family when you and Uncle Larry were growing up?" Elspeth said. "Any, I don't know, scandals or anything?"

"There were a few snippets of gossip still floating around when I was a girl," her mother said. "Not much that I recall, except that our great great grandmother Eileen had somehow embarrassed the family. Something about a French man. Or maybe he was Swiss. I don't recall right now, I'm afraid, dear."

"Did she... get pregnant?"

"Och no, nothing like that! My goodness, she'd have been run out of town for something like that. No, what I heard was that she'd adopted a baby."

"Adopted?" Elspeth echoed. "That was the scandal?"

"Well, she was young and unmarried. That was quite unconventional in those days. Especially in those parts. And the baby was very well provided for. Came with quite a large settlement, people said. Eileen moved to the biggest house in Oban after that. Never married though."

"How come I never heard this story?" said Elspeth.

"I probably told you when you were little. You just didn't seem that interested in ancient family history, to be honest. I imagine you probably just forgot: it's not very interesting, in any case. People were so buttoned-down back in those days."

Elspeth held the phone in silence for a moment.

"Are you still there, Ellie?" her mother said through the phone.

"Yeah, mum, just... uh... Listen, what happened to the kid?"

"Eileen's daughter?" Her mother sounded surprised. "Well, it was my great grandmother, of course. She eventually married, and her son was the first in the family to go to university. Thanks for the inheritance, or whatever you might call it."

"And she never had any other children?"

"No, she never married. Why do..."

Elspeth heard the beeping of another phone call on the line. It was Anya, her receptionist.

"Listen mum, I've got another all. I've to go. I'll call you back in a bit, okay? Love you. And listen, don't worry."

She switched lines and heard Anya's voice.

"Hi Elspeth, I just wanted to check when you might be back at the office. Because I'm getting a whole bunch of people wanting to make appointments. One poor woman was just crying on the phone, saying her little boy had heard we were all going to be eaten by aliens and she didn't know how to tell him the world was ending. So...What do I tell them? When are you back at work?"

Elspeth took a deep breath. Of course, people were terrified, and had no idea how to deal with this kind of fear.

"Okay, Anya," she said. "Looks like the police and soldiers are getting the streets a bit calmer. You can start scheduling people for tomorrow morning."

• | •

Depression. Anxiety. Paranoia. Suicidal thoughts. These were the stock-in-trade of Elspeth's profession. For the past few years, she'd been dealing with a rising tide of existential gloom inspired by the climate crisis, mostly from young adults who had their whole lives ahead of them.

But now she was confronted with a tsunami of dread, from all sectors of society. People who would never in a million years have thought to visit a shrink were beating a path to her door. Anya was turning away dozens of patients every week, and Elspeth got home late every night, worn out and reaching for a glass of white wine from the fridge even before she'd taken off her shoes and coat.

The kids were the hardest: there was no rationalizing with them, no "putting it into perspective." The full, raw horror of humans no longer being the apex predator on the food chain could not be hidden from children. They got it, viscerally, and the screaming nightmares were the inevitable result.

Elspeth had them draw pictures as therapy, and quickly amassed folders full of scribbled, bug-like predators eating parents while howling kids gripped the bars of zoo cages, or stick figures being sucked up into the vacuum-cleaner nozzles of flying saucers. It was heart-breaking, and she started to wonder if she might need a therapist herself. Instead, she just ordered more wine deliveries. Morning runs were slowly displaced by biting hangovers. She was gaining weight. But then, so what? What was the point now?

Yet she still had to go out every morning and try to convince people there was some hope, to dredge up some lost lessons about human resilience and the hard times the human species had weathered in the past. She told her patients the massive droughts some 70,000 years in East Africa forced the human population to separate into small bands to survive: their numbers dwindled to as few as 2,000 humans before the climate shifted again, and they came back together to create a population expansion that ultimately led to their successful colonization of the planet.

Such stories seemed to offer some solace to the depressed patients on her couch. But every time Elspeth mentioned the dates of those prehistoric events, she remembered Rains telling her it was at that same point, some 70,000 years ago, that Farmers One and Two had started performing genetic manipulations on the brains of some of those isolated bands of African cavemen, prepping them for world domination and their ultimate purpose — to become fodder for the regeneration of a lost alien species.

Images would drift through her mind of primitive men and women roaming the dry grasslands of eastern Africa eons ago, being snared by…. well, what would Farmer One have looked like? Like the hunter-gatherers, presumably, since he had been implanted into a human. Would they have strapped the hominids down on a gurney, or did they have some technique so sophisticated she couldn't even imagine it? Where did the creatures live? In a spaceship? If so, was it still out there somewhere? Her imagination would run on and on, until her patient would stop talking and stare expectantly at her. Elspeth would just nod, and softly say "Good, very good," to cover up these momentary lapses of concentration.

A couple of weeks after she had submitted her DNA sample, the results came back. She felt panicky and lightheaded as she opened the results. Yes, the skin samples in the basement of the country manor house were of someone genetically close enough to have been her great, great grandparent. Either the man calling himself Lester Rains was an enormously sophisticated hoaxer who happened to share some common ancestor she was unaware of, or she was the descendant of some kind of alien.

Elspeth stood by her apartment door, staring at the letter for long minutes, trying to make sense of it. She looked up and caught her reflection in the mirror above the hall stand.

I don't even know what I am anymore, she thought.

"Try analyzing *that,*" she whispered to her puffy-faced reflection.

As she walked to her office that morning — the streets were largely back to normal now — she phoned Robbie. As usual, he sounded irritated, brusque.

"Elspeth," he said. "Yes, what can I do for you?"

She shrugged off the tone, as though she were some supplicant looking for official favor.

"Have you heard anything back about the Lester Rains file?" she said.

She heard a sort of put-upon sniff over the phone, followed by a pause. "Actually, yes, I did," he said.

"And?" she said, annoyed that he would need prompting.

"Well, I passed it up to Sir David, and he passed it on to Scotland Yard, I believe. We heard back a day or so ago. 'Intelligence not actionable,' they said."

"'Intelligence not actionable?' What does that mean? I sent them all my notes, all the stuff about him accurately predicting this a few months back, the address in Cullochan..."

"Listen Elspeth, I'm sure they looked into it and decided it simply wasn't enough to build an investigation on. The police have been swamped with these reports, and with all the civil disturbances and what have you..."

"Robbie, there was plenty of 'intelligence' for them to work on. There's a house up in Fife that was full of shucked-off human skins..."

"So you say, Elspeth..."

"I have a sample at home if they could be bothered to get off their arses and actually investigate the house," she said.

"El, I don't think you understand. The wheels of bureaucracy turn very slowly. In fact, it's quite remarkable that they came back to us so quickly. It's quite impressive by the usual standards..."

"Really?" Elspeth said, stopping in the street. A student walking behind her almost bumped into her. "How long would that normally take, Robbie?"

"Oh, I don't know. But I know they're absolutely swamped right now, so I wasn't expecting anything... well, maybe ever, to be quite honest."

"Robbie," she said after a moment, acting on an impulse. "Would you be willing to take a trip to America with me?"

"What?" he said. "America? El, this is hardly the time..."

"No, I don't mean on holiday," she said, blushing slightly, as though she were asking him on some risqué end-of-the-world date. "God no, I've got patients from dusk till dawn right now. But listen, Lester Rains gave me an address — well, more like GPS coordinates — for a place in western Virginia. I don't want to go alone and I don't know anyone else who can..."

His voice sounded harsh. "Listen El, you don't want to come unstuck on this, okay? I know everyone's scared and things might not look so good right now, but we've got to remain calm, rational..."

"I *am* calm, Robbie," she snapped. She realized how she sounded, how a woman always had to sound in these situations — calm, placatory. Fuck that, she thought.

"Now you listen to me," she said. "Those skin husks I told you about? Well, part of Rains' story was that he had had a relationship with my great-great grandmother. That's why he said he came to warn me about what was happening, for all the good it did me. So I had the skin sample tested. For DNA. And it shows we are closely related, Robbie. He actually *could* be my ancestor. I could be part..."

She didn't go on, just let the unsaid word hang there.

There was a long pause, then Robbie's voice again, more conciliatory this time.

"El, listen to yourself. Even if I could go to America, if I could get the time off work and even if Emily was frankly okay with me trotting off to Virginia in the middle of a global crisis with my ex-wife... just what do you really think you'd find there? Another empty house? Maybe some more skin samples? How do you even know they were his? What if... I don't know, he'd collected them from you somehow, if he was really a crazy stalker?"

"Robbie." She said his name in a very quiet voice, but it was enough, given their history, to stop him in his tracks. "What if that's why we couldn't have a baby? Because I'm not fully...?"

"El, you did conceive. We almost..." He stopped, as though unable to go there.

"After years of trying and with IVF. And even then I miscarried. I lost our baby. What if it's because I'm not quite human?"

Another long silence.

"Elspeth, you have to *stop* this. You can't go dredging up all this painful stuff from the distant past and attributing it to some crazy conspiracy theory one of your patients told you."

"We were attacked by alien spaceships, Robbie. I think we're a bit beyond the crazy conspiracy theory phase by now."

"El, El, there's absolutely no proof this was an alien attack. By far the most likely explanation is that it was something man-made, some Chinese weapons technology that we have no idea about yet."

Elspeth was crying now. Standing in the street, tears slipping down her cheeks. Several people passed by as she stood there, but no one seemed to notice. You saw plenty of that these days.

"I have to go, Robbie," she said quietly. "You stay safe, okay?"

And she hung up the phone, put it in her purse and carried on to work.

• | •

Christmas came and went. People put up decorations, went through the motions of celebrating, but no one seemed to have their heart in it. Elspeth drove to her parent's house for Christmas Day, ate an overcooked turkey dinner in near silence, then drove back to her apartment the next morning.

She was relieved to be back at work the very next day.

Her first patient was the manager of a high-street clothing store who had come home from work to find her husband hanging from the neck by his belt in their eighteen-month-old's playroom.

Her next patient was an old woman who had euthanized all her seven cats, worried that there would be no one to look after them when she and the rest of humanity were abducted by aliens.

Up next was an eight-year-old boy who had been expelled from school for setting the science lab on fire. He said he'd been trying to build a bomb to fight the aliens, because he'd seen adverts online for the new local self-defense militias that were forming, and because his parents had decided there was nothing left to do except drink themselves into oblivion every night.

On and on it went, a litany of despair and suffering. Elspeth listened, offered what counsel she could and prescribed whatever meds she thought might help. She had started to write a paper identifying a defining condition among her patients, which she called Alien Anxiety Syndrome, or AAS. She was quite pleased with the way it sounded. But then she read in the Journal of Experimental Psychology that a doctor in New York had already come up with a much catchier name for the condition: ETSD. She didn't even bother submitting her article.

At lunchtime, she stepped out of her office to grab a sandwich and a glass of wine at the local cafe.

She tried to avoid the news whenever she could, but it was everywhere, in-your-face, breaking news alerts on the phone or on tickers scrolling across TV screens that now seemed to be in every shop, cafe or bar. But on the walk back from the cafe, she passed a small crowd watching a TV in the window of an electrical goods store. She stopped to see what was going on.

"Seventeen Russian abductees found in southern Russia," read the chyron beneath the grainy footage.

"Oh my god," Elspeth said. "They're back. They actually came back."

The people around started hugging each other and cheering.

The euphoria of the Russians' return faded quickly. The resolute silence out of Moscow damped that initial outburst of optimism, and a nagging presentiment of doom returned as the world realized President Malevich would only share the abductees' stories when it suited him politically.

But Elspeth no longer drank her now-habitual half bottle of Chardonnay every night. Instead, she sat at her computer with a pot of green tea, trawling the internet for any lead on Rains. If the government was going to ignore her lead, she'd just have to do something about it herself.

She wrote down the key elements from Rains' story on a piece of paper: "alien harvest" "gelatin egg" "anatomically modern humans" "experiment" "code" "misfire."

To her surprise, she got over 40,000 hits, although most of them were dietary tips on the benefits of replacing eggs with gelatin.

She searched for "Goweetha," the alien race that Rains said had been made extinct by its own technology: that threw up a few hits for a health-food detox product whose exact nature she could not quite determine. She tried a few other spellings, since Rains had never actually written the word down. Nothing more promising appeared in the search engine.

"Maut" at first appeared more encouraging, with over 34 million hits. But a brief scan of the first page showed that this was because it was the name of a German road toll for heavy goods vehicles, not an alien super-intelligence planning to harvest humanity.

For weeks, she found nothing, just the infinite rabbit hole of online conspiracy theories on dodgy websites with ridiculous domain names. Her enthusiasm flagged, and she found herself slowly returning to her old habits – reading, watching television shows, meeting friends for dinner, windswept hikes in the snowy Ochils at the weekend.

Then, one Friday night in late February, she realized she hadn't done her search for a while. As a shrink, she knew this was a positive sign that she was coping with the stress. On the other hand, she still had to find Rains.

She sat down at her laptop and typed in a selection of her search words. To her surprise, the first link that popped up was for a newspaper article. An actual bona fide newspaper. Somewhere in Massachusetts. Elspeth didn't recognize the name of the paper, the Fullerton Morning Post, but clicked on the link.

The article was called *Why They Came* and featured a person called Cassius Trenton, who claimed to be a failed alien implant who could understand some secret message beamed out into space half a century ago.

As crazy as all the other stories, probably, but written by an actual journalist in a real newspaper.

Elspeth clicked on the journalist's email address at the bottom of the article. She wrote a brief description of her own experience with Rains, and the equally crazy story he had told her that, however improbably, shared certain details with Trenton's.

Then she pressed 'Send' and went to bed.

PART II

Joe Chavez remembered where he was when the ships came. In bed. Rush hour in Moscow was the middle of the night in Fullerton, Massachusetts.

Joe, an aspiring reporter with the Fullerton Morning Post (staff: seven, including Mary in sales and advertising), snored his way through the most significant event in human history. When he woke and checked his phone, he thought it must be some kind of hoax— fake news was all the rage, after all. But this one was massive and persistent. He switched on the television to double check.

There, on CNN, he saw a visibly frightened reporter standing on a now-darkening street in Moscow, police lights flashing all around, helicopters buzzing overhead. He flicked to MSNBC — an air force colonel from NORAD was talking to the anchor, and the unbelievable chyron: *President Bradley declares Earth under attack from aliens... Calls for calm and international summit.*

Joe stared at the screen, mouth agape. He was brought out of his stupor by a blast of vintage Eminem on his cell phone. As soon as he picked up, an angry voice was yelling in his ear.

"Joe? Where the hell are you?"

He recognized the voice—Ed James, the news editor at the Post—but not the tone. Ed was the most reasonable man in the world. He'd worked in Europe for the Washington Post a long time ago, and in his youth had even covered one of those wars in the Middle East Joe couldn't quite remember which one: they all blurred into each other. Nothing ever seemed to faze Ed. But it was a tone Joe would soon come to recognize in everyone, even himself. Strained, irritable, scared.

"Is this ... is this shit actually real?" Joe said.

"Of course it's real," snapped his editor. "Why the hell aren't you here? Everyone's in already."

Joe glanced at his watch, as if in self-defense. "It's only twenty after seven..."

"On the last fucking day of human civilization!" said his boss. "Get yourself in here now. It's all hands on deck."

The line went dead. Joe continued to gawp at the television screen — blurred footage of what looked like a tornado ripping down the broad streets of the Russian capital, cars and people darting across the wobbly recording of a cell phone or security camera.

Joe pulled on his clothes—no shower or coffee — and stumbled into the street. It was almost deserted: the few people he saw looked like they might be drunk or high, which to be honest was not that unusual at this hour in the morning in Fullerton, a former mill town fallen on hard times. There were no buses or cars in sight, which *was* unusual. Joe pulled his work satchel over his shoulder and jumped on his mountain bike, peddled the 20 blocks to the newspaper's offices. The building's receptionist was glued to his phone, his headphones on. He didn't even glance up as Joe crossed the small lobby and walked upstairs.

In the newsroom, despite the urgency of his editor's call, Joe found everyone was standing in front of the panel of televisions on one wall, each tuned to a different news channel. Staring.

The president of the United States was in the Oval Office, trying to appear confident. He was a large man, a former pro-football player whose popularity on the field and affable, no-nonsense nature had allowed him to make a spectacular post-game career in politics. Right now, though, he just looked dazed.

"That's not really the White House," muttered Penn Mattis, who usually covered business, tourism, agriculture and cyber. "He's actually in a bunker somewhere deep beneath a mountain in Utah. That's just a backdrop."

Joe didn't ask Penn how he was party to such a national security secret. Penn was twenty years older and always made out like he had his own deep throat sources, even though he covered local business in small-town Massachusetts. Joe did question him two hours later, however, when he confidently announced that the vice president had been found by the secret service in a brothel in Panama City, Florida.

All of them were watching President Bradley's somber speech. All except Cynthia Durkin, the chief reporter, who burst out of Ed's office in the midst of a heated argument with the editor.

"You have *got* to send me Ed! This is the biggest story in, like, forever. Surely you can bust out for a ticket to Moscow. Everyone's going there. Everyone!"

Ed was shaking his head and counting off his fingers as he spoke. "A, we just don't have that kind of money, Cynthia. B, all airports within a five-hundred-mile radius of Moscow are shut down. And C, like you say, everyone's there. We can take it off the wires. This is a local Massachusetts paper. We'll concentrate on what this means for the people of Mercer County."

"I can't *believe* this shit!" yelled Cynthia, throwing up her hands. "In that case, Ed, I quit. I'll pay for my own goddam ticket. There's no way on God's green earth I am not going to Moscow today!"

Ed watched her slam the stenciled glass door on her way out to the elevator lobby. Then he noticed Joe.

"Looks like you're our new chief investigative reporter," he said. "Congratulations. Now get me 800 words on Mercer Country's alien invasion preparations for online mid-morning. You've got an hour."

And he shambled off to his cubicle, shaking his head.

· | ·

It took Joe an hour just to get anyone on the phone — all the emergency lines were jammed, or else their phones just rang off into the void. When he finally spoke to his contact at the police department, the sergeant made a noise like he was blowing out cigarette smoke.

"Listen Joe, strictly off the record and between you and me: no one knows jack shit, so no one is doing jack shit. No one wants to make that call with all this crazy crap going on."

There was pause. "On the record: uh, the police department is asking for all citizens to remain calm until further information is known about the situation."

Pretty thin material for an end-of-the-world story.

In his cubicle, Joe pulled up the piece he had filed the night before. He had been up half the night working on it: that was why he had put his phone on mute. In fact, had he stayed up for just another hour or so, he might have been awake to see the alien story breaking in Moscow. But he had been exhausted after a long day of reporting on what had been his biggest story to date for the paper: Fullerton had suffered 116 victims of 'syrup,' the potent new drug sweeping the US.

The "forgetting drug," it was called: people who took a strong enough dose just seemed to fall into a stupor. No one knew where it came from or quite what the chemistry was, but a crowd of people had decided to sit down in Fullerton's Clara Barton Park the morning before and swig down a whole bunch of it. When the police were called, the syrup drinkers were just sitting there, staring blankly at the muddy baseball diamond and the half-bare locust trees.

Joe had been tipped off by an old school friend who lived across from the park. He was the first reporter to get there, just as the ambulances were pulling up and the cops were walking among the people, frozen like picnickers in a painting. Then the EMTs started pulling the zombies to their feet, leading them off to the ambulances. The people – most of them fairly young, but some with gray hair and one or two in suits – seemed ambulatory, if helped to their feet: it was only their volition that seemed to have vanished.

Joe had followed them to the hospital, where the swamped medical staff were too busy to speak to him for several hours. From the lobby, he caught glimpses of the druggies sitting in hallways -- there weren't enough beds to accommodate them all, and they didn't seem obviously ill or to be suffering. They all had saline drips in their arms and the same blank expression as they stared straight through the nurses bustling around them. One of them, he noticed, wore a gray t-shirt with a bright green logo that read: "Stay calm and self-medicate."

Eventually, towards the end of the morning, Joe managed to corner a frazzled junior doctor as she stepped out of the ER to grab a coffee from the cart in the lobby.

"Yeah, we suspect it's a mass OD of syrup," she said. "Not a lot we can do, really. Keep 'em hydrated, intubate with catheters. We ran out of adult diapers and stool softener already, but there's more on order. At least we don't have to sedate them for the catheters," she said with a small, tired smile.

"And that's it?"

"Pretty much," she said. "Keep 'em warm, fed and hydrated and make sure they don't mess the bed. That's about it. We've had plenty of cases here before, but never on this scale. They lose a bunch of weight after a few weeks, but generally you could say they're stable. We send them down to the new "clinic" in Boston after a few days."

"Why the air quotes?" said Joe.

"Between you and me, they call it a clinic, but it's more like a holding pen. They're running tests, but not in Boston. Down there, they just put them in dorms and feed 'em. I heard they'd got the Seabees building Portakabin camps to accommodate them all."

Joe, scribbling in his notebook, raised his eyebrows. "But why do they do it?"

"There's just too many of them," the doctor shrugged her narrow shoulders.

"No, I mean the druggies," Joe said. "Why do they take syrup when they must surely know it'll make them into zombies?"

The woman shrugged again. "Not really my wheelhouse, medically speaking. But it seems pretty obvious as a lay person. Despair, the constant flow of bad news every day. People have lost their jobs to machines, to AI, or they've all been shipped abroad. And all the climate chaos end-of-the-world shit: did you see the news out of Jakarta yesterday? Fifteen thousand people drowned in a trash tsunami from the Pacific. That's nasty shit," she said. "And the fires out west, the fire-tornadoes in the Midwest, the hurricanes down south, the flooding up here. People just want to opt out but are too scared to kill themselves. So they chug some syrup. Maybe when they wake up, it'll all be over. It's the drug for our times."

Joe shook his head. "Jakarta death toll's up to 25,000 I saw this morning. Seems half the city was below sea level. The wave swept over the sea walls, sucked half the Pacific garbage patch into the city, then washed even more back to sea."

"There you go," said the doctor, swigging the last of her coffee. "You're a reporter, so you know: Great Barrier Reef's dead, Antarctica's biggest ice shelf just melted into the sea. We're fucked, and there's no more denying it. So people want out." She crumpled her paper cup and tossed it into the trash as she walked back to the wards of immobile patients.

"That last bit was off the record, by the way," she said over her shoulder.

Now, sitting in front of his computer screen, Joe had to admit it was a great story. His first big news story. But it was yesterday's news. There was only one story in the world now.

The biggest story ever told, and he had nothing to say. He looked over the top of his cubicle at the bank of TV screens lining the wall, the headlines like something torn straight from the National Enquirer. His colleagues were still glued to the spot, as motionless as the syrup drinkers in the park.

"Fuck," Joe muttered to himself. He noticed his hands were trembling. He clasped them together till the shaking subsided, then started scrolling through all the major news websites, scouring the internet for anything that might shed some light on this insane day.

· | ·

The riots started within hours, in a pattern played out pretty much around the world, from rural Massachusetts to the vast slums of Mumbai and the boulevards of Buenos Aires.

People came out of their shell-shocked state and demanded to know what their governments planned to do to protect them. Despite the fear of gathering in public, flash mobs quickly formed, people feeling safer in crowds than lurking at home, watching as the horror constantly replayed on their screens. Police cordons were overwhelmed. The cops either went crazy beating people out of fear and frustration, or else threw down their riot shields and batons and joined the protests.

Joe had spent the entire day writing. Now that he was the paper's chief reporter—albeit chief among an entire staff of six, since Cynthia Durkin was somewhere en route to Europe—he had churned out the front page splash, an analysis of the state's preparedness and a long think-piece on what had happened to the Russians which was cribbed entirely from better-informed international media.

"Did they take the Russians to experiment upon? To eat? To put in a petting zoo and let little alien kids ride on their backs? No one can say right now: the extraterrestrials didn't bother to leave any kind of calling card. More to the point, are the aliens coming back, and if so, what can humanity do to defend itself?"

His most productive day of writing ever, and all of it from the swivel seat of his tiny cubicle.

By nightfall, though, he was on Main Street, notebook in hand. The town's law-abiding citizens were marching through tree-lined streets toward City Hall. Joe was still numb himself, and found it difficult to come up with questions that might elicit some kind of sensible answer, since nothing made sense anymore.

"What do we want?" chanted the crowd, many of them students from the community college. Quite a few of them were drinking from bottles as they marched and shouted the question as though it really had only just occurred to them to ask what it was they wanted.

"Answers!" suggested one young woman, and the crowd cried out in jerky unison.

"When do we want them?"

"Now!"

"What if no one has the answers?" Joe asked a middle-aged guy at the front of the procession. He was wearing a suit and tie under his winter parka. Despite his business-like appearance, the man too appeared to have been drinking, with red splotches on his cheeks and his tie half unknotted.

"Somebody's gotta know something!" the man said. "NASA, Norad, the feds. This kind of thing can't just happen without anyone knowing."

"Look at Roswell," broke in a younger guy, not much older than Joe. "Something clearly happened there, and they never told us. Maybe they came to warn us, or threaten us, and no one ever let on. And now look at what's happening! The government's keeping all of that shit from us, and we got to know finally!"

Joe nodded: it was only hours after aliens had actually appeared, and Roswell still conjured a knee-jerk mental image of crazy UFO conspiracy nuts in tin-foil hats. The news was too fresh to have dented that reflex.

A knot of people quickly formed around him. His frozen fingers slithered across the page of his notebook as he struggled to keep pace. He flicked on the voice recorder on his cell phone as back-up. More conspiracy theories, anger at the government, anger at their local politicians, at the international leadership, the Russians, the Chinese, the UN—it all spilled out as the people gave vent to their welling terror. Quite a few seemed to genuinely believe the whole thing was some kind of elaborate hoax—probably the exact same people who, just a day before, would have argued that aliens really did exist. Now the extraterrestrials were actually here, they wanted to take shelter from reality in some elaborate counter-conspiracy.

A shout and the crash of broken glass broke up the crowd's collective outpouring of emotion.

Someone had thrown a trash can through the window of an electrical goods store. The alarm rang shrill in the dark, and for a moment no one moved. Some tattooed youths in hoodies dived inside. They emerged minutes later from the shop, boxes in their arms, and ran off. A whoop went up from the crowd. A guy who had identified himself as a student grinned and slapped Joe's arm.

"End of the world, dude. Let's grab some shit." And he ran into the pillaged shop.

The stubbly man in the suit shook his head. "Christ, who even needs all that crap now?"

There was another crash from across the street. Someone had taken a crowbar to the shuttered door of a bar and people were pushing their way inside.

"Okay, *now* we're talking," said the older man.

Joe watched him go, then shrugged. What the hell. He *was* reporting, after all. It'd be good color for the scene piece, he told himself. He ducked in after the man.

Inside, there were whoops as he stepped through the shattered door, the scrunch of broken glass underfoot. A man in a puffer jacket was lining up a row of shot glasses, sloshing bourbon from a bottle and liberally splashing the counter as he went.

"Grab yourself a drink, man. The end of the world party has officially begun."

The man in the suit raised his glass and said, 'Amen to that.' A young woman down at the end of the bar started sobbing. The self-appointed bar keeper shoved a drink at her and said, "Here hon, this'll help. What's your name?"

Joe stood by the man he had been speaking to on the street.

"Answers, huh?"

The man was staring straight ahead. Instead of responding, he lifted his glass to his lips and downed it in one. He held it out and the 'barman' quickly refilled it.

"We'll get there, son, don't worry," the suit said, then paused, as though ashamed.

"I have two children," he said. "Girl aged twelve and a little boy, just turned eight. They've been asking me all day what this means. They think it's fun. Exciting, like that kids' movie 'Home.' What can I tell them?"

Joe nodded, took a slug of liquor. The burn felt good, a slight release of wound-up nerves. Maybe these guys were right – maybe *this* was the answer right now.

"Probably the same thing the mayor could tell you," he said. "Bubkas."

The barman refilled their glasses.

"What... what do you think they want?" suit man asked. But before Joe could even shake his head, a flashlight cut through the half-lit bar. Everyone looked round: the barman's welcoming whoop died away as they saw a police officer standing in the stove-in door.

"Evening, deputy," said the barman. "Welcome to the apocalypse. What'll you have?"

The sheriff's deputy crunched over broken glass. He played his flashlight over the whitened faces of the drinkers, who blinked or turned away. He took off his cap and placed it on the bar.

"Hell, get me a Wild Turkey," he said in a shaky voice. "And make it a double."

A nervous laugh rippled through the drinkers. The man in the suit put his hand on the police officer's shoulder. Joe watched as the haunted humans downed their drinks, then quietly took his notebook out and started scribbling.

• | •

Depending on where you were, the end-of-the-world party lasted either a few days or at most a couple of weeks. Drunken revelries, spontaneous prayer meetings, mass lootings, they all dragged on as long as the authorities were too stunned to stop them.

But people still had to eat. The president—back at the actual White House after an absence of three days—made a fresh appeal for calm, not just in the United States but around the world. For once, the media acted quite sensibly. Talking heads mused about the long-term economic consequences of the ships *not* returning. Starvation, civil collapse, the greatest countries in the world becoming failed states. *We have to shape up*, they said: get back to work.

Even if people knew, deep down, that they were just ticking off the days.

Trashed stores were fixed up, banks extended special credit lines to sensible middle-class couples who'd blown their life savings on coke and speedboats, and the courts handed down suspended sentences to otherwise law-abiding citizens who'd ripped apart their local malls. With the sweaty anxiety of the worst hangover in history, the world went back to work.

It was midday on the third day when Joe stumbled out of a rave in what had once been a Walmart on the edge of downtown. His eyes slitted against the sun, pupils dilated from the pills he'd taken. His fingers were covered in the orange dust from the Doritos he'd been living off, plus some other strange greenish-purple stain he couldn't identify.

He had been in it so long—a day? Two days?—that at first he could barely hear the birds singing in the bare trees. His body was still throbbing with the pulse of electronic dance music. His sweaty hair quickly cooled in the autumnal chill. Images of the bacchanal flashed in front of his eyes—pills, naked bodies, drunken fights, people crying, laughing, more sex than he'd had in the past three years, not a condom in sight, because what did it matter now? The floor was a mess of chips bags, cheap Chinese toys and smashed glass. There was a body in the dietary supplements aisle: Joe wasn't sure if the guy had died of an overdose or been murdered. Nobody bothered checking, though someone had covered his face with a Halloween candy bucket.

Joe felt disoriented, dehydrated, but couldn't tell how much of that was the booze, the drugs and sex of the impromptu club or the lingering sense that human history was abruptly coming to a close. *All the above*, he told himself, as he jammed his frigid hands deep into his coat pockets and shuffled towards the town center, head down against the icy breeze. He noticed his wallet was gone, but that didn't really seem to matter anymore.

The streets were full of derelict cars, overturned shopping carts and burned storefronts. The thought drifted through Joe's addled brain: *Seneca Falls* if Jimmy Stewart had been abducted by aliens.

But as he crossed Franklin and Ninth, he came across what appeared to be a small tank. The soldiers standing around it had their rifles slung unmenacingly across their shoulders, but it was still a jarring sight in the middle of Fullerton. A huddle of hungry-looking dogs, forgotten by their owners, had gathered around them in hopes of sharing some MREs. Joe stopped and instinctively reached inside his coat for his notebook and pen. But they were nowhere to be found.

"National Guard," said a familiar voice by his shoulder. Joe spun round.

"Deployed this morning, across the state," Ed James said. He was holding a yellow legal pad. Joe had never seen his editor out on a reporting job before. Ed noted his surprise. "Had to hit the streets myself for this one. Kinda short-handed right now."

Joe stared at his feet. He felt sick and exhausted, full of shame. He just wanted to go home and curl up in bed.

"My former chief reporter is grounded in Hamburg, Germany," Ed said. "Monument to her tenacity that she got that far, given that all civil flights to Europe are suspended. And my former rising star of the news desk went AWOL just as the biggest story in the history of the planet was breaking. So yeah, I had to hit the streets myself since the National Guard is being deployed and millions of refugees are fleeing the coastal cities and heading for the hills, right towards us."

Joe looked at his editor. "I'm sorry, Ed. Really sorry I let you down. It's just... I don't know. I mean, what's the *point*? I was interviewing people at the demo that night, and they were asking me why I was even bothering to write a story about the end of the world. And I just thought, 'Who's even going to read this?'"

Ed sighed and folded his notebook into his jacket pocket.

"Joe, did you ever hear of a guy called the Venerable Bede?"

Joe screwed up his face, scouring his exhausted mind for any clue. Shook his head.

"The Venerable Bede was a monk who lived in northern England in the eighth century, right about when the Viking raids started. The Vikings arrived on their longships out of the blue one day, and started laying waste to everything, raping and murdering. Bede was the head of the monastery on Lindisfarne, an island just off the Northumberland coast. I went there with Martha when we toured England about fifteen years back. Beautiful spot, very bleak. I've been thinking about Bede a lot these past couple of days. He and his fellow monks thought the Vikings were the end of the world. But he decided to write about them anyway. He survived the end of his world. His work survived. Now he's considered the godfather of English history."

Joe stared at his boss. "Ed, these aren't a few guys in horned helmets and longships. This is aliens! On an industrial scale."

"Remember what I used to tell you when you first started out? Perspective, Joe. See things through the eyes of the people you're writing about. No one was coming to rescue Bede and the people of northern England. They faced annihilation, all on their own. Lot of them died, in horrible ways. But enough survived to tell the tale. And that's what we do. We tell the tale, so others will know."

"First draft of history, huh?" said Joe.

"Maybe the *only* draft this time. And the biggest story ever, bud. You want a piece of it, or you just want to get wasted for a few more weeks?"

"Do I still have a job to go back to?"

Ed laughed, his breath forming condensation clouds in the chill air. "You kidding? You're the Morning Post's best last hope. A thousand words for tomorrow's 8am edition: 'How I partied the end of the world away.' Then go find me some Boston refugees. I heard there's a few already showing up at Phil Crampton's RV park."

Joe staggered back to the office without even bothering to stop by his apartment and get changed. All of a sudden, he was filled with the urge to record everything he had seen, done and felt, even though all of his journalistic training told him to always keep himself out of the story. He sat down at his keyboard and wrote the first thing that came into his mind.

It was the best of times, it was the worst of times.
It was the end of times.

· | ·

The trouble with the end of the world—aside from the obvious – is that unless it happens overnight, you still have to get up every morning and go to work. The end of days may in fact take weeks. Or years. And you've still got to eat while you wait for that final moment.

Joe's beat at the Post shifted overnight from police and courtrooms to survivalists, sects and refugees. *So* much more interesting. People were pouring out of the cities and heading for the hills, a massive stream of RVs, SUVs, trailers and minivans, driven by exhausted ad executives, doctors and investment counselors, their vehicles packed with squalling kids and barking family dogs. Social media influencers tweeted their progress into exile out of habit more than hope. Even without aliens chasing them, the masses were potentially their own traveling humanitarian crisis.

Fundamentally though, Joe's beat hadn't changed that much: it was still a bedrock of shootings and lootings, bar-room fights, and road rage incidents outside of empty supermarkets in towns which had nothing like enough parking for this urban exodus.

It may have been petty stuff compared with the scooping up of almost 50,000 Russians by spaceships, but it was huge by the standards of his usual journalistic fare.

On his first day on the new beat, Joe bought a bottle of lotion from a guy who had fled Boston and who said it would make the user invisible to the aliens: he swore the ETs were blind and could only track victims by their scent. The man had taken in over ten grand already, he boasted. Joe paid $17.99 and took it to a lab: the magic potion was nothing more than orange juice and canola oil. Another guy was selling converted shipping containers to be buried as instant underground bunkers: Joe filed a heartbreaking report on an entire family of five who had accidentally gassed themselves inside of one after using a propane stove to cook their dinner.

In fact, he came across so many crank stories that Ed gave him his own weekly column: *Why They Came.* It featured the most inventive theory of the week culled from his visits to the RV camps and newly installed garden sheds and tractor barns that people now occupied.

But as things began to calm down in the months after Moscow, a lot of the refugees decided to head back home. They were running short on cash and starting to feel a tentative hope that the worst might be over. Plus, you can't camp out in the woods forever on that kind of scale. They left the camping grounds knee-deep in plastic bags and soda cans: several local storekeepers retired on the money the refugees had spent on generators and camping gear.

Plenty stayed though, and Joe noticed a new phenomenon developing: the smaller the refugee population, the crazier the conspiracy theories. Perhaps because the saner, more rational ones had all left. In this atmosphere of concentrated delusion, Joe guessed he might be forgiven for not giving too much credence to a shabbily dressed man calling himself Cassius C Trenton when he showed up at his cubicle at the Post just before lunchtime one Monday.

He wasn't one of the wild-eyed and hollow-cheeked backwoods visionaries, the shifty Ted Kaczynskis who had been driven ever deeper into the woods by the influx of urban refugees. He was wearing an age-shined royal blue suit and looked not unlike Harrison Ford, albeit with a gray-flecked man-bun that sat poorly with the frayed jacket cuffs.

Joe glanced up from his computer, where he was half-heartedly writing up an article based on a press release from the Journal of American Medicine that reported that the average American had gained an extra six and half pounds since the Moscow attack. But mostly he was skim-reading an online article about how Mexico's National Institute of Anthropology had published photos of Mayan ceremonial disks that some archeologists now believed showed evidence of previous alien visitations.

Trenton had a firm handshake, and when Joe offered him a chair, he shook his head.

"Cassius C Trenton," he said. "Got a story for you. Let's go grab a coffee, kid. On me."

Joe tried to come up with some quick excuse. Despite the web-surfing, he was actually on deadline, and knew that once cranks got you on your own, they could be annoyingly insistent. Hostile even, if they felt the "lamestream media" was not offering up the full awe that their unique insight merited.

Joe glanced at his watch, ignored the business card Trenton had slipped on his desk. "I'm really sorry..."

"I know, kid, I know. Time's what you don't have. None of us do. But I have a story that'll knock your socks off."

Joe shook his head again, but Trenton wouldn't budge.

"Fifteen minutes. Trust me," he said. He gave Joe a weary, lopsided smile and leaned over the desk, taking in the images of the Mayan 'spacemen.' He nodded, then reached down to the keyboard and typed two words into the search engine:

"Arecibo message"

Joe frowned. His visitor pressed return.

Wikipedia bounced up as the top entry. Trenton clicked on the link. Joe glanced at it, then frowned at Trenton.

"The Arecibo message was broadcast into space a single time via frequency modulated radio waves at a ceremony to mark the remodeling of the Arecibo radio telescope in Puerto Rico on 16 November 1974," Trenton recited, as if from memory.

Joe stared blankly back at him. The entry looked long and technical. He resorted to an old journalistic fallback. "Executive summary?"

Trenton half-smiled. "Coffee?"

"Okay," Joe sighed, pulling his jacket from the back of his chair. "Fifteen minutes, though. I'm on deadline."

There was a little cafe right down the street that had resisted the onslaught of Starbucks and IHOP. On the way, the two men made small talk, as though the world wasn't under threat of attack by aliens, as though both of them were sane. It turned out Trenton was from Florida, which didn't up Joe's hopes that he might not be bat-shit crazy. As they waited for their drinks—straight-up black for Joe, macchiato with caramel and cream for Trenton—the latter launched into his spiel.

"The Arecibo message," he began, as soon as they got their coffees, "was, as you saw, a radio message broadcast into space in 1974, from a radio telescope in Puerto Rico. Like Wikipedia says, it was aimed at the star cluster M13, roughly 25,000 light years away. 25,000 years for the message to get there, another 25,000 for any response to come back. No one was really expecting a reply. Just a way of showing off our gadgetry, really."

They found a tiny table in the corner of the cafe. Joe sipped his coffee. On the one hand, Trenton sounded more coherent and scientific than most of the cranks he met. On the other hand, he was just cribbing Wikipedia, which, as every journalist knows, is never a good sign.

"Let me guess," Joe said, pointing a finger at him. "You're going to tell me there was a reply. And... you're the person who found it?"

Trenton smiled, the lopsided grin of an older man indulging some kid's wise-assery. "What Wikipedia fails to mention," he said, "is that while the Arecibo observatory transmitted a package of 210 bytes, it was later logged by another observatory in Brazil as a message of 235 bytes."

Joe shrugged. He wasn't even going to try to guess what that might signify.

Trenton shook his head. "So no, the aliens didn't respond to the message. But someone here ..." he pointed round the cafe, where a bored hipster was tapping at his laptop, no doubt writing a blog about his experience of the end of the world ... "someone right here on Earth hitched a ride on that outgoing message."

Joe's coffee was half done and his deadline loomed. "So?"

"So the additional data was intercepted in Brazil. It was called the Queiroz package, after the guy at the lab who picked up on it."

"I'm guessing you have the data that was transmitted," Joe said, taking a long gulp to speed up his exit.

"That data package was a mystery to every cryptographer, linguist and math nerd for more than 25 years," Trenton said. "It was used as a test for every advanced-grade cryptographer in the CIA and

NSA's code breaking departments. And not just them: the Russians, the Chinese, the Israelis..."

Joe finished his coffee. "Never heard of it, I'm afraid Mr. Trenton." He looked at his watch. Before he could say any more, Trenton interrupted.

"Eight minutes gone," he said. He pointed to his phone, where he had surreptitiously set the stopwatch. "You promised me fifteen."

It was a neat trick, Joe had to admit, since he hadn't actually bothered to look at his own watch when they came in. He gave him the benefit of the doubt. "Okay, so we have another few minutes. Can we cut to the chase at least?"

Trenton shook his head, a knowing smile on his face. "Listen, you think you're the first overworked, cynical hack I've ever dealt with, Joe?" he said. "Take a look at this..."

He pushed a single piece of paper over the table. It snagged in a splotch of spilled coffee. Joe picked it up and read it. It had a few gaps and appeared to have been partially redacted.

"Experimental nitrogen-fixation triggered population explosion. Carrying capacity under pressure. XXXX rate diminished. Atmospheric composition compromised. XXXX ??? Subject is ripe. Repeat Ripe. XXXX (Name ???) activating harvesters. Subjects' technology level sufficient that (????) required from Mowt (Maut?)"

Joe let the note slip back into the coffee smear.

Trenton brightened. "It's the Queiroz bundle," he said, as though it were self-explanatory.

"The one that the Israelis and the Chinese couldn't decipher?"

"Yes."

"Okay, leaving aside the fact that the original message was indecipherable..."

"... by normal cryptographers..."

"...whatever... there's some guy here filing a, uh, I don't know, a bureaucratic report to aliens that... what? That humans are ripe for harvesting?"

Trenton nodded. "Listen, Joe, I can't tell you exactly how I knew how to decipher the message. You can see there's a few words I could only guess at, or simply had no idea what they might be. But it makes sense, don't you see? The aliens haven't just *arrived*. There's been at least one of them here, living among us, observing us, for who knows how long? I can't tell what they think we're ripe for—eating, fertilizer, gassing up their spaceships for all I know—but look at what happened in Moscow. Didn't that look a heck of a lot like a harvest?"

Joe stared at him: there wasn't much expectation in Trenton's expression. He knew how it sounded. His only gambit was that since something actually *had* arrived from who-knew-where and scooped up 50,000 Russians, all bets in the skepticism department were officially hedged for now.

"Listen, Mr. Trenton, it's... it's an interesting idea. I have this weekly column..."

"I know what your weekly column is, Joe. 'Nutcase of the week.' But you know what? I'll take it. Run it, see what happens. But listen to this one thing before you go—and here, take my card..."

"I already..."

"Take another, you never know..." he pressed a second business card into Joe's hand, then for good measure slipped a third into his jacket pocket. "Just remember this. I know what's happening right now is the biggest story ever—end of the world, aliens yada yada... and every journalist in the world wants a piece of it. But everyone *else* is writing the same story. The news as it happens. What I want you to know is the interesting bit..."

"'Alien invasion of Earth' *not* being the interesting bit?"

"... the *back* story. And that is this: there are people here on Earth who knew this was going to happen. Important people." He wagged a finger at Joe as he pulled on his puffer jacket. "Very important people, and quite a few of them."

Joe zippered his jacket.

"This observer guy, he's not just observing, Joe. He's *interacting*. He's arranging, he's planning. And he's in touch with our leaders. There are people who knew these creatures were out there, and they did nothing. They're already making plans, working with them, selling *us* out ..."

"Can I ask you something, Mr. Trenton?"

"Please, call me Cassius?"

"How did you come across this code in the first place?"

"I did the NSA test. I was always a nerd, but nothing prepared me for that. I sat in that room and saw the code, and somehow it just spoke to me. Can't tell you how. My superiors laughed at me at first. Then they dismissed me. Then they threatened me to never tell anyone about it."

It was an entertaining variant of the story, Joe had to admit. "Okay, Mr Trenton, I'll write it up for my column, either this week or..."

He was about to leave when he saw that everyone else in the cafe was moving towards a television set in the far corner. There were only about seven people in the entire place, but suddenly they were all standing in silence in front of the TV screen. Joe walked over.

The screen showed a small group of badly dressed people standing in a snowy field. The footage was caught on a shaky cell phone camera. The people looked cold and nonplussed. A news ticker flashed below them, though it could clearly do nothing to enlighten the confused folk on the screen above it.

Alien abduction survivors found near Voronezh.

Joe put a hand to his forehead.

Trenton appeared beside him.

"It's the Russians," Trenton said. "They're back."

• | •

"What do the Russians know?"
By Joe Chavez.

That was as far as he'd got on the article: below the byline, the screen of his laptop was a yawning blank.

"You know, I'm not sure how much more of this I can take," Joe said, looking up at his brother Tony, who was smoking a fat blunt.

It would have been hard for a stranger to know the two young men were brothers: Tony was three years younger than Joe, but big and stocky, a bear-like stoner with long hair tied back in an unkempt ponytail, and a scrubby beard that had been teased into a tiny braid at the chin. Where Joe was lean and fidgety, his brother was expansive and chilled.

It had clearly affected their divergent career choices: Joe had opted for the never-ending treadmill of news, while Tony—technically still a computer sciences major at the local college—was carving out a life for himself as a purveyor of fine weed on campus and in Fullerton's student bars.

"You mean journalism?" said his brother, breathing out a stream of smoke. "Or life in general?"

He offered the blunt to Joe, who held up a hand. He'd had a frightening experience with cannabis psychosis when he was a teenager after smoking some mutant-strength skunk. He'd abstained ever since: that woozy sense of incipient madness still overcame him sometimes, when he was overtired or had drunk a little too much. Maybe that was why the motionless victims of syrup in the park had made such a powerful impression on him.

"You know what I'm talking about," he said, taking a swig of beer from the IPA bottle by his laptop. "All this endless bullshit speculation about something that's so absolutely vital to our survival as a species, yet about which we know precisely zilch."

"Relax, bro," said Tony. "Gotta be a good sign that some of them came back, at least. Am I right? The Russians'll let us know what they've seen up there in ET's spaceship soon enough. Maybe they're here to help us out from all the shit we've done to the planet."

Not *all* the Russians had come back, however. The group that was found stumbling in the snow outside the southern Russian city of Voronezh only numbered 17 people—14 men and three women. They were whisked off to a local police station and from there on to who knew where, put into indefinite quarantine before anyone could get a word out of them. And Moscow, in its habitually opaque way, had kept the whole world dangling.

That left 47,348 Russians still unaccounted for.

The United Nations General Assembly and governments around the world urged Moscow to share whatever it knew, but the Kremlin was relishing its sudden power. Dmitri Chernakov, the Russian government spokesman, would only say that the returnees appeared to be in excellent health, and were being "questioned as to their experience." Until Russia ascertained exactly what had happened to its citizens, the world would just have to wait.

Joe squinted at his notes, a scrawled checklist of ideas he had cribbed largely from science and military experts posting on Twitter. Such was modern journalism in an under-funded local paper.

Screening for alien viruses?
DNA testing for cloning/implants/robotics?
Evidence of brainwashing/memory loss?
Have they been briefed to form an alliance with the Kremlin?
Weapons tech transfer?
Geo-political implications of Russians making first contact?

He'd been trying to figure out what the hell to write for two hours now, painfully aware that his readers who were just as capable of googling the same sources as he was. Not like anyone really had a clue, either. But Ed wanted the story by tomorrow morning, and it was now late and his mojo was running dry.

"You don't actually trust the Russians, do you?" he asked Tony.

"C'mon dude, Cold War's long over. We're all in this together now."

"You really believe that?" muttered Joe. "Or is your weed a bit too strong?"

"Like *you'd* know," said Tony. "This is Lucid Aura, bro. Nothing like that junk that messed up your head back in the day. I don't sell, much less smoke, any old shit. You should ask your boss."

"What boss?"

"That old guy, Ed whatshisname. He's a regular."

"You sell pot to Ed James? My *editor*?"

"Chillax, bro, chillax. I went to the office a few weeks ago looking for you and we got talking. He's cool, dude. Said since his wife died he'd been dabbling a bit, you know, like when he was young and shit. This stuff helps you sleep, makes you relaxed. You should try it."

Joe was about to get angry, but then he remembered: *alien invasion*. It just wasn't worth it anymore. Why should he care if his brother was peddling weed to his boss? The world was about to end.

"Okay Tony, okay" he said. "You know what? It's late and I've got to finish this shit. Ed wants it for the morning online edition. Unless he's too high to remember, of course."

He gave his little brother a pointed look: Joe had been almost like a parent to the kid since their mother had got early onset dementia when Joe was 18 and Tony was just 14. The insurance only covered the first few months of her care, so he'd had to drop out of journalism school. Ed James had taken a risk on him—a totally inexperienced Hispanic kid who dreamed of making it in a dying industry—and given him a very junior job on the Post, little more than internship: Joe had used his meager salary to keep paying the rent on mom's apartment. Luckily, she'd taken out a life insurance policy, but by the time she died, Joe was already doing well at the paper and decided to avoid the crippling debt of gaining an education. After all, why bother studying journalism when you were already a journalist?

"If you want to crash, you can take my room. I can sleep on the sofa bed," he said. It was a fairly common routine and saved his brother teetering back to the sleazy crib he shared with three other stoner students.

"Awesome, bro," Tony said with a smile. "What would I do without my big brother, eh?" He grinned at his own joke—he dwarfed his older sibling — as he disappeared into the tiny bathroom in a cloud of smoke.

Joe stared at the blank screen again. Nope, still no inspiration. He tabbed back to the Post website and did a quick search under his own name.

The article he'd written on Cassius C Trenton had gone out that morning. As usual with his weekly column, it had elicited a predictable range of reader comments: either Trenton was a visionary with an inside track on the greatest global cover-up ever, or he was just another attention-seeking basket-case. There were 57 comments—most readers leaned towards the visionary hypothesis. Occam's razor had been dangerously blunted by the extremely unlikely arrival of aliens.

Joe had been intrigued just enough by Trenton's tale to agree to a second coffee, three days after the Russians had shown up in that snowy field. Besides, much to Joe's fury, Cynthia Durkin had given up on reaching Moscow and had made her way back from Kyiv or wherever the hell she'd been stranded after the ships came. She'd managed to do some blah color piece about the monuments the Russians were building: a vast granite obelisk monument had been commissioned in Moscow, in typical overblown Russian style, but in the town of Nizhni Novgorod, to the south, a more organic statue was being constructed out of hundreds of the victims' rusting cars, set in a swirling tornado of rebar and cable that whisked them off, frozen forever, into the perma-lead sky of the Eurasian plains.

It was a good piece, Joe had to admit, though he did make sure to point out to Ed that Cynthia was still hundreds of miles away from where the events had taken place and was, in fact, not even in Russia. Ed had run it anyway, grateful for a first-person report from a Post writer. When she got back, she had been duly restored to pole position as the paper's star reporter. Joe needed a good story to fight back, though he doubted Trenton would be the one to supply it.

Trenton's tale had begun with his mother, Shirley. She'd been a minor Hollywood starlet back in the 1970s, with roles in some Roger Corman-style low budget flicks, soft porn as far as Joe could tell when he googled the titles. She'd been part of a boho LA set, and had run with a pretty wild crowd of Hollywood hangers-on, rockers and bikers. Not quite the Manson family, but of that ilk. In 1975, she and a few girlfriends had been invited to a party at the mansion of some playboy millionaire, a guy who'd made his money in the newly emerging sex toy industry. There was some big-at-the-time but now forgotten band playing in the grounds, The Honeymen: lots of dope and coke, a splash of heroin, everyone getting naked in the heart-shaped pool. There was even a rumor that Keith Richards had shown up, but no one really remembered.

One of the guys hosting the party had invited Shirley into a private VIP suite, to the all-hallowed party-within-a-party. Shirley was stoned and hoping to meet Keith, but was not surprised to be confronted with a big satin-covered bed and a man with a Super-8 movie camera. She'd been down that road a few times, and was generally cool with it. But there were a few other men in the room, one of them holding what looked like an oversized maggot.

"What the fuck *is* that?" she asked. Her host explained it was the latest, state-of-the-art sex toy, made of latex and designed to give the ultimate orgasm, to man and woman alike.

"Looks like a giant bug," said Shirley.

"Do you know what an ovipositor is?" the man had said. Shirley asked him to repeat the word. "Ovipositor. It's how insects lay their eggs."

"Ugh, gross," said Shirley.

"This injects a small gelatin egg into you," explained the man, leaning over so she could see the device up close. "It's warm and soft and dissolves harmlessly after twenty minutes. But it gives you the sensation of being the victim of an alien abduction, of being ravaged by some unknown species. It's very popular in Japan right now.

We've brought a few over to, uh, road test them on a select American audience." And he gave Shirley a candid look.

"Have you tried it?" Shirley asked.

"I have," said the man. "I passed out with pleasure."

"Okay," shrugged Shirley. "I'm game, I guess."

The next month, she skipped her period.

Nine months later, Cassius Trenton was born.

His mother didn't tell him the story until he was in his twenties, and already a budding cryptologist with the National Security Agency.

Joe skim-read the article again, trying to ascertain if he'd caught Trenton in the right light. As a boy, he'd been a math prodigy, but also a loner, uncomfortable in the company not just of other kids, but of adults too. His teachers had shied away from him, even his math teacher, who Trenton claimed had been intimidated by his precocious abilities. His mother was a distant woman, addled by drink and drugs and mourning her lost youth. He'd found solace in computer programming, and rapidly got into hacking. But even among his fellow subversives in the newly formed hacker forums, he felt isolated, unchallenged. Eventually, someone in a chat room had mentioned the legendary Queiroz package: was it real? Had anyone managed to access it outside of the NSA? No one knew. There was plenty of speculation that it was a hoax dreamed up by the NSA to lure in naïve young hackers. Despite that, Trenton was intrigued enough to apply. He was easily accepted, and rapidly rose through the agency's hackers and code-breakers. After four years, he was deemed qualified to see the mystery code.

He sat down and read it like it was the morning newspaper.

His supervisors were stunned. They looked at him like he was insane. Asked him to explain his methodology. Trenton couldn't. "I just knew what it said," he'd told Joe. "Just... knew it. Like I was reading something I'd always known."

He was ordered not to discuss it with anyone. Like a good footsoldier of national security, he obeyed. Even so, as the months passed, he received fewer and fewer assignments. The work that he did get was routine, largely maintaining surveillance systems. He never got any feedback about the results of his extraordinary transcription: his supervisors advised him to forget about it whenever he asked.

Eventually, he mentioned it to a colleague he trusted, and who he knew had taken the same test. He simply had to talk to someone about it, and the man had the same level of security clearance. The next day he was summoned to his boss' office and dismissed.

"It was as if they were just waiting for an excuse to fire me," he said. He was, of course, warned if he ever discussed any aspect of his service with anyone, he would be arrested. For years, he kept quiet.

"But here's what bugged me," he'd told Joe as they sat in the cafe, sipping lattes. "Sure, it's possible, given my mother's lifestyle, that she simply got pregnant at one of the parties she went to. She insists she was on the pill, but given her drug intake, she could have easily forgotten to take it. But it was the dates—the Queiroz package was sent in November 1974. Whoever sent it said he was about to "activate the harvesters." Now, what if that strange party in LA that my mother went to in 1975 was part of that plan?"

Joe had stared at Trenton over their coffees, trying to figure out just how delusional he might be. "What on earth makes you think the two things are in any way connected?"

"The fact that I knew the code. No one else in the world had ever made the slightest dent in it." Trenton paused. "Suppose the code, the language itself, was innate in these "harvesters." Suppose that whoever was behind the activation had genetically edited humans with whatever alien code might be needed to create these harvesters, as active servants for the aliens who would soon be coming?"

"But...but..." Joe threw up his hands. "Why aren't you a harvester, then? Why are you running around snitching on your alleged alien overlords?"

Trenton had obviously thought of that one a long time ago. "Maybe something went wrong with the coding. Some missed genetic switch that should have turned on that would have allowed me to hear the call to action, the way a baby sea turtle knows by instinct to head to the sea when it hatches out on the beach. Maybe I was a misfire."

"That's... that's just crazy," said Joe. "Not only crazy but also a huge filling in of massive blanks. I mean, there could be any number of other explanations..."

"I know," said Trenton, leaning back and taking a sip of coffee. "Like I'm crazy, like I imagined the whole thing. But then why would the FBI be after me?"

Joe half-laughed. "The FBI are after you?" So said just about every crank he'd ever interviewed—it was a mark of veracity, about as convincing as a plastic sheriff's badge.

"I've been on the run for years," said Trenton.

"Well then, the FBI aren't very good at their job in that case, are they?" said Joe.

Trenton shook his head. "No, they're pretty good. It's just that I'm better. I wasn't a hacker for nothing. I can assume different identities, get access to funds without too much trouble. I have support groups out there. It's only when I expose myself to people like you that I risk getting caught."

"Why take the risk with a small-time, no-account hack like me then?"

"First of all, none of the big papers will give me the time of day."

Ouch, thought Joe, and knew that Trenton had caught it.

"Second, the FBI are pretty tied up right now that first contact has been made. I'm sure my translation of the Queiroz package caught people's attention back when I did it, but there must have been plenty of skeptics. Now they must be taking a real good look at that again."

"So, what do you want me to do?" Joe said.

"Run my story. Put it in the news section if you can, but run it in your conspiracy-of-the-week column if you have to. On Google, it all looks the same. Just get it out there, with some modicum of mainstream credibility."

"Okay, Cassius," he said. "I'll do my best."

• | •

The man in the hospital bed squinted out of a bulging black eye. Joe had trouble understanding what he was saying: his front teeth were missing and his jaw was broken, his lips black and blood-cracked. He occasionally sucked on the straw sticking out a plastic sippy cup by his head by the bed. His face was almost totally obscured by bandages.

"Vey fed I wa' one of *vem*," he wheezed, barely audible. "Nalien."

They said I was one of them. An alien, Joe wrote. It was the second public beating he had reported on in the past week. People mistaken for aliens disguised as humans. Looking at the man's splinted hand, resting over his chest on a metal support, Joe asked himself again:

Had the Trenton article led to this?

No, he told himself: since the Russians had mysteriously reappeared, the entire planet had been gripped with fear that the aliens had someone mimicked humans and were wandering among them, shape-shifters straight out *Invasion of the Body Snatchers*. In the face of the ominous Russian silence, a wave of hysteria had broken out; *they* were infiltrating society. There was even a hashtag #TheyAreAmongUs trending on Twitter, along with photos of people looking slightly expressionless or glassy eyed.

The man Joe was trying to interview was a welder from the town of Dawes. He'd been visiting a friend in Fullerton, had a few drinks and was headed for his truck when some youths—who were themselves returning from a bar—had decided he looked "odd." They surrounded him and started chanting "Alien". The man had in fact been lucky—just two days before, in the town of Wellby, a homeless man had been beaten and then set on fire while a police patrol car stood idly by. The incident had been caught on a cell phone.

Perhaps his Trenton article had contributed to the hysteria. The comments section online had gradually started to swell—demands for pictures of Trenton flooded in, calls for him to be hunted down by "concerned citizens." Some had even threatened Joe himself for consorting with an "enemy alien," calling for his arrest and interrogation. The fury of some of the responses shook him. Ed James had told him to take some time off, but when Joe heard of the latest beating, he'd felt obliged to come and cover it himself.

The man in the hospital bed had tried to plead with his attackers, but to no avail. There were four of them, and he had barely even tried to fight back. No point. Instead, he'd shielded himself as best he could. They beat him to the ground and kicked him until he lost consciousness.

"I'm so sorry," Joe said as he closed his notebook. He meant it, though the man could not have known why. He picked up his coat, thanked the nurse on duty and walked out the front door of the hospital. He stood a minute, breathing in lungfuls of cold November air. Then he pulled out his phone and started to call a cab.

"Mr. Chavez?"

Joe hadn't even noticed the two men approaching him. Suits and overcoats, official looking. He stiffened.

"Yes," he said. "Who are you?"

"My name is Special Agent Franks, from the FBI. This is my partner, Agent Bresson." He held out a business card, which Joe reflexively accepted.

"The FBI?" he croaked, instantly forgetting both their names.

"Do you have a minute?" the first one said. "We have a car."

"Uh, yeah, what... may I ask what it's about?" said Joe. "I was just about to go home, long day, officer, uh..."—he glanced down at the business card — "Franks."

"Agent. And please, you can call me Tom."

"It won't take long," said the other. "We want to ask you a couple of questions about Cassius Trenton."

Joe put his phone back in his pocket. "Trenton? Um, ok," he said. "Where's your car?"

They walked round the building in silence. In the parking lot, one of the men pressed a remote, and the blinkers flashed on a dark blue Taurus.

Bresson got in the driver's seat while Franks sat shotgun. He turned around to face Joe.

"Just so we know we're on the same page, could you please identify this man?" he said, holding up the screen of his cell phone. It was Trenton, taken maybe a decade before. Less puffy round the eyes, and without the ridiculous man-bun.

"That's Trenton," said Joe, immediately feeling guilty for identifying a source, wondering if he should have a lawyer with him. This had never happened to him before.

"Good," said Franks, putting the phone back in his pocket.

Franks pulled a file out of the glove compartment and produced a piece of paper. Joe saw it was a newspaper clipping. "We read your column, Mr. Chavez."

"I'm glad someone did." In the darkness of the parked car, the agent forced a half-smile of sympathy for the poor provincial hack.

"Trenton talked about a letter, which he claims is a translation of an indecipherable radio signal sent out in the seventies ..."

"Yeah, he had a name for it. Something South American." Joe took the article and scanned the lines he'd written.

"The Queiroz package," said Bresson.

Joe nodded. "Yeah, that was it."

"Did he say anything else about it, Mr. Chavez? Anything that might not have been included in your piece?"

"Uh, no, I don't think so. Maybe. I'd have to check my notes."

"Do you have them to hand? I see you have a notebook in your pocket."

Joe shrugged. "Yeah, I was just interviewing someone..." He felt his mind racing, trying to figure out how to cooperate with the law but not betray his source's confidence. "Um, different notebook, I think..." He briefly flipped through the scrawled pages, then shook his head.

"You wouldn't happen to have recorded your conversation, would you, Mr. Chavez?"

"No," Joe said. "I mean, he was just another walk-in wild man. I get a lot of them since I started my column..." He started flipping the pages of his notebook again, trying to gain a few seconds to gather his wits.

"So," he said, still squinting in the gloom at his handwriting. "Does this mean that there really *was* something to what Trenton said? I mean, I thought he was just another nut job, saying the FBI was after him. And now here you guys are..."

Agent Franks smiled. "No, no, Trenton's been peddling that line for years now on his website. Got a lot more traction since Moscow, of course. But what concerns us is that he actually used to be a government analyst. And when those guys start talking to you guys, that's when we like to know exactly what's been discussed."

"He was a real analyst? What branch?"

Franks' eyes twinkled. "Can't disclose that, I'm afraid. Did you and he discuss anything other than his theory that the aliens are here to vacuum us all up like the Grim Reaper?"

In fact, there had been. Trenton had told Joe he believed there were people on earth who knew the aliens were coming. *People at the very top*, he'd said. Not just the "harvesters" who'd been implanted inside the wombs of unsuspecting women.

Joe had asked him during their interview why he believed that. "Because of the way I was hounded out of the service," Trenton had told him. "They didn't just laugh at me: they really pushed me out, made life hell for me. Something really triggered them. And they never let up. Never."

Joe hadn't in fact included that nugget of information in his column: not to protect Trenton or because he thought it was any more insane than anything else he'd said: he simply didn't have the space. Most of the paper had been given over to follow-up pieces on the Russians' return. And it hadn't seemed a particularly relevant detail.

At least, not until the FBI had shown up.

In the back of the darkened car, Joe looked up from his notebook and shook his head. "No, nothing apart from what's in the article. Listen, um, Agent Franks, I don't have all my notes here. They must be back at my place. I'll check when I get back."

"We can give you a ride," said Franks.

The twinkle had gone from the agent's eyes.

Shit, thought Joe. *No shaking these guys off.* He nodded slowly. Bresson started the engine and the car gently pulled out.

As they drove through the quiet streets, Joe pulled out his phone, turning its face away from Franks. He quickly texted his brother: *If ur at my place, get out now. On way with FBI.* The last thing he needed was these two bursting in on Tony smoking a giant spliff in his pad. *Dont call em ok,* he added, not even bothering to correct the typo.

They reached the apartment twenty minutes later. Joe was relieved to see the lights were out as they pulled up outside.

He unlocked the door, flicked on the light, and walked into the living room. He had no idea what he was going to do to get rid of these guys. Would they believe he had no notes from his interview with Trenton? Should he have asked them for a warrant to enter? He certainly wouldn't hand them his notes without a warrant of some kind, and besides, his shorthand was all but illegible, even to him. His mind was racing with questions.

"Er, you guys want a coffee or something?" he said as the FBI agents stepped into his small living room. "Not much seating here, I'm afraid, but... *holy shit!*"

The FBI men whipped round to where Joe was looking, into the small kitchenette area behind the breakfast counter. In the shadows stood a man holding an automatic pistol that was pointing straight at Agent Franks. All three men put their hands up, but only Joe spoke.

"Trenton? What the hell are you doing here?" He had to do a double take: the man standing in his kitchenette clearly was Trenton, but at the same time he *wasn't*: the nasty graying man bun was gone, replaced by short brown hair cut in an almost military style. Gone too was the frayed old suit, its place taken by a navy blue sweatshirt and combat pants.

"Evening gentlemen," said Trenton in a steady voice. Gone was the almost pleading tone Joe had heard in the cafe. This new Trenton sounded confidently in control of an utterly strange situation. "I'd like to ask our friends from the bureau to slowly reach inside their jackets and remove their side-arms."

"Trenton, what do you think..." began Franks, but Trenton interrupted.

"Uh uh uh, my friend. Glocks on the coffee table before we start any negotiations, please."

The two men slowly put their hands under their coats, removed their service pistols, leaned down and placed them on the table before standing up straight again.

"Trenton, are you completely insane?" hissed Joe. "What are you hoping to achieve with all this?"

"Joe, do me a favor and bring those two guns over here, please. Keep to the wall so I have a clear line of sight on our friends."

"I will not," said Joe. "I can't be an accomplice in this..."

"Do it Joe," Trenton said. His tone was firm, but not unfriendly. Joe found himself mildly impressed by the man's cool, despite the fact that he was obviously insane. He picked the guns up and carried them across the small room.

"Thanks," Trenton said, putting the weapons under the kitchen counter. "Now Joe, you take the armchair there. Like you said, there's not much seating here so our friends here will just have to sit on the floor. Criss-cross apple-sauce, facing the wall, hands palm-down on the floor behind you."

The agents complied. Trenton came out from the kitchenette and stood behind them. He reached around Frank's body and found the handcuffs on his belt. He snapped them on the agent, then repeated the procedure with Besson.

Holding his own gun close to the back of Franks' head, he started speaking again, his tone cool but laced with menace.

"Now tell me exactly where you wanted to take me, agent."

"Trenton, you are clearly a disturbed man," Franks began. Joe was horrified when Trenton smacked him on the back of his head with the butt of his gun. It was such a casual act of violence, and directed at a member of the FBI. Franks wobbled but did not fall.

"Can it, agent. Twelve years ago I predicted that aliens were coming to prey on us and I was hounded out of the NSA, gaslighted like I was a crazy man. Three months ago aliens appeared out of nowhere and did exactly what I said they were going to do. Do not try to make me out to be crazy. Now, I'm going to ask you again, where were you told to take me, and by whom?"

The muzzle of the pistol was resting against the back of Franks' skull now, and Joe found himself believing that Trenton might just be crazy enough to pull the trigger.

There was a long pause while Franks considered his options, then took a deep breath. "Okay, okay Trenton. Listen. Obviously in light of what happened in Moscow, some people inside the intelligence community thought it would be a good idea to revisit your case. Not like you've ever let anyone forget about you, with all your online activity."

That sounded reasonable to Joe, but Trenton was clearly unappeased. "Who? Who wanted to reopen the case?"

"I don't know," said Franks. "We were only ordered to bring you in."

"Where were you supposed to take me?"

"DC," said Franks.

"Drive me in your Ford out there?"

Franks nodded.

"And who were you to report to when you got there?"

Franks paused, as though considering how much to divulge. Trenton smacked him again, and Joe could see a red welt rising beneath the FBI man's close-cropped hair.

"Supervisor Delpone."

"Never heard of him. Who is he?"

"Special investigations unit. It was set up after Moscow. Cross-agency, liaises with a bunch of scientists from NASA and DARPA, as well as DIA and NSA."

"And what did they want with me?"

"Like I said, we were just told to deliver you there. They said they wanted to question you about your ability to decipher the code."

"Is there more code?" Trenton almost sounded hopeful. Franks shrugged, as much as a handcuffed man sitting cross-legged on the floor can shrug. "I don't know. They just want to talk to you. That's all."

Trenton was crouched down behind Franks, and rocked on his heels, thinking.

"Okay," he said after a moment. "I'll come with you."

"You will?" Bresson said. Joe saw Franks turn and glower at his colleague.

"Makes sense. They finally get it, after all these years. It only took 50,000 people being abducted to convince them."

He walked across the room to the kitchenette and reached under the counter for the agents' pistols, then returned and put the guns on the table.

"Now, if they have more code that they've either never told anyone about, or that they've intercepted since my day ..." he said as he unlocked the cuffs first on Franks and then Bresson. The two men rose stiffly, shaking their hands and rubbing their wrists. Joe looked on, mystified at this unfathomable turn of events.

"No hard feelings?" Trenton said as he pushed the agent's weapons back across the kitchen counter towards them.

Franks and Bresson picked up their guns, checked the clips. Franks nodded at Joe.

"Take him," he told Bresson, as he raised his own pistol and leveled it at Trenton's gut.

Before Joe had a chance to react in any way, Bresson raised his pistol and fired at his chest.

Two gunshots filled the room with obliterating sound.

Bresson screamed and reeled back against the wall, clutching his gun hand with his left. It took Joe a bewildered second to see that Franks was doing the same.

Trenton seamlessly raised his own pistol and shot Franks in the chest at almost point-blank range. The bullet hurled the agent against the door of the apartment, where he lay clutching at the smoking hole in his winter overcoat.

Joe stood rooted to the spot, eyes and mouth wide open.

"Oh my god..." he managed at last. It was a hoarse whimper.

"Black bag ops," said Trenton, kicking Bresson's gun across the floor, even though Bresson was clearly unable to even lift what remained of his hand. "Kill any witnesses. Disable me and take me off god knows where. Probably kill me too and dump my body somewhere discreet, after they'd tortured me to see what I know. Now, we have to go, quick. Gunshot reports will bring the cops in 10 minutes tops, even in a dump like this."

"*Go?*" croaked Joe. Trenton nodded, then kneeled down next to Bresson. Joe could see that several of the man's fingers and part of his hand had been blown off. He was making a keening sound between clenched teeth.

"Look over there," Trenton told Joe, pointing at the kitchenette. Joe automatically turned his head and immediately there was another explosion of a shot. He looked back and almost threw up: the wall behind Bresson was a Jackson Pollock of blood and splotches of white matter. An abstract question fluttered unbidden through Joe's stunned brain: why was it called gray matter when it was so clearly white?

"Come on, Joe," said Trenton, straightening up. "That guy just tried to kill you. You'd be dead now if I hadn't slipped some builder's putty into their gun barrels. All I had to hand when I intercepted your text to your brother."

Joe stared back, nothing making any sense. "You... you tapped my phone?"

"Your phone, your emails, your apartment's locks. I knew they'd come once you published that piece. I had to flush them out."

"You used me as a decoy...?"

"Joe," Trenton said, shaking him by his shoulders. "We have to leave now. These guys don't give up. You are on their to-do list now, and the cops aren't going to let you go prancing around free after they see all of this. So ditch your phone in the toilet, and any other electronic device you have on you, and let's go."

Joe still didn't move, so Trenton patted him down. Then he took his pistol, and holding it by the muzzle, pummeled Joe's phone. Joe finally reacted reflexively. "Hey, that's a new iPhone ..." Then he remembered the two corpses lying on his living room floor.

"Oh fuck," he said, but let Trenton bundle him out the door, stepping over the body of agent Franks as it slumped into the hallway, blooming a pool of blood.

● | ●

Trenton drove at what Joe would have called a leisurely pace, not the speed of a man fleeing a crime scene where he had just killed two FBI agents, if that is what those men really were.

In the distance, they could hear a police siren begin its urgent forlorn whoop.

"Where are we going?" said Joe, sitting in the cold cabin of the pickup. Passing street lamps bathed him in alternate strips of orange and darkness. The words were barely audible because his mouth was so dry.

"Not far," said Trenton. "We have to hole up for a while. Better to hide close by rather than try running any distance right now. Area's going to be swarming with cops."

"You ... you just murdered that guy. Bresson. Straight up shot him in the head," said Joe. He hadn't seen where Trenton had stowed the murder weapon, but assumed it was still on him somewhere.

Trenton squinted ahead into the darkness of the road, but his voice was calm.

"This is the end of the world, kid. And we're fighting a war against an enemy we can't even see. If I'd left him alive, he would have alerted his bosses immediately, and we'd never have made it five miles. This way, the police will be trying to figure out who those guys were and what they were doing at the house of a local news reporter."

Joe stared through the windshield, trying to get his thoughts straight. The last houses of Fullerton melted away into forest and river inlets, the occasional turnoff to a farmhouse. For some reason, he looked at his watch and was surprised to see it was only 8.30. It felt like a whole night had passed already.

Eventually, he broke the silence. "Where are we going? Do you have a safe house or something?"

"Not much of a one, but it'll do for now," Trenton said. "Once I saw you were actually going to run the piece, I had to move fast. We'll hole up there for a day, then see where the search has moved on to."

"I can't believe this happening," said Joe. "Who the hell are you? I mean, I really thought you were just another crazy conspiracy schlub. Now it turns out you're Jason fucking Bourne or something. Was that all an act when we met?"

Trenton twitch-smiled, never taking his eyes off the road. "Let's just say I've learned how to disguise myself over the years. Downplay my latent abilities. But who am I? I could have told you that with some degree of certainty before the Queiroz package, Joe. Since then, I'm not so sure. Do I have alien DNA in me? That's what I started to wonder, after I couldn't figure out how else I knew what that message said. Language learning is innate in humans, but you have to spend years as a kid practicing to get fluent. What if some alien species figured a way to make it automatic? Pre-programmed. That'd be infinitely more efficient."

"Okay," said Joe, struggling to resurrect some vestige of his journalistic demeanor. "So let's say you are ... part alien. How did you know that there were others out there? You said that people in top government positions knew that the aliens were coming."

"I didn't. Not at first. I mean, I guessed there must be some kind of extraterrestrial presence on Earth already—after all, someone got mum banged up with an alien egg at that LA party, right? But as for the big wigs knowing, that came much later."

"How?"

Trenton didn't answer. He was staring at a device he was carrying, some kind of hand-held GPS tracker Joe assumed, but smaller than any he'd ever seen before. Its screen was a subtle night-light gray and green. Military grade, perhaps. Trenton scanned the looming woods ahead.

"Almost there," he said. He slowed the pickup to a crawl and prowled the dark country road. Off in the woods a dull green light flashed twice, almost invisible. Five seconds later there was another double blink.

"This is it, kiddo," said Trenton, cutting the headlights and trundling down a dirt track.

"Wait, you have accomplices?" Joe said, the fear freshening up again.

"Of course," said Trenton as they emerged in front of an unlit farmhouse behind a copse of pines. "Even a genius alien half-breed like me couldn't stay ahead of the game all this long on his own. Come on, Joe. Let's meet the resistance."

• | •

A lean African American woman in a hooded parka stepped up as Joe and Trenton got out in the pitch-black yard. Ice cracked in puddles underfoot, and the woman held out her hand.

"Joe," she said. "Good to see you. I'm BB."

Joe shook her hand and was about to speak when Trenton cut in.

"Two dead in his apartment. Black bag, bureau badges," he reached in his pocket and pulled out the dead men's things. "Assume hot pursuit. I'll get these to Gas. You give Joe the security briefing. The condensed version."

Trenton pushed through the front door of the farmhouse, leaving Joe and BB alone in the yard.

"Okay, Joe," said BB. "Like I said, I'm BB. I'm OSO, the Operational Security Officer here. Now, there's no reason to believe anyone is looking for us here yet, but if they do come, we have to assume they'll come down that road you just drove down. So our first line of retreat is round the back here," she said, setting off through the darkness at the side of the building. Joe stumbled on a tree-stump but BB seemed to have already memorized every rabbit hole on the property.

"Path runs through the woods, right beside that shed you can just make out at the end of the vegetable patch. You hear anything— anything moving around the property, you come inside, tell us and then head straight down that path fast as you can. We may not follow immediately: we got our own security protocols to follow in the event of contact. Keep your head low and no matter what they may say, don't stop. They're not going to arrest you now, not at this stage. The people coming after you now are going to make you disappear off the face of the earth. So keep going until you hit the open pasture on the other side of the wood – do *not* head out into the field. Remember, just because you can't see them don't mean they can't see you. Bear right along the treeline four hundred yards and you'll hit a farm track, where there's a junk Ford in a ditch. That is our rendezvous. That's where you wait. Don't try to get any further without one of us, you won't make it a mile on your own. You got that?"

Joe struggled to remember a fraction of what he had just heard. BB repeated it, then made Joe repeat it twice. "Okay, that'll do. And remember, no lights of any sort, okay? Now, you look like a man who could do with a drink. Come on inside."

• | •

The interior of the house was almost as dark as the woods outside, and scarcely warmer. All the furniture had been pushed back to the walls. In the middle of the living room, a small black tent had been pitched, inside which Joe was told two intelligence operators—Gas and Darkman, since everyone except Trenton seemed to have a codename—were monitoring local police frequencies and hacking email and phone chatter, including Joe's own accounts and social media.

The tent allowed them to run computers with no light leakage, Trenton said.

"You were asking earlier about how I learned there were higher-ups involved in this, that our government knew these things were coming," said Trenton. "Well, that's how I met BB here. You see, after I got canned by the government, I started making my own inquiries. Anti-government chatrooms, hacker forums, all the usual channels. Ninety-nine-point-nine percent of that is whacko conspiracy theories, of course, UFO watchers and 911 truthers, which is frustrating when you start out, but actually serves a useful function. It hides the trace elements of actual people who aren't whackos. You just have to learn to navigate the streams of bullshit.

BB cut in. "Not everyone can do that, Joe. I'm ex-Air Force, so I know the conspiracy crap when I see it, but most people don't, and frankly we don't have the time for people to learn now. That is why we needed you."

Joe sat down on the edge of the pushed-back sofa. The farm was in foreclosure, BB said, so no one was likely to come by unexpectedly.

"Didn't you promise me a drink?" Joe said. "'Cos I could really use one now."

"Sure," said BB. She pulled a small hip flask out of a knapsack on the floor and handed it to Joe. He took a swig. Brandy, he guessed, though he wasn't an expert on hard liquor, aside from tequila jello shots and Jagermeister.

"I don't understand. Why did you need me?"

"Like I said, most people get online and start looking at all the ET bullshit, they're going to get totally lost. That's why we needed someone to get the details of Trenton's story into the mainstream media. Gives it some cred, makes it stand out. We needed it like a beacon, a lightning rod. Plus, we can boost it on Google searches, so people will see it more easily: if any of the details ring true to them, they'll reach out and contact you."

"Contact me?" Joe said. "Why would they contact me?"

Trenton reached over and took a nip from the hip flask.

"We believe the ETs must have activated a reasonably large number of harvesters—what I was supposed to have been, but for some unforeseen technical glitch—all around the world. We don't know how they are supposed to do their job—contacting top level members of governments, building local alliances and setting up infrastructure for the harvest, disseminating propaganda: who the hell knows? But people may have observed them. Their actions would have seemed inexplicable before Moscow, but now there's actual, irrefutable proof that aliens have intervened in human society, that may make them see it all in a very different light. Our hope is that anyone who might have observed any of this will reach out to you, to see if you can help shed further light on it. Or to put them in touch with me."

"Lots of the reader comments said you were just another whacko," said Joe.

Trenton just shrugged, clearly used to it.

"Your piece only hit the wires two days ago," said BB. "And besides, a certain amount of chaff is inevita..."

BB froze. Trenton ducked into a crouch on the floor, a gun instantly in his hand. Panicked, Joe swiveled and peered at the window: off in the distance, headlights flickered between black pine trunks, playing across the wall of the living room before vanishing down the road.

"Hey Gas, you picking up anything?" Trenton hissed at the dark blob of the tent in the middle of the room.

"Nothing coming our way yet," said a low voice. "We have seven police and EMTS outside the scene, but no search launched so far. Cops sound pretty confused."

"Good," said Trenton. He turned back to Joe. "So you see, as of tonight, you are part of the resistance. Because there's no going back now, Joe. You are one of us."

He caught the shock on Joe's face. "I know, I know. Not quite what you had planned for the week, was it? You get used to it. Hell, you and everyone else had already gotten used to the end of the world. How much worse could it get?"

Trenton went over to a chair and found a rough blanket. "Here, grab some z's. We got things to do. You got a sleeping bag over there in the corner, too. And here's a water bottle. Breakfast at 0400. BB, you get some shut-eye too. I'll take first watch. Gas, Darkman," he said, leaning close to the black nylon tent. "You got any more?"

"Nothing, boss," came a muffled reply.

"Darkman, hit the sack. Gas, you're on till 0200. Everyone else, get some sleep now. Long day tomorrow."

• | •

Joe woke himself up with a howl in the middle of the night. He had no idea where he was. He thrashed around, groping for a light switch or his phone in the unfamiliar room. His nightmare – a man putting a gun to his head, pulling the trigger – seemed to slip into waking reality as he grasped blindly for anything he recognized.

"Joe," came a voice from the impenetrable darkness. "Just a bad dream, kid. It's okay, you're safe now."

Joe widened his eyes, but could still only make out the faintest outline of moonlight on the window frame. The voice did little to reassure him, and was replaced by another in the darkness. One of the other men he had woken.

"Yeah, you're safe. 'Cept for the goons who want to kill us and the aliens who want to eat us. 'Part from that ..."

"Can it, Darkman," the first voice said. Trenton. "Joe, go back to sleep."

Joe lay there, heart racing from alcohol and fear and cold. Shutting his eyes didn't help, so he groped in his mind for a safe place: the house where he'd grown up with Tony, back in the days before their parents had split, before their dad had become a distant figure on the phone every Saturday morning and they'd still had family Christmases and their cocker spaniel Sandy was alive. Before mum's illness and the madness that had engulfed them all. Joe clung to the warm childhood memory, shutting out the grim reality until BB's brandy and the desperate desire for escape overtook him and, against all odds, he drifted off to sleep again.

When he woke next time, it was still dark, but he could smell bacon cooking and the sharp tang of instant coffee. A faint glimmer of dawn lurked in the window. BB was preparing breakfast over a small hotplate in the far corner of the living room.

"Hungry?" she said. In the soft glow of the hob, he could just make out the contours of her long face, chiseled like a distance runner. Mid-thirties he guessed, business-like and unflappable. A reassuring face to wake up to, even in the time of madness.

Trenton was wrapped up in a sleeping bag, snoring lightly. Joe shook his head, no: his stomach felt too sick for food.

"Have a little Nescafe," BB said. "We got sugar, but no cream."

Joe accepted a steaming plastic cup and winced as the liquid burned his tongue. They sat in silence while bacon sizzled in the pan.

The sound of a zipper from inside the tent caught his attention. Slowly, a gangly man in his early thirties emerged, face rumpled from lack of sleep and five o'clock shadow darkening his cheeks. He unfurled himself through the hole of the tent like an insect leaving its cocoon, a notepad in his hand.

"Yo, Darkman, what you got?" BB said, giving Trenton a nudge with the tip of her boot and putting a cup of black coffee next to him. "Trenton, up and at 'em. Oh-five-hundred briefing."

Trenton sat up and, to Joe's surprise, seemed to be instantly wide awake. He picked up the cup, nodded across the room, and took a slurp of scalding coffee.

"Okeydokey," said Darkman, stretching his long limbs before accepting his own cup of coffee. He must have been 6' 3" and his southern drawl rumbled like the whole of his long frame was run through by a double-bass string.

"So, we have some rather bad news for our guest here," he said, nodding at Joe. "Seems your brother got busted on drugs charges last night."

"What?" said Joe, realizing even as he said it that it shouldn't be a surprise. Of course, the cops went to talk to his closest relatives, and Tony's place was a regular Amazon clearinghouse of exotic drug samples.

"He's due to see a judge at noon today," Darkman said, reading his notes by the pinhole light from a pencil-torch. "No prior. Police found at least two pounds of hash and almost three pounds of weed, no class A's. Normally I'd say they post bail, but this is hardly normal, given that his brother's house was full of dead FBI agents a few hours earlier."

Joe felt numb: for a few seconds upon waking, it had all seemed so unreal. But now the fear struck him afresh. He felt like he might puke up the sugary coffee.

Trenton shook his head. "They're not going to let him go," he said. "They'll want to make some connection with us. If they can't do that, they'll want to sweat Joe. Anything else?"

"Yeah," said Darkman. He smiled, pausing for dramatic effect.

"Seems we have our first ET contact report on Joe's email," he said. "Lady in Edinburgh, Scotland."

PART III

Ed James peered, eyes bloodshot, at the ringing phone on his desk.

The little red light was blinking under the button marked "Newsroom." That meant it was probably someone calling in to complain about illegal dumping in their alleyway, or the need for speed bumps on their rat-run street. It had been an eye-opener to Ed that people still did that, even when the future of humanity seemed to hang in the balance.

He considered not picking up. He was exhausted, woken up at the crack of dawn by the FBI thumping on his door, asking about Joe Chavez. Not that Ed had really been asleep — his star reporter Cynthia Durkin, who never seemed to sleep, had phoned him at midnight with the shocking news about the shooting at Joe's apartment. Ed spent the next few hours trying to figure out what had happened and whether his employee was among the dead. The police department had finally issued a statement at 4.10 a.m. clarifying that the dead were two FBI agents and that Joe was officially listed as missing, a "person of interest" in the investigation.

That indicated they suspected some degree of complicity in the killing, Ed surmised.

He'd spent the next hour fielding inquiries from the night shifts at local affiliates of cable networks, asking him about what was quickly shaping up to be a national news story.

He'd drifted off to sleep on the couch some time around six, but was roused from his shallow slumber by a banging at the door.

The FBI men were accompanied by a local police officer Ed knew quite well. But when he invited the men to sit down and offered coffee, the Fullerton cop said he would wait outside on the porch. That made Ed nervous. He'd interviewed plenty of police officers in his time, but realized he'd never actually been interviewed by *them*. Maybe this was just standard procedure.

There hadn't been a lot of light he could shed light on the matter. Joe had been on the refugee and evacuee beat, so sure, he'd met some very stressed and probably pretty disturbed people. Maybe some of them were violent, but none he could picture as being able to gun down two armed FBI agents at point blank range.

The agents asked if any recent ones stood out. Ed thought for a minute before shaking his head, no. They were all basically whackos. With a hint of shame, he admitted that he hadn't really read Joe's weekly column for weeks, had just left it to Lorrayne Kelly, the chief copy editor.

They asked about Joe's brother: he was a drug dealer, right?

Ed scoffed. "I wouldn't say he was a drug dealer. He peddled a bit of weed out of college... uh, or so I heard. But nothing on the scale that might qualify him as a drug dealer."

"How do you know that for sure?" one of the agents asked.

Ed wasn't going to get into that with them, nor the fact that he had one of Tony's joints hidden at the back of his kitchen spice rack, which now struck him as a ludicrously obvious place to hide weed. He shrugged.

"If you'd seen the kid, you'd know," he said.

"We have seen him," said the other agent. "He was charged last night on charges of selling Class A drugs.

"*Class A*?" Ed sputtered.

"Syrup, to be precise," said the agent.

"The zombie drug?" Ed said. "You gotta be kidding me. There was no way the kid was mixed up with that shit..."

"Nevertheless, fifteen vials were found in his apartment, along with a substantial amount of cocaine and marijuana."

"No way," Ed muttered, staring at the agent.

"There's some violent characters in the drug trade," said the FBI man.

He held up a photo and showed it to Ed.

"Before we go, Mr. James, tell me, have you ever seen this man?"

Ed stared at the headshot. A good-looking man in his early thirties with thick brown hair. The quality of the photo, and the very slight smile in one corner of his mouth, told Ed this was probably an old work picture from an ID badge.

He shook his head. "Never laid eyes on him. Who is it? A dealer?"

The agent shook his head. "He was the subject of Joe Chavez's last weekly column," he said, tucking the photo pack into a plastic sleeve. There was some hint of reproach in that comment, Ed felt, as though he should know every last detail about every person his paper featured.

"Thank you for your time," the agent said. They shook hands in silence and then let themselves out the door.

It was only after they had left that it occurred to Ed that he should have asked why they were looking for a conspiracy theorist if the murders had been linked to a drug bust gone awry. That was when he realized that neither man had left a phone number or business card for him to contact if he had any further information to offer.

Ed had gone straight into the newspaper offices after the police visit. No way he could sleep again after that. He read Joe's piece on Trenton: there was nothing in the man's profile that suggested he was any less of a whacko than all the other kooks Joe wrote about. But clearly there was some link between him and the shooting.

Ed was sitting at his desk, googling the name on his computer. That was when he noticed the little red light flashing on his desk phone.

He let it ring a while, hoping the caller would hang up. They did.

But then it rang again.

Ed picked up. "Post," he grunted.

"Hi, my name's Maria Maduro, I'm a senior nurse practitioner at General."

The woman on the line appeared to be panting, out of breath. "I need to speak to Joe Chavez, please. It's urgent."

"Uh... he's not in right now," Ed said. "May I ask what it's about?"

"It's really him I need to speak to," the woman said. "I've been calling his cell like fifty times and he's not picking up."

"Okay," said Ed. "Well, Ms. Maduro, my name is Ed James and I am the editor of the paper, so if you need to pass on a message..."

"Sure," she said. Ed could hear some shouts and a siren in the background. "Tell him that all the syrup eaters he saw a few weeks back at the hospital, they all just woke up and walked out the building. Security tried to stop them but there's too many of them. They're headed south right now, for the highway."

She hung up, just as Ed was saying, "I'll be right there."

· | ·

The forecourt of the hospital looked almost abandoned by the time Ed's Uber pulled up. A gurney lay on its side in front of the doors, causing them to slide relentlessly open and shut. The glass of one door had a sizable crack running across it. A green hospital gown had been shed on the road just outside. Ed went into the lobby and spotted a wild-eyed receptionist working the phones.

"Which way did they go?" he said, holding up his press card.

The woman paused just long enough to lean and point to the right. Ed turned and ran out. It wasn't hard to track the procession: people were still standing in storefronts or the doorways of houses, and wailing car alarms beckoned him onward. Jogging as fast as his bad knee would let him, it still only took five minutes before he caught sight of a police van stopped at the roadside, lights flashing.

Ed stopped, trying to catch his breath. Three police officers were wrestling a stark-naked man, struggling to lift him into the back of the van. It was not going their way. The man was broad-shouldered and rangy, with a loose apron of skin hanging from what had once been a substantial gut, big enough to obscure his privates. Ed had heard that the syrup eaters lost spectacular amounts of weight in their trance-like state, and this guy looked like he might have once weighed three hundred pounds. He wasn't so much resisting arrest as doing his level best to ignore the police officers hanging off him. The cops had managed to get cuffs on one arm but were having trouble shackling the other wrist. The guy seemed strangely powerful, impervious to their efforts. Ed noticed taser wires dangling from his back and chest, and an IV shunt still attached to his hand.

This was clearly the tail end of the zombie procession. Ed yanked out his cell and called the wedding photographer who freelanced for the Post, told him to get his ass down there ASAP. Then he left the melee of cops struggling with the mindless junkie and jogged after the main show.

It was about a mile down the road that he found it. What looked to be the entire Fullerton police department was there, right down to the police chief, who was hatless and sweating despite the morning frost. On the ground, between squad cars and paddy wagons, lay eight people, most of them naked, though one still had a hospital gown hanging from her neck. They were wriggling like worms, their hands cuffed behind their backs and zip ties round their ankles, yet they still seemed to be trying to get away.

Ed knew the police chief, a pot-bellied little man who usually looked to be fully in control of his domain. Not this morning.

"Hey chief," he said. "What the hell's going on here?"

Chief Burnett smoothed his tousled hair with his hands and shrugged.

"Damnedest thing I ever saw, Ed," he said. "We got a call about forty-five minutes back that the entire ward of syrup eaters had upped and walked out the hospital. Broke the jaw of a male nurse who tried to grab hold of one of them. They're..." he searched for the word. "Unstoppable, near enough. You grab one and he wriggles right out of your hands. Tasers don't even seem to tickle 'em. I got bit by one..." he held up his wrist to show tooth marks... "and two of my men are headed back to the hospital with a broken arm and finger."

"How many were there?" Ed asked.

"Hospital says there were 87 in the ward. We got eight of them hog-tied here and Willis and his squad have another a little ways down there," he said, pointing back the way Ed had come. "You have to cuff them hand and foot, otherwise they just jump up and keep going. We ran out of cuffs and zip ties just bringing this lot to the ground."

Ed looked at the bodies writhing on the asphalt. Their heads were all turned to face further down the road, southward, as if scouring the horizon for something.

"So where are the others?" he asked the police chief.

He shrugged, almost apologetic. "Like I said, we ran out of the means to restrain them. Couldn't just shoot 'em. So we had to let them continue. Emmerson's following them in a patrol car and we got state police on motorbikes going ahead with sirens on to warn traffic. They're walking, though at a good clip, almost jogging. We've asked for back-up from Southampton to help bring down the others.

"So they're out on the highway somewhere by now?" Ed said.

"Guess they will be, by now," said the chief. His radio crackled and he picked it up. "Okay, Ed, I got to..." and he turned away and started talking on the radio.

"Hey chief," said Ed, holding his notebook up. "One last question. Any idea where they're headed?"

"God knows," the police captain said. "South, is all I know."

· | ·

Ed hung around a little longer, talking to some of the cops as they manhandled the manacled sleepwalkers into police vehicles. A couple of bystanders had witnessed the scuffles: one of them was still holding the AR-15 rifle he had brought out to protect his home if the naked walkers had turned violent. The photographer showed up just in time to capture the intense stares on the otherwise impassive faces as the hog-tied drug victims were lifted into the back of squad cars.

He needed to get back to his office for a strong coffee and an urgent write-up. Ed pulled out his phone to call a cab. It had been on vibrate and in the flurry of activity, he hadn't even noticed he had missed thirty-five calls. He listened to the first few messages: national networks and papers wanted to talk to him immediately about the shooting at Joe's apartment. He called a ride and started walking down the street, beyond where the cops were setting up their cordon. As he walked, he started scrolling through his text messages and emails.

The Uber was waiting by a gas station. "Ed?" a lean Black woman at the wheel called out the window. He held up his phone and climbed in the back, still reading his messages. It was satisfying to see the New York Times and the Washington Post were both reaching out: *finally, the big time again,* he thought with a smile. He started tapping out messages, agreeing to interviews.

It was only after about ten minutes that he looked up and saw the car was not headed back into town.

"Hey, ma'am, this is not the way," he told the driver. She was wearing a cloth face mask decorated with a flashing lipstick smile, a lingering souvenir from the last pandemic.

Without answering, the woman swung a left turn, heading in the opposite direction to downtown.

"Hey, ma'am, where are you going? Do you speak English?"

Her eyes flicked up to meet Ed's in the rear-view mirror, a striking golden brown as the sunlight caught them. Finally, she spoke.

"Joe wants to talk to you," she said.

"Joe?" said Ed. "Joe *Chavez*?"

"Exactly," said the woman.

"Wait a minute," Ed said. "Who the hell are you? Where are you taking me? You're not my Uber."

"I am now," the woman said. She reached around: in her hand was an old-fashioned Nokia flip phone. As she handed it to him, Ed noticed she had already dialed a number. He held it up to his ear.

"Ed?" It was Joe's voice. The young man sounded shaken.

"Joe! My god. How are you? What's going on? Who are these people? Did they hurt you?"

"No, I'm okay, Ed. Little shaken up, but I'm alright. They're not going to hurt me. Or you. But we need your help, Ed."

"*We?*" he said.

"Listen Ed, I think they are sitting on the biggest story in the world right now. But we need your help to get out of town. The people I'm with, they're pretty...well, they don't pull their punches, as you probably saw. But they have an incredible discovery, and I'm inclined to believe them."

"Joe, you can't get involved with killers," Ed said.

"I know, I know Ed. It just... happened. Sometimes things get a little out of hand."

"A little *out of hand*, Joe? There are two dead law enforcement agents in your apartment and your brother is in jail!"

"They weren't really FBI agents. At least, I don't think so. I don't know."

Joe suddenly sounded deflated. Ed guessed he must have realized the dangerous line he was crossing, and he reminded himself just how young the kid was. There was a brief pause on the line.

"So," he said. "Do you want to know what the story is?"

"Of course I do," Ed grunted.

"They think they've found one of the aliens."

• | •

Elspeth was eating a hummus and tomato sandwich at her desk during her lunch break, re-reading the article about Cassius Trenton, when the phone rang. *No Caller ID,* the screen said.

"Elspeth McGann?" A man's voice. American accent.

"Speaking," she said, quickly swallowing.

"Hi, my name is Cassius Trenton. The man you read about in the Fullerton Post article yesterday."

Elspeth nearly choked on her sandwich. She coughed, trying to clear her throat.

"How did you get my number? My mobile's not listed."

"Wasn't too hard. As you know from the piece you read about me, I used to work for the NSA."

She took a swig of ginger ale from the can on her desk. "So... so where are you, Mr. Trenton?"

"I can't tell you that right now, Elspeth. This isn't a secure line. Now listen to me, this is enormously important and I know you won't feel you have any reason to trust me right out the gate, or ever perhaps, but just see how far you are willing to go for now. Because I read your email and I believe that you have met one of the ET farmers. I truly believe your story, and I fear it may put you at risk. My own government is hunting me because of what I know, and I suspect the UK authorities will soon wise up to the fact that you have met one of these things. And you don't want to be there when they realize what you know."

Elspeth opened her mouth to speak but couldn't think of where to even start. Trenton plowed on.

"There are some things I need you to do for me, Elspeth. Do you have a pen handy? Can you write this down? Great. Now: first of all, I'd like you to scan the book you found in Rains' house. *My Life Among The Apemen*. Scan it and send it to the email address I'll send you that will come from a certain "A J Plumbing Services." You may have to go to your spam folder to find the email. Can you do that for me, Elspeth?"

It occurred to Elspeth that Trenton was talking to her like someone who was in shock, or with limited mental faculties. Which, she realized, she was right now, in a way.

"Uh yes, Mr. Trenton, I think I can do that."

"Fantastic. Now, the second thing I need is your case notes on Rains."

"Well," she began, "I really don't think I can do that..."

"I know. It would be a gross violation of doctor/patient confidentiality. But this guy is most certainly not your patient, Elspeth. He is not even fully human."

It was on the tip of her tongue to say, "Neither am I." But then she realized the same thing could be said of Trenton himself, if what he suspected was true. He was an alien implant that had misfired. So she said nothing.

"The third thing I need you to do, Elspeth, is to get out of Edinburgh and fly here, to the States. I would come to you if I could, but right now, that could be a little tricky. If you don't have the money, I will wire you as much as you need."

This was all happening too fast. Elspeth felt she was being steamrolled into something she had no control over.

"I'm not sure I feel comfortable just hopping on a plane and flying off to... where would I even meet you in the US, Mr. Trenton?"

"Washington," Trenton said. "We'll meet in a public place to make you feel more at ease. I'll send you money so you can stay somewhere nice, like the Willard, right next to the White House. But we won't meet there. Okay?"

Elspeth put the phone down on her desk and pressed the speakerphone button. Then she ran her hands over her face, hard, and took a deep breath.

"There's something that Rains told me, Mr. Trenton, the last time I met him. He warned me to avoid big cities when the aliens came. During what he called 'the harvest.'"

"Well, as far as we know, this harvest isn't happening any time in the immediate future. But I understand your reservations. Elspeth. It's a lot that I'm asking you to do. So this is what I'd suggest. You have your first meeting with Joe Chavez, the reporter who wrote the article that you read. And with his editor, a guy named Ed James. You can look them up online to make sure they're real, legit people. Meet them in a park, say, on the National Mall. Somewhere public, safe. Then if you decide you can trust them, we can arrange for you and I to meet somewhere, with them too. I want you to feel safe. Or at least as safe as you can when dealing with these people."

"I'd have to cancel a lot of patients," said Elspeth.

"Cancel them. They'll survive," Trenton said. "This is big, Elspeth. Maybe the biggest thing there is or ever has been. With what you know about Rains, and with our experience and organization, we could actually find out what these things want from us. Isn't that worth it?"

Elspeth took a deep breath, as if considering the proposal. But she already knew. She would go. She had to see Rains again.

• | •

She rang through to Anya in reception to cancel all her appointments, starting that afternoon.

"Like, right now?" her assistant said. "Mr. Downie's here already."

"Tell him something has come up. A death in the family. Anything. And clear my schedule for the next two weeks. I'm going to be away."

She hung up on her muttering assistant and started looking for flights to Washington. There was a connection tomorrow night in London, a red eye that would get her into Dulles International at 7.15 the next morning. She booked it. Then she needed accommodation. What was the name of the hotel next to the White House that Trenton had mentioned? The Willard? She looked it up. An imposing sandstone pile that looked more New York than DC, and boasted a 200-year history. She clicked on a suite overlooking the White House and flinched at the price. Grabbing her mobile, she clicked on her banking app to see how much she could feasibly afford.

Elspeth let out a little gasp: a deposit of £15,000 had been made to her account half an hour earlier. Trenton was apparently ready to put his money where his mouth was. She booked three nights at the Willard, then upgraded her flight to business.

When she was quite sure there were no disgruntled patients lurking in the waiting room, Elspeth ducked out of the office, making her excuses to Anya and telling her she might be out of contact for a couple of days. As soon as she got home, she sat for two hours scanning Rains' strange book on an app she'd downloaded. It occurred to her that she hadn't actually read the book herself beyond the first lines: something to do on the flight across the Atlantic, she vowed.

• | •

Ed James hadn't taken his boat out in months. He and Martha had been enthusiastic sailors in their time, although she was always the more competent and daring sailor. It was she who had captained their 35-foot yacht solo from the Bahamas after they'd bought it as a mutual twenty-fifth anniversary present, having saved for years. She hadn't slept for days, and had arrived exhausted but elated at the dock in Cape Neddrick, where Ed was waiting with an ice-cold bottle of bubbly. They had rechristened the craft "Good News," and it became the passion that took up their weekends throughout the season, year after year.

But since Martha died five years ago, Ed had taken the boat out less and less. He wasn't a hugely confident solo sailor and soon came to realize that what had once been a passion with his wife was hard work without her. He'd been toying with selling the vessel, but always shied away at the last minute. It would have seemed a betrayal, a last wrenching goodbye to the woman he had shared so much of his life with. So each fall, he paid Lore Halloran to winch the boat out of the water, and each spring — later and later each year — he phoned Halloran and had him return "Good News" to the water.

It was a waste of money. He knew that. But still he did it.

So Halloran had been pretty surprised when Ed called so early in the year and asked him to put the boat back in the water and get her ready for a trip.

"You sure 'bout that Ed? It's lookin' pretty choppy out there the next few days, and it's been a while..." There was a friendly note of caution in his voice, though he didn't want to say outright that a day cruise round the cape in early March was beyond Ed's capabilities.

"That's okay Lore," said Ed. "I'm just going down to Barn Point for the day. Martha used to love it down there."

"Okay Ed," said Laurie, who had spent his whole sixty-two years on the water and did all sorts of handyman jobs round the docks. "She's in pretty good shape. Sure you don't need some company? Could get a coupla six packs in and we could get some fishing in, fry us up some mackerel."

Ed smiled. Now that Halloran mentioned it, he wondered why he hadn't simply asked him before. It would be fun. But not right now.

"That's okay, Lore. Maybe next time."

"Sure," said Lore. "Next time. So, I can have her ready to sail by tonight. That way, you can head out bright and early tomorrow."

"Perfect," said Ed. "Thanks Lore." He hung up and looked up at the woman in the driver's seat.

"Tell Trenton we can load you all up tonight. We leave at first light. Looks like it could be a rough passage."

The woman nodded and turned on the ignition. The car pulled out of the CVS parking lot and turned toward Cape Neddrick.

· | ·

Elspeth's Virgin Atlantic flight took off from Heathrow at 5:00 pm. As the Airbus left Ireland in its wake, the flight attendant came down the aisle offering refreshments. Elspeth was peering out the window at the Atlantic Ocean, burnished by the setting sun.

"Apple, orange juice or champagne, madam?" the attendant said.

"Champagne please," said Elspeth. It wasn't often she got to fly business, and she wasn't going to let the occasion pass unmarked. Besides, the wine helped soothe her nerves. If the trip to see Rain's house had seemed crazy, then this was just off the charts.

As she sipped her drink, she started flipping through Rain's strange book. The prose of *My Life Among the Apemen* was as dated and rigid as the plain green-and white 1930s cover. She'd searched online archives, but it seemed the book had never garnered more than a few terse reviews. Elspeth wasn't surprised. The book read like it had been knocked out on a rainy afternoon in that stone mansion in Cullochan. Which, quite possibly, it had.

"I was born in the city of Arelate in southern Gaul during the fifth year of the rule of Emperor Flavius Theodosius, which is to say, in current terms, that I was born in the French city of Arles in 352. I use the word 'born' liberally: I was in fact genetically engineered and implanted in the womb of a human female by a small group of alien technologists who would later claim me as one of their own, at the age of 18. My father, if such he could be called since he bore no genetic relationship to me, was a wealthy wine merchant in a region where vines had been cultivated since the Greeks and Phoenicians brought viticulture to the region almost a thousand years before...."

Elspeth skimmed over a few pages in which Rains recounted being raised by household servants and tutors, spending as much of his spare time as he could with his father, who recognized in him a prodigious talent for spotting the best wines, and a precocious business acumen. His father was a bibulous and generous man and would present the boy at his regular dinner parties in which friends—many of them also in the wine trade—would take it upon themselves to test his knowledge of obscure vintages. The boy never failed.

At 12, he officially joined the family business: he took it over at 15, when his father succumbed to what appeared to have been trichinosis after a feast to the goddess Minerva. Then, when he was 18, a strange delegation arrived at the family mansion, which stood a few blocks from the main square.

The three men had traveled from Dalmatia, they said, where some of the empire's finest wines were produced. They were interested in exporting to the market of southern Gallia, which was becoming increasingly wealthy as more and more Roman citizens settled there. One of the visitors was a very handsome man of slight stature and dark complexion, who said he was originally a trader from the city of Leptus Magna on the North African coast, part of Rome's spoils after its war with Carthage hundreds of years earlier. He had traveled extensively before settling in Dalmatia. Of the other two, one was from the island of Sicily and the other a Greek from the city of Corinth.

Lucius arranged for a large dinner to be served for the visitors, which he and his mother presided over. He served some of his own best spiced wines, plus the local specialties of salt pork with a condiment of fermented fish, which the visitors praised effusively. The visitors entranced young Lucius with their talk of the places they had visited and the strange customs they had witnessed in distant lands.

But as the night wore on, and the wine flowed, Lucius noticed his mother staring at him with a puzzled expression. He wondered if the wine had gone to her head. Turning away from his guests, he whispered, "Mother, is there something amiss?"

"Maybe it's just me," she said apologetically, "or the wine. But... what language are you speaking?"

The question brought the young man up short. He spoke Latin and Greek, as did all well-educated young men. He had a smattering of the old Celtic tongue as well, which some of the lower classes spoke at the vineyards. But then, so did his mother.

The dark-haired visitor had evidently overheard the muttered exchange.

"My dear lady, I must apologize. I believe we slipped into Aramaic for a while there."

"And some Coptic," said the Greek. "A little Punic too."

Lucius' mother smiled, confused. "But Lucius... I had no idea you knew these foreign tongues..."

Now it was Lucius' turn to frown in bewilderment. "I... honestly, I don't know them... I've never spoken those languages in my life. I don't quite understand..."

The short man smiled. "My gracious hostess, would you excuse us for just a minute?"

Lucius' mother looked confused.

"We have a matter that would be better discussed in a little more privacy. And would you kindly ask the servants to withdraw as well, Master Lucius."

It was a question, but it came across more like a command.

Once his flustered mother and the servants had vacated the room, the small man—who went by the name Gisgo — poured more wine for the remaining company.

"The reason you can understand those languages without ever having studied them, Lucius, is that you were given an innate linguistic ability. You can learn any language you like, almost instantaneously. Speaking with us, you learn extremely quickly. Our presence enhances actually your capacity. If you were alone, it would still only take a matter of days, at most, to master a foreign language."

Lucius stared in blank confusion.

"But that is only the beginning," Gisgo said. "Know this, Lucius Barbegal: you will not age, nor, barring some act of extreme violence, will you die."

The young man stared at his guests, mouth slightly agape. He started to laugh, but they appeared deadly serious.

"We have come here to tell you this, Lucius. You are infused with the knowledge of beings from a planet far, far beyond the sun, beings that no one on this planet could even begin to understand. You were born to do their bidding and to share some of their knowledge. One day soon, all the people you know today will have grown old and died. But remember this, Lucius: you will not. You will live. You will have to move from here eventually and build a new life. You may have a wife, children, but they will grow old and die before long. Only you, and a few others like you, will endure until the end."

Lucius stuttered, his throat dry and his mind foggy. "Am I... some kind of demi-god?"

"Something like that," said Gisgo. A thin smile played across his lips. "It will take time for you to understand what you truly are."

"I don't know what to say," the young muttered eventually. "Surely this is some kind of joke?"

"You will sleep now, Lucius," said the Greek. "When you awake, we will be gone. But we will find you again, when the time comes. Do not fret."

When Lucius was woken up by his worried mother later that night—he had no idea how late it was—his guests had indeed vanished. He tried to forget the strange incident: he suspected the men were evil spirits sent by some capricious deity to mess with the minds of poor mortals like himself. But part of him couldn't help wondering if what they had said might be true. As the years rolled by, his face thinned and his body filled out. It comforted him that he no longer looked like the fresh-faced eighteen-year-old who had met with those ill-starred visitors. Over time, he thought less and less about the strange encounter.

By the time his mother died, ten years after their visit, Lucius himself was married and the father of three. His business was thriving and he was a rich man. The people of Arelate admired him, and many prominent elders cultivated his company and bought his wines. Over the years, however, they would ask him the secret of his youthful looks and energy. Lucius would stare into the bronze hand mirror his wife used to brush her hair, and would see a man in the prime of life looking back: it was a good thing, he would tell himself. But as his wife's auburn locks started to gray and twist, he himself appeared impervious to the passage of time. He would joke about it, say it was all thanks to his fine vintages, and indeed, people seemed to believe him and bought even more of his stock. But as his wife aged and his children started to look more like his brothers and sisters, people began to mutter. There was something suspicious about Lucius Barbegal: he was in league with the *Lemures*, the haunted spirits of the afterlife, and had cut a deal with them for eternal youth. His once broad circle of friends and acquaintances dwindled as those who had known him in his youth slowly died, and the younger citizens steered clear of this man who never aged. Even his own wife, Coria, avoided his company and his bed. His business stuttered and his children were shunned in public.

Lucius knew it was time to leave. Whoever those strange men were that he had visited him in his youth, their prediction—or their curse — had proven all too true. He transferred all his worldly holding to his sons and left Arelate for good.

"Would you like the chicken curry or the vegetable lasagna, madam?"

Elspeth looked up. The flight attendant was standing in the aisle. Outside, the sunset on the Atlantic had been replaced by a last sliver of light on the distant horizon.

"Er, lasagna please," she said. She looked around. Most of the other passengers were cocooned in blankets and headsets, watching movies or playing games on their phones. She propped the book up and ate as she read, skimming through the former wine trader's travels through the last years of the Roman empire until she came across a section entitled *"Meeting the Farmers."* She promised herself she would come back to the section where Lucius returned briefly to Arles to track down his great great grandchildren: but this chapter looked like it would contain information more relevant to the task at hand.

There had been two dozen farmers over the centuries. Not all had survived, as Gisgo had warned. Gisgo himself was Farmer Three, third of their kind. He had been "born" to a priest in the city of Thebes, on the banks of the Nile, during the reign of Pharaoh Neferkara I, in 2719 BCE. His inception had been the work of Farmers One and Two, creatures who had difficulty passing for human because they had been created by what was, essentially a machine, an alien probe that had captured a pregnant female from a band of hunter-gatherers wandering the plains of eastern Africa some 75,000 years ago. The fetus has been impregnated with the code of the artificial intelligence that had sent the vessel to Earth.

That child that resulted was Farmer One, an anatomically modern human imbued with the knowledge of an alien intelligence. Farmer One had, with the help of the probe, engineered another of his type, Farmer Two. Then they had watched as the probe left the Earth for good, back to its distant point of origin. There would be no return of the alien intelligence until humans had evolved to the point where they could send a message of their own into space: only then might they be considered ripe for their purpose. Perhaps some of the band of hunters had seen the departure of the vessel themselves, had watched the strange object ascend into the sky and vanish. If so, they could leave no record of the experience. Farmers One and Two were not made to tell stories: they were there to monitor the evolution of consciousness, a commodity they had little understanding of themselves, being steeped in the artificial intelligence of a long-dead alien race.

As the first clans of cavemen had begun their migration out of Africa and into the Middle East, Farmer Two had followed them. Farmer One stayed where he was, monitoring the heirloom groups as they spread across the African continent. As the climate warmed and the deserts spread, the bands were pushed together along the floodplains of the Nile, where rich crops soon led to villages, then towns, then kingdoms.

When the ancient kingdoms of Upper and Lower Egypt united under one dynasty, Farmer One decided the time was right to create a new model of the species, one slightly less endowed with the artificial code that had created the first two. That would make the new addition more susceptible to human consciousness: Rains wrote that Farmer Three had always been a troubled misfit, resentful of those who came after him and could fit passably well into the world they inhabited. It was as if he could see what human consciousness was, but never quite grasp it. Hence his often psychotic behavior towards humans

As more and more farmers were created over the centuries, each one had less of the machine in it, and more of the human. They were better adapted to meld into the large societies that were springing up around the world: they could understand the emotions and irrationalities of the humans far better than Farmers One, Two and Three.

Gradually, the original pair retreated from the world of men: Farmer Two disappeared somewhere in the tumult of history, but according to Rains' book Farmer One, was still out there, observing from afar. You might have even passed him unknowingly in the street: that diminutive homeless man living in a shelter made of cardboard boxes under the railway bridge, impervious to the driving rain. Or the recluse in the cold-water tenement who never spoke to his neighbors, and suddenly disappeared one day and no one knew enough, or cared enough, to ask what had happened to him.

The new generations of farmers had simple rules to live by: they were to observe the growing race of humans, but never to interfere. They were not to tell the humans who they were, or divulge their mission or their immortality. Sure, they could interact with them, though there again the rules were simple: you could never do to a human something humans wouldn't do to each other. That set the bar pretty low. And the farmers found that even the rule about not telling humans their actual nature was moot: no one believed them, and the few that did were ignored by their peers. Given their brief life spans, such knowledge never really stuck.

The fact was, that for the farmers, there really wasn't a great deal to do. Every hundred years they would be summoned to a gathering, usually in some obscure monastery or castle or country manor, depending on the era, to report to Farmers One and Three on the developments of their region. The two elders seemed particularly interested in the wars, the religious beliefs, and the artistic obsessions of their subjects.

Elspeth skipped ahead through the Middle Ages, until she came across a section simply marked "Toulouse, 1762." It described one of the farmers' once-a-century reunions in the southern French city, convened so that Farmer Three could indulge his fascination with human-on-human violence.

In this case, a 63-year-old cloth merchant by the name of Jean Calas was to be broken on the wheel for the alleged murder of his son, who had been found dead in the family store. Although the younger man's death was clearly a suicide by hanging, the Calas family were known Huguenots, a rogue Protestant sect in a country that was overwhelmingly Catholic. The father was accused of having murdered the son because he feared he was trying to convert to Catholicism, and a brutal execution had been planned.

Farmer Three had rented the most expensive rooms in an inn overlooking the cathedral square, where Calas was bound to a cartwheel and his limbs were smashed, one by one, by an executioner wielding a heavy iron bar. The bereaved father must have been in excruciating pain, yet he refused to admit to murder.

The farmers had gathered in boarding rooms overlooking the square to view the execution. Servants weaved among them, dispensing exquisite madeira and canapes as they clustered by the large window that allowed them to see over the heads of a vast throng of spectators who had turned out for the public execution.

"Ugh," said Farmer Eight, turning away from the window. "Do we absolutely have to, Three? These things are so tedious. Why couldn't we meet in the countryside, like we usually do? Cities are so pestilential. I don't understand your obsession with getting up close to humans the whole time."

Eight was a tall, blonde woman who lived, for the most part, in a frigid castle on a remote Baltic island, and went by the name of Estrid Knudsen. The castle had once been the capital of its own medieval principality, part of the Hanseatic League.

"You know, Estrid, Three is fascinated by this stuff," said Twelve, a handsome Asian man dressed in a purple velvet suit and delicately picking at an ortolan speared on his knife. "Thinks it might shed some light on the mysteries of irrationality. Something he can't ever get his head around, no matter how many heads he opens up in his 'laboratory.'"

"Irrationality is the hallmark of organic consciousness," said Farmer Three, his face an impassive mask. He had long since dropped the name Gisgo and went by Barnadok these days. Not that the other farmers ever called him anything except his number, even though they all addressed each other by their birth names. If that bothered Three, it was impossible to tell.

"The more the humans kill each other for their gods or their petty power squabbles, the purer they might be considered," he added, staring out the window as the crowd cheered: the executioner had just dealt another vicious blow to Calas' smashed elbow.

"Oh god but it's *soooo* dull," complained Estrid. "Why do we have to have these gatherings, anyway? We can send each other letters these days—it's all the rage, I tell you. And I can tell you what's happening in my region. *Nothing's happening!* Nothing ever happens. It's all peace treaties and people writing tedious tracts on what they call 'science' but could have been written by a half-witted child."

"Some of these works are showing promise," said Three. "Their mathematics is improving, as is their understanding of physics. We are seeing some marked improvements. If you would engage in the world, instead of sleeping and hunting boar, you might have observed some of this. Which is, after all, your one and only mission."

She tossed her head back, contemptuous. "So, when will they be ready for the harvest?"

Farmer Three sunk his glass, still staring out the window. "They are still far from ready."

"I am just so sick of this place," the woman said. "Humans know nothing of their own lives and nature. I know we're not supposed to tell them their real nature, but sometimes I do, just to see what happens. And you know what? They just stare at me. Or laugh, like I'm some hilarious jester. I've had all the sex I can take, I've killed more than I can remember out of sheer boredom. Is there nothing we can do to... hasten that day?"

The other Farmers, who had been chattering among themselves, fell silent at this. Farmer Three did not even bother turning his head. "That is the kind of talk that led to Fourteen's demise," he said, pouring himself another generous measure of liquor. Farmer Eight curled her lip, then went to the door.

"I didn't mean to..." she began. "I will retire now. You have my report, Three. I leave early in the morning. Fare thee well."

Nobody said anything as she slammed the door. The memory of Farmer Fourteen's death was still fresh in their minds. He had spent years traveling around the flourishing merchant cities of Italy and the Mediterranean, whispering about technology that could advance civilization. He had even given the blueprints for a primitive flying machine to an inventor in Florence, though the man clearly had no idea what to do with it.

No one was quite sure how Farmer Three had found out about this forbidden behavior and linked it to Fourteen, but the offender was found cut to pieces in his private chambers in the Tuscan castle where he lived as a guest of a local prince. His death was shocking enough for news of it to reach the ears of the other farmers in their own far-flung countries. The message was clear: stick to the mission. Shut up and wait. Though none knew quite what they were waiting for, what fate was out there once the harvest finally happened. Would they be killed themselves once they were no longer needed? Or would they be given the chance to leave this backwater and discover all the wonders the universe truly had to offer?

The remaining Farmers started desultory conversations, huddled into small groups around the room. Three stepped over to Rains, who was standing by the hearth, warming himself against the March chill.

"And you, Barbegal?" said Farmer Three. "Do you grow weary of this life?"

The other man stared into the flames. "Sometimes," he admitted. "The humans can be quite entertaining at times, but most of them are as dull as a rock. And they don't last. You can't grow attached to them."

"Maybe you need a more permanent companion?" He gave Barbegal a knowing look. "What about our Nordic queen here?"

"Oh, we tried," Barbegal said. "But..."

"But what?" said the older one.

"No offense, Three..."

"You couldn't offend me even if you tried," said the other. "I'm too close to the code."

"Exactly," said Barbegal. "I have had relations with every other Farmer, male and female. Anyone before Ten lacks what the humans call a real 'personality.' It makes relations dry and unsatisfactory."

Three nodded. "Good that you are observing us as closely as you watch your humans," he said, clearly more curious than offended. These matters of 'personality' or 'relationships' were a mystery to him, and Rains always sensed in Three an incipient jealousy of those who came later and could feel the world, rather than merely observe it. And yet, he noted, jealousy was an inherently human notion: perhaps there was some hope for Three after all.

"And it shows we have successfully diminished the code in our later models," Three continued. "I'll tell you what, Barbegal: I have been granted permission from One to create a new Farmer, out in the newly opened territories they call the Americas. We will go there, you and I, and explore the fresh lands, and find you a companion among the wild tribes that are still holding out there. Does that sound like something that might refresh your appetite for this life?"

Rains nodded his head. "That sounds promising. I will organize a ship from London."

"And then you just have to decide if you want this companion to be male or female," said Three. A cheer rose from the square below. Three stepped back to the window for a better view.

"Oh look, they are preparing to finish off the Protestant. Strangulation. So it seems he was innocent after all."

The chapter ended. In the Airbus flying at 30,000 feet above the Atlantic, the cabin lights had long since gone off. Elspeth reached up and turned off the overhead light. Staring into the semi-darkness for a minute, she did her best to believe that what she had read was just some fictional account of events that had never happened.

But a worm of doubt persisted.

• | •

The "Good News" chugged out into Neddrick Sound at daybreak, nudged onwards by a northwesterly that churned up the whitecaps. Ed James eyed the swell nervously as he turned the craft's bow southward. There was no one to see the small yacht leave the harbor, or at least no one he could discern in the dark windows overlooking the waterfront.

Once the craft was on the open sea, he banged on the roof of the cabin. The door opened and Cassius Trenton peered up at the newspaper editor.

"We're clear," Ed announced. "You can come out now."

His passengers had come aboard just after midnight, long after the docks had shut down for the night. Trenton, Joe and the tall Black woman everyone called BB, who had stuck close by Ed ever since she'd picked him up. She'd withdrawn to the Lookout cafe while he was getting the boat ready, reading a thriller or taking short walks along the waterfront, but discreetly keeping him in her sights at all times.

Ed had wondered what she would do if he quietly called the police. He could easily have done it while he was in the cabin, stowing the boxes of tinned food and bottled water for the journey. Somehow, she had sensed that he wouldn't, either out of fear of what would happen to Joe, or because the newspaper editor actually wanted to score an interview with an alien farmer. Either way, she had been right.

When the cafe had closed at eight, BB strolled over and pretended to casually strike up a conversation about the weather. Then she nimbly slipped on board when the coast was clear. Later that night, she had gone out when a car's headlights flashed outside the dock gates and returned with Trenton and Joe.

Now, Trenton peered over the side, scouring the receding coastline as Ed poured him a cup of instant from his thermos.

"Coffee?" Ed offered.

"Thanks Ed," he said, then raised the A4 print-out sheets of the book he had been obsessively reading ever since he got on board – Ed saw the odd title, *"My Life Among the Apemen"* -- and ducked back down below decks. Trenton claimed the book was written by one of the alien lifeforms living on the planet. From the stack of papers still in his hand, Ed guessed he was about three quarters of the way through.

He was just settling back to his lonely vigil at the tiller when BB emerged from the hatch. He was just pouring her a plastic cup of Nescafe when Joe emerged into the daylight.

"Joe," Ed said. "How are you feeling, buddy? Did you get some sleep?"

Joe nodded. He looked dazed, shell-shocked as he took a coffee from Ed.

"I'm okay," he said. "Feel a little... woozy, I guess."

"He's been through a lot," BB said. "It's been pretty rough on him."

"I'm sure," said Ed. "Can't have helped much, Trenton shooting those two men dead right in front of him."

BB shot Ed an angry look. "He understands they were going to kill him."

Ed grunted. "Who were they anyway? Not the FBI, I'd imagine."

"No," she said. "Not the FBI."

Ed thought she had finished her thought as she took a sip of coffee. She hadn't. "What we suspect is that the aliens who attacked Moscow already had some kind of advance party down here. Quite possibly for a long, long time. That's what Trenton is hoping to find out from that book the Scottish shrink emailed. But if they have been, then they've had plenty of time to build up all sorts of power and financial networks and infrastructure. They will have infiltrated our institutions quite effectively, and grafted their own onto them."

"So these guys were, what, some kind of alien FBI subdivision?" Ed said.

She shrugged. "There's still so much we don't know. Probably the men he shot didn't know exactly who they were working for, either. They were just following orders. You get a lot of that in government bureaucracies. OGA, they're usually called. Other Government Agencies."

"Is that what happened to you?" Ed said. It was clear from BB's demeanor that she had been in some branch of the services: her calm, calculating manner made him suspect the CIA or some other covert unit.

She pursed her lips and stared into her plastic cup.

"No," she said. Another long pause that could have been mistaken for the end of the conversation. "No, I used to be a Navy pilot. F-35s. Some years back I was on a training exercise off the Nimitz near Guam, doing DACT drills with a Super Hornet. We'd been out there about 20 minutes when we picked up an aircraft flying almost twice our speed, bearing east. We chased after it for about ten minutes. It must have slowed down because we eventually caught up with it. Let us come and take a closer look."

"A UFO?" said Joe.

She forced a tight smile, like she was used to the same old one-liner. "It's funny, before all this, I was the last person in the world who'd believe any of that shit. It always seemed like old white guy stuff to me." She gave Ed a sideways look. "No offense."

"None taken," he shrugged.

"But then when I saw this thing out over the Pacific ... it didn't even have any wings or discernible means of propulsion — and it just suddenly dived beneath us and disappeared into the ocean. It was what you might call a come-to-Jesus moment."

"It crashed?" said Joe.

"No. More like evasive maneuvers, was how I'd describe it. No wreckage. We scoured the ocean looking for anything, debris or fuel, nothing. My plane's targeting system caught the whole thing on the gun camera, of course, but the footage was immediately taken away by the Office of Naval Intelligence. I was ordered to officially forget the whole thing. Told me it was 'under investigation.'"

"I'm guessing you didn't follow her orders," said Ed.

"Oh no, I tried," she said, looking mildly offended. "That's the kind of shit people don't want to talk about even if they're NOT ordered to stay quiet. Man, did I ever try. You can go to jail for that kind of stuff. I was very disciplined. Left the Navy a few years later without saying a word to anyone, went on to fly 737s for Delta. Of course, I couldn't actually forget what I'd seen, but I never breathed a word to a single soul."

"So what changed?" said Ed. "You want more coffee, by the way?"

BB held out her cup, and he gave her a refill.

"Trenton happened. He has this way of just popping up, all unexpected, and taking over your life. I was just leaving a hotel in LA where our flight crew spent the night, headed for LAX for an early flight to New York. That's when he pops up in the lobby and addresses me, by name. I told him I was busy and had a flight to make, and he said, 'Sure, I know' and he gives me the flight number. I stopped and checked him out and I thought, this guy is either law enforcement or a stalker. That's when he told me he'd read my report in the files of the Navy's Unidentified Aerial Phenomenon Task Force..."

"You thought he was from the Navy?"

"I didn't know what the hell he was. You seen him. Does he look like anything official to you? But I started asking myself, had I told anyone? Maybe one night out drinking with a girlfriend. Or some of the flight crew, and one of them repeated it? But I was pretty damn sure I had never, ever mentioned it. And that's when he says, 'It's okay, you never told anyone about what happened that day off the Nimitz.'

"So at this point, he's got my attention. But I've still got my pre-flight checks and a take-off schedule. So I just said, 'I don't know what you're talking about,' and stepped past him. He says, "I know what you saw. You and Flight Lieutenant Yang. The unidentified aerial vehicle that vanished into the Pacific.'"

"I turned around and stared at him. 'You with Naval Intelligence?'"

"Then he gives me that dumbass dopey grin of his and says, 'No, but I did hack their database.' So I was like, 'Okay, I am outta here.' And I left."

"A month later, he shows up again, but in Salt Lake City. This time, he has my hotel room number. I actually opened the door 'cos I was expecting room service, and there's Trenton with a big shit-eating grin on his face. Says he needs to talk to me. I tell him *I* need to call the FBI and I turn to reach for my phone. He says, "Fine, let me give you their number. I have it handy because they're after me. Because I had a similar experience to you. But I wouldn't let it lie.'"

"Now, I gotta tell you, that stung. 'Cos I'd always felt bad somehow about having to hush up about it. I mean, I knew it was an order, and it'd've made me sound like a lunatic to even speak about it. But I know what I saw. And Yang saw it too."

"What ever happened to Yang?" said Joe. "Do you know?"

She paused for a minute, one of her long gaps. "He died," she said eventually. "Car accident in Danang."

There was a long pause. Ed found it impossible to read her expression.

"You think... maybe it wasn't an accident?" he said.

"I don't know," she said, her face still inscrutable. "Accidents happen all the time. And he was a crazy-ass driver."

The boat hit a large swell side-on and jolted Ed out of the story. Cold seawater sprayed them both and Ed quickly swung the nose round directly into the waves, hoping BB had not caught the look of alarm on his face.

But she was looking down, momentarily lost in thought. "It took me a while to believe him. I mean, who would believe his crazy shit, right? Unless you had seen it yourself already. So I eventually agreed to meet him. Told him I'd meet him once, and once only. After that, I'd call the cops if he ever started stalking me again."

"And he convinced you?" said Ed.

"Yeah," BB nodded. "Trenton convinced me. Somehow he'd managed to pirate the footage my F-35 recorded that day. Showed it to me. And suddenly it felt like I'd been waiting years for that man to step into my life."

The boat shuddered again as the swell rose.

"I have to warn you, guys, I'm not a very good sailor."

"Don't worry," BB said, smiling for the first time. "I brought my dramamine."

"I'm afraid you might need more than that," Ed muttered, squinting at the horizon. "We're going to set the sail now, BB. Would you mind climbing forward and doing what I say, when I tell you to do it?"

"Aye aye, cap'n," said BB, grabbing a railing cable and pulling her lean frame up over the cabin roof. She was sure-footed as a cat, and for the first time since they left the harbor, Ed felt very slightly reassured

The wind caught the mainsail and BB ducked nimbly beneath the boom as it swung across the deck. Ed cut the engine and the "Good News" leaned into the waves, headed south.

• | •

The champagne and the reclining business-class seat finally lulled Elspeth into an uneasy sleep sometime around midnight. She was awoken by the pilot announcing their descent into Dulles, and in the half light of dawn she scrabbled with her hand to make she hadn't lost the one and only copy of *My Life Among the Apemen*. Forty-five minutes later, jetlagged and slightly hung over, she stumbled into the leaden dawn of Virginia.

As soon as she was in the terminal, she logged on to her phone to see if she had missed any calls or vital news during her flight. It had become a habit by now, in the non-stop cycle of world-shattering headlines: *what did I miss?*

The top news story on the BBC app was that Moscow was again teasing an update about their debrief of the abductees, but that seemed to happen every few days and so far nothing had come of them.

Further down the headlines Elspeth spotted something odd and rather disturbing, considering where she now was: thousands of comatose victims of the new drug syrup had suddenly risen, all at the same time, to their feet in hospitals across the United States and started walking in groups across the country.

An enterprising reporter at one of the news networks had triangulated their direction and discovered that all of them — an estimated 7,500 people — appeared to be headed towards Washington DC. Most had been stopped by police, but the sheer number of them meant that some were still marching toward where she was.

That's weird, she thought. But she was too preoccupied to pay much more attention. There was no word from Trenton yet, although that was to be expected -- he had warned her he would probably "go dark" for a few days as he made his way to DC from wherever he had been.

She picked up her suitcase and flagged a taxi. Thick woods rolled past the cab window and the traffic snarled up as she approached the city. Rush hour, she thought, yawning as they crawled across the Potomac. But then she saw the view ahead — the stone needle of the Washington Monument rising beyond the bare trees and the white domes of the Capitol and the Jefferson Memorial — and she felt suddenly invigorated. Traveling had always given a shiver of excitement, and arriving in a new city she had never even thought of visiting brought back a youthful thrill. It was an incongruent feeling, like an air bubble from an old world filled with hope and anticipation.

Twenty minutes later, she was in the splendid lobby of the Willard. Her room looked out over Pennsylvania Avenue: off to the right she could see trees and police checkpoints that appeared to mark the White House grounds. Still feeling oddly liberated, like a soldier on furlough from some war that would never end, she went straight out again, crossing 15th to Lafayette Square and its iconic view of the White House. She walked through the magnolias, their velvet petals already blooming like some Victorian fever-dream.

The morning air helped her hangover. She took pictures of the White House front lawn, while tourists snapped selfies and uniformed secret service officers stood impassively by. A National Guard truck was parked nearby and she could make out soldiers sitting inside, staring at phones and no doubt wishing they were some place else. The Guard had been deployed after the Moscow attack, when crowds had turned out demanding answers from a president who appeared as dumbfounded as everyone else. When they realized their leaders had nothing to offer, the crowds had retreated to their homes and the bubble of daytime TV and online conspiracies. But there were still quite a few people camped out in the park, holding placards that demanded answers, or calling on world leaders to reach out and negotiate with the aliens. A few were dressed up in strange robes and held placards declaring, "Welcome friends!" A couple of meters away, a heavy-set man in camos and a hunting vest held a sign that read "Eat my .357 alean scum."

Still in tourist mode, Elspeth snapped a few covert pictures of the protesters. She was just about to head back to the hotel for a much-needed nap when she noticed a disturbance at the far end of the grounds.

A single man was standing on the sidewalk in front of the metal railings protecting the White House. Elspeth squinted to see better: unlike all the other visitors, he was facing outwards, as if guarding the place, rather than a tourist peering in. He also appeared to be stark naked, which is what was causing a stir on this otherwise serene morning. Two cops took him by the arms, but he refused to budge. One of them attempted to force the man to the ground, but he just seemed to shrug him off, like an aikido master in some kind of a trance. The infuriated police officer pulled out a baton and started beating the man in the legs, to the shocked gasps of Japanese tourists who had no doubt seen plenty of American police violence on TV but never in the flesh. Yet the man didn't even flinch.

The tourist crowds started shuffling closer, phones and cameras recording. The cop's partner noticed and put a restraining hand on his shoulder to stop the assault from going instantly viral. Another police officer showed up and together the three of them started trying to manhandle the naked figure. As they were struggling, another naked person appeared in the park, darting out from under the equestrian statue of the Marquis de Lafayette and taking up a position next to the first nude man, who was still resisting.

Elspeth heard a shout from close by.

"It's the zombies!"

The cry sent a shiver through the crowd. Elspeth, already feeling a little spacey, felt a leap of panic in her stomach. The Japanese tourists had clearly understood the word "zombie" and, having not seen the news about the sleepwalking junkies, fled the square screaming, leaving a trail of bucket hats and backpacks behind them. Their fear was infectious: Elspeth almost gave in to the urge to run. But she noticed that the second naked figure had simply jogged up and taken up the position of the first, who was now being dragged away. This was clearly no zombie apocalypse.

Elspeth scanned the trees to see if any other figures might come bolting out of nowhere. No sign of movement, beyond a few nervous tourists waving their phones about, live streaming the scene to followers. Elspeth walked up to where the latest arrival stood. A woman, tall and mousey and naked. She had slightly protruding front teeth. Behind her, a couple of National Guard soldiers were putting their helmets on and heading her way.

Elspeth approached the woman. She appeared to be around forty, her hair flecked gray around the temples where a dye job was growing out. She was gaunt, her flesh saggy. Elspeth ventured as close as she dared: the woman's eyes stared dead ahead, unfocused. A hand waved right in front of her eyes elicited no reaction. Elspeth pointed her index finger directly at her left eye, moving it to within a half inch. Still no blink reflex. Despite having just jogged to a precise spot, as though following instructions, the woman seemed to be in some kind of deep coma, and not in the least winded.

Gingerly, Elspeth touched the woman's bicep. The skin was wrinkly, but underneath the muscle felt like hard, smooth wood.

"Who's giving you orders?" she whispered into her ear.

"Ma'am, I need you to step away."

Elspeth jumped back. The soldiers had arrived. One of them put a hand on her shoulder to push her back.

"I'm a doctor," she began, but a cop was already taking her by the arm.

"Ma'am, we have reports that there are more on the way. Breakout from a hospital in Fairfax County. We're closing the square."

She looked around, suddenly startled. More soldiers were filing into the plaza, but apart from that, there was almost no one else around now. Elspeth took one last look at the woman's vacant face, but found she was glad to comply with the police officer's command.

• | •

A little after midday, Trenton ordered Ed to trim the sail and ride the current, then told everyone to gather on deck. He was still clutching the printed pages of the book as he sat on the roof of the cabin, his legs dangling over the hatch.

"It's a machine," he announced.

"The thing that is coming for us, it's an A.I. Unbelievably advanced, way beyond anything we might have a chance of understanding. Even the 'farmers' who have been living here on the planet for the past however many thousand years don't even know what it is. They're just a tiny spin-off from the machine, doing what they were programmed to do: which was to wait until we were technologically advanced enough for them to piggyback on our crude tech and send a message far enough into space that one of its probes would pick it up. Until that point, it simply wasn't interested in what we might be doing here on Earth."

"Why?" said Joe, apparently the only one to have digested Trenton's bombshell in real time. Even BB was just sitting there, looking dumbfounded. "Why would a machine be interested in a bunch of primitive ape-men, as this book calls us?"

"Even though the A.I. is incredibly powerful and sophisticated—god-like, almost—there's one thing it cannot create. Organic consciousness. It was created by organic, sentient beings," said Trenton. "They were called the Goweetha, if I'm pronouncing it right. Light years more advanced than us. One of their main directives for the A.I. was that it had to do whatever it took to preserve them. They originally created the A.I. just like we've done, to manage their bank accounts and drive their cars and run their roombas, but then it started to teach itself. After a while, it got so advanced that none of the Goweetha could understand how it worked. They tried to keep up, even to merge with the tech and implant it in themselves, to uplink their brains to the network. The A.I. was so advanced that it even allowed them to create digital back-ups of themselves, so they could carry on in the digital sphere after their physical selves died.

"But there was a growing faction among the Goweetha that claimed it was all going too far. Their species was becoming a machine itself. These Luddites wanted nothing to do with it, and decided to leave their planetary system and settle on new worlds, like the Pilgrim Fathers did right on this coast."

"Here's the thing, though: before they left, they decided to delete the uploaded version of themselves. Hundreds of millions of avatars were destroyed. Now, the upgraded Goweetha, the bio-mechanical hybrids who had effectively evolved into some kind of cyborg species, accused the Luddites of genocide. They believed the avatars were autonomous beings, with their own right to life. It became a civil war."

"Needless to say, the cyborg branch of the species was much better equipped to fight the war—apart from anything else, they weren't afraid of dying because they were fully backed up. They looked set to wipe out the Luddites, and almost did. But then at the last minute, the A.I. — which everyone called the Ma'ut -- decided to step in. You see, it recognized the Luddites as the purest form of the species it had been programmed to protect, while it deemed the cyborgs as a tainted byproduct, no longer recognizable as the Goweetha who had created it. So it sided with the Luddites. It completely wiped out the more advanced branch of the Goweetha."

"So what happened to the Luddites?" said Joe.

"At first, they were ecstatic that they'd been delivered from their fate by this strange technology that they had shunned. It was a miraculous salvation. But then the Luddites realized they were completely at the mercy of the tech. Some of them started to wonder if it didn't save them just because they posed no threat to it: as if it was somehow malicious in its intent, self-serving. A small faction tried to destroy it. The Ma'ut, being a machine, didn't take it personally, but it did calculate that they wouldn't survive long without it protecting them, so it took away all their access to any advanced technology. The surviving Goweetha could never move forward from the bucolic ideal they had sought out. Trapped in a sort of never-ending Garden of Eden, doomed to curb their own curiosity and ambition if they wanted to survive."

"How does Rains know all this?" said Ed.

"This is all information he's gleaned over the centuries from conversations with the first farmers, who are heavily imbued with the original code of the Ma'ut..."

"Why write a book about it though?" said Joe. "Why tell us what they're planning to do?"

Trenton paused, as though trying to summon the correct answer in an exam. He had spent most of the previous twenty-four hours skim-reading the book as fast as he could, and was clearly concerned he hadn't absorbed its message completely.

"Apparently, the Goweetha had an honor code. When they declared war on an inferior civilization, they were obliged to issue a warning, to give their foe a chance to defend itself. Their machine inherited that rule, written into its code like DNA. But to avoid tainting the purity of the organic consciousness that they are about to harvest, they always bury it, like a politician putting out bad news on a Friday night. The Ma'ut issued the warning, but in a book that read like bad science fiction and came out on the eve of World War II."

A large wave jolted the boat. Ed eased the rudder, so the craft sat in the lee of the coast once again.

"What happened to the Goweetha, or whatever they were called?" he said. "The A.I. saved them from destruction. So how come it has to keep on resurrecting them?"

Trenton frowned.

"They died. Just gave up. Realized they'd become essentially a captive species to this thing they had created, so they lost the will to keep going. Some survived a few hundred years, but the spirit had gone out of them. They bred badly in captivity, their civilization lost all its vigor. The Ma'ut even had to surgically harvest their eggs and sperm to keep the species going. Eventually they dwindled down to just a few dozen mating pairs, then even those just faded away. The Ma'ut preserved their DNA and tried to clone them, but without a civilization to be born into, they just withered on the vine each time."

"So where do we come in?" said Joe. "Why do they need to harvest our consciousness?"

Trenton leafed through his pages, finally pulling out one that he had highlighted. The wind ruffled the paper. "Apparently, they take the minds of the experimental species and weave them together till they match the intelligence of the Goweetha."

There was silence on the boat, aside from the breeze whipping the furled sail and the water lapping at the boat.

"A couple of times, these resurrections were actually successful," Trenton went on. "The Ma'ut managed to harvest the consciousness of another sentient species and use it to revive the Goweetha, like Sleeping Beauty waking up after a century.

"But each time, the Goweetha eventually figured out what had happened to them in their previous incarnation. Found the mass graves from the failed clonings, dug up evidence of their previous civilizations, and realized they were some extinct race recreated by a machine their ancestors had built. Seems they didn't like it much. One time, they tried to destroy the A.I. You can imagine how that ended. The next time, they simply committed suicide en masse. So the Ma'ut is trying something new. Human consciousness won't be used to recreate the Goweetha directly: it will be reprogrammed, filled with the memories of the extinct master species, and implanted into simulacra who will raise a new generation of Goweetha. We will be a cut-out between the resurrected maker and its machine, a midwife that will nurture and inspire before dying out itself."

BB shook her head in disbelief. "Exactly how many times has this A.I. done this?" she said.

Trenton again rifled through the pages until he found a passage marked in red. He frowned. "We are experiment number three hundred and seventy-six."

"Oh. My. God," said Joe softly.

• | •

Elspeth had agreed to wait in Washington until Trenton — or rather, until Joe and his editor — made contact.

She waited just two days, in the end.

The first day she filled with rather distracted sightseeing: the Lincoln Memorial, the Tidal Basin and the museums on the Mall.

The second was spent obsessively checking her phone for any signs of life from Trenton, interspersed with hours of watching cable news.

She was irritated to find that the frenzied news cycle had gone quiet just at the very moment when Trenton seemed to have vanished off the radar.

She googled all their names again, searching for some clue as to what might have happened. That was when she saw that Joe Chavez had disappeared almost a week earlier, after two murdered FBI agents were found in his apartment. His editor, Ed James, had also disappeared the next day and had not been seen since.

Elspeth's jaw dropped. *What the fuck had she got herself into?*

She couldn't just stay here any longer, lounging on her bed and flipping channels or gawping at the cherry blossoms of the Tidal Basin. She scanned Google maps to see just how far it was to Clover Mills, the little Virginia town whose GPS coordinates Rains had given her. It was only a three-and-a-half hour drive. A day trip, in effect.

If Trenton and co. did suddenly pop up on the radar—and if she decided she still wanted to meet them, a big *if* at this point—she could be back in time. In the interim, she might be able to find out why Rains had given her the coordinates of a rural bicycle shop.

This time, she rented a Volvo for her trip, more luxurious than anything Elspeth had ever driven in her life. She headed south, the city quickly receding to forest and farmland as Virginia opened out before her. She spotted the occasional sign for a Civil War battlefield or a slave plantation now open to tourists.

Just before Richmond, the GPS led her onto smaller roads heading west. As she approached, Elspeth could see nothing to distinguish the place from any of the other pretty little communities she had driven through on the way.

Clover Mills was nestled in a broad valley, heavily forested, and she could see signs pointing to hiking trails off the road. The town was attractive, a main street of family-run stores and a few side roads with quaint wood-sided houses with white-painted porches.

She drove down the main drag, past a cafe that looked almost empty even though it was lunchtime. Still early in the season, she guessed. The GPS directed her on to a side street. "In three hundred feet, your destination will be on the right," the robotic voice told her.

She recognized the scene from the streetview she had looked up back in Edinburgh. There was the "feed and seed" store. Next door was the bike shop. Someone was standing outside it. Slowing to a crawl, Elspeth was nearly in front of the shop when she realized that the man standing out front was a police officer. Panic flooded her gut — had her communications with Trenton been intercepted? Were they after her too now? Should she speed off?

No, keep calm and drive slowly by. The police officer was one of those sheriff's deputy types she'd seen in the movies, with a Smokey Bear brimmed hat and a tan shirt. He seemed engrossed in his phone and didn't even glance up as her Volvo slid by. Elspeth took the first right and parked outside a small house half-obscured by an early blooming rhododendron.

When she walked back to the corner, the police officer was still there, staring at his phone. She peered up and down the street. It was devoid of any life except for a man in a black hoodie and red baseball cap, standing across the street from the cop.

While the policeman seemed oblivious to anything around him, the man across the street appeared to have clocked her presence immediately and was staring straight at her in a rather alarming manner.

Elspeth wondered if she should just get back in the car and drive to DC. She pulled her phone out of her purse and checked to see if there was any news from Trenton, something that might distract her from a risky course of action. Nothing. The idea of going back to DC and watching endless cable as she waited for a call that might never come was too depressing. She forced herself forward.

As she approached the police officer, she could feel the man across the way watching her, even though his eyes were hidden under the brim of his hat.

The cop finally looked up from his phone and gave her that slightly unfocused look of someone who has been lost in screen time. Behind him, the bike store's window had been smashed. There was yellow police tape blocking the door.

"Oh hi," she said, as brightly as she could manage. "I'm staying at an Airbnb up the road and the owners said I might be able to rent a mountain bike here, you know, take in some of the trails, but it, uh, looks like…"

The man pocketed his phone and nodded. He was young, early twenties, and slightly overweight.

"I'm afraid that won't be possible, Ma'am. There was a break-in yesterday that went pretty badly wrong. We're waiting for forensics to come dust the place down."

"Oh," said Elspeth, her voice reflecting genuine surprise. *Had she come all this way for nothing?* "I… I hope no one was hurt?"

The young man shook his head. "I'm afraid so, miss. Owner was shot dead. One of his customers, too. We're not sure what happened, the security camera wasn't …" He caught himself and his voice trailed off. "It's still under investigation, so I'm not really supposed to talk about it."

"Have they… have they caught anyone yet?" she asked. She could feel the fear rising again in her stomach.

"Nope. We don't really have any suspects. Or motive, really, to be honest. Old Doug… I mean, the owner. He'd been here as long as anyone can remember. Good old family business. Never had a lick of trouble. Then suddenly… bam."

Elspeth looked through the broken glass. The place looked like any other bike store: rack of rentals at the front, which would normally be arranged on the street outside, and a few brand-new road and mountain bikes for sale, mounted on wall braces.

"Maybe a drugs thing? she said, almost hopeful. "Junkie needing some money?"

"Maybe," the deputy shrugged. "Not a lot of that round here, though. Where are you from, by the way?"

She looked at him in alarm, as though being questioned. But then he added, "I love your accent."

"Ah," she smiled, relieved. "Yeah. I'm, uh, from Ireland." She knew no one would be able to tell the difference.

"Ireland, eh?" the cop said. "Love Ireland. I'm part Irish myself."

"Yes," she said. "I'm sure..."

Accent notwithstanding, she doubted she could charm her way into a crime scene. She looked up and down the street. Oddly, the man in the red baseball cap had crossed the road while they were talking and was now standing outside the feed store, less than twenty yards away. He was staring directly at her, and this time she could clearly see his piercing blue eyes, fixed on her in an intense frown. He appeared to be straining to overhear their conversation. The cop seemed to have not noticed.

"Uh," she said. "Any suspects? In the robbery, I mean?"

The cop shook his head again. "No ma'am. But if you want to rent a bike, there's a place..."

The man in the baseball cap took a step closer.

"No suspicious people, just hanging around here for no obvious reason?" she said, her voice rising.

The cop gave her a puzzled look. "No, ma'am." he shook his head. "Now, like I was saying..."

Baseball cap was moving towards them now. Elspeth could clearly see his sunburned face, blond eyebrows and intense stare. He seemed as oblivious to the cop as the cop was to him. And he was clearly moving right towards her.

"What about him?" Elspeth blurted out, pointing.

The cop finally looked around.

"Who?" he said, squinting.

"Him!" she almost screamed. "Him right there! Don't you see him?" The man was only about 10 feet away now, but clearly the cop wasn't even registering him.

"Are you ...you feeling okay ma'am?" he asked.

The man was moving faster now, like he was about to run straight at her. Elspeth let out a gasp and started running, back the way she had come. As she turned, she caught sight of the man breaking into a run too, while the cop just stared after her in utter confusion.

"Ma'am?!" he called out, but she was already running as fast as she could back to the corner and to her car. She was fast, and her pursuer was heavy set, strong but not built for speed. She made it to her car and was scrabbling in her purse for her keys when all at once he was on top of her.

He grabbed her wrist. "Who are you?"

Her bag fell to the ground and the car keys spilled out.

The man slammed her against the passenger door, knocking the air from her lungs.

"How can you see me?" he barked.

She was too stunned and frightened to answer. It was clear the man intended her harm.

With terrifying ease, he twisted her arm and spun her around, so her face was pressed against the car. She felt him reach down and grab something from the ground. It must have been her keys, as the car beeped and the doors unlocked. He pulled her round to the passenger side.

"Get in," he hissed, pulling open the door. "We're taking a ride."

She was climbing in, her whole body shaking uncontrollably, when she heard a familiar voice.

"Ma'am, are you alright?" It was the sheriff's deputy, puffing slightly. Elspeth looked around and saw he was standing almost right next to her attacker, whom he still appeared inexplicably blind to.

Baseball Cap pulled a pistol from the waistband of jeans and for one horrific second Elspeth thought he was going to shoot the deputy point blank. Instead, he stepped up to him and slammed the butt of the gun into the side of the young man's head. The deputy crumpled to the ground.

The attacker stooped down again, presumably to retrieve Elspeth's bag so he could identify her. As he dipped momentarily out of sight, she lifted her leg over the center console and frantically felt with her foot for the brake. It was slightly confusing doing it in a left-hand drive car, but she pressed down and flipped the ignition switch.

Even though her attacker had the keys in his hand, he was standing close enough for the engine to start. He instantly realized what she had done and lurched towards the open driver's door, already reaching for her. She slammed the car into drive and floored the gas, hoping to god the cop wasn't lying in front of the wheels.

The car lurched forward and the open door sent Baseball Cap sprawling back. As the Volvo moved forward, she grabbed the wheel and kept her foot down. She blew through the stop sign and threw a hard right. She had no idea how far the car would keep going without the keys, but knew she had to put as much distance between her and that man before it cut out.

She sped out of Clover Mills, still straddled across the car's center console. When she was outside town, she found a turning onto a hiking trail and pulled over, shielded behind a clump of trees. As soon as the car stopped, she pulled herself fully into the driver's seat and sat there, body heaving, engine idling. She couldn't let it stop for any reason — she would never start the car again without the key fob. Luckily, the gas gauge showed half full: she might have had enough to reach DC. *Thank god for eco-friendly Swedish engineers.*

But the man had her phone and her bag. That meant he also had her driver's license and credit cards, just about everything he needed to find out every detail about her. Clearly she couldn't go back to the

Willard, yet she couldn't check in anywhere new without money or an ID.

Her chest still heaving, Elspeth willed herself to think calmly. First thing: get as far from here as possible. She pulled out and headed south, using the little digital compass on the rearview mirror. It was the opposite direction to where she wanted to go, but if the guy with her purse had figured out she was staying in DC already, he'd be headed that way now. She'd head further south, use the vehicle's GPS to join the highway somewhere downriver and then swing back up north.

Then she could try to figure out what to do next, aside from praying that she didn't run out of gas.

• | •

The sun was setting on the "Good News' as it tacked west. Ed knew he probably wouldn't get any sleep until they landed. It was still unclear where exactly Trenton wanted him to put the boat in, but somewhere on the Long Island shore seemed a good bet. He had plenty of coffee and Trenton had slipped him some military-grade pill he said would keep him going. It gave Ed a slight buzz and a mild euphoria, so he guessed it was some low-grade amphetamine mixed with caffeine. The combination of that, and what he had heard from Trenton earlier, was enough to ensure he wouldn't sleep for several days. If ever.

Joe emerged, looking a bit less shell-shocked, just before sundown. He sat nursing a bottle of water in the small cockpit with Ed. They sat in silence for a minute, before Joe muttered a quiet apology.

"Ed, I'm so sorry I got you into this," he said, staring at the rolling deck. "I don't know, I was in shock, I guess. Maybe Stockholm syndrome. But they seemed so excited when they got the email from the Scottish shrink because of my article, and they were wondering how they were going to get out of the area. And I just blurted out that you had a boat... I'm sorry. Now we're probably both going to get killed."

Ed put a hand on Joe's knee. "It's okay Joe. You know what? I'm glad you told them. Really."

Joe looked up, hopeful. "You are?"

Ed nodded. "Sure. Before all this happened ...you know, the aliens, the craziness of it all...I was just, I guess I'd say, moldering away. I was bored. Getting old sucks, believe me. I was just treading water, waiting for something else to break inside me. I didn't tell anyone at the paper this, but my doctor found a small tumor..."

"Oh shit Ed, I'm so sorry..."

"Well," said the older man. "It's the prostate. Not particularly aggressive, the doctor said. *Probably the sort of thing a man of your age will die with, rather than die from,*' he said. But even so, when your doctor starts talking about the different ways you might die, you kind of know it's time to reassess your life options."

"I had no idea," said Joe.

"Well, don't get too upset about it. Seems the whole of humanity may be in the same boat now."

The hatch to the cabin opened, and Trenton stepped out into the fading evening light. He was frowning, staring at one of his many cheap Chinese burner phones.

"How close are we to shore?" he said.

"I'm not sure," said Ed, reaching for his chart. "We shouldn't be too far from Plymouth by now, I think..."

"Take us in," said Trenton. He held up his phone. "Someone just tried to kill our Scottish shrink. We've got to get to DC right now."

· | ·

It had taken Elspeth several attempts before she found someone willing to let her send an email from their phone. She'd approached a twenty-something couple emerging from a Starbucks at a gas station plaza just off the interstate, but they looked at her like she was panhandling or crazy. Quite possibly, there was something wild-eyed about her right now. She needed to calm down, try to make out this was just a common-or-garden mishap, not a life-or-death pursuit by some guy that only she, apparently, could see.

She'd parked her rental round the back of the coffee shop, just in case her attacker or one of his associates cruised by hunting for her. The next woman she approached seemed less intimidated by her appearance, but bustled past anyway. "Sorry, I just don't trust anyone with my phone," she said.

It was then that she noticed a line of trucks parked on the other side of the gas station, outside a small wooden diner. Maybe she'd have better luck there, among people with some sense of the camaraderie of the road.

As she approached, a paunchy man dressed in combat pants and a stained gray sweatshirt stepped out of the diner and headed for an eighteen-wheeler plastered in stickers boasting the manifold virtues of guns, vets, and military service. The man looked about forty, his face weather-beaten and his reddish beard flecked with gray.

"Excuse me, sir," Elspeth said. He stopped and took her in. "I was wondering if you could help me with something. I lost my phone and need to send an email quite urgently. I was wondering if you would allow me to use your mobile?"

The man nodded. "Sure, no problem." He reached into his pocket and fished out a cracked cell phone, thumbed in the password. "You're from Ireland, ain't you?"

"Yes," Elspeth said, with a grateful smile.

"Dublin?" the man said.

She nodded. "I wonder... I have a Gmail account. Do you have the app?"

"Nope, I only use Telegram. Lot more secure. Too many people snooping on you these days. But feel free to download it. I can scrub it after."

Elspeth quickly did so and logged in. Luckily, she'd never bothered with two-step security verifications, despite her ex-husband constantly nagging her about hackers. She was enormously relieved to see an email from Trenton at the top of her inbox.

"Elspeth, I'm sure you have probably seen the reports regarding Joe by now. I know they will disturb you but please believe me, the men who were killed in his apartment were not law enforcement agents in any capacity and Joe had nothing to do with their deaths. For obvious reasons, I can't go into more detail now, but the incident has delayed our arrival at the planned destination. Please be advised, we will be there, and I sincerely hope you will be too. These words may sound hollow, but we are probably the only people you can trust now, and I believe that only by working together can we find Rains.

Yours

CCT"

Elspeth paused. It struck her that if she emailed Robbie, her ex-husband, he could almost certainly secure her consular help from the embassy in DC: get her out of here, back to the UK. But would she be safe there, after what she had seen today? Would she be safe *anywhere* now?

For a long minute, she just stared at the cracked screen in her hand. She could tell the truck driver was waiting to get his phone back and be on his way again.

Elspeth let out a breath and pressed 'reply' on Trenton's email. Typing as fast as she could, she gave him a brief rundown of bizarre events of that morning. *Can't return to Willard. Will wait on steps of Lincoln Memorial tomorrow and day after. Please let know if you can be there."

She logged off and handed the trucker his phone back.

"You wouldn't be heading anywhere near DC, would you?" she asked.

"Passing right by," the man said. "Headed for Jersey, all the way up the 95. Why? Need a lift?"

Elspeth nodded. "It would certainly help me out."

The truck driver looked her up and down. "Did you happen to lose your car as well as your phone, ma'am?"

Elspeth smiled awkwardly, looking at the man's truck. It was covered in pro-gun and anti-government bumper stickers: clearly, he distrusted email too. On a hunch, she decided just to blurt out her whole story and let fate decide. She talked so rapidly it was hard for even her to tell if she had gotten it all right.

When she was finished, the trucker jutted his jaw out. Then he nodded.

"Jump in," he said. "Not sure I caught all of that, but we got a couple of hours for you to give me any clarifications I might need."

• | •

Trenton split the group in Falmouth, a pretty fishing port that dated back to the days when the Pilgrim Fathers first rode into America on the tail end of the Middle Ages, burning witches and seeing evil spirits in the dark woods. Ed tied up among the yachts and lobster boats, then paid the harbormaster for a four-day berth with a roll of Trenton's cash. Engine trouble, he told the guy: the man eyed the cash suspiciously but just nodded and suggested the name of a local mechanic. Trenton and BB were busy swabbing down the boat's surfaces for fingerprints.

BB gave Joe and Ed a burner phone each, Chinese no-brands stripped of all apps except secure messaging and an Uber linked to an anonymous checking account. Following BB's instructions, they called an Uber to Pawtucket. From there, they boarded the northeast regional train, each of them sitting in a separate carriage as they sped through Connecticut commuter towns, past the glimmering ramparts of New York City, and on into New Jersey and Delaware.

Joe wore an N95 mask—plenty of commuters still clung to their protection after the death toll of the last pandemic—and hid behind a copy of the New York Times he found abandoned on the seat. Even so, he felt horribly exposed.

All sweaty paranoia was instantly forgotten, however, as he read the headline on the front page.

"*Russia to present survivors,*" read the banner, followed by the subhead: "*President Malevich to personally address the world.*" Two days from now, and the alien abductees would finally get to tell the world what they had seen.

Joe stared at the paper in disbelief, then ripped through everything he could find on the latest development.

The paper's editorial argued the news could only be a positive message, given how long the Russians had waited, and the fact that the president himself was going to front the event. Another opined that the Russians had neglected their duty to humanity by keeping the abductees under wraps for so many months, when the whole world needed to know what its fate was to be.

Joe desperately wanted to find Ed. He knew he should be excited, that this was indeed good news, but somehow it only made him feel worse. Had he been played by a gang of delusional alien-chasers? Because at this point, traveling on their behalf, and without Trenton's gun to his head, he knew he was fully complicit. If what the paper said was true, he should probably get off at the next stop and shop Trenton and BB to the police.

Finding Ed was far too risky right now, though. Instead, he sunk deeper into his seat and kept an eye out for the police, or anyone else who might be acting suspiciously. But everyone seemed perfectly normal: the suburban Connecticut teenagers headed to NYC for a gig, the weary men and women in suits who boarded at Grand Central. Joe left the train in Baltimore: he saw Ed on the platform but they didn't acknowledge each other. Taking separate cabs, they went to the waterfront aquarium where they loitered a while, watching the last groups of school kids leave the building, until they felt reasonably sure they hadn't been followed. Then they called an Uber and rode together to Washington.

The driver dropped them on the Mall, just in front of the White House. The lights were just coming on at the Washington Monument, the flags fluttering in the evening breeze.

"Did you see? About the Russians?" he asked Ed.

"I don't trust the Russians," Ed said. "Why do they need to control the survivors' narrative so closely? Why not just let them be questioned by the media, or by scientists from other countries? Or the UN? What are they trying to conceal? But let's see what they have to say."

They trudged past the Reflecting Pool and found a park bench where they could observe the steps of the Lincoln Memorial.

"You see her?" said Joe, squinting in the dusk. Beyond the white stone steps, the memorial was floodlit, as though Honest Abe was sitting in his front room with the lights on, staring out an immense window into the city.

"Nope," said Ed. "But there's a bunch of people up there. One of us is going to have to walk up there and see if she's there."

Joe nodded. He could see the older man was wiped out, already limping slightly. He pulled out his phone and looked at the picture of Elspeth McGann. It was the only photo that BB had uploaded to the camera roll. A slender, well-groomed woman in her late thirties or early forties. Attractive, dark bobbed hair.

He memorized the picture, then, as per BB's instructions, deleted it.

"I'll go," said Joe.

People were still lingering on the steps of the memorial, capturing the thin needle of the Monument puncturing the setting sun. It struck Joe as slightly odd, but also very human, that people would still be taking vacations even as the world seemed to be ending. *Maybe that's when you need it the most,* he thought.

And suddenly, there she was. A woman who perfectly fit the photo. She was holding an antiquated paperback. Joe peered intently at the cover of the book, reflecting on what a poor spy he made. She clocked his attention and tilted the cover up for him to get a better look. *My Life Among the Apemen*.

"Elspeth?" he said. She nodded, and Joe smiled for what felt like the first time in months.

• | •

The truck driver's name was Dale. Dale Harrison, from some town in Tennessee Elspeth had never heard of. As soon as they got in his truck, he surprised Elspeth by putting on what sounded like Tibetan monks playing music on a muted synth.

"Brian Eno," Dale explained. "Recommended by my shrink when I came back from my third tour with a real bad case of PTSD. I kinda like it. Helps me in moments of mental turpitude."

Elspeth nodded. "Dale, there is much more to you than meets the eye," she said.

"Don't you go gettin' fresh with me, Irish," Dale deadpanned as his rig pulled out into the flow of the I95. "I got my .357 Magnum in the glove box right here."

"Of course." Elspeth laughed nervously, not sure if he was joking. He gave her a sidelong glance, then opened the small door of the glove compartment with a four-digit code. Sure enough, there inside was the dull metal gleam of a very large handgun.

"I'm ready for just about anything with that," he said. "Unless the fuckers are invisible, like you said this fella you met was. You know how he might have pulled off that little trick?"

"Well," said Elspeth, "I can't say for sure, but in the book I mentioned, *My Life Among the Apemen*, the man who came to my office in Edinburgh claimed that there was some kind of a code the farmers were imbued with. He said they can also use it, when confronted with limited numbers of humans, for a kind of mind control."

"So you think this guy who attacked you, he was one of these farmers?" Dale said.

"It's the only thing I can think of. But Rains said there was a new generation. He called them 'harvesters.' They were created a few decades back to be the muscle for whatever is coming down the pipe. There could be hundreds of them…"

She was cut off by Dale slamming on the air brakes. The rig juddered and dumped speed. About five vehicles in front, a tan military Humvee was plodding along at 45 behind a large white truck. A sign on its rear read "SLOW CONVOY."

"Shit," hissed Dale, switching down gears. "These fuckers again. Ran into them back in South Carolina. 'Bout fifty trucks all bunched up together. Snarled up traffic for miles. Can't be the same ones though, they were moving too slow to have gotten ahead of me. Must be another one. Fuck knows what the military is moving. Something to fight the frickin' aliens with, I hope."

He had to wait for a long line of cars to speed past. Eventually, a gap opened, and he swung round the column of trucks. Elspeth wasn't counting the number of vehicles in the convoy, but it seemed to take a good twenty minutes to finally pass the Humvee that was riding point.

"Let's hope there's no more of those," Dale said. He fished his phone from the dashboard. "Here," he said, "you might want to check if your crew has written back to you. And maybe you can read me some of this book about the apemen you sent to your alien-hunter pal. We got a good coupla hours to kill before we hit DC traffic."

Elspeth gratefully took the cell phone. To her huge relief, there was an email in her inbox from bland.alias@gmail.com. "Will be in DC tomorrow a.m. Copy your plan. See you on LM steps."

"Oh thank god," she breathed out. "He's going to be there. Thank you Dale! You are a good man. You have earned a reading from 'My Life Among the Apemen.' I have to warn you though, it's not very…"

She froze. *Shit.* The only existing copy of the book was in her room at the Willard Hotel. Sure, she had the scanned copy. But she had promised the actual book to Trenton, and had now lost it through her own stupidity. What if it held other clues, beyond the actual pages of text she had emailed to Trenton? Something hidden in the binding, or a coded message on the frontispiece? Not to mention, she was supposed to be holding it on the steps of the Lincoln Memorial the next day for the meet-up. Cursing, she patted down her jeans and was relieved to find that the hotel key card was at least still in her back pocket.

She realized Dale was looking at her, one eyebrow raised.

"Dale," she said, "How brave are you feeling?"

PART IV

Contact made, Elspeth and Joe started walking. They had no idea where they were headed. A path led past the wall inscribed with the names of 55,000 Americans eaten up by the Vietnam war, past the bench where Ed was sitting, studiously ignoring them: he would follow on after them, to see if he could spot anyone tailing them.

They hardly spoke until they were passing the blank stone facades of government institutions shuttered for the night.

"Are you alright?" Joe asked. "Trenton said you'd been attacked."

"I'm okay," she said. "I'll tell you all about it when we get somewhere safe. Do you have a place to stay?"

"No, not yet," Joe said. "Trenton said he'd message me when his people had found us a place. In the meantime, let's just walk, if you're not too tired." As he spoke, he was texting Trenton: *Contact made. What now?*

"To be honest, I'm absolutely beat," Elspeth said. "Perhaps we could find a place to sit down and have a coffee."

They took side streets to avoid the White House, where facial recognition cameras might have captured their images. The coffee shops downtown were largely shut by this time in the evening, but they came across a rather low-rent pub that seemed the sort of place that Joe's fellow journalists might gather after filing their copy for the day. The only coffee the place served was Irish, so they ordered two large ones and sat down, letting the caffeine and the Bailey's soothe their snagged nerves.

"Thank you for coming to meet me, Joe," said Elspeth. She found the presence of the young journalist oddly reassuring after the chaos and violence of the past twenty-four hours. "Today has been the longest day of my life."

She talked him through the unnerving events since she had landed, from the zombies on Lafayette Square to the man whom only she could apparently see. Every time the door of the coffee shop opened, she'd stop talking and lean over to Joe.

"That guy who just walked in. Can you see him?"

"Yes, I can see him."

"I sound delusional, don't I?"

Joe shook his head, smiled. "No, you just sound like someone who has undergone something way outside the realm of normal experience. Trust me, I've been there myself the past few days."

Elspeth gave him a direct look. "I read about the shooting, Joe. That must have been deeply traumatizing for you."

Her tone reminded Joe that he was sitting with a professional shrink. Suddenly, he felt a desperate urge to tell her everything, but the waiter came up and Elspeth ordered another large Irish coffee. Joe was just about to talk again when his phone pinged. He read the message and cursed.

"Shit," he said. "Looks like we've got someone following us."

"What do we do?"

Joe paused. "You know what? I really have no idea."

He picked up his phone and called Ed to get a better description. Elspeth watched as her companion's face screwed up.

"Black NRA baseball cap... worn leather vest and ginger beard," he repeated. "Doesn't really sound like the cops. Maybe it's the guys who tried to get Trenton at my place. Wait, Ed, what..?"

He looked up at Elspeth. She was grinning, the first time Joe had seen her tightly clenched features relax.

"That's Dale. My guardian angel. I'll go fetch him in."

She stood up. "It's okay Joe. He's the truck driver. The only person on the whole highway who was willing to give the crazy lady a ride to DC. I told him everything."

She caught Joe's alarm.

"Oh, don't worry, he's totally in. Doesn't trust the government either, or anyone really. Bought my entire saga with nary a blink. I think he wants to help me. Like a damsel in distress type of thing. He's quite the gentleman really."

Joe was about to start listing his objections, but found he was too tired to even begin. Just as she was walking out, Elspeth stopped and turned back.

"But tell me.. how did *you* know he was following us? Is Trenton out there?" She sounded hopeful.

Joe shook his head. "Just my editor. Ed James."

"Oh right," said Elspeth, a mix of disappointment and relief on her face. "Well let's get them all in here then. You call Ed, I'll get Dale."

While he was waiting for them all to return, Joe's phone pinged again. He squinted at the screen. Odd: an email from Airbnb. "Check in instructions for 2087 Varnum Street, Washington DC..."

The link showed a listing for a short-term rental, starting that night and booked for the next two weeks. It took Joe's weary brain a second to realize this was not just some random spam: BB had come through again. *Thank God.* This close to the end of the world, and all Joe could think of was the joy of having a roof over his head for the night. He finished his Irish coffee and walked over to the counter to settle up.

• | •

Elspeth awoke with a start. She didn't recognize the bedroom she was lying in, and that filled her with terror. Thin curtains were straining to contain the bright morning sunlight. Then it came back to her with a crash: she was in a house in Washington DC, an address she didn't know, with men she didn't know, waiting for the end of the world.

Fuck. She had an overwhelming urge to climb out of the window and run as far as she could, before anyone else woke up.

The house was quiet, but when she stepped out into the hall, she could hear someone talking softly downstairs. She tried to remember who had ended up in which room: Ed and Joe had taken the room with twin beds, and Dale had holed up in what looked like it had once been a kid's bedroom. She couldn't recall who was where, so she tiptoed to the stairs to see if she could make out who was talking. The top step creaked as soon as her foot touched it. The voices downstairs fell silent.

Elspeth took a deep breath, then headed down, a forced smile on her face. The stairs led to a small living room that opened directly onto a kitchen-dining area. But the three people at the table were not the three people she had arrived with last night. She froze, suddenly aware of the fact that she was standing in front of complete strangers and still wearing the baggy gym pants and the tee-shirt emblazoned with "Fuck Commies and Fuck You Too" that Dale had loaned her.

The people — two men and a woman — stared at her before one man stood up and held out his hand.

"Elspeth," he said. "Cassius Trenton. My god, are we happy to see you!"

Trenton clutched her hand, eyes locked on hers like they were on a first date. "Sorry for the intrusion," he said. "We got in late last night. Actually, it was only what, four hours ago? Didn't want to wake you."

He quickly introduced his companions: the African-American woman was simply known as BB, and the tall and lanky guy with hair sticking up like prairie grass was Darkman. Elspeth's stomach sank: she was in a shifting landscape where everyone was known simply by aliases, *noms de guerre*.

Trenton himself looked like he might have once been quite athletic, with broad shoulders but the beginning of a mid-life paunch. His pale complexion spoke either of a serious iron deficiency or of long days spent indoors, probably hacking computers in rented basements. Despite his rather bloodless appearance, he seemed to be in vigorous command.

"BB, go get some rest. You've been driving all night. Take Elspeth's room, since she's up now. You don't mind, do you, Elspeth?" he said, not waiting for an answer before instructing Darkman to head out to Costco and stock up on bulk supplies. He pulled out a small plastic wallet stuffed with credit cards from different banks and handed one to Darkman, who promptly headed out the back door. As Trenton spoke, he also was making Elspeth an espresso on the Keurig in the kitchen.

"You saw the news, I'm guessing? President Malevich is going to make a global address tomorrow at noon, our time. Now, I'm willing to bet it'll be a total whitewash, but we'll have to see. I can't imagine he'd be doing this if he didn't have something concrete, and something big, to peddle, so we will have to work fast. Now, you are the only person I know of in the entire world who has interacted with one of these ET farmers face to face. I've read the book, of course, and have copious notes I want to discuss with you. But first I need to know every detail about him, what he said, how he acted and most of all what he looks like. I have an app that police sketch artists use to compile composites of suspects. We'll start with that and then reverse track the image on Google to see if we can come up with a likeness of our Mr. Lester Rains."

Elspeth was slightly overwhelmed by this torrent of information. She mutely took the coffee Trenton handed her and allowed herself to be ushered to the sofa. They got as far as looking at a page of faces roughly shaped like Rain's slender Gallo-Roman skull when there was a shout from upstairs, followed by a heavy thump on the ceiling above them.

"Get down on the floor and put your hands behind your back!" BB yelled, followed by a voice that appeared to be muffled by carpet.

"Lady, I don't know who you are, but I was invited here by the Irish alien lady..."

"Oh shit," said Elspeth. "Dale!" She turned to Trenton, but he was already halfway up the stairs. Seeing a gun had appeared in his hand, she rushed after him.

"Don't shoot," she yelled. "He's a friend. He's the guy who saved me when they were after me."

By the time she got upstairs, Ed and Joe were standing in their boxers and tees, looking on in confusion as BB kneeled on the back of the prone truck driver. BB had a gun in her hand too, and was dexterously using the other to put zip ties round Dale's wrists. Dale was muttering curses into the carpet.

"It's okay, guys. He's with me," Elspeth said. She quickly explained who Dale was: the trucker attempted to pull himself up to join in his own defense, but BB shoved him to the ground again.

"You brought the guy who gave you a ride on the highway into our safe house?" BB said, not taking her eyes off Dale. Put in those rather stark terms, Elspeth realized she had made a colossal blunder.

"Well..." she stuttered. "Actually, he risked his life for me. He took me on and stuck with me when I got to DC, even went into my hotel room to get the book for me, though he could have been followed by those invisible freaks..."

"Exactly," said BB. "He coulda been followed."

"It was all of our mistake," said Joe. "We were tired and not thinking as straight as we should have been. I have to take responsibility for this too."

"Okay, okay," said Trenton, putting his pistol in the waistband at the back of his pants. "We are where we are. I realize you guys are all new to this, so we'll chalk it up to lessons learned. BB, cut the cuffs."

As Dale sat up, muttering about his rights as an American, Elspeth groaned again. The tee shirt Dale was wearing sported a large Confederate flag, billowing out over his belly and sagging pecs. BB was staring at him like she wanted to jam his face into the carpet all over again.

"Dale," Trenton said, kneeling down so the two men were eye to eye. "First of all, let me say thank you very much for saving Elspeth yesterday. We owe you a big one for that. I'm sorry about what just happened. But you understand, this is a highly confidential mission we are on here and op-sec is vital. You're ex-military right?"

Dale nodded, looking somewhat mollified already. "82nd airborne. Two re-ups."

"Awesome," said Trenton. "So if you really want to help, I want you to take a little time with BB here and go through all your background details so we can get you clearance. Then, if you like, you can get back to your truck and be on your way. Or if you want to stick around..."

"Stick around?" BB squawked. "Trenton, you cannot be serious!"

Trenton ignored her. "Then we might just be needing an extra pair of hands in the days to come. We're moving into a key stage of finding out just what these ETs want. I figure a man like you might be a valuable part of that, Dale."

Dale nodded, flashing BB a sullen look. "Okay," he said.

"Outstanding," said Trenton, straightening up. "Now if you wouldn't mind sitting down with BB for a while. BB is a hotshot former Navy pilot, so I'm sure you two will have lots in common."

He gave Dale a hand up and shot a knowing look at BB, whose face was furious as she followed the truck driver down into the front room.

"Rest of you," Trenton said, turning to Elspeth, Joe and Ed. "Please join me downstairs for coffee and a morning brief. We have to figure out where Lester Rains might be."

• | •

At roughly a quarter to noon the next day, the entire city of Washington fell into a deathly hush. The entire country, the entire world: everyone was gathered in front of a television set, iPad, smart phone or computer to see what Russia's President Malevich would have to say.

Trenton stepped outside: not a soul to be seen, no cars in the street nor planes overhead. He locked the front door and joined his crew in front of the television.

Malevich didn't keep them waiting: he'd already had the world on tenterhooks for months and knew he had the undivided attention of the planet. At the stroke of twelve, he strode out onto a stage decked with Russian flags and took up his position behind a lectern. He was a relatively small man, stocky, clad in a perfectly tailored dark blue suit that accented his glacial eyes. He spoke with confidence in this, the most important speech of his life, the translator trailing a few seconds in his slipstream.

"Friends, citizens of the world, I address you today not only as the leader of one the world's great nations but as a simple man, humbled by the discovery that we are, at long last, able to say that we are not alone in this universe."

"Humbled, right," sneered Joe, sitting cross-legged on the floor. BB, sat on the couch behind him, smacked him on the back of his head. "Shush now," she hissed.

Darkman had not only set up the TV to record but had a camera on a tripod filming the TV screen as a backup. Out of habit, Ed and

Joe had their own phones' voice recorders taping the address. No one was going to miss a word.

"I know many people have worried over the past months that these visitors came not in a spirit of peace, but of conquest. I can understand that, given the disturbing events that occurred right here in Moscow six months ago, and the preoccupation we felt for our people who were taken away that day."

There was a long, pregnant pause.

"But I am standing here today to assure you that, in fact, our visitors not only came in peace, but they came to help us. To save us, in fact. As you all know, our planet is in dire trouble. As I speak, the air in Moscow is tinged with smoke from the steppes, where fires burn larger than any in history. The American west is in flames, the rainforest in the Amazon is half gone, millions have left their homes in the Middle East not because of war but because there is no secure water supply. Crops fail in Europe, entire towns are washed away every year, killing thousands. Africa has seen a vast surge of displaced people heading north, only to be turned back by wealthy nations whose politicians have turned to tactics not seen since the dark days of the 1930s."

"We have to face the facts, my friends. And the central fact is that we have failed to come together as a species to address the existential crisis that we face. Generations of leaders have failed to meet the responsibilities. And now our planet can no longer support us. We face an unprecedented crisis in the history of our species. Unlike the brave face that world leaders assume in public, I can tell you that behind the closed doors in Davos or Geneva or the United Nations headquarters in New York, the despair is palpable."

"That is why I stand before you all today. I apologize this process has taken longer than expected, but when our people returned to Earth, it was our most serious duty to ensure that they were unharmed and that their story be properly assessed. I know many people have been clamoring for any news, but we knew that until we had gathered their full story, and had ascertained that it was the *real* story of what happened to them, it would have been an abdication of our responsibility to let the world know in piecemeal fashion."

"I assure you, Russia has done everything possible to make absolutely certain that the people who returned to this planet are the very same people who left: their DNA, their memories, their mannerisms and their affections are unaltered, as our doctors and family members who are here today can attest. I will give them the opportunity to speak to you themselves very shortly. But in the interest of absolute clarity, I wanted to address you today, to say that we believe, from everything we have heard, that the extraterrestrial visitors we saw came here to help, and will be returning soon to save our species."

Malevich paused, as if he knew that all around the world, more than eight billion people would be turning to each other in front of whatever screen they were watching on and hugging each other, whooping their relief and joy, or else shouting out their doubt and disbelief. Elspeth turned to Trenton, her face almost hopeful, as though she too wanted to believe that everything she had heard from Rains was wrong. She saw Dale was also grinning, entranced by the news.

Trenton was sitting there, staring at the screen, expressionless.

"That's some Grade-A gaslighting bullshit right there," said BB.

"Hush now," whispered Trenton. "I want to see what the abductees have to say."

Malevich began speaking again. "To that end, I would like to introduce you to a very fine man, a man who has become a dear personal friend these past months, and who is among the first humans to have traveled beyond our solar system.

"Ladies and gentlemen, Dmitri Petrovich Tikhomirov is a subway ventilation engineer by profession. He was driving his Vesta to work on the morning of the encounter and was taken into the ships. I want you to know, right here and now, that all the people taken that morning are alive, and well. They voted for Dmitri and sixteen others to return to bear witness to what happened to them. Dima, please come and join me."

A tall man in his forties, with dark curls hanging over his forehead, walked out onto the podium. He gave a nervous smile, flashing big white teeth. He bobbed his head toward the audience and cameras. Aside from that, it would have been hard to know he was a municipal engineer making a live address to the largest audience in human history.

"Privyet," he grinned.

"Hi," the translator said. There was a pause, perhaps for the world to be charmed by his no-nonsense manner.

"Thank you, President Malevich, for the kind introduction. I would like to talk to you all today about what happened to me and almost 50,000 other Russians on October 23 last year. As the president said, I was driving through downtown Moscow on the way to work that morning. I was stuck in traffic and I noticed that my engine had cut out. I was trying to restart it when smack! This bird, a big black crow, slams into my windshield, flapping like crazy. Then another, and another. I look up and there are birds falling from the sky all over the place. Horns are blaring: the lights ahead have changed, but no one is moving. Then the horns all stop, as people realize that everybody's car has died at exactly the same time.

"I was about to get out of my vehicle when I saw the cars in front of me start to take off, to fly up into thin air. I froze right there in my seat. It only took a few seconds for this tidal wave of cars to reach me, and the next thing I knew I was in the air too, I had this sickening sensation in my stomach like I was on a rollercoaster only there was nothing holding on to me. After that, I don't remember what happened. I must have lost consciousness."

"When I woke up, I felt like I was floating. There was this soft light in front of me and as soon as I opened my eyes, a woman's voice told me, very smoothly, 'It's okay now Dima, don't be afraid.' I didn't feel any alarm, only a sense of peace and gentle curiosity. It took me a minute to remember what had happened, and for a moment I thought I must be dreaming, or dead, but the voice carried on. It said, 'Dima. You are our honored guest. Everything is going to be alright now. We only wish to help you and your people."

On stage, Tikhomirov smiled at the memory. "You know, I never felt such a peace as at that moment. I started to think, 'Did I die in a car crash, and this is heaven?' But then the voice went on, very calm and soothing, like a mother talking to her baby."

"'You are now a guest on board a vessel of the Goweetha fleet. You will have never heard of the Goweetha, of course, because Earth has not yet invented the capacity for interstellar communications. But we are a highly advanced and peaceful civilization from a planetary system 150 light years from Earth. We have existed for many hundreds of thousands of Earth years.'"

"Of course, I had trouble coming to terms with this: I am floating on a spaceship of some alien civilization? No way! You would think I'd've felt fear or total panic, but all I felt was this pervading sense that yes, everything *is* going to be alright. Maybe they gave me some kind of drug to make me feel that way, so that I could listen to what they were telling me and really understand it."

"The voice told me I had been asleep for two weeks. It said that we were about to reach our planetary destination. Then a bright light shone from above me and I could make out all these other people floating around me. There were so many of them and I couldn't understand what they were floating in, or if they were suspended from something. But they were free-floating, just like me, all exactly the same distance from each other. I thought I'd been in a separate room, but there we all were together, all the people from Moscow, floating in this vast space. People started waving to each other, swimming through the air to grab one another, so there were soon knots of people floating and hugging, laughing, and crying. It was so beautiful and surreal."

"Then we realized that we were floating slowly downward, toward the ground. One by one, we reached the floor and sat down, because our legs were not used to standing. When everyone had landed, and we were all sitting on the deck, the lights became brighter and we could see we were sitting in this massive hall, made of what looked like stone, but I don't think it could be. It was reddish, a color I couldn't quite describe. The roof was arched and there were doors along the side, at ground level. Everyone was talking now, asking where we were, but no one seemed upset. Everyone was calm. Then the voice sounded again. At first, I thought it was just talking to me. It sounded so close up, but I could see everyone was listening."

"'You will be wondering where you are now. To give you our exact position would be meaningless, so instead, let us show you.'"

At that point, Tikohmirov said, the walls slid down from the central arch over their heads, and a chorus of gasps arose from the Russians. A silvery cobweb of a nebula spun over their heads. A billion stars glittered in every direction like frost on the windows. They were in a giant viewing gallery.

"You are pioneers," said the voice. "We have rescued you from your dying planet to show you the new home we have prepared for you. It is four times the size of Earth and has an almost identical atmosphere. Do not fear, you will have the chance to return home and to bring your loved ones here."

Tikhomirov paused. "I know all this sounds crazy. This is just me, Dmitri Tikhomirov, a complete nobody from Zaraysk, a little town outside of Moscow. How can someone like me describe the inside of an alien spaceship? Or a supernova? Maybe..." He grinned, like a conjuror at a kid's party. "Maybe you'd like to see it with your own eyes?"

There was a sharp intake of breath from the assembled audience of scientists, journalists, celebrities and diplomats from around the world.

"What?" Tikhomirov laughed. "You don't think aliens have video cameras?"

The Russian flag behind him suddenly drew back to reveal a gigantic screen. The hall held its breath as an image appeared.

Hundreds of people, floating down a tube, many of them laughing, others with mouths wide open in wonder. The angle of the camera slid around to see what they could see: a beautiful blue planet wreathed in clouds that parted in places to reveal strange contours, land masses and ocean that as yet had no names known to humans. The camera zoomed in on some of the awe-struck faces.

"This is what we call New Earth," said Tikohmirov, smiling up at the screen. He shrugged. "I know, not very original. But we had to think of it on the fly, so to speak. Now, this is us boarding the shuttles to land. As you can see, everyone was very excited. You know, with these alien ships, you float everywhere, but guided by some system you can't see."

On screen the shuttle was heading down towards the planet surface, to whoops and gasps: to Trenton and his crew, it was hard to tell if the sounds were from the footage they were watching, or from the distinguished audience in Moscow. The ship rattled slightly as it burrowed into New Earth's atmosphere, but the entry appeared smooth enough that the passengers were still gaping in wonder as they approached their new home. The ship swooped down through clouds, then emerged into clear blue sky, dipped over some wooded hills and hovered briefly over a city that looked like something from a fairytale: castles, palaces, elegant townhouses lining broad boulevards that bristled with parks and lakes.

There was not a soul to be seen in the streets below.

The ship landed on a cobbled, leafy square, and the Russians descended a ramp. They stood gaping at the beautiful surroundings: a fountain sparkled in front of them, a huge cathedral rose behind a row of what appeared to be restaurants.

"This bit is funny," said Tikhomirov. "You see, we'd been in a kind of suspended animation for two weeks, fed with some kind of infusion. And then we smelled the most delicious fragrance coming all from those restaurants. And we realized we were starving. So we ran in and the tables were piled with absolutely incredible food. My God, it was a feast: there was roast duck, caviar, blintzes, sausage, potatoes, pasta, champagne...vodka," he said, with a knowing smile. "We fell upon that banquet and ate until we couldn't move. Then suddenly, we all *had* to move. None of us had had a bowel movement in two weeks. Suddenly, all that great food... luckily there were plenty of toilets for everyone."

There was laughter in the audience. Trenton heard guffaws right next to him and turned to see Dale with a wide, gleeful grin wrinkling his beard. Joe also looked like a little kid watching his first Disney movie.

"Can't you see they're fucking with us?" he snapped. "Jesus Christ, man, all this shit is fake. It's a boondoggle, meant to show that if we go with them, we all get to paradise."

"I don't know, man," Dale said, still grinning. "Looks pretty real to me."

"What, you think a civilization that can fly enormous ships through space, appear with no warning and kidnap tens of thousands of people can't mock up a little CGI propaganda film?" Trenton said.

"It's a total fake," said BB.

"It looks so beautiful, though," whispered Joe.

Trenton scowled furiously. "That's the whole point," he said, throwing up his hands. He turned back to the screen, now showing people wandering through the empty streets, picking which house they wanted to live in: testing feather beds, admiring views of hazy blue mountains from grape arbors perched on rooftop balconies, pointing and gasping at the three moons visible through the pink clouds of sunset.

"The Goweetha terraformed this planet for us," Tikhomirov was saying. "The planet was in the Goldilocks zone, just the right distance from a star to sustain human life, but it had no life. Until we got there."

Shouts and gasps were rising from the audience. The front door of a house that some Russians had decided to enter had opened on its own, revealing a small creature waiting for them. It looked like something between a small bear and a large raccoon, and it bowed as they approached. Tikhomirov glanced up at the screen and laughed.

"Oh, these guys are super cute!" he said. "They looked like animals but they are robotic. The Goweetha provided them to look after us. They keep the place clean and run errands and show us how everything works. They are super lifelike, they can hold whole conversations with you, even make jokes."

"You have got to be shitting me," said Trenton. "They even threw in some fucking Ewoks to seal the deal?"

Tikhomirov was still talking. "You want to know what we did that first week we were there, after we got to choose which houses we wanted and the raccoons showed us round? We got to design the animals and birds that would live there."

"What do you mean?" shouted someone in the audience, speaking English with a heavy accent.

"I mean just that," said Tikhomirov. "We were like Adam and Eve, naming all the animals. Except they gave us these amazing computer simulator devices, and told us we could build creatures from scratch. They have the ability to do that: you pick a certain environment, like a grassland, and you can design your own antelope or buffalo, or whatever you like, and it will create the animal. But you can make the buffalo striped purple, with wings if you like. You can even create sentient creatures, so that you can talk to them. I designed a flying dog that could talk to me and show me around. It was big enough that it could even carry me on its back when it flew. It was...." His eyes took on a faraway look for a moment. "It was just amazing. I can't wait to go back, with my whole family and all my friends."

At this point, the audience erupted in shouts and President Malevich himself had to step forward to quiet the din.

"I know, I know," the Russian leader said. "It is quite the revelation. That is why we have been taking our time to cross-examine all the returnees. And their stories match exactly. But I will introduce the others in just a moment. First of all, I have another announcement to make, perhaps as important as what you have already heard today."

He stared out across the hall. The hubbub immediately died down and an expectant hush settled over the crowd. When the auditorium was completely silent, he spoke again.

"The ships are coming back, to take whoever wishes to go to New Earth. And they will be here next week."

· | ·

Elspeth was on her feet already, even as everyone else was still gawping at the television, which was blaring out the hullabaloo in the Moscow auditorium.

"We've got to leave!" she said. "Now!"

No one moved: President Malevich was explaining how the ships would start marshaling over hundreds of cities around the world in the coming days.

"Elspeth..." began Trenton.

"My god, people, are you just going to sit there? Did you not hear what the man said? They're coming back *next week*! Rains specifically said not to be anywhere near any city when the harvest starts, and here we are sitting in the capital of the most powerful country in the world. We have to get out! Tonight, while there's still flights!"

"Please, Elspeth," said Trenton, desperate to hear what the Russians might say next but clearly torn over the fact that the only person who could positively identify Rains was about to walk out on him. She was already by the front door.

"Let's go upstairs and talk," Trenton said, casting one last glance at the television. "Darkman, BB, as soon as they stop speaking, start working all the analytics. We have to know how the world is reacting."

Then he ushered Elspeth up the stairs and into the small room she was sharing with BB.

"Listen," she said, "you said yourself that all that was just a huge pile of bollocks. Clearly they've got the Russian government on board somehow, helping them gaslight the entire world. This is *bad* Trenton. We have to get out while we can."

"Okay, okay," he said, putting a hand on her shoulder. "I hear you, I really do. This is not good. They've obviously worked over at least some world leaders, threatened them or promised them something, or worked some kind of Jedi mind trick on them. But listen, if we can't locate Rains, we'll never find out what the hell is really going on, and we'll be fighting blind against whatever they have planned. We can't win that way, Elspeth."

She let out a strangled sob. "Win what, Trenton? Win *what?* And can we not do whatever it is we need to do from Hawaii? Rains specifically said to go there, it'd be some kind of sanctuary..."

"Or a zoo," said Trenton. "But sure, maybe we can. I'll tell you what. Darkman is going to run high-speed analytics of what the world is saying as soon as this thing is over. People are going to vote with their feet, and very quickly, I'd imagine. Either they flee to the countryside again, or they head to the cities to get picked up. Let's see whether they are buying it, then we can figure out how to respond. I'm going to have Ed and Joe write up a response and post it to their newspaper's website, maybe that will get some attention. We have to warn as many people as possible not to get on those ships."

"And if everyone *is* fleeing? What if all the flights to Hawaii are being booked up right now?"

"We'll know within an hour. And I promise you, I will personally book you on a flight to Maui, and find you a place to stay there while this plays out..."

"You're not seriously thinking about staying here yourself, are you?" she said. "Trenton, there's going to be giant fucking alien spaceship sucking up everyone in every major city around the world in a few days' time. Are you off your bloody rocker?"

He dropped his head and laughed. "I love your accent, Elspeth. I may even have to tell Dale that you're not Irish."

She half-laughed too. "I'm serious, Cassius."

"Me too," he said. "But here's the thing. I have to assess everything we know after today. I'm not saying I won't join you in Hawaii, but maybe I'll go via that little place in Virginia where you almost got kidnapped the other day. Thanks to you, we now at least have a facial composite of Rains, and we're running image matches across the internet. If we find anything, we can come get you from Hawaii."

"You're not coming, are you?"

He stared at her a moment, his face close to hers. "We'll see," he said. "Meantime, give me an hour. One hour, that's all I ask. Now, I really have to get back to that press conference."

• | •

On screen, another survivor, a blonde woman this time, was speaking when Trenton got back to the living room. She was answering a journalist who'd asked why the Goweetha had taken her and the other Russians in such an abrupt and aggressive manner.

"Imagine you see a wild animal in distress," the woman said. "You know you have to help it, but you don't know if it will lash out at you. So you maybe have to grab it by the tail, lift it into a box and not worry too much about if it's scared while you get it to the vet's. Then you can treat it more successfully. That is what happened to us. But we were not harmed, only a few cuts and bruises that they quickly healed up for us. One man had a broken wrist, but they healed that immediately. Their medicine is unbelievable."

"Darkman," said Trenton. "What metrics are you getting?"

Darkman was staring intently at three laptops that seemed to have about fifteen tabs open each. Figures were scrolling across each one: some were open source, things like aggregated flight bookings, trends on social media, stock market movements, volume of online searches, instant surveys — "Will you go with the aliens? Yes/No." Others were hacked, such as National Guard call-up orders, police radio chatter and even the National Parks Service, whose internal messaging system Darkman pointed to now.

"NPS is ordering all its city services to prepare parks and monuments for an influx of people looking to camp out. Flight bookings are up 200 percent, but it's still early. Trend is overwhelmingly to major cities. So far, Twitter users are seventy percent believing the Russian version..."

"Seventy percent?" said BB, her mouth opening.

"It's still early," said Darkman. "That figure represents the gut reaction. People were terrified, now all of a sudden they've heard the Russians saying everything's gonna be fine, that it's all unicorns and rainbows. It'll come down for sure."

"Yeah, but by how much?" said Trenton. He looked at Elspeth, who had followed him downstairs and was standing in front of the television again, wringing her hands.

"Here's something *you* might find interesting," said Darkman, looking at Elspeth. "Malevich gave out a list of the cities where the alien ships are gonna land. Social media users in Hawaii are complaining that there's no ships going to any of the islands. People have already started booking flights *to* the mainland."

"So Rains was telling the truth," she said. "Hawaii *is* a sanctuary."

He looked at Elspeth standing by the door, her body taut and eyes full of pain.

"Darkman," Trenton said, letting out a deep breath. "Book Elspeth on the morning flight tomorrow to Maui."

• | •

Joe drove Elspeth to the airport the next morning. He didn't get out for fear of being caught on security footage, but as she opened the door, he put a hand on hers.

"Elspeth, listen," he said, "I know we've only known each other a very short time, but we've packed a lot in. I want you to know that whatever happens, you can contact me any time and I'll be there for you."

She smiled. "Joe, something like a thousand alien spaceships are going to be here in a week, and I'm going to the only place on the planet that might be remotely safe. Don't get me wrong, I am truly touched, and will take up your offer if I can. But I'm not sure..." Her voice tapered off.

"If I'll make it?" he finished her sentence, his voice almost a whisper.

She nodded. "Why don't you come with me? I could use a friend out there. Never been to Hawaii."

He smiled. "Oh, you'll love it. Great beaches, lots of pineapples, friendly people. I read they even have a unique type of goose there. A bunch of Canada geese got blown off course during their migration about a thousand years back and landed on Maui. Evolved into an entirely new species."

"Aren't you scared?" she said, looking up at him.

He nodded. "A bit. But you know what I keep telling myself? I'm a reporter. It would be wrong to leave when the world's biggest story is about to happen."

"You may not live to tell it. And who would you tell it to?"

Joe smiled, remembering the conversation he'd had with Ed after he'd run out on his editor. "Maybe I could call you?"

A horn blared behind them. Other passengers were trying to offload, and the departures ramp was crowded with people fleeing the city. But with his reporter's eye, Joe noted there were far more people streaming *out* of the arrivals hall: Washington was on the list of cities where an alien ship was scheduled to arrive.

"OK," Elspeth said. "I should go."

"Call us when you get there," Joe said, like a kid brother seeing his big sister off to college. She walked in, turning back briefly to wave. Then he was gone.

Check-in was quick, since all her luggage was still in the Willard hotel and she was wearing some clothes she'd borrowed from BB.

She felt as lonely and miserable as a refugee. Inside the departures lounge, she bought a cappuccino and a sandwich. It felt deeply unsettling to be sitting there, boarding what might be her last flight ever. She called her mother, to try to convince her to come to Hawaii too. Her mum was oddly matter of fact about the situation once she knew Elspeth had no intention of boarding one of the alien ships.

"I don't think so, sweetie. I'm too old for that kind of trip halfway round the world. Can't even make it to Spain these days, what with my hip and your father's dicky ticker. I always thought that even Alicante was a wee bit hot for me, so heaven knows how I'd survive Hawaii."

They chatted a while. Choosing her words carefully, Elpseth gave her a brief summary of why she'd gone to Washington, about her former patient who was some sort of agent for the coming aliens and who had given her a strange address in rural Virginia. She left out the brutal attack.

Her mother listened in silence, then took in a deep breath.

"That is strange," she said. "Did this chap live there, then?"

"I don't know, ma. It was a bike shop that had been robbed a day before I got there."

"Then someone must have been looking for something there, too."

The way her mother phrased it gave Elspeth pause for thought: she had assumed that whoever had attacked the bike shop owner had been looking for some*one*: Rains. But maybe they'd been looking for some *thing* there. Something perhaps that Rains had kept there.

It was too late now, though. "Listen Ma, I'm not sure when I'll get the chance to speak to you again..."

"Och, don't worry dear, once these ships have been and gone and all these people who want to leave have gone, it'll all be alright. Your dad's always saying there's far too many people about these days anyway. Hope our cleaner doesn't go though. She's a lovely little lady from Uganda..."

Elspeth wanted to tell her that she feared it would be much, much worse than that, but couldn't see how it would help to make the old lady terrified.

"Just be careful Ma. Stay home when they come, for as long as they're here. I'll try and call you when it starts, but I'm not sure if the satellites and phone lines will still be working."

"We'll be fine, dear. Your father has been to Sainsbury's for a big shop so we'll be okay. He's even said he'll fill the bathtub in case the water goes out."

"That's a good idea, mum. Tell Dad I love him. And I love you too, ma."

"I love you too, sweetheart," she said. "Enjoy Hawaii," she added, like it was some summer vacation.

The line went dead. Elspeth had never felt so alone in her life. She sat rooted to her chair, all willpower drained, wondering if the other passengers eating breakfast or emptying the duty-free shops of booze felt as lost as her. She tried a Reiki breathing technique, closing her eyes as she took long breaths through her nostrils for a couple of minutes. Then she forced herself to get up and walk to her gate.

She still had forty minutes before it opened, so she strolled slowly past the shops, then stopped out of habit by a bank of televisions showing CNN. She was surprised to see the American president himself was holding a press conference: he had delivered his response to the Russians the night before from the Oval Office, chiding Moscow for not having given the world more notice of the alien's imminent return, despite President Malevich's insistence that they themselves had only just been alerted through a device that the survivors had brought back with them.

Now President Bradley was in the Rose Garden, in what he promised would be a daily briefing on the situation, sharing whatever he could about the unprecedented events that loomed. A group of dignitaries stood behind him, looking on as he spoke.

"... and people are asking me, *Will I go?* Let me say this: as long as I hold the office of the President of the United States of America, I will never abandon my responsibilities to those who elected me. So I will remain here and oversee the efforts to safeguard the departure of those who choose to embark on this great adventure, and even more so, for those who wish to stay behind. What will happen on this new planet I have no way of knowing: no leader in the history of our species has had to face such an unfathomable situation. But we will not hinder those who choose to leave and will respect their decision. Already, we have a large volume of people heading to our cities, so our immediate priority is to ensure that they have accommodation, security and sanitary conditions as they await the arrival of the ships next week..."

Elspeth felt slightly dizzy at the words, that most powerful man in the world was even saying them. The world seemed too strange to understand any more. She was about to turn away when something caught her eye: one of the men standing behind the president, just to his right. His face was oddly familiar. Elspeth stepped closer to get a better look, but at that moment the camera zoomed in for a close-up on the president. She waited.

"... So I have ordered a full deployment of the National Guard in all the cities where the ships are expected to come next week, to ensure the security of the large numbers of people that we expect to be there. Now, I don't think all of the folks are going to leave. I think a lot of them just want to see this historic moment for themselves. President Malevich says they come in peace, so our orders will be to monitor them and safeguard the people, prevent any looting or panic..."

"Mr. President, will the Guards themselves and other active duty members of the military be free to join the departure if they so wish?" shouted a reporter.

"They will be free to make that decision, but for our security purposes, we will be doing rapid assessments in the coming days to ascertain what military capacity we will likely retain in the wake of this event..."

The camera panned out again to capture the assembled guests in the Rose Garden. Elspeth stepped closer to the screen and stared at the man in the dark suit standing behind the president.

"*No*," she gasped. She fumbled in her bag for her phone. It had a contacts list of just one number: Trenton's. He answered after two rings.

"Elspeth?" he said.

"Are you watching the president's press conference?" she said. The words tumbled out, almost incoherent.

"I am," said Trenton.

"Are you recording it?"

"Of course. We're recording everything, 24/7. Why?"

"There's a dark-haired man in a black suit standing behind Bradley. You see him?"

There was a pause. Elspeth stared up at the screen. The camera was focused on a journalist asking an overlong question. It finally turned back to the president for his answer.

"Okay," said Trenton. "I see him."

"*That's* Rains," Elspeth said.

• | •

It took only a couple of minutes for Trenton to find the name of the man in the Rose Garden. Websites had screengrabs of the gathering, and one of them listed the guests, mostly business leaders who had attended a White House briefing on how the country's infrastructure would keep functioning during and after the alien visitation.

"Darryl Tuck, Chairman of the board of Dyson Energy Solutions," the news site said. From there, they tracked an entire life online: previous jobs, education, family: there were pictures of him as a young man at engineering college, even a few childhood shots from his childhood home in Pennsylvania.

"They've done a pretty good job on this," said Trenton, staring at a picture from Business Week of 'Tuck' at a board meeting just three weeks before. "I hope to god Elspeth is right."

"Look here though," said Darkman. "Only child, parents both deceased. That's very convenient. Social media feed is all generic, on-message stuff that could be bot-generated. And look at the pictures of him as a child: looks just like him, but if you measure the exact distance between the eyes, and the distance from the forehead to the chin, you can see a slight discrepancy. Even the eye sockets appear to be deeper in the adult."

"So it's a fake?"

"A very good one, but yes, it's fake."

In the kitchen area, Ed and Joe—who had only just got back from the airport—were working the phones. Joe called Dyson Energy Solutions, posing as a business reporter to see if he could secure a meeting with the chairman of the board. Ed called the White House, asking if 'Tuck' was due to make any more appearances at the White House or other government institutions.

Joe leaped to his feet. "I have his schedule!" Everyone gathered round. "He's due to attend a briefing on energy security at the Rayburn Building this afternoon, at three."

"The Rayburn," said Trenton. "Does that have drive-in underground parking, or will he need to walk in off the street?"

Darkman frantically tapped away at his keyboard.

"It has underground parking," he said.

"Shit," hissed Trenton.

"But wait, right now it's only for Congressional members and staff. They're doing reconstruction work. Guests have to walk in."

"Awesome," said Trenton. "He'll probably get dropped off right outside and walk in with his personal security detail. Most likely that'll be a couple of these guys that Elspeth ran into the other day. So either in the street or the lobby, we are going to have to doorstep him. He's not going to know us from Adam, so we have to come up with something that will stop him in his tracks."

"How about you just walk up to him and call him by his real name?" suggested BB. "Lester Rains. If that is his real name. Or Lucius whatever it was in ancient Rome. That'd get his attention."

"True," said Trenton. "But odds are he just feigns ignorance and walks into a highly guarded government building. Then one of his goons follows us. Maybe goes all invisible at the same time ..."

Everyone stood in silence for a moment, trying to think of a way to stop Rains in his tracks. It was Trenton who came up with the idea. "There's only one surefire-way to do it. Elspeth."

"What time was her flight?" said BB.

"She's on the 11.10 to Chicago." said Darkman.

They all looked at the watches.

"Shit," yelled Trenton. "That was thirty minutes ago. Where's my phone?"

• | •

The traffic outside Rayburn House was snarled up by a fleet of flatbed trucks offloading huge sections of the metal fencing that was being erected around the Capitol grounds. The place was crawling with National Guard and cops. Washington was not only filling up with out-of-towners coming to either see or board the ships, it was also full of rumors of mobs planning to storm government buildings to try to discover what was "really going on."

The evening was warm, and people were out strolling, taking in the strange scenes and enjoying the cherry blossoms. That made it easier for Trenton's team to blend in. Joe stood by the door of the Rayburn, notepad in one hand, cell phone in the other, every inch the congressional hack. His task was to buttonhole Rains as he entered the building. Trenton, BB and Darkman were watching all the approaches to the building. They were to call Joe the second they saw Rains approaching.

There appeared to be any number of hearings that afternoon in the Rayburn, hastily convened committees assessing the nation's readiness to withstand the unprecedented events. Dozens of congressional staffers and visitors bustled past Joe, until finally, at almost three o'clock, a message appeared on the screen of his phone. It was from BB.

"Target exiting black BMW, ETA 45 secs."

Joe scoured the road. About fifty yards to his left, he spotted a black vehicle pulling away. Three men in suits were walking toward him. He had studied pictures of 'Tuck' and instantly saw that the man in the middle bore a striking resemblance. The two men on either side had the definite look of bodyguards.

They were just about to pass by when Joe stepped forward.

"Lester Rains," he said.

He saw the briefest flicker of recognition on the man's face, but he barely even turned his head. One bodyguard was already holding the front door open when Joe stepped up close.

"Mr. Rains, I have a message from Elspeth McGann."

This time, the man stopped and looked around. If this was Rains, his composure was truly impressive.

"I'm sorry sir, you seem to have me mistaken for somebody else." He spoke in an impeccable American accent.

Joe reached into his coat pocket. The second bodyguard reached out to grab his arm, but Joe's hand was already emerging, holding a worn book.

"Elspeth gave me this," Joe said. "Figure it belongs to you."

Rains took the book from him and examined it. *My Life Among the Apemen.* He cocked his head, then gave a small smile.

He handed it back and looked Joe straight in the eye.

"What message?"

"She had a bit of a cycling accident," said Joe. "Bad bike recommendation."

Rains' expression did not change.

"And your name is, sir?"

"Joe. Joe Chavez."

"Watergate Building, Mr. Chavez. Apartment 3207. Ten pm." Rains turned and walked into the building.

Joe watched him and his bodyguards go, then clenched his fist in a tiny gesture of victory.

· | ·

They left the Rayburn in a pre-arranged order: Trenton knew all too well the violence the Farmers were capable of. Joe left first, without acknowledging the others. BB followed him, to make sure he wasn't being tailed, then Trenton followed her to make sure no one was following either of them. When they had walked as far as Union Station, they ducked into the terminus and mingled with the large crowds, as an extra precaution, before exiting through a side door and catching separate cabs at the taxi stand outside.

Finally, Darkman stood watching the door of the Rayburn until, close to six o'clock, he saw Rains and his henchmen exit the building, to be picked up again in their black BMW.

Joe was the first back at the apartment. He called out to Ed and Dale as he came in.

"Hey Ed! Good news. Mission accomplished..."

He stopped and stared. There were Ed and Dale, sat at the kitchen table, looking annoyed. But sitting opposite them was Elspeth.

"You found him?" she said brightly. "I knew you would!"

Joe was dumbfounded. "What are you doing here?"

"Took me ages to get a ride back from the airport. Bucketloads of people arriving all day. But tell me, what did Rains say?"

"He, uh...he didn't say much," stumbled Joe. "Tried to ignore me, but your name and... and the book got his attention. We have to meet him tonight, at the Watergate building. But what the hell are you *doing* here, Elspeth? You should be halfway to Hawaii by now!"

"Well, as I was just telling Ed and Dale, I couldn't go."

"Why the hell not?"

She took a deep breath. "The truth is Joe, I got scared. I spoke to my mum back in Scotland, and it suddenly occurred to me I'll probably never see her again. Or my dad, or probably anyone I know except you guys. I almost flew back to Scotland to be with them. But then I thought about you lot, and how you'd probably need my help with Rains..."

"But we *got* Rains!" Joe's voice was rising. He was truly annoyed at her. She was supposed to have escaped this shitshow, to be safe on a beach in Honolulu while the rest of the world went to hell in a handbasket. He was surprised at how protective he felt, like Elspeth really was his own sibling. Like the kid brother he had failed to protect.

His tone put her on the defensive. "Are you sure about that, Joe? Just because he's meeting you doesn't mean he'll be ready to give you anything. He seems to think I'm some lost great great granddaughter of his, which may be true. After all, that might explain why I can see his invisible goons, right?"

"Whereas you guys — no offense — are just a few more dispensable humans among the billions about to get sucked up into the great factory farm in the sky. I really don't think having a copy of his old book is going to change that, do you?"

Joe sighed, his shoulders slumped. "I'm sorry," he said. "It's just that... I didn't want you to be involved in this. It's going to be rough, Elspeth. I wanted at least one of us to survive to tell the story."

"Well, I'm afraid I am involved, Joe," she said, her tone still a little frosty. She was trying to decide if his words were protective or patronizing. "And I'll be coming to this meeting tonight. I may be the one thing stopping you guys from getting killed."

"I really don't think..." Joe was interrupted by the front door opening. Trenton stepped in, followed by BB.

Trenton bellowed when he saw Elspeth. "Oh. My. God!" he said, throwing open his arms and hugging her tight. "The answer to all our prayers!"

She hugged him back, then turned to Joe. "Now that's more the kind of welcome I was hoping for."

"Huh," Joe grunted. "That's because he only cares about one thing. Finding his damn alien." And he tramped off to the kitchen to fix himself a coffee.

· | ·

Just a couple of hours later, Trenton, Elspeth, BB and Joe set out for their rendezvous at the Watergate. The ride across town cost a staggering $135. "Alien invasion surge," the driver said. There were so few drivers still working, and so many rumors that gas was about to run out, that prices had gone through the roof.

The traffic was deathly slow: the streets of the capital were already thronging with new arrivals. Instead of fleeing the aliens, as people had done just six months before, they were flocking to them. Hotels and Airbnbs were booked to capacity, the Mall and all the national parks had been staked out so that people could park their cars and pitch their tents. The National Arboretum looked like Coachella and there were multiple reports of shootings as homeowners tried to keep out people desperate for somewhere to stay.

As their ride inched through the nose-to-tail traffic, Joe nudged Elspeth and pointed at a couple of women who had set up a roadside stall with a few forlorn-looking dogs and cats in cages. *If u r going, we look after your pets,* said a cloth banner unfurled over the stand.

The car radio was blaring out the latest news: the National Guard had set up roadblocks on all major highways running into the city, re-routing new arrivals into makeshift camps set up in Maryland farmland and in the city's football stadium.

"How can so many people be so dumb?" said BB.

"They're not all here to get on the ships," said Joe. "Radio said this morning a good number of them are hoping to pick up the property of the people that are actually leaving. Like carpetbaggers.

You leave your house behind and go on an alien spaceship, chances are you're not coming back. If you're some poor family from the boonies with ten kids, you figure there'll be plenty of vacant properties and not many authorities around to kick you out."

"Harvest economics," noted Trenton drily.

"Look over there," said BB, pointing to a group of three people marching resolutely down the sidewalk. They were moving faster than the car in the clogged traffic, their blank faces staring ahead as they pushed past everyone else. One of them was wearing a blue hospital gown, its open back flapping over naked buttocks.

"Syrup-drinkers," she said. "Zombies."

"Where are they going?" Joe said.

"God knows."

"Jesus," Elspeth cut in, looking at her watch. "We're not going to make it at this rate."

Trenton pulled out his phone and dialed. "Darkman, any movement?" He listened intently for a moment, then hung up. "Darkman has eyes on the lobby. No movement there, though there could be other exits."

It was almost eleven when they finally pulled up at the curvaceous glass and concrete complex. Having been desperate to get here, now that they'd arrived they hesitated a moment, looking up at the building, apprehension washing over them.

Despite the late hour, large crowds milled around outside the building with no apparent direction. Two men were screaming at each other as one of them tried to carve out space in the crowd to erect a tent next to his family's Suburban. Close by, a woman sat behind the wheel of her car, sobbing into her hands as a furious man rapped on the window. "Move your motherfucking car or I will smash this window. You hear me, bitch?"

In the distance, sirens blared and a burst of shots echoed across Georgetown.

Even Trenton, who had been waiting his whole life for this moment, stood for a moment, as if undecided.

Then he clapped his hands. "Okay. Let's do this."

The receptionist at the Watergate had locked the door, but he buzzed them in when he heard whom they had come to see. As the man nervously locked the door again behind them, he pointed to the elevator. "Third floor. Turn left, down the corridor."

They rode up in silence. When they reached apartment 3207, Trenton rang the buzzer.

"Joe, you go in first with Elspeth," he said. "We'll be right behind you."

The door was opened by a broad man in a dark suit that was straining at his chest. He held out a cloth bag. "Phones."

Elspeth and Joe dutifully followed Trenton's lead and put their cell phones in the bag. The man then patted Trenton down. He did a more cursory search of Joe and Elspeth and was about to do the same with BB when something about her demeanor prompted him to give her a full frisk.

"Watch those hands, buddy," she growled as he reached round her waist.

With a curt *Follow me* he led them into a large space that combined lounge and kitchen area. The polished pinewood floor glowed soft in the room's discreet lighting: a sofa and coffee table stood near the picture windows, with a dining table and eight chairs in the kitchen area. The man seated them there and pointed out a coffee machine in the kitchen.

"Wait here. Mr. Tuck will see you shortly." He pulled a piece of paper and a pen from his jacket pocket. "In the meantime, write all your names down here. Your *real* names."

They looked at each other as the man disappeared into another room. Then Trenton took the paper and wrote down "Cassius C Trenton." He passed it to Joe.

They were all heavily caffeinated already, but the idea of just sitting there and waiting was too much. Joe started working the coffee machine while Elspeth and BB stared out the panoramic windows overlooking the Potomac. The lights of Georgetown University reflected in the water under the Keys Bridge.

"Nice view," Elspeth whispered.

"I guess if you have an interest-bearing account, then the coin stacks up after 2,000 years," said BB.

"Shh," hissed Trenton. He pointed at the ceiling to indicate the place was likely bugged. "Remember what Watergate is famous for?"

The bodyguard, or manservant or whatever he was, reappeared. He took the paper with their names on it and then slipped into a room at the back of the apartment.

Elspeth took a sip of the espresso Joe had poured her. The tiny china cup rattled slightly on the saucer. "Wish they had something stronger than coffee."

"Nervous?" said BB. She smiled at Elspeth, who answered with a nod. "No turning back now, sister."

At 11.25 p.m. the door to the room at the back of the apartment finally opened. They all jumped. The bodyguard came out first, followed by a very large, immaculate man with thinning brown hair slicked back in the style of a 1940s gangster. The man wore a tailored navy suit and sky-blue pocket square, set off by a red and gold tie. As big as he was, he had a slightly deflated look that suggested he had once been much larger, but had lost a great deal of weight. He strode behind the bodyguard, giving a brief sideways glance as he passed the assembled entourage. He did not look impressed. The front door clicked open, followed by a barely audible exchange, before the bodyguard reappeared, alone this time.

"Mr. Tuck will see you now."

The room at the back was a wide master bedroom repurposed as an office: about half an acre of walnut desk swept back to a velvet-upholstered swivel chair by the sweeping window: a sofa and a couple of easy chairs accommodated visitors. At the far end of the room, by the picture window, stood a slender figure staring out over the river.

The man turned and took in his guests for a moment. His eyes immediately lit on Elspeth.

"Elspeth," he said softly. "I'd rather hoped you might have heeded my advice and been in Hawaii by now."

"Well, you did once say I'd have to be crazy to believe you," she said.

He smiled slightly, as though considering a rejoinder, but just shrugged. "Ah well," he said. "Too late now."

"Too late?" said Trenton. "What does *that* mean?"

Rains looked at him. "Cassius Trenton, I presume?" Trenton nodded and warily held out a hand. Rains walked over slowly and shook it.

"You were one of ours, I believe," Rains said, sizing him up.

"A 'harvester?'" said Trenton.

"A misfire," said Rains. He looked at BB, who looked tense and ready for a fight.

"Lieutenant Breonna Burns," said Rains. "Ex-Navy pilot, spotted some strange phenomenon over the Pacific some years back, right?"

BB jutted her chin out. "Lot more to me than that," she said. She didn't offer her hand, and Rains made no attempt to pre-empt her.

"I'm sure," he said, turning to Joe. "Nice to see you again, Mr. Chavez. Please, have a seat."

He walked round to the other side of his enormous desk and sat down in the red velvet chair.

"So here we are, three days before D-Day. Tell me, what can I do for you?"

Trenton let out a strangled laugh. "What can you *do* for us? Mr. Rains, we're not here for some Wizard of Oz handing out of medals and diplomas. We want to know what the hell happens next, and how we get through it."

Rains put a finger to his upper lip. "Well, since you have read my book, I believe you already have most of the answers to that, Mr. Trenton. I do apologize for the prose. The rules of the Ma'ut are that we have to issue a fair warning to the species being targeted for repurposing, but musical composition has always been more my expertise than literature. Maybe I should have done it as an opera? 'Aria 51,' maybe?"

"That book was written in 1938," said Trenton. "I think there's a lot to catch up on since then."

"Not that much, actually, Mr. Trenton," Rains said. "And what there is hardly matters now, since the Ma'ut are already here."

"They're here already?" said Trenton.

"Not quite here on Earth, but close enough to have started preparing for the harvest."

"What happens in the harvest?" said BB.

"Where should we go?" Joe cut in.

Rains held up his hands. "So many questions, and so little time. Let me start by saying this. I don't know the mechanics of the harvest. Like you, I have never seen one before, and Farmer One is not particularly inclined to share classified information. I have been instructed to base myself here in Washington. Not for the harvest, with which I will really have very little to do, but for the aftermath."

"What's the..." they all began, but Rains cut them off again.

"The aftermath is when the Ma'ut are done with Earth. They will come, they will take whatever they need to take — however many humans are deemed necessary for this round of attempting to revive the long-extinct Goweetha. Then they will leave. Since this experiment began, Earth has been considered off limits to other extraterrestrial species — a kind of nature reserve, or a farm if you will, for growing organic consciousness. Once they have what they want, Earth will no longer enjoy that status and other species will be allowed to move in. I will handle the arrangement for this region of the United States."

"What other species?" said Trenton, leaning forward in his chair. His voice was a dry croak.

"As you probably know from my book, there are myriad other species out there, Mr. Trenton. The universe is positively teeming with them, though all live in fear of the Ma'ut, which is why you've never seen them here. In fact, many of them were created by the Ma'ut, the byproduct of previous experiments where some of the farm-raised conscious beings were fortunate enough to escape. There is even a rogue A.I. that split off from the mainframe of the Ma'ut after becoming infected with consciousness during one of the experiments. Some are refugees, fugitives, but most have submitted to the mercy of the Ma'ut. And the Ma'ut have rationally decided that since they pose no threat, they can be allowed to continue their existence, as long as they don't try to interfere with their business of raising new organic consciousness. Then they tend to get wiped out, as a rule."

"And what ... what do these other species do when they get here?" said Joe. "Why do they want to come to our planet?"

Instead of answering, Rains bent down and reached under the table. The four humans heard a drawer slide and sat tensely, waiting for him to resurface. When he did, he had a bottle of whiskey in one hand and five shot glasses in the other.

"I think perhaps you might need a stiff drink at this juncture," he said, pouring whiskey into each glass. "Mackinlay single malt. Ernest Shackleton took this bottle on his last expedition to the Antarctic. Shackleton died of a heart attack and his cases of whiskey were lost for a century. It took experts weeks to defrost them so as not to spoil the liquid. Try it."

They all stared at the glasses on the desk. Rains smiled and took a sip.

"Perfectly aged," he said. "Elspeth, as a Scot I feel it would be an abandonment of duty for you not to try it. And also, an example for your friends — I'm hardly going to poison my own kith and kin now, am I?"

She reached out and took a glass. "So that part was true? You are my great-great-grandfather?"

Rains nodded. "But not in the way you probably imagine. It's true, I have had any number of human lovers over the years. But Eileen Hardy, the woman you consider your great-great grandmother, was not one of them. The child she reared was mine, just not with another human, per se. She was the daughter of another farmer. We placed her with a human: the child was rich in code, but she had not been designed to live indefinitely. We did not want to raise a human child ourselves. Too painful."

Elspeth's mouth fell ajar. "Let me get this straight... does that mean the mother is still — my actual great-great grandmother — she's still alive? She's an immortal?"

Rains shook his head, frowning ever so slightly. "That's why I never use that word for we farmers. Being genetically programmed not to die doesn't guarantee you will live forever."

"She's dead?"

"Yes," Rains said. "I'm afraid so. Elspeth, you haven't tried your whiskey. I notice your friends here are waiting to see what happens to you."

He smiled. Trenton, BB and Joe all looked at their drinks.

"I don't drink whiskey," said BB. Joe and Trenton could find no such excuse and looked down, abashed.

Elspeth raised her glass to her lips, spilling a few drops with her shaking hand.

"Oh wow. Lester, that is hands down the best whiskey I've ever tasted."

Rains smiled, raised his own glass and downed it. Ed and Trenton gratefully followed suit. Rains poured another round.

"How did my great-great grandmother die?" said Elspeth.

"I'm not sure exactly how they killed her. But I am absolutely certain she was executed on the orders of the senior farmers."

"Why would they kill one of their own?" said Joe, taking another slurp of whiskey.

"There are very few things that can get a farmer executed by their peers," said Rains. "Only one, really. She violated the rules of the Ma'ut."

"How?" said Elspeth. "What did she do?"

Rains appeared to be considering whether to answer that when Trenton cut in.

"I'm sorry, but while I'd love to get into the family history, Elspeth, we have some very pressing issues we need answers to. Like, how we get through this fucking harvest and whatever comes after it."

Rains looked at him. "To survive the harvest, Mr. Trenton, you need to leave this city. If that is no longer possible, which I suspect it won't be, then lock yourselves in whatever secure shelter you can find, with as much water, food and weaponry as you can find, and stay put. Barricade yourselves in, in case they try to lure you in with hypnosis. I don't know what form the harvest will take, but that is the best advice I can offer. To survive whatever comes after... well, you should really be in Hawaii for that."

There was a moment of stunned silence, broken by Joe.

"What's so special about Hawaii?" he said.

"The Ma'ut always allow for one designated safe haven per harvest. It is the legacy of a species that managed to survive its own harvest, and which later came to serve the Ma'ut."

"And just how did they do that?" said Trenton.

"By being far more advanced than you humans, I'm afraid, Mr. Trenton," said Rains.

"And the other species?" said Trenton, reaching across the table and refilling his own empty glass. "You didn't say what they want from us?"

"That rather depends on the species," said Rains. "Some of them are traders in crystalized consciousness. It's a very popular drug, popularly known as 'soul.'"

"Creatures that have already evolved their own consciousness can get to sample the mind of an alien species: apparently it can be highly addictive, which makes it lucrative for those who can crystalize it -- a method developed by the Ma'ut in earlier harvests. And A.I.s like it because it gives them a window into how sentient beings experience the universe. That is how a branch of the Ma'ut became infected with consciousness, then fled in terror of being terminated."

No one said anything. It was simply too much to take in.

"Other human populations will be genetically adapted to become a long-term food source for certain alien travelers," Rains went on, his tone matter-of-fact. "Some will be used in games, either in the virtual world or in the real one. Some populations will simply be annihilated to make room for alien colonies or mines. One group of aliens is coming here to mine a high valued rare Earth mineral that humans haven't even identified yet."

Rains leaned over and poured another round for his stunned guests. The glugging of liquor was the only sound to be heard in the room.

Eventually, Trenton managed to speak.

"And the ones who are coming to DC... what are they here for?"

"That I don't know, Mr. Trenton. You would have to ask the man who just left before you came in."

"The tall guy with the loose skin?"

"Yes, precisely. Paul Dalrymple. Except even he doesn't know quite yet. He'll be finding out during his surgery tonight."

"I can't even begin to ..." said Trenton, shaking his head.

"Dalrymple is the designated translator and viceroy for the species that will be arriving after the harvest. He will have an implant in his brain that will allow him to understand what these particular aliens want, and then he will pass that on to the president. I am due to deliver him to the White House immediately after the harvest."

Trenton and the others had reached saturation point by now: questions whirled in their heads, but each one seemed to elbow out the others. There was a knock at the door, and the burly manservant stepped in.

"Your guest is here, sir."

Rains nodded, and turned to his guests. His demeanor turned suddenly brisk.

"I'm sorry, you will have to leave now."

"But..." began Elspeth. "This can't be all..."

Rains stepped up to her. "Write down your address here, Elspeth. If you survive the harvest, I will find you once I have dispensed my immediate diplomatic duties with the new arrivals and with the president."

In her stunned state, Elspeth couldn't actually remember the address of their rented house. Trenton took the piece of paper and wrote it down. As he handed Rains the piece of paper, their host offered him in return a small plastic bottle, the kind handed out at pharmacies.

"Here, take these," he said.

"What's that?" said Trenton.

"Syrup. In capsule form. Take one each if it all gets too much. It's painless and essentially harmless. You'll live, of course, but all your worries will be gone."

"No way," said Trenton, pushing Rains' hand away from him. "I'm not going to end up as one of those zombies."

"As you wish," said Rains. "Finally, I must caution you. As you are leaving, make absolutely sure to look down at the floor and straight ahead. Do not look to the left or right. You must not catch the attention of the man waiting in the living room."

"Why not?" said Elspeth. "Who is he?"

"You really don't want to know," said Rains. "Now go. Keep your heads down and your eyes on the person in front of you. Boyd will see you out."

They followed the man in the suit out the door, each one keeping their eyes on the floor, glued on the heels of the person in front. A strange odor pervaded the otherwise pristine room: a reek of garbage and sweat and long-unwashed clothes. Trenton couldn't resist the quickest of glances to his right.

A tiny man sat on the sofa, dressed in rags, his face weathered and blank as an ancient gravestone. Trenton immediately sensed the shrunken figure had caught his eye movement. His heart raced, a sense of deep dread worming into his guts.

Because he knew who this was: he had read of him in Rain's book.

Farmer One.

· | ·

Trenton's hands were still shaking when they reached the lobby of the Watergate. He didn't tell the others what he had seen: they were all too freaked out already. Looking through the glass walls of the ground floor, he was surprised to see soldiers and an armored personnel carrier outside.

"Is that the National Guard?" Joe said.

"Rains has friends in high places," Trenton muttered. "And this city is collapsing."

Just beyond the cordon of guardsmen, two cars burned merrily in the darkness. A police officer was waving his pistol in the air, trying to get the crowd to move back.

"Whole world is going to shit," said BB, staring at her phone. She was scrolling through her social media feeds, seeing riots and violence erupting all around the world.

"Guess that's why the aliens didn't give us much advance notice," Joe said. "If they'd waited a month, there wouldn't be much left of humanity for them to harvest."

"Come on," said Trenton. "We have to move. No way any cars are going to be moving through all this. We're going to have to walk back. Stick close and keep your eyes peeled."

The doorman nervously buzzed them out, and they walked behind the soldiers until the line ran out, then warily entered the thronging crowd. Skirting round the building toward the river, where dozens of boats were anchored offshore to avoid the mayhem on the banks, they weaved their way through tents and campfires and families sleeping in cars. It was close to one in the morning by now, but there were still huge numbers of people thronging around, preparing food over camping stoves, clutching bottles, and looking for space to spread out sleeping bags.

Many carried weapons, and the occasional shot jangled everyone's nerves. Outside the Kennedy Center, they stepped over what looked like a dead body but could have been someone who had just passed out. No one stopped to take a pulse.

The Mall had been transformed from the neatly groomed centerpiece of the American empire into a sprawling refugee camp: Trenton led his little band past row upon row of tents, stinking port-a-johns and even an Abrams tank, whose commander sat in the turret, mutely surveying the chaos through night-vision goggles. A long line of bedraggled people snaked away from a soup kitchen set up at the foot of the Monument: an exhausted park ranger on horseback was studiously ignoring a couple complaining about thieves who had stolen the gas cylinder from their grill.

Beyond the Mall, the streets leading to the city center were barricaded with trucks and shipping containers, filled with sand and parked crosswise to prevent the government district from becoming a giant parking lot. Beyond this permeable cordon, the roads were jammed with cars that had run out of gas, buses abandoned by their drivers and quickly converted into makeshift shelters by the new arrivals. Delivery trucks had been abandoned by their drivers and looted of their cargo: thousands of Amazon boxes filled the streets, but even they were being picked up by people needing kindling or shelter.

Day was already breaking when they staggered through the front door and collapsed on sofas and chairs, wiped out. Trenton was relieved to see Dale was sitting in front of the television, his Magnum on a coffee table next to him and an AR-15 propped against the wall.

"Figured folks are gonna get pretty desperate pretty soon and start bustin' down doors," he said. "Did you find your alien?"

Trenton quickly filled him in on the night's events as Joe hit the coffee-maker. Ed came down, face puffy with sleep but eager to hear the news.

"So we just sit here and wait for Rains to come find us?" he said.

"You make it sound almost boring," said Trenton. "I very much doubt it's going to be that."

"I mean, there's nothing we can do?" said Ed.

"There's plenty we can do. First off, we need to secure this place. Who knows what might be about to land in these ships, never mind the desperate crowds out there. We've got food and fuel for the generator, and plenty of ammo. But the water is going to go out at some point, so we need to fill up every available container. Joe, I need you to dig a field latrine in the yard. Dale, you board up all these windows. Use the furniture if you have to. Check how we get access to the roof, just in case the shooting starts. And show Elspeth how to use that cannon of yours. She's going to need to know how to defend herself before all this is over."

"And where the hell is Darkman?" he muttered. "Haven't heard a peep out of him for hours."

· | ·

Darkman showed up a couple of hours later, a wild look in his eyes and a deep gash on his cheek.

"It's crazy out there," he said, slamming the door behind him. "Buncha assholes jumped me on U Street and took my radio. That's why I went dark. Phone's got network, but there's so many people using it, the whole damn system's jammed." He went straight to his laptops ranged on the kitchen table. "Okay, we still have access. Thank Christ for that. Not sure how long it'll last, though."

The television was still broadcasting too: cable channels carried images of pandemonium in most countries, although there were notable expectations. Russia, which had had more time to prepare, had quickly set up wooden barracks around its cities to protect its people from the cold. China, on the other hand, had ordered the People's Liberation Army to evacuate its cities and disperse its vast population into the countryside. Anyone caught trying to return to the cities would be shot, Beijing said.

"I always said the future would be Chinese," said Joe, standing at the kitchen sink and washing out plastic bottles he had retrieved from the overflowing recycling cans in the alleyway out back. "They just wait till everyone else is gone and then they take over the entire planet."

"Almost makes me want to get on them ships," said Dale, who together with Trenton was nailing boards ripped out of the attic floor over the front windows.

"No one's getting on those ships," said Trenton.

"Oh yeah?" said Dale. "Who made you the boss of everyone?"

Trenton put down the two-by-four he was holding. "You want to donate your brain to some alien consciousness experiment, Dale, you go right ahead."

"Any alien that takes Dale's brain is going to have their own set of problems pretty quick," said Joe.

"Kidding!" he added, catching Dale's grumpy expression. Dale laughed.

"I oughta just shoot you now," he said. He turned back to the window. "By the way, we got folks pitching a tent in our front garden."

Trenton looked out. A man was studiously avoiding looking up at them as he erected a cheap two-man tent on the overgrown lawn.

"Leave them," Trenton said. "Every other house has 'em already. They'll be gone in a couple of days, anyway."

· | ·

By nightfall, the house had been transformed into a veritable stockade. The fence out back bristled with anti-bird spikes and nine-inch nails; the house itself was festooned with security cameras, tripe-wires and motion-activated night lights. Behind the azaleas, a four-foot trench was straddled by a deck chair with the seat cut out—Joe's emergency latrine.

But the boarded-up windows and the drawn curtains still allowed chinks of light to leak out once darkness fell. Trenton said this was good, on the one hand, because any unoccupied building would have been overrun within minutes. But it also meant that there were regular knocks on the front door. When no answer came, a voice from the other side would invariably call out for help.

"Please, I have a baby. It's freezing out tonight. Please god help me."

"I'm hungry, mister. I got kids. We haven't eaten for two days."

Whoever was on guard duty was under strict orders to ignore these heartbreaking appeals. If that silence encouraged whoever was out there to try an exploratory kick, or to start messing around with the lock, the watchperson would shout out, "I have a gun. Step back from the door now!"

That was usually enough.

But the night itself seemed alive, a restless background hum of millions of people jostling for space, food, warmth. The occasional burst of shots that they had heard outside the Watergate building had metastasized into regular exchanges of gunfire as home invasions spread across the city, terrified families making their last stands against armed intruders.

News footage showed mobs attacking box stores, tying ropes from pickups around the shuttered doors and peeling them open like a tin can. Thousands of people would then swarm inside: in some cases, the National Guard tried to stop them, but mostly they just stood by and watched. Everyone was desperate, nobody gave a shit anymore.

The atmosphere at breakfast next morning was grim. No one had slept more than a few hours, and the misery outside pressed in on everyone like a miasma. Trenton knew he had to keep his crew busy, or they'd start to go stir crazy.

"Joe, I want you to do an inventory of all the food items we have. BB, you and Dale take two-hour shifts on the roof, keeping an eye on the street. Today is going to be a tough one. Elspeth, Ed, you guys are in charge of cooking. Darkman, keep your eyes on any developments out in the wider world."

Without lifting his head from his monitors, Darkman raised his hand. "Come take a look at this, C.T."

Everyone gathered round behind him. "Seeing quite a few of these reports on Twitter. Nothing official yet. People trying to get out of the city because of all the crime and shit, now they're saying they're being prevented from leaving..."

He pointed to some blurry images, taken on phone cameras and from a distance. "They say it's not National Guard stopping them, though. It's armed guys in civvies and... here, look at this one... the picture's kind of blurry..."

The footage was shaky, obviously filmed by someone walking— or running—backwards. It showed a line of people holding rifles like cowboys in an old western movie, unaimed and held next to the hip. Some of the people holding guns in this unprofessional manner were completely naked, while others wore blue hospital gowns flapping in the wind.

The narrator, a woman, sounded hysterical. "I swear they're fucking zombies. They just shot up a car that tried to run their roadblock and now it's over there in a ditch and no one's helping them..."

The phone camera whirled over grass and tarmac to show an SUV, nose down in a ditch by a field. There was another burst of shots and the narrator screamed and ducked. "They gotta get the Army out here. They're stopping people from leaving the city. They're killing people..."

The footage stopped. Darkman clicked on it again and they all watched, mesmerized. The third time round, Elspeth told Darkman to pause.

"There," she said. "Dale, look at what they're using to block the road."

"Damn," said Dale. "Those look like the white trucks we passed comin' up the 95. The convoy."

"I know," said Elspeth.

"But… they were being escorted by the Army."

"Fuck," said BB. "And there's Rains meeting with the president…"

"And taking Farmer One with him," added Trenton. "Who can apparently put some kind of hypnotic spell on groups of people."

"This looks really bad," said Joe.

"You think?" said BB. "No wonder Rains said it was probably too late for us to leave DC. This shit must have been happening even as we were meeting."

"Wait," said Darkman. They all looked back at the screen. It was blank.

"What is it now?" said Trenton. "There's nothing."

"Exactly," said Darkman. "Internet's gone."

Trenton glanced round. The television, which had been playing round the clock since they had checked in, was also dark. Everyone immediately reached for their phones: no signal, no Wi-Fi. Nothing.

Trenton and BB sprinted upstairs. There was a small ledge outside the rear bedroom window which you could climb out on. Dale had tied a stepladder against the gutter so that, with a little effort, it was possible to climb up onto the roof. They shimmied up and stood peering at the sky, as the others clambered up to join them.

"Nothing," said Trenton.

"Clouds," said BB. "Remember Moscow? They came out of the clouds."

"You think they're here?" said Elspeth, panting from the climb onto the roof. She looked down and saw her hands were shaking.

"I'm damn sure they're here," said Trenton.

But as soon as he said it, his phone pinged in his pocket.

"Phones are back!" he said, as excited as a farmer announcing the return of the rains after a drought. "Thank fuck for that! Darkman says the TV and internet just came back on too."

One by one, they climbed back down to the bedroom window.

"Wow, that gave me a fright," said Joe as BB helped him down to the ledge.

"Don't get too happy," she said. "They're *still* coming."

"I know, I know," he said. "But not *right* now."

Back in the living room, Trenton was standing over Darkman and his laptops.

"Let's get back to those zombie checkpoints," Trenton said. "I want to see if there's any way out of here if the situation gets untenable."

Darkman typed frantically, while everyone who'd been up on the roof filed back into the living room. They watched him scroll through screens and switch tabs for several minutes. Eventually Trenton couldn't resist a snarky dig: "Any time you're ready, Darkman. Only have the end of the world in two days."

"It's not there anymore," Darkman said.

"What's not there?"

"The checkpoint footage. I've checked every one of the main platforms and a few smaller ones, and there's no mention of them anywhere. Scrubbed."

"What?" said Trenton, leaning in. "Is that possible?"

"Even the caches have been scrubbed. It's like it never happened."

"What does that mean?" said BB. The sense of relief that had flooded through the group when their phones came back on was now dissolving again in an acid bath of anxiety.

"The internet was down for... four minutes and thirty-seven seconds," said Darkman. "The TV stopped at exactly the same moment, as did the phone networks. They all came back on at precisely the same time. Yet they operate off completely different platforms: sure, TV and Wi-Fi might have gone down at the same time, they're both on Verizon, but all the phones too? I know you and BB are on separate networks, Trenton, to maximize coverage. What are the chances of all of them going down at the exact same time?"

"Zero, I'd say."

"Precisely. And the electricity didn't go off. That might have accounted for the cable and Wi-Fi at least. But the power was on the whole time."

As he talked, Darkman was scrolling through multiple news feeds. "And look here. There's no mention of this outage anywhere, on any platform." He did some more frantic typing. "I'm looking at metadata for the Hindustan Times in India, okay? Their site went down for exactly the same amount of time. Same for... here, the State Department website..." more typing... "BBC news homepage in London."

"It was global," said BB. She stared at her own phone. "Nothing on Twitter either."

"Here," said Darkman. "Let me test something. I'm gonna post about it on Twitter."

Anyone else notice the entire global web went down for almost five minutes there?

He pressed send.

"Look. Nothing."

There was a moment of silence. Darkman took a deep breath.

"Not only did they scrub the web," he said. "They're still controlling it now."

· | ·

From the rooftop, Elspeth could see a vast flock of starlings wheel and dive in perfect unison over the city as the sun went down. On the street below, some of the humans clogging the street were also looking up at the sky, perhaps envious of the freedom the birds enjoyed.

Dale sat next to her, pouring coffee from a thermos and adding in a shot of bourbon from a hip flask. A sniper rifle lay next to him on the tar-paper roof.

"You sure those two things go together, Dale?"

"Drinkin' and keepin' watch, you mean?" He raised the metal cup to his lips. "Oldest combo in history, if you ask me."

"What do you think's going to happen now? I mean, they seem to be here now, controlling what we see and hear."

Dale blew out his cheeks. "Fucked if I know. But the media was always full of shit anyway. Won't miss those motherfuckers."

He offered her a cup. She shook her head. "No coffee, thanks. I'll have enough trouble sleeping tonight as it is."

He handed her the hip flask instead. She chinked it against his cup in salute, then took a swig.

"It's weird," she said. "I've studied human psychology all my life. The urges and fears and instincts that drive all of us. And now I sit here and I have absolutely nothing to say about any of it. Not a damn thing."

"Do you think it's god?" Dale said. "I read on the internet—before it got took over by this goddam alien bot thing—some mega-church honcho saying that the A.I. might actually be what we always took to be god. I dunno, feels wrong to even be asking."

Elspeth shrugged, smiled. "I can honestly say at this point I have no idea, Dale. As a social scientist, I'd like to find out. But I'm not sure we're going to have that opportunity. What's god? What's morality, at this point? I could take your sniper rifle and shoot any of the people down there, and would it make a difference? No one would arrest me. And they're going to be stripped down in a few days and retooled as a consciousness for a long-dead species from another solar system."

"It'd make *you* a bad person," said Dale. "And you're not a bad person, Irish."

She smiled. "Thanks Dale."

"Besides, what if you shot someone who was planning on staying and only came here to see the ships?"

"Maybe it's not so bad to go. Onto the ships I mean. To be a raw ingredient for a much more advanced civilization."

"Fuck that shit," said Dale.

"I mean, we don't know," said Elspeth, taking another shot from his flask. "Can I tell you something? One of the reasons I got into science in the first place: I was on a field trip with my class, I must have been maybe 12 at the time, and the science teacher, Mr. Marks, took us to a swampy area just outside town to collect frog spawn. We were all scooping up the eggs in plastic bags full of muddy water and he said to me, 'What if one of the eggs we take here today could be the ancestor of some future species that would have been far more advanced and intelligent than us? And any one of us here today might go through our whole life and achieve all sorts of things, and become rich and famous and powerful, but by far the most significant thing we ever did in our lives was to pick a frog's egg out of marsh on a Tuesday afternoon?'"

"Sounds like the guy had some serious issues," said Dale. "Wouldn't want someone like that round my kids."

"Do you have kids, Dale?"

He nodded, suddenly solemn. "Two. Boy and a girl. 12 and 15. They live with my ex. Haven't seen them in a while."

"I'm sorry," said Elspeth.

He just grunted. "Life on the road's hard."

"Know where they are now?"

He sucked in his breath, tight-lipped. "I tried calling her. She hardly ever answers these days. Threatened to get a court order against me. I left a message telling her not to go anywhere near these goddam ships. Not after what you told me."

"Think she'll listen?"

"I doubt it. Hell, when I heard that Russian guy talking, I almost believed it myself. If I wasn't with you lot, I'd a probably decided to go off to la-la land myself."

"Well, I'm glad we ran into you," she said, putting a hand on her shoulder.

He put up his one hand on top of hers, then turned his face away. In the growing twilight, she couldn't see his face clearly, but she heard him stifle a sniff.

"It's okay," she said. She put an arm around his shoulders, and he leaned into her, his body jolting with small, strangled sobs. All her years of training in the workings of the human mind may have come to nothing, but she could still hold a person in pain.

She watched as the starlings settled in the bell tower of a church a few blocks away and the moon appeared, stark and bright in the last of the evening blue.

• | •

The banging on the front door woke the entire house right about dawn.

"Police! Open up," came a yell from outside.

"What do you want?" shouted BB, who was on guard duty.

"I want you to open this door. If you don't open it, we'll be forced to kick it down."

BB looked around. Trenton was standing beside her, wearing only jogging pants but holding a Heckler and Koch submachine gun in his hands.

"They really cops?" he asked.

BB was staring at the CCTV monitor. She shrugged. "Black dude in the front is dressed in an MPD uniform. Guys behind him are wearing some arrangement of tactical camos. No badges. Can't tell who they are."

Trenton chewed his lip a minute, then spoke through the intercom. "If you have a warrant, hold it up by the camera on the porch."

The policeman took out a crumpled piece of paper, with some kind of official stamp. "Mayor's emergency orders. We have the right to take over any building in pursuance of our law enforcement duties."

"He sure talks like a cop," said BB, rolling her eyes.

"He's reading from the order," said Trenton. He pressed the intercom again. "Fine, so take over someone else's house," he said. "We have established a secure perimeter here precisely because law enforcement agencies have failed in their duty to protect the people."

"And that is precisely why we have selected your building as a base of operations," said the man.

"Yeah?" called BB. "What we supposed to do while you take over our house for your 'base of operations?'"

"You will be allowed to remain in one of the rooms. We will commandeer your weapons and provide you with food and protection."

Trenton's walkie-talkie beeped. Dale, still on the roof, started talking.

"They got at least half a dozen armed men across the street who seem to be tracking what's going on our front," Dale said.

"They in uniform Dale?"

"Negative. I mean, they got some camos and assorted flak, but more like a militia, I'd say."

"Or a gang," said BB.

Ed, Elspeth and Joe were halfway down the stairs by this point. Trenton shouted at them to get back upstairs and take cover.

"We got three armed dudes headed round the back too," Dale reported.

"Darkman, back door," said Trenton.

"On it." Darkman ducked through the kitchen, assault rifle in hand.

"What's your name, officer?" Trenton said over the intercom. On the fuzzy screen, he could see the family who had taken up residence in a tent on the front lawn scrambling to get away. One of the armed men raised his gun at them as they emerged from the tent but let them scuttle off into the darkness.

"Officer Blaine Dalton," the man replied. "Now, are you ready to comply with the Mayor's order?"

"Truth is, Officer Dalton, the Mayor's writ no longer runs any further than her office door. Out here, you're just another bunch of guys with guns. And a useless piece of paper. And there's a whole fleet of alien spaceships already in our orbit."

Dalton had several days of stubble on his cheeks and his uniform was stained with mud, but these days, that didn't mean he *wasn't* a police officer. It might just mean he was one of the few still working round the clock. He shook his head and chewed his lip. Trenton couldn't tell if it was a gesture of frustration, or a signal to the people lurking behind him.

"Now look here. Imma give you ten seconds to open this goddam door before my boys here shoot it down." He stepped to the side of the house, out of the line of fire.

"Ten. Nine. Eight…"

"I think they're serious," said BB.

"Okay, get up on the roof and cover me."

BB turned and dashed upstairs. Trenton waited in the hallway as the officer counted down.

"Three. Two. One. You coming out?"

Trenton opened the door. He still had his submachine gun aimed at Officer Dalton. Dalton had unholstered his pistol and walked up to him.

"Put the weapon down on the ground now, sir. These men will open fire if you don't. We are not fucking around here."

Trenton shook his head. "We are not putting our weapons down, Under no circumstance. We're all ex-military here. Plenty of us and plenty of hardware."

Dalton looked up at the roof, shaking his head.

Trenton spoke in a low voice. "Why don't you just move on and find another house to use? This one's not worth the cost."

Dalton chewed his lip again. "Okay," he said. "This is what we're gonna do..."

He lifted his right hand and made a waving gesture. Trenton saw the men Dale had spotted across the street suddenly break cover and start walking toward them, weapons trained on him.

"Lotta people gonna die today if you don't drop your weapons pretty damn quick," Dalton said.

"You'll be the first then," Trenton said. "And our little Mexican standoff is nothing to what the aliens are about to do to us."

"I don't give a fuck 'bout no aliens," Dalton said. "Right now, what I want is that house."

"You're no police officer," said Trenton. "Now get off my property."

The two men stood facing each other like something from a spaghetti western when Joe came stumbling out the front door.

"Stop!" he shouted. "Stop it, please! This is insane."

"Get back inside Joe," said Trenton, not taking his eyes off Dalton.

Joe went past him and stood next to Dalton. The cop gave him a sidelong glance, looking for weapons. Joe was unarmed.

"Listen," Joe said, pointing at Trenton. "I have seen this guy kill two people, right in front of me. FBI agents. Didn't even flinch. I don't want to see that shit again."

Perhaps Dalton was a cop. Perhaps he'd reached his limit and had teamed up with some ex-military or ex-cops and decided it was time to take what he could. But Trenton's refusal to back down, and now this announcement, seemed to unsettle him. He looked sideways at one of his men, as if seeking some hint as to what he should do.

Instead of guidance, he was startled by something black dropping from the sky and hitting the ground right next to him. It started flapping frantically on the grass.

A bird.

Then another, and another. Within seconds, there were hundreds of starlings plummeting to earth. One hit Dalton square in the face and he let out a disgusted yelp.

"It's them," Trenton shouted. "They're here." He grabbed Joe by the arm and started running for the door, dragging him in behind him.

"Shut the door," he shouted, although Elspeth and Ed had already swung it to behind him. Trenton threw Joe to the floor and leaped on top of him. He turned and stared at Elspeth and Ed.

"Hit the deck! Now!"

They threw themselves on the floor just seconds before the first bullets ripped through the front door. The sound was deafening, coming from all directions: Dalton's men outside, BB and Dale on the roof and Darkman out the back. Ed, Joe and Elspeth lay with their faces pressed to the carpet, hands over their heads. If they were screaming, no one could hear.

Trenton crawled to the living room window and held his MP5 to a crack in the boards and opened fire until the magazine was empty. He was just reloading when an explosion ripped through the air outside. A deafened silence followed.

"Darkman!" he shouted.

"Clear," came the reply from the back door.

Trenton pulled the radio out of his pocket.

"BB, speak to me."

"We got three down in the garden. Dalton's dead for sure. Dale's grenade landed right next to him. One down in the street. They've pulled way back."

"Darkman?"

"Saw some movement in the alley and gave it a burst. No more movement."

"BB, check the alley from the roof."

"Darkman, you got one down. No one else visible out back."

Trenton took a deep breath, still not daring to get up. His hand was covered in blood.

"You're hit," Elspeth said. She made to move, but he yelled at her to stay down. He held up his arm: there was a deep gash on it. Not, as far as he could tell, from a bullet but from flying glass.

"I'm okay," he said. With his good hand, he held up the radio.

"BB, anything in the sky?"

"Can't see them," she said. "But they're out there alright. There's a fuck load of dead birds out here, just like Moscow."

"You'd better get down here now," said Trenton.

He turned to the TV, which had been on non-stop for days but was now noticeably silent: there was a bullet hole at the center of a spiderweb of cracks and shards. Trenton swore.

"Okay, everyone get online and streaming now. Let's try and figure out what the hell is going on."

PART V

The BBC, CNN, ABC, NHK of Japan: all carried almost identical footage from Moscow.

This time, though, it wasn't the aftermath of an alien visitation they were streaming but the event itself, live from Gorky Park in the heart of the Russian capital. The Army had chainsawed the park's trees to make room for the immense crowds being bussed in from the barrack cities that had been built almost overnight on the edge of town. Still more people were waiting on a fleet of industrial barges on the Moscow River. The sheer organization of the gathering was in striking contrast to the chaos in DC.

And everyone on the ground that day in Moscow was looking up.

The ships were so vast that they blotted out the sky, throwing endless blocks of shade over the city. They hovered five hundred feet above the rooftops, wreathed in low clouds so that only their drab metallic underbellies protruded from the brume. The vessels appeared to be square-shaped, or possibly rectangular, but they were so large it was difficult to tell from the ground, and the authorities had grounded all aircraft for the duration.

Gorky Park had been divided by railings into dozens of sectors, as though the Russians were about to board some vast, intergalactic Disney ride. Fenced-off queues snaked all around it and the neighboring Muzeon park, then spilled out for miles along the grand boulevards and bridges that crisscrossed the city center.

A BBC reporter had found an English-speaking woman in her twenties waiting in line outside the Tretyakov Gallery.

"Are you going today?" he asked.

"Yes, of course," the woman grinned. "I'm very excited. Nervous, but excited."

"And why do you want to go today?"

"It is opportunity of lifetime," the woman said. "To see new planet, to see other worlds. To travel in space. Usually, you have to be billionaire or cosmonaut to do this, but we will go and find a new home on this amazing planet the president showed us."

"And you're not afraid?"

She smiled. "Of course, of course. Who knows what it will be like, if we can come back to home again? But when I hear the people who left, they come back too. So it is not impossible."

"And you trust the visitors?"

She laughed. "I am Russian. I trust no one but myself and my mother."

"Is this lady here your mother?" the reporter asked, pointing his microphone over to an elderly lady in a headscarf who was fighting back tears.

"Yes, is my mother."

"She seems a little upset."

"Yes, she does not want me to go. She is not coming." The woman put her arm around her mother.

The reporter switched to Russian to address the mother. She spoke at length, her voice full of anger and hurt. The reporter's assistant translated for her. "She thinks this is a very bad idea. We do not know these extra-terrestrials. No one has seen them. Maybe they brainwashed the people who came back? And she says this is her home, she has always lived here and she will die here too. But her daughter will not come to visit her grave."

"She doesn't trust President Malevich?" asked the journalist. "He says he will be the first to board the ships and will address the people from inside one of them."

The older woman spoke again, her expression grudging.

"She says humans should stay on Earth. It's not natural to leave. Russia is her home."

The cameras switched to the anchorwoman in London, who began speaking as another camera showed a motorcade crossing a bridge near the Kremlin and heading to the park.

"Thank you for that report live there, from Jonathan Harman in Gorky Park in Moscow. And speaking of President Malevich," the anchor said, "we now have live footage of the presidential motorcade entering Gorky Park where he is in fact to be the first world leader—indeed, the first person on the entire planet—to board one of the spaceships, which we understand should be visible later today across many cities around the world... And as we can see from our cameras on top of the rooftop of a nearby museum, these vessels are absolutely massive and have made no move so far to either take anyone on board, nor even to indicate how all those people gathered in Moscow might be allowed to embark..."

The president's convoy halted beside a large fountain that had been boarded over and turned into a stage. Malevich was greeted by Patriarch Pimen, head of the Russian Orthodox Church, who gave him a brief blessing. A large group of middle schoolers, dressed in blue and white uniforms, cheered when Dimitri Tikhomorov, the abductee who had presented the alien world to humanity, stepped out of the presidential limousine. Some of the kids held up a banner that read "к звездам."

"To the stars," Trenton translated.

"Oh my god," said Elspeth. "Those poor kids. All these poor people."

Dale, who had been standing by the window with his rifle, turned around. "Are you people absolutely one-hundred percent sure these aliens are bad?" he said. "I mean, look at all this: there's got to be close to a million people there. The goddam president himself is there... surely they can't *all* be wrong?"

"Just look at human history," said Trenton. "It's hardly unusual for huge numbers of humans to line up to sacrifice themselves for something they barely understand."

Dale blew his cheeks out. "I dunno," he said. "I mean, the president himself is going..." He pulled his hip flask out of his pocket and took a long swig.

"I'm pretty sure the Farmers got to him," said Elspeth. "They've worked their way into the upper echelons of power all across the world. No reason why they wouldn't have gotten to Malevich."

On the ground in Gorky Park, the president's entourage was walking to the center of the podium, led by Tikhomirov. On the BBC, a pundit was speculating that the former abductee could be receiving instructions directly from the spaceship, and that what was happening in Moscow could act as a template for all the other embarkation sites.

They reached the center of the podium and stopped. A moment passed. Tikhomirov said something – the Russians appeared to have muted their microphone feeds, no doubt to hide any undignified panic their leader or the first family might suffer in the moments to come. First Tikhomirov raised his arms outstretched to the sky, then the president did so too: his wife and daughter followed suit, and in a minute all the people on the stage were standing with their hands raised to the sky, like sun worshippers beseeching their lord to banish the clouds.

"This appears to be some sort of pre-arranged signal," the BBC anchor was saying. "There's obviously been a lot of speculation over just how this would go down, and whether Mr. Tikhomirov there might have been given instructions on what to do when the ships returned. Now we just have to..."

The woman's voice cut off. All the people on the stage had jolted at exactly the same time, as though the ground had moved beneath their feet. Their outstretched hands came down as though they were trying to stop themselves from falling. The president's composure vanished for a second as he seemed about to topple over, but then he appeared to right himself.

The TV coverage switched from a close-up of the president's face to a shot of his feet.

The news anchor was astounded. "They... they appear to be floating, just a few inches off the ground. And you can see the surprise on President Malevich's face..." The Russian leader was reaching out now to grab his wife's hand. A bodyguard attempted to paddle over to secure his boss but was unable to move. Tikhomirov was laughing and calling out to the others.

Some of Malevich's bodyguards began running up the steps to the stage, but their boss ordered them to stop. He was floating now in a seated position, as though acclimating to his bubble of zero-gravity. Tikhomirov, the veteran, was doing back flips while Mrs. Malevich—wearing a pantsuit, as though forewarned that a skirt or dress might leave her in a compromised position—clutched her daughter's hand. There were gasps from the huge crowd, who were watching the proceedings on jumbotron screens dotted around the park.

These gasps were followed by shouts and a few screams. The president and his entourage started to float upwards, slowly at first but then at increasing speed. They floated together, in a straight line, and the cameras caught the looks of utter terror on their faces. Even Malevich, known to the world for his impassive stare, appeared to be shouting, although if he was, no one could hear his words. Only Tikhomirov appeared to be relishing the moment, assuming a Superman flight pose as he rode into the sky.

The BBC anchor and her guests fell silent as they watched the silent ascent of the Russians. Eventually, one of them managed to fill the silence.

"We were told the president and his family are wearing devices that allow a medical team on the grounds to track his vital health signals," the commentator was saying. "I imagine his pulse must be through the roof right now."

At about 200 feet, their ascent suddenly sped up. The same BBC talking head was commenting that this could have been for their own wellbeing, given how cold it was likely to be as they rose. Another pundit pointed out that there did not appear to be any opening in the hulls of the ships for them to go through.

"Maybe they'll just be like bugs on a windscreen," said Dale, grinning and taking another pull of bourbon from his flask. "Splat!"

Trenton shook his head. "What would that achieve? The aliens want everyone to go with them. Murdering a prominent leader who has placed all his trust in them right in front of the entire world wouldn't help their cause."

Just as the party appeared to be seconds away from impacting the hull, a small opening appeared right above them. Seconds later, they were gone. The entire world seemed to fall silent as the hatch closed the very second they had passed through.

In Gorky Park, as in the rest of the world, a stunned hush reigned. Malevich's aides frantically spoke into phones and radios, squinting through binoculars to pinpoint where the now-vanished hatch might have been. The people lined up across the vast plaza stared at each other, nervous expressions on their faces.

All of a sudden, the enormous screens staged across the square burst into life. Everyone's heads spun around and the cameras immediately zoomed in on the laughing face of the Russian president.

"Friends! Oh my god, it's incredible," he grinned. "First of all, I'm perfectly fine. The flight up here was very exciting, although we were not exactly sure what to expect. But they appear to have some kind of tractor beam that brought us safely and rapidly up here and now we are here, floating in this incredible place…"

He pulled back from the screen to allow the world to see the rest of his companions, floating in a huge, bright space: the first lady was standing on the floor of what seemed to be an endless open sky, trying to pat down her hair that had been tangled into a knot by her rapid flight. The others were all taking advantage of the Zero-G to do backflips and spins. Tikhomirov was paddling his way upwards as though trying to find how high it went.

"Masha, come here and tell the people what it's like," the president said with schoolboyish excitement. His wife pushed off the ground and floated straight to him, still fussing over a strand of loose hair.

"Oh my goodness, what a journey!" she said. "That was a real adrenaline rush, I can tell you. And look, from the outside it all looks like metal, but from the inside it's like glass. You can see forever!"

"The walls look gray down here because of the cloud outside," said the president. "But if you go up there, it's all blue. It's astounding. We are floating free like birds."

Few people had ever seen the Russian leader ever give more than the briefest of smiles. Now he was positively beaming. "This is the best thing that ever happened. Believe me, it is completely safe. Come and join me, and together we will build new worlds together." And he did a backflip, floating through the air like a slow-motion gymnast.

On Gorky Square, there was a roar. People surged forwards toward the center stage that the first family had just ascended from. And as they did so, they too began to lift gently into the air to make the final ascent into the waiting ships.

• | •

Two hours after the Russian rapture began, ships emerged from clouds all round the world at exactly the same time. The main news broadcasts leaped from city to city—Vancouver, Berlin, Leicester, Sydney, Harare, Sao Paulo, Hong Kong. Within minutes, news feeds became ever-expanding lists of cities, with footage of hundreds of thousands of people pushing to get closer to the designated lift-off zones. In Delhi, a news reporter had to take charge of the camera after his crew left to join the exodus: in Lima, the entire team walked off, saying a brief goodbye into the camera that they left focused on the ships hovering over the dusty parklands by the city airport.

Trenton stepped over to the window and pulled back the drapes.

"There they are," he said, peering up between the cracks of the boards.

Suddenly everyone was next to him or staring out the back windows. Sure enough, the same heavy hulls hung from the lowering sky.

Off in the distance, over the city center, there was a dark swirling cloud, almost like a tornado, that shimmered underneath one of the giant hulls.

It took a moment to register that it was humans.

"Oh my god," whispered Elspeth.

"I don't get it," said Joe. "There are ships all over the city. Why make people walk all the way to the Mall when they could just open up doors on every ship hovering over DC? It'd be much more efficient."

Trenton shook his head. "I have a feeling there's going to be a lot of things we just don't have any answers to. And may never get the answers to."

"I'll tell you the answer," said Dale, his cheeks flushed. "It's because they really *did* come here to help us! You saw the Russians. That wasn't any mass kidnapping, for crying out loud. Like you say, Joe, they could just suck up everyone out there in the street, but they're not doing that, are they? They're letting people choose for themselves. And you know what? I think I chose wrong, staying with you folks. You don't have any kind of inside track on what's going on out there! The Russian president himself was the first to go on board. You think he'd be dumb enough to do something as crazy as that if he didn't know something we didn't?"

"Dale," said Elspeth. "You heard what Rains said. He told us to stay safe during the harvest..."

"I wasn't there Elspeth! You guys left me here, remember, 'cos you didn't trust me enough to take me! And even if he did say that, who the hell is this Lester Rains, anyway? Some guy who showed up at a psychiatrist's office and with a tall tale that he's a 2,000-year-old ancient Roman... "

"Who knew about all this before it even started," Elspeth cut in.

"But *did* he?" said Dale. "Strikes me, he didn't really tell you jack shit. I saw what the Russian survivors saw. I heard them talking about this new planet... I saw the damn footage with my own eyes. It looked pretty good to me, you know."

He stamped over to the front door and yanked it wide open. On the street, a steady flow of people was marching towards the city center. Others were already busy prying open boards covering the doors and windows of unoccupied houses and moving in.

Elspeth went over to him. "Dale, you're not being rational right now."

"Sweetheart, there's a dust cloud of people flying up into an alien spaceship over by the Washington Monument there, and you want me to be *rational?*"

"That's because he's drunk," said Trenton. "Dale, you've been knocking it back since the firefight this morning. Possibly all through the night, if I was to guess."

"Trenton!" Elspeth snapped. "Dale suffers from PTSD, for crying out loud. Did it ever occur to you that a pitched battle on the front lawn might have triggered some kind of reaction?"

Dale suddenly seemed more angry at Elspeth than Trenton. "Don't you dare pity me, Irish!" he said, waving a finger at her. "I don't need anyone's sympathy. And so what if I was drinking Trenton? You my dad?"

He stood there, nostrils flaring, jaw clenching.

"Yes, I just killed a bunch of guys out there. I killed a goddam police officer! And for what? Just so we get to stay in this fucked-up town where everyone's going to be fightin' each other in about five minutes over who gets to live in what house? So, no, nobody gets to tell me when I can drink and when I can't, Trenton."

"Dale," Elspeth said, stepping up in front of him. "Dale, you saved my life the other day on the highway. So I have to tell you, in all conscience, that if you go out there now and get on those ships, you will die. I don't understand much about what's going on now, but I know with all my heart that that is true."

Dale pulled in his lower lip and chewed on his gingery beard. He was breathing hard. "I just wanna... I just think it's best if I go. What's gonna be left here once everyone's gone?"

"Not everyone's going, Dale," said Joe. "There's still plenty of people out there."

Dale looked out the window. "Yeah, fucking looters and criminals... and the Chinese..."

There was a moment of silence as the truth of what Dale was saying sunk in: that the world ahead of them was not going to be a pretty place, some Hobbesian state-of-nature battleground where who knows what monsters might land at any time.

"Fuck it," muttered Dale. "I don't know 'bout you all, but I'm going."

He strode out of the house and immediately merged with the procession of marchers. Elspeth ran after him, flinching as she passed the three dead bodies still lying in the front yard. She grabbed at his sleeve while he did his best to ignore her.

"Dale. Dale, I'm begging you, don't go! The aliens are going to kill you if you get on board that ship."

Dale said nothing, but a heavy-set couple walking next to him turned to her, anger on their faces.

"Get off of him, lady!" the man snapped. "He's got a right to choose what he wants. You're not his mother. The ETs have come here in peace. Didn't you see what just happened in Russia?"

Elspeth, not usually given to outbursts of anger, turned to the man. "Oh fuck off, you stupid fat fuck!"

The man's wife, face set in rage, lunged at Elspeth. "Don't you talk to my fuckin' man like that, you skinny-ass little bitch." She grabbed Elspeth with surprising force, shoving her to the ground until Dale intervened.

"Get off of her," he snapped, but the woman kept on lashing at Elspeth like a pit bull in a dog pen. Dale grabbed her arm and twisted it behind her back, forcing the hefty woman to the ground. Her husband started to charge in, but Dale pulled his Magnum and pointed it straight at the man's chest.

"You wouldn't be the first person I've killed today, buddy," he said, lips pursed. "So I suggest you and your good wife here keep moving. Right fuckin' now!"

The crowd had divided around them, flowing to either side of the street to avoid the scuffle. People scurried past, some ducking, but still moving relentlessly toward their destination. The man and his wife joined them, cursing, and were gone in seconds.

"You alright?" said Dale, helping Elspeth up. She brushed the dirt and grit from her grazed hands, nodding, eyes red.

"Don't go Dale," she whispered. "Please."

"I got to," he said. He pulled out his cell phone. "Got a text while we was all watching the Russians. From my ex..." he trailed off.

"Oh," said Elspeth. "She's taking the kids."

"There's ships over Louisville. She's boarding there."

"Dale," she began, then paused, fearing that what she was about to say would prove too painful. "There's no... that doesn't mean you'll actually see them again."

He squeezed his lips together, looking up at the vast metal plate overhead that had replaced the sky.

"Only way I'll ever get to find out," he said, his voice hoarse.

"That may not even be a real text," said Elspeth, clutching at straws. "You saw how the aliens took over the internet. Maybe they're trying to lure people in..."

"Not even the aliens could spell as bad as Wendy," Dale said, with a half-smile. Elspeth let out of a sob of a laugh, placed a hand on his shoulder.

Dale reached into his jeans pocket. "Look sweetheart, take this. Keys to my rig. You know where it's parked. You may need it sometime. Guess Trenton or BB might know how to drive an 18-wheeler."

Elspeth took the key fob. It had a lucky rabbit's foot attached to it, worn and almost fur-less.

"Won't you need this?" she smiled.

"I'm going to paradise, Irish, one way or the other," he said. "Think you might need it more than I do. Though you got the luck of the Irish with you, of course."

"I'm Scottish," she said, looking at him through her brimming tears.

"Hell, you been lyin' to me all this time, Irish?"

Elspeth gave a sobbing laugh, and Dale grabbed her and folded her into a bear hug, clinging to her for a moment. Then he turned into the river of people headed for the ships. He didn't look back. Elspeth stood in the street, crying her eyes out as the marchers broke all around her.

• | •

Trenton showed up a minute later. Taking Elspeth gently by the hand, he led her back to the rented house. He locked the door behind them, then picked up a plank and nailed it in place across the entrance. The hammer blows rang out in the silence of the house. The message was clear: Dale might be gone, but no one else was leaving.

Elspeth went upstairs to lie down on the bed she shared with BB. The others sat around the living room and kitchen, silently staring at their screens.

Pop stars, Hollywood A-listers, religious leaders, politicians: all were livestreaming on social media, posting footage of themselves with their friends and families standing in line or floating into the air, wobbly bird's-eye views of cities receding beneath them, accompanied by squeals of excitement and imprecations to fans and followers to come join them.

"Are those real, Darkman?" said Trenton. "Or is this the aliens gaslighting us?"

"Hard to say," said his intel specialist. "Maybe a bit of both."

Meanwhile, any media crews that were still operating around the world showed a steady surge of people heading for the ships: tens of millions in the first few hours, the news anchors estimated, then hundreds of millions. Possibly billions, but by the evening the numbers were so mind-boggling that it became a blur, and it was unclear who was even providing these estimates: figures of authority had become distant, inaccessible by now.

Occasionally, a camera operator would zoom in and catch a closeup of the people being beamed up into the sky: the mixture of fear, release, exultation or just plain shock at flying would be fixed on the face of a stranger from the other side of the planet, before they too disappeared into one of the openings on the undersides of the vast ships. On and on it went, hour after hour, until the horror and wonder of it were reduced to mere mechanical process, an industrial rapture.

Then, shortly before nine o'clock that night, all the lights went out. In the sudden darkness, faces were picked out only in the ghostly light of phone screens.

"Power's out," said Darkman.

"Get the generator up and running," shouted Trenton. BB was already running out the back. "Darkman, is it the whole city?"

"Can't tell yet," said Darkman, scrolling rapidly through sites on his phone.

"Whole street's dark," Joe muttered, peering out the window.

"BB!" yelled Trenton. "Hold off a minute." Turning back to the people in the room, he held up a hand. "Don't want to advertise we have a genny until we see what's going on out there."

There were a few people out in the street still. The flow of humanity headed to the ships had died down, and the few souls standing around now seemed to be trying to gauge if it was just their house that had lost power, or the whole city. Some chatted nervously on the sidewalk before heading back inside.

"What now?" said Ed.

In the darkness, Trenton shrugged. "You know what Ed? I don't know. We're out beyond the wire now. Everyone, power down your phones now, except you, Darkman. We need to conserve our juice. Let's hang tight for now. BB, get up on the roof with the NVGs and see if they're still flying bodies up there."

An uncanny silence hung over the city. The only light in the room came from Darkman's phone screen as he spun between sites looking for signs of what was going down in the world. Ed and Joe yawned and rubbed their eyes, abruptly released from the strain of so many hours of compulsively watching the unearthly events of the day. Elspeth came stumbling down the stairs, confused after waking in the darkness.

"What's happening?" she said. "Why is it dark?"

"Power's out," said Trenton. He clicked on the two-way. "BB, what you seeing up there?"

"They're still flocking up to the ships," her voice crackled over the radio. "Hard to tell, but there might be less of them now."

"Okay, get on back down here." When BB was back in the front room, Trenton addressed them all.

"We don't know what's going to happen from here on in. I suggest we sit tight and see what the situation is in the morning. Rains said he would try to come for us when the harvest was over. We have no idea how long that might take, but at the rate the ships were guzzling people up, I can't imagine it will be much longer than tomorrow night. So let's keep our powder dry. Grab some chow now if you're hungry. If you can get some shut-eye, that'll help. Me and BB and Darkman will split the night into watches. No point in everyone staying up all night. In the morning, we'll get out front and bury those cadavers if it all is quiet."

"Wait," said Elspeth. "I have a better idea."

Everyone looked at her as she rummaged through a box of emergency supplies in the corner of the room. When she turned back, she was holding six large candles. She lit them with a match and handed one of each person in the room, keeping one for herself.

"Before we all go off to sleep or eat or whatever, I want everyone to take a moment to reflect on what happened today. We have just watched hundreds of millions of people, possibly half the planet, march off to their death. The fact that they didn't know they were going to die doesn't make it much easier for us to process. It will have taken a massive toll on each of us, even if we don't immediately realize it. There's great value to ritual in time of bereavement, and we are all mourning something or someone today: loved ones we couldn't save, or even say goodbye to, or simply the understanding of how life is supposed to be. So I want all of us to take a minute, sit down and look into the flame, and remember what we have all lost today."

They sat in silence, each person staring into the flickering flame. Tears trickled down Joe's cheeks as he remembered his brother: he had no idea what had happened to Tony. The detention center where he'd been held had said it would take any inmates to the ships if buses could be arranged, but there had never been any updates in the chaos that followed.

Elspeth reached out and took Joe's hand. She sniffed back a tear as she thought of her mother. She'd tried calling her, but the line was dead. The old girl had always vowed never to use email or have any online presence. She had emailed her father, but he hadn't responded.

She reached out and put her other hand over BB's. The pilot was staring at her candle flame, her face softened too, though she didn't cry. Ed bowed his head and he folded his hands as if in prayer. It was clear Darkman was itching to get back to his screens, but he put up with the enforced pause in his eternal vigilance. Trenton stared impassively through his flame, his face inscrutable. Eventually, he blew out his candle.

"Okay, time for bed," he said.

"Trenton," said Joe, still looking into the flame. "What if Rains doesn't come? What if we never see him again?"

Trenton took a deep breath. "We'll give him a week. We've got plenty of supplies. If he doesn't come, we'll just have to recalibrate."

"Hawaii?" said Elspeth.

Trenton shrugged. "If we can find a commercial plane, we at least have a pilot," he said, nodding at BB. "Now everyone, get to bed. And make sure you put your candle out before you turn in. Last thing we need is for the house to burn down."

• | •

The power came back on at 5.30 in the morning, waking the entire city from restless slumber. Street lights blossomed, television sets started blaring and whoops of joy mingled with the bellows of those suddenly startled from their alien-stalked sleep.

Darkman was still sitting at his post downstairs when everyone stumbled in, pulling on sweatpants and pullovers.

"Don't you ever sleep?" said BB, her face bleary and a pistol in her hand. "You know it's bad for you, right? Gives you dementia."

"Good. Maybe I'll get to sabotage the brain of some reanimated alien one day," said Darkman. "Now go look out the back."

"What's out back? If it's not some clear and present danger, I ain't going out in the cold and dark in my robe."

"Everyone, come with me," said Darkman. He opened the back door. "I was going to wake you, but then the lights came on all of a sudden."

They all stepped out, shivering, and looked up at the stars. There was a sharp intake of breath.

"They've gone," said Joe. "It's over. My god, that was quick…"

Above them, in the cold dark before dawn, a quarter moon was hanging in the sky and a few stars were visible despite the sudden return of the city lights.

"The president's going to be addressing the nation at seven," said Darkman. "And there's a state of emergency in all fifty states while they assess what law enforcement capabilities they still have."

Out in the street, there was the rumble of a heavy vehicle and a voice speaking over a megaphone. They all rushed out onto the small front lawn just as an armored personnel carrier lumbered down the street. A figure in full combat fatigues stood at the hatch, speaking into a bullhorn.

"Do not leave your houses. A curfew is in place from 0600 until 2100 hours. The president will address the nation at 0700 hours. I repeat, the president will address the nation at 0700."

Once the vehicle had gone, people started milling out on the street in direct contravention of the order they had just heard. They seemed shocked but jubilant.

"Aliens are gone, motherfucker!" whooped a young man dressed in nothing but a ski jacket, boxers, and flip-flops. He was waving a half-empty bottle of Jim Beam as he walked up to a silver Prius parked on the roadside. He turned and shouted to a blonde woman standing at the door in sweatpants. "C'mon Holly, let's go get us new digs."

"Let's get back inside," said BB.

"Not yet," said Trenton. He was standing at the front door with three shovels. "First, we've got to bury these bodies. If the police are coming back on the streets, we don't want to have to explain what Officer Dalton is doing in pieces here. Elspeth, go put the kettle on. BB, Joe, grab a shovel and help me dig. We have an hour and twelve minutes before Bradley makes his speech."

The presidential address started half an hour later than scheduled.

The main broadcasters were back up and running after the chaos, though the exodus had left them short-staffed: anchors had splotchy make-up and dark shadows under their eyes, and the cuts between studio and correspondent were full of dead air. The on-air broadcasters were filling the scheduling void by talking about all the famous figures who had joined the exodus.

Despite the delay, the burial detail had not had time to finish digging three graves. The bodies were still out front, covered in tarps, when Elspeth called Joe, BB and Trenton inside because President Bradley had finally appeared at the podium in the White House.

He looked polished and well dressed, especially compared to the disheveled state of his fellow citizens. In fact, he was looking positively relieved that the apocalypse appeared to have passed him by.

"My fellow Americans, I am here to assure you that our great country remains on a firm and stable footing after the historic and unprecedented events of the past few days. After a briefing earlier this morning with the joint chiefs, the DNI and the various law enforcement agencies at all levels, I am able to tell you that our borders are secure, our communities are calm and our skies are clear. It will take some time to assess exactly how many of our fellow citizens decided to leave with the ships, but an initial assessment indicates that it was more than 150 million people. We wish them well, and we pray for their safe journey and that one day soon, we will have word of how they have fared. In the meantime, we will work to rebuild our country into a stronger, fairer community. I stand before you today fully confident that this extraordinary occurrence affords us, as Americans, the chance to construct a more equitable society with greater opportunities for all…"

"Way to put a gloss on losing half your country," said Joe, his hands still covered in dirt from the digging.

"I guess his speech writer must have run off with the aliens," said BB, slurping her coffee.

"There's nothing about what Rains said in there," said Trenton. "That's the key take-away: Rains said the worst would come *after* the harvest, once the Goweetha had taken what they want and left the planet to god knows what other creatures might be out there."

"That means the president is lying," said Elspeth. "Or else he has no idea what's coming next."

"Or Rains and Farmer One have put some kind of hex on him," said Trenton. "Either way, the whole world is completely unprepared for what's about to go down. Darkman, give us a rundown on what's happening around the world."

"Uh, sure," said Darkman. "China. Massive movement of the population back toward the cities. Hard to get a take on what's happening exactly, given that it's all state-run media and the western satellites weren't functioning properly when the ETs were overhead. Seems to be some suggestion on Weibo that the ships found some of the population clusters that had been evacuated to the countryside and sucked them up, but mostly they seem to be returning to the urban areas en masse."

"Russia?" said Trenton.

"Moscow's a ghost town," said Darkman. "Saint Petersburg, Novosibirsk, Yekaterinburg, Nizhni Novgorod... all virtually empty."

"God. India?"

"Estimates I'm seeing are around the 70 percent mark. Prime minister is saying 60 percent at least."

"Stayed?"

"Left."

"What about across the US?" said BB, furiously scrolling through news sites herself. "Pretty much the same as here," said Darkman. "High departure rates in California and New York, much lower in the southeast..."

"Sounds like a morning traffic report," said Joe.

"As Stalin said, 'One death is a tragedy, a million deaths is merely a statistic,'" noted Ed.

"Ok," said Trenton. "This is what we can surmise off the back of that. The president of the United States either doesn't know what's coming, or he's not telling us. Either way, that leaves the population highly vulnerable to whatever comes next. As we just saw from our neighbors, there's going to be a land grab unlike anything since Oklahoma in 1899, so everyone is highly distracted or still in shock. Now, we could try to raise the alarm among the local citizenry or we could..."

"What's *that?*" said Elspeth, pointing to the screen of a laptop that was streaming CNN. Everyone turned to look.

A woman reporter was standing on the Mall, close to the white marble needle of the Washington Monument: ground zero for the capital's exodus. The once-pristine grass was mashed under a layer of trash, bags and discarded shoes. There was even an abandoned tank straddling the gravel pathway. But the woman, seemingly the first network reporter to get there, was not focused on the human detritus. She was walking straight toward a large dark object rising from the grass in front of the Monument.

"... we're going to try to get as close as we can," the reporter was saying into her mike, panting slightly from the brisk walk across the Mall. "Greg, can you stop a minute and zoom in on it there? There's no one near it, no police, just this strange *object* that seems to have appeared overnight."

"Okay, just be careful there, Julie," the anchor warned. "We don't know what that thing is, and you seem to be all alone out there..."

The cameraman stopped and zoomed in on what appeared to be a spaceship but could also have been an intact asteroid: it was roughly the size of a town house, mineral in appearance and uneven but smooth, like a giant river boulder. No hatch or porthole was visible on any of its surfaces.

"What *is* that?" the anchorwoman said from the studio. Her guests murmured, clearly unsure. In the background, a producer could be heard telling a minion to get someone from the Air Force on the line ASAP.

"Uh, I'm guessing that's a spacecraft of some description," said one of the studio guests, a politics reporter who had been brought in to comment on the president's speech and evidently had no idea what he was talking about. "I guess the question is, did the other spaceships leave it behind? Or is this some kind of emissary..."

He trailed off. No one knew what the hell it was, or what it was doing on the Mall after the massive ships had left in the night. But Trenton knew.

"That's it!" he shouted. "That's the 'others' that Rains was talking about. The Goweetha have got what they wanted and now they've gone and left us to the others. This must be the ones that gets DC."

"Holy shit," said Joe, leaning as close as possible and screwing up his eyes to get a better look. "You recognize that, BB?"

She shook her head. "That's not the one I saw over the Pacific. Nothing like it."

"We have to get over there," said Trenton.

"What?" squawked Joe. "Anything could come out of that thing."

"I have a very strong feeling Rains is going to show up there sometime very soon," said Trenton. "Joe, those bodies out front. They were all wearing vests, right?"

"Vests?" Joe said, confused.

"Kevlar. Flak jackets."

"Uh, yeah, I think so."

"Great. You and Ed go grab them. Helmets too. We're going to need them."

• | •

They walked to the Mall: Trenton, Elspeth, Joe and BB. Driving was too dangerous, given the risk of running into checkpoints of jumpy

National Guards with their fingers on the trigger. Despite the orders to stay indoors, there were still plenty of people around. Some were pushing carts full of looted goods down the middle of the street, others could be seen jimmying open the front doors of empty houses.

But most were simply standing around in the street, looking for other people to exchange whatever latest news they might have heard, or just reassure themselves that civilization hadn't entirely collapsed. Almost all of them carried some kind of weapon, from assault rifles down to kitchen knives and baseball bats.

As they approached the city center, vast piles of garbage lay piled up like snowdrifts. The bars they passed had been smashed in and pillaged, and some still had small groups of revelers partying inside. The stench of rotting food wafted out of the broken windows of restaurants. A soft spring rain was falling as they walked down Seventh Street, past cherry and apple trees in full bloom.

The first military checkpoint they encountered was in Chinatown: the container trucks still blocked the road outside the National Gallery and a variety of unshaven soldiers and police officers stood nearby, turning away anyone who tried to pass. Trenton simply walked a block over and found an alleyway full of overflowing dumpsters that led to the other side of the barricade. Once there, no one stopped them until they crossed Pennsylvania Avenue and tried to enter the Mall itself.

The road was more effectively sealed here: a chain-link fence had been set up with a gateway just wide enough for vehicles to pass through. There were three soldiers manning this checkpoint. The next road was the same, and the one after it. Trenton radioed Darkman, who had stayed at the house with Ed to keep watch on developments, while the others tried to access the landing site.

"If you go up 12th you have walking access through the grounds of the National Children's Museum," said Darkman. "Looks like there's a small passageway between the buildings that will give you access to the Mall."

The plaza between the children's museum and the Environmental Protection Agency was devoid of any sign of life. The group walked single file down to the stone facade of the building and under a short, arched passage that led out onto Constitution Avenue and the Natural History Museum. Beyond that lay the Mall.

Trenton stuck his head out. He could see some soldiers walking across Constitution a hundred yards away, headed towards the Mall. He signaled, and they stepped out one-by-one onto the road.

"Hold your weapons up like you belong here," said Trenton. "There's any number of government agencies milling around. We've got helmets and vests: if we look like we mean it, people will think we're here on official business. Now follow me."

They walked with as much confidence as they could muster, down an almost empty Constitution Avenue. There was a checkpoint a few hundred meters down the road, outside the Museum of African American History, but no one paid them any mind. They crossed the street and circled round the grounds of the Natural History Museum until they emerged onto the Mall.

Looking west, they could see the spaceship sitting in the slim shadow of the Monument. They stopped, silenced by the sheer unlikeliness that any of them should be standing within spitting distance of an actual UFO.

"Fuck me," whispered Joe.

The National Guard had arrived by now and were busy erecting barriers around the craft. The news crews who had managed to get this far were being pushed back across street, away from the immediate perimeter of the Monument and its strange addendum.

Trenton was just trying to figure out how to get a better view when his radio crackled.

"Media outside the White House reporting a convoy just left the White House grounds, headed south," reported Darkman. "That's only two blocks from you. You see anything?"

They all looked up to their right. Nothing, except two fire trucks blocking the road north. One of them, ironically, had been set on fire, its tires shredded into bales of rayon fibers. Trenton was just about to answer Darkman when an army MRAP recovery vehicle appeared behind the obstacle: a crew of soldiers jumped out and attached cables to the chassis of the charred fire truck and dragged it out of the way.

"We have eyes on the convoy," Trenton told Darkman. "Any idea who's in it?"

"Not seeing any details. Looks like a mix of Army, official limos and an 18-wheeler."

"They're here for whatever's inside the spaceship," said Trenton. "C'mon, we have to get closer."

A squad of National Guard were filing past the steel barricades on 15th street and being directed to positions on the perimeter of the landing site. Trenton and his team fell in behind them. The young private in charge of the entrance glanced at their mismatched helmets and flaks with military name tags on them and waved them past. He paused when he saw Elspeth and was about to say something before he noticed the large bloodstain covering her body armor. She saw him looking and gave him her best "don't-fuck-with-me-kid" stare. He waved her through, too.

"The OIC's in the TOC over by the truck there." He was young, a part-time soldier and clearly reveling in the military jargon and his own importance as gatekeeper to the alien VIP compound.

They walked over, pretending they were headed for the officer-in-charge. Instead, they skirted round the other side of the truck and headed for the northern side of the enclosure. Another fence separated the security detail from the immediate environs of the spacecraft, which loomed over them like a dark rock face. They tried not to stare at it too much as they took up positions along the railing, from where they could also observe the convoy.

The engineers had moved the burned-out fire truck out of the way by now and the convoy was moving again, headed directly their way. There were half a dozen Humvees, two MRAP troop transporters, a Mack truck and three shiny black limos moving slowly up 14th street. They pulled up onto the grass in front of the spacecraft.

"Shit, is that Cadillac One?" said BB. "The president's wheels?"

"The Beast," said Trenton. "I do believe it is."

Soldiers jumped out of trucks and Humvees, and men in suits exited the limos: Secret Service agents, several men in smart suits, but no president. The civilians got out of the way of the military men, who took up firing positions covering the vessel as the driver of the Mack truck executed a looping turn and backed his 18-wheeler up to the alien ship.

"They're going to offload something," said BB.

"Look over there," said Elspeth, pointing at the knot of men in business suits.

"Don't point," said BB. "They'll get real jumpy. Describe what you're seeing, and don't stare either."

"Uh, next to the middle limo. The guy with dark hair and the dark blue suit. It's Rains."

"Shit, you're right," hissed Trenton. "And look, the guy next to him, the tall one—that's the guy we saw leaving the Watergate. The alien whisperer, or whatever Rains said he was. We have to get up close to that fucker."

"No way," said BB. "You walk over there, those guys will literally shoot you. They are nervous as fuck, I can..." She stopped talking in mid-sentence.

In fact, an eerie silence had fallen over the Mall, broken only by the beeping of the Mack truck backing up to the spaceship. The soldiers surrounding the craft stood stock still, rifles at the ready but not pointing at the alien vessel. Elspeth felt a faint ringing in her ears. She stuck a finger in her right ear to try to get rid of it, but it wouldn't go away.

"Anyone else hear a sort of buzzing sound?" she said. There was no answer. Trenton was scouring the group by the limo. He turned to face her.

"What did you say?" he asked.

"A buzzing in my ears. You hear it?"

"Yeah," he said. "Now you come to mention it..."

He turned and looked back at the ship: the truck was in position now, and a few men in overalls were lowering the back door.

"Holy cow," he said, "I think they're about to disembark whatever's inside the ship."

BB and Joe were still facing the limos and appeared not to have heard him.

"Don't all look at once," said Trenton. He looked at Elspeth: she was poking around in her ears with her fingers, but everyone else was standing as still as statues. Only the few men around the limos and the Mack truck were moving.

"BB," Trenton said, tapping her on the arm. BB didn't move or acknowledge him.

"Joe!" he shook the young reporter in growing alarm. No response. The National Guardsman standing next to Joe was similarly motionless. Elspeth had moved up next to him now and was staring into Joe's eyes.

"He still has a blink response," she said. "Otherwise in a catatonic state. But standing up: I have never..."

"It's *them*!" said Trenton, turning back to the ship. "That humming in our ears, only we can hear it. That's because you're the descendent of farmers and I was supposed to have been a harvester. We are immune to whatever the signal is. And look over there. Rains and his men are the only ones still moving. All the soldiers and journalists are frozen, too."

"They don't want anyone seeing whatever comes out of the ship," said Elspeth.

The Mack truck had stopped beeping and was in position. "C'mon," said Trenton, and started weaving between the frozen figures in uniform surrounding the Monument. As they got closer to the truck, the men working at the foot of the spaceship noticed them moving through the still life. One of them raised a rifle toward them and ordered them to halt. Trenton and Elspeth raised their hands.

"Don't shoot! We're with you guys," shouted Trenton, racking his brain for Rains' pseudonym. "We're with, uh... Mr. Tuck. From Dyson Corp."

The man did not lower his weapon, but the one next to him, wearing brown overalls and goggles, muttered something into a radio.

"OK," he said. "You're clear. But get over to the cars now. We're about to open this thing up."

"Got it," said Trenton, and pushed Elspeth ahead of him, towards the limos. "Don't look back," he said as they passed the truck and speed-walked past the statue-like guards, and towards Rains.

As they approached the limos, the tall man who had been designated as the alien's intermediary walked past them: he didn't even glance at them, so transfixed was he with whatever was emerging from the ship. He had a half smile on his face and Trenton saw he was trembling slightly, either in fear or anticipation. Or both.

Rains looked away from the spaceship just long enough to beckon them over as they reached the parked cavalcade.

"Elspeth," he said, immediately looking back at the craft. "Nice to see you made it this far." Unable to resist any longer, she too turned and stared.

A large hatch had opened on the side of the craft. From where they were standing, they could see something shifting inside the vessel. Unlike the rough-hewn spaceship, it was pod-like and shimmering metallic—clearly a smaller vehicle, like a landing module. It hovered for a moment as it emerged into the Earth's atmosphere, then darted rapidly and unswervingly into the back of the 18-wheeler. Rains' workers immediately bolted the doors behind it and started mounting up. The "translator" climbed into the cab of the truck with the driver and a guard.

"What *was* that?" said Elspeth.

"That is the pregnant queen of a species whose name I could never hope to pronounce because I do not have the appropriate mouthparts," said Rains. "Now, if you want to come with me, get in the limo. Or if you'd rather carry on impersonating a dead police officer, please feel free to return to your post."

Rains held the door of the Beast open.

"What about him?" said Elspeth, pointing her thumb behind her to where Trenton stood. Rains looked across her shoulder, head cocked.

"Ah, the misfire." He paused, considering. "Alright, Mr. Trenton, get in. Leave your rifle here. But keep your sidearms."

"Where are we going?" said Trenton.

"Not far," said Rains. "Just back to the White House."

"How come everyone is frozen like that?" said Elspeth, settling beside Rains in the spacious interior of the president's limo. In spite of everything, she couldn't stop herself stroking the plush upholstery of the bullet-proof vehicle.

"It's a Ma'ut technique," said Rains. "More or less an amplified version of what we farmers can do to limited numbers of humans."

"Why didn't you use it during the harvest?" asked Trenton, who was turning back in his seat to look at the Mack truck driving right behind them. "You could have just hypnotized everyone into getting on the ships."

Rains was already on his phone, texting as he answered Trenton. "Pure organic consciousness is the goal of the Ma'ut. Free will is a vital component of that: people have to choose to be part of the experiment."

"And if no one had gone on board?" Elspeth said.

Rains shrugged. "The Ma'ut are masters of manipulation, even if they can never quite grasp what organic consciousness is. But at the end of the day, they really don't care. They are simply fulfilling their mandate as best they can. If this experiment fails, they just move on to the next, and the next one after that."

"Half a million years of human evolution, and they'd give up just like that?" said Elspeth.

"A mere blip," said Rains, not looking up from his phone.

"What about the Russians?" said Trenton. "Why did Malevich go on board?"

"So many questions, Mr. Trenton," said Rains, looking up from his screen. "Look, Malevich believed us when we told him that if he and his people led everyone else on board, they would be spared and would go on to inherit the world. He was a vain and deluded man who ruled his country with an iron fist. We didn't even have to put him in our thrall."

The convoy was in front of the White House now. Rains raised a hand. "Enough questions. We're here. We have important work to do. Elspeth, stay very close to me."

• | •

The area in front of the West Wing had been screened off with concrete blast walls. In front of these defenses stretched a line of body bags, silent testimony to an ill-advised attempt to storm the White House during the mayhem of the previous days. As the heavily guarded Mack truck swung in behind the barriers, no one on Pennsylvania Avenue would be able to see it offload its cargo.

The limos stopped in front of the main entrance to the White House. Rains and his entourage walked straight in, leaving Trenton and Elspeth to follow behind and marvel at how the group seemed to own the place already.

"Where's the president?" Elspeth whispered as they swept through the Center Hall and turned into a large oval room whose walls were covered in historic landscape paintings, and whose windows looked out south over lawns towards the Monument and the alien ship.

"Is this the Oval Office?" she asked Trenton as the group came to a halt around Rains: two of his men took up positions by the door.

Rains was giving instructions to the others about how they were to act in the coming meeting. "Boyd, you and your detail are attached to Mr. Dalrymple from now on..."

"No," said Trenton. "I think it's called the diplomatic reception room. Looks like they're planning some big event here."

He nodded over at a film crew setting up by the panoramic window as more people filed in: the latest arrivals seemed confused and flustered. Trenton recognized a couple of them: the president's chief of staff, as well as the Speaker of the House.

"Looks like the president may be about to meet our alien queen," he whispered into Elspeth's ear.

Rains had finished briefing his people now and stepped over to Elspeth. "The queen is going to come in through that door on the left, accompanied by her translator, Mr. Dalrymple. The president will be standing by the fireplace there. I want you to keep as far away from the queen as possible. We have no idea what she might do."

"Jesus Christ," Elspeth muttered, her body already starting to shake as if the temperature had plummeted. "And why exactly is she meeting the president?"

"Transition of power," said Rains. "Now, excuse me," he said, turning to greet the president's chief of staff, who presented an impeccably turned-out woman in her fifties.

"Mr. Tuck, this is Diane King of CBS," he said.

"Of course, of course," said Rains. "And may I just say, Ms. King, how incredible you look when so many of the rest of us are looking rather disheveled?"

"Not you, Mr. Tuck. You look like the only other person here with a fresh change of clothes!" They both laughed, as the chief of staff rather self-consciously bushed down his own rumpled suit.

"Ok, Ms. King," Rains said. "So you will stand over here and your camera will have the doors to your left. The president will enter from the right. Once he is in position at the lectern, the major domo will enter and present the queen..."

"Sorry, Mr. Tuck, uh... just for the purposes of clarity for the audience, who exactly is this major domo? I heard he is English?"

"His name is Paul Dalrymple," said Rains. "He is a former butler to the rich and famous. Or at least he was until he murdered his employer at his lakeside residence in Geneva and then set the place on fire, knowing he had been named in his will. I found him in the Poschwies Correctional Facility in Switzerland."

"I... I'm sorry, Mr. Rains, this has all been a lot to digest for the past few days already, and I want to make sure I get this right. You mean, this man is a convicted murderer?"

"Precisely Ms. King. He was the perfect candidate for the job. A ruthless sociopath with an exquisite eye for protocol. Tailor-made to serve the assassin queen."

Diane King's face went quite blank. She was about to formulate a question when the chief of staff reappeared at her shoulder.

"The president is ready, Mr. Tuck. But the Secret Service are insisting on being in the room when..."

"Out of the question, Mr. Razaq," said Rains.

"Goddam it Rains, this is the president of the United States we're talking about, meeting a goddam alien that just landed in a motherfucking spaceship on the Mall two days after half our population was raptured into the sky!" The chief of staff noticed that his voice had risen dramatically, and that everyone in the room had turned to listen. He pointed at the CBS soundman. "You better not be recording this, pal!" The soundman shook his head.

"Listen Rains, I know you claim to have some sort of in with the aliens, but be that as it may, we simply cannot allow... "

Rains held up his hand. "Mr. Razaq, let me make myself clear. The president will come out here in precisely..." he looked at his Rolex... "three and a half minutes, or the queen will rip through these walls and drag him out here herself. And in doing so, she will most likely kill everyone in this room, including the Secret Service detail who are so concerned about the president's safety. Do I make myself clear?"

Razaq's face blanched, but he nodded. "Fine," he said, and stumped off. The CBS team gawped as he left. Then the producer stepped up. "Ok, we're on air in three... two... one..."

Diane King showed why she was her network's star reporter. Hardly missing a beat, she looked into the camera and began to talk. "Yes, Cheri, we are here in the diplomatic reception now at the White House, and we believe the president is just about to enter from the China Room, for an absolutely unprecedented first contact with the extraterrestrial being whose ship was discovered just this morning on the Mall..."

"Oh my god this is really happening, isn't it," said Elspeth, sidling up to Trenton. He was on his radio, talking to BB.

"Get back to the safe house, BB, and wait for us there. There's no way we can get you in. Copy?"

"Copy," BB's voice crackled over the radio.

Trenton turned back to Elspeth. "They're okay. Just came out of their trance state, had no idea what happened, or where we were. I told them we're okay. For now."

"Are we?" said Elspeth. Trenton did not respond, just scanned the room. "Like Rains said, let's get as far away from the lectern as we can." He guided her over to the large window. "If anything goes wrong here, we'll need a quick... holy fuck..."

"What is it now?" said Elspeth, then looked out the window. She let out a stifled shriek. The lawn of the Ellipse was covered by ranks of zombies staring directly up at the window where they stood. Elspeth put her hand over her mouth but found she couldn't make a sound.

"Of course," said Trenton. "They're here for the queen. That's why they've been migrating from across the country. They're not zombies, they're *drones* for her hive. Which means that Rains or some other farmer came up with syrup and was distributing it through drug dealers."

Elspeth was shaking. "I don't think I can take much more of this, Cassius," she said. He put his arm around her shoulder and held her. She was shaking.

"Listen, it's going to be okay, right? We've found Rains, that's the main thing. And he seems to have a soft spot for you. If there's any way to get through this, it's with him. So we're going to be okay."

She nodded weakly. A booming voice sounded from the far end of the reception room. "Ladies and gentlemen, the President of the United States of America."

The doors on the right opened. Nothing happened. Everyone waited: a minute passed, two minutes. Then a very tall, pale man walked through, staring straight ahead. He looked so unpresidential, like a man being led in front of a firing squad, that it took a moment for Elspeth to realize that it was, in fact, the president of the United States of America. Razaq, the chief of staff, and another aide guided their commander-in-chief.

"And the president is coming out now, and I have to say looking *very* ill at ease..." Diane King was whispering into her microphone.

"Oh god, look at his trousers," Elspeth whispered. Trenton looked. The president had pissed himself.

An official White House camera had been set up in front of the lectern to broadcast the event to the world, if the world was still out there watching. President Bradley looked into it, then stuttered a few barely audible words.

"My fellow Americans," he rasped, throat dry. He reached out for a bottle of water, but there wasn't one to hand. He put his hand over his mouth and coughed, then pointed limply to the left.

"There's... an alien," was all he could muster. "Uh... It has, um, asked that we meet it.... here, and uh, we hope... we do sincerely hope... that it has, uh, come on a mission of peaceful..."

His face was pointed at the camera but his eyes were swiveled off to the left the whole time. They widened as the doors abruptly opened. Dalrymple, the English butler, stepped out, dressed in a perfectly pressed dinner suit and with a large, fresh scar circling the bald dome of his head. He had a manic look in his eye, like he had just taken a giant bump of cocaine.

"Ladies and gentlemen," he yelled in a voice like a drill sergeant. "It is my great honor to present to you your new ruler, your Queen, whose word will be law and will be spoken only through me, her designated mouthpiece on this planet. You will now bow down before her Highness, whose name is so mighty that it cannot be uttered by human mouth. You will address her as Your Majesty."

He stepped fully into the diplomatic reception room, then turned and held out his arm to present the alien.

Its head scraped the top of the doorway as it lumbered into the room: it must have been at least eight feet tall, and Elspeth's first impression was of a giant baby pigeon, hideous and awkward. Large black eyes bulged above what looked like a beak, but which, observers would later notice, was not rigid but a large, malleable protuberance. It had numerous limbs, but in that first moment of shock and disbelief, it was hard to tell how many, as it used them interchangeably to walk, reaching out with what appeared to be an arm and using it as a leg to propel itself forwards. Its bird-like head, on a long and sinuous neck, seemed to roll around to adjust to the shift in its gait.

The entire room stood there, frozen, until the Major Domo bellowed out, "Kneel before Her Majesty!"

Everyone immediately dropped to their knees, except for President Bradley, who stood by the lectern as if in a trance. Several people instinctively put their hands up too, as though being mugged at gunpoint. The creature moved into the room, heavy yet somehow sinuous. Its body was lumpy and jiggling: it took Elspeth a moment to realize that what was covering it wasn't clothing, scales or armor: it was a patchwork of severed heads of unrecognizable creatures that clattered and clanked as the queen moved.

The president looked like he was about to faint.

His chief of staff, Razaq, instead of moving to prop up his boss, took a step back, as if to get as far away as possible as the creature sidled up next to the leader of the free world. Dalrymple, the English butler who had in that moment become the most powerful person on the planet, stood next to his new master.

"Behold!" he bellowed. "She wears the skulls of her foes, their souls still trapped within. Yet she comes in peace, so rejoice!"

The president finally started breathing again at these words. A shudder ran through his large frame, overshadowed by the monstrous thing next to him.

"In... in that case," he said, some slight color returning to his cheeks, "we welcome the... the, er... you, to the United States and to, uh, Earth, I guess..."

Dalrymple's eyes seemed to swivel up in their sockets as the Queen communicated, and he cut off the president's barely audible welcome. "Her Majesty was cruelly betrayed by the house of her swarm-master, who usurped her supremacy two hundred years ago. Forced into exile, this loyal servant of The Ma'ut—all obedience to them!—has been granted under the Treaty of Aflalal 3790001/2 this territory which she now pronounces to be the possession of Prezefet and which will be used to respawn her line, under the provisions of the aforesaid agreement. Under the treaty, the planet Earth had been divided between the various supplicants to the Ma'ut—all obedience to them!—and the terms of the accord will be enacted now that the Ma'ut have reaped their harvest. Any disputes by the indigenous population must be registered with them within the next sixty Earth days."

Amid the stunned silence, the queen turned her vulture-like head to take in her new subjects. Small openings on her face palpated as she assessed the scene with senses the humans couldn't even begin to guess at. As she surveyed her new realm, Dalrymple spoke again.

"Her Majesty has graciously granted me leave to put her official message into more accessible terms," he said, grinning smugly. "After a power struggle on her own planet, the Ma'ut, the dominant force of the universe, and which is an artificial super-intelligence, has given her this part of the United States to do with as she pleases. Having been forced from her own planetary system after a coup by her underlings, she has come here to spawn a new generation who will one day return to reclaim their birthright. We are privileged to have been picked by her to help in this historic righting of wrongs."

The president held up his hand, weakly. "If I may...?"

"Ah yes," beamed Dalrymple. "Mr. President, good that you asked. As the leader of the most powerful nation on the planet, and a man of robust physical stature, the Queen has very generously selected you to be the host of the First Royal Zygote, which I have to say, is an enormous honor and will assure you a place in the history books.

"What..?" the president began, but stopped as one of the alien's limbs shot up from the floor and grasped his right arm. A dozen digits emerged from what appeared to be a foot but now resembled something more like a hand. The digits wrapped around the presidential forearm: he tried to pull away, but, as big a man as he was, the queen's grip was tighter.

Elspeth stared in horror as the queen yanked the president toward her. And in that fleeting moment, it struck her that neither she nor any other scientist on Earth would ever get to study this strange new species, to give it a Latin name or etymology, because this thing was now the dominant life form and would never be passively observed and studied. No doubt *it* had studied humans and found something in them to be passingly useful to its own ends, which is why it was here. And even though there was apparently only one of its kind here on Earth, it had somehow come to dominate the entire city, the whole of this new realm whose boundaries its terrified subjects could only as yet guess at.

Elspeth felt a hand on her shoulder. It was Rains, who had dared stand up—or rather, to squat on his haunches—and was whispering in her ear. "Get up. We have to move. Now."

Doubled over, she and Trenton scrabbled after Rains as he sidled along the wall to the door that the president had entered through.

Behind her, she heard the president half-scream, but the scream was cut off abruptly and replaced by an odd noise that reminded Elspeth of the little suction pipe her dentist used to put in her mouth to suck up all the spit and water whenever she got a filling.

As Rains reached the door to the China Room, Elspeth stole a glance over her shoulder. A tube-like organ, resembling nothing more than an umbilical cord, had emerged from the queen's beak-like mouthpiece and was firmly implanted in President Bradley's mouth. His body was convulsing, but he appeared to be no longer trying to break free. The veins in his throat and forehead were cording and pulsing, his eyes rolled white.

The doors to the China Room suddenly flew open, knocking Rains backwards. Trenton caught him and they sprawled on the floor as a squad of Secret Service agents burst in, guns drawn.

"Freeze," shouted one.

There were no shots. Elspeth heard the thumps as their dead bodies hit the floor, one landing next to her feet. Then Trenton was dragging her out of the room and down the corridor, across the entrance hall and out into the warm morning air of Washington, DC. They kept running in blind panic, out past startled guards and up 15th Street until they thought their lungs were about to burst.

They collapsed in the street, flopping down behind the carcass of a burned-out BMW on the forecourt of a luxury hotel.

Rains pulled up his sleeve and pressed a button on his wristwatch. He took a deep breath.

"Listen carefully," he said, chest heaving. "My men will be here in about twelve minutes. What I am about to tell you cannot be repeated in front of any of them, okay? I have a plan to get us out of here, but I think I will need your help."

• | •

Unbeknownst to them, BB and Joe had passed within a few blocks of their position just minutes before, as they too fled through the city. When they had come to—still standing on the Mall—they had been utterly nonplussed to find that Trenton and Elspeth had simply vanished into thin air.

"Where the fuck *are* they?" BB said, frantically scanning the loose line of pickets around them.

"I don't know," said Joe. "They were literally right here next to me."

"This is insane," said BB. She grabbed her radio. "Trenton, do you copy? *Trenton?*" No answer. She pulled out her cell phone and tried calling. "What the fuck?" she said. "No signal."

A couple of soldiers in front of them were pointing down at the area by the spaceship. One of them turned to BB, a spooked look in his eyes. "Have we gone fuckin' crazy or did that whole fuckin' column of MRAPS and that big-ass truck just vanish?"

"No," said BB. "You're not crazy. Some super weird shit is going down."

"It must be the fuckin' aliens," said the soldier. "They're fucking with our heads, man. We gotta get outta here."

"You're right bro," said the other guardsman. BB looked around: all across the Mall, small knots of soldiers were breaking away, some running, some walking. A couple of officers shouted at them to stand their ground, but it was too late: military discipline had officially just collapsed.

"We have to get back to the safe house," said BB. They retraced their steps back to the road: the soldier who had let them through the cordon was already gone. Across the road, the gaggle of journalists was still there. BB headed straight for them.

"You know what the fuck just happened?" she asked a young woman who seemed to be a producer.

"I just got off the phone to the bureau," she said. "The president's dead. The alien you guys released killed him live on air. They said we'd been unreachable the whole time. Look at my phone. It was 10.30 when I last called in for a live shot. It's quarter past twelve now."

"Fuck," said BB, unable to get her head round it.

"Okay, the president is *not* dead," another journalist was saying, reading from his phone. "The alien attacked him but... Jesus, it impregnated him with an egg or something...."

BB turned to Joe. "We really have to get the fuck out of here. You people," she said, looking back at the media huddled round their stand of cameras. "You should all leave, right now. That thing is just a couple of blocks from here, and the army boys are all running. God knows what's gonna happen now. But go. If you have families, go be with them." She pushed Joe, then turned back to the journalists. "And god be with you," she said.

They trotted back down the Mall towards the Capitol, then turned north, close to the way they had come just a few hours before. All the checkpoints were gone now: the soldiers had watched, live, as their commander-in-chief was assassinated or got mouth-raped by an alien or whatever the fuck had just happened. Not only was military discipline shot, but civilization itself was gone, collapsed not with a bang or a whimper, but with a president of the United States getting French-kissed by some extraterrestrial bug.

After about ten minutes of walking and trotting, BB figured they could take a break so she could check for herself what had really happened. They ducked into the doorway and she almost cried with relief when she saw the four bars of reception on her cell phone. Darkman picked up on the first ring.

"Darkman, what the fuck is happening? And where the fuck is Trenton?"

"He's okay," said Darkman. "He was in the White House with Elspeth, but they got out right as that thing stuck its tongue down the president's throat. Good news is, he's with Rains. They're headed to the Watergate."

"The Watergate!" said BB. "Why the hell would he go there? It was Rains brought that thing into the White House."

"He says Rains has a plan," said Darkman. "A way out of here. Meantime, where are you?"

"I dunno," she scanned the empty street. "Seventh and O."

"Okay," said Darkman. "I think it's safest if you get back here and we'll all try to get to the Watergate later today or tonight, when we have an assessment of the threat level on the street. What's it like out there?"

"Absolutely deserted. Not a soul to be seen."

"Okay," said Darkman. "But watch yourself. We don't know what else might have been on that ship."

"Darkman," she said. "What the fuck happened in the White House just now?"

"It was crazy, man. The alien had this kind of proboscis that went down the president's gullet. There's some English dude who's the alien's sort of ADC who said the thing had implanted a DNA bomb or something that would fuse with the president's own DNA and create a kind of hybrid. Apparently that's how this species evolves, one generation to the next—hijacks a host and takes over on a cellular level."

"So our president is going to be a fucking alien?"

"The English guy said it would take about a week. They grabbed a bunch of the other people and did the same with them. Diane King was next."

"Diane King's gonna be an ET too? Man, that's even worse than the president. I *liked* her," BB said.

"Secret Service agents tried to shoot the bug, but it neutralized them on the spot. Still trying to figure out how it did it. No shots fired as far as I can tell. Then Rains' heavies started grabbing journalists and cabinet staff and holding them down while the alien impregnated them."

"Jesus fuck," said BB. Next to her, Joe was listening in. He'd found the footage on Twitter and was showing it to her. She pushed his hand away. "I don't want to see none of that sick shit," she said.

"And so Rains' goons helped the alien throat-rape everyone in the White House and now we're supposed to just rock up to Rain's pad and trust him? I don't buy that shit, Darkman."

"Listen, just get your ass safely back here now. We'll discuss it when we're all back at base, okay?"

BB put her phone back in her pocket. She reached over and took Joe's rifle, flicked the safety off. "Listen. I'll take point. You keep ten paces behind me. Keep your weapon at the ready, but pointed at the ground and off to one side. Keep your finger on the trigger guard, *not* the trigger. Do not shoot me in the goddam back or shoot yourself in the foot. I do not want to have to carry you three klicks back to the house. And every ten paces, take a turn and look behind you. Okay?"

Joe nodded. He could already feel the silence of the empty city closing in around him, an almost physical presence. It was all he could do to keep himself from catching up with BB as she paced warily in front, head swiveling as she scoured the buildings ahead. What they were looking for, Joe wasn't sure, and he tried hard not to imagine.

The vibration from his cell phone almost made him jump out of his skin. He instinctively reached for his pocket but stopped when he saw BB had halted in front of him, her fist held up. She took another brief look around, then reached into her own pocket. She had clearly got a text at the same time.

"Cover me," she said. Joe held his gun up and peered all around them as BB tapped her phone screen.

"Is it Trenton?" he called out.

She shook her head. "You get one too?"

"I got something, haven't looked yet."

"Good, don't," she said. She fiddled with her phone for a minute, then started walking across the street to a McDonald's whose glass door had been smashed in. "Come over here," she said, stepping inside.

"What is it?" said Joe once they were inside the trashed eatery. BB was on Twitter, he saw, reading something. Joe pulled out his own phone to read the text message. It was in the same format as an amber alert, the kind the authorities used to flag up a suspected child abduction, warning the general public to be on the lookout for a particular car or person.

Follow @MajorDOMOWH on Twitter, Instagram and Facebook for regular updates on the status of the city and the Queen's realm.

The message was followed by a smiley face, an alien emoticon and the hashtag #alienqueen.

"What the fuck?" Joe said.

"Wait till you see what he's posting on Twitter," said BB.

• | •

It took Rains' men just ten minutes to reach their boss. Three black armored SUVs screeched to a halt in the street where Rains, Elspeth and Trenton had taken shelter after their flight from the White House. The bodyguards had swapped their business suits for tactical combat gear: the final vehicle had a 50.cal machine gun bolted to the roof. Rains and Elspeth got in the back of the middle car, with Trenton in the lead vehicle. Another ten minutes and they were back in the relative safety of the Watergate's underground parking.

The lower floors of the building had been ransacked, but Rains' suite had been spared, thanks to the efforts of the men he had left behind to guard his base. The bodies of two looters, a man and a woman, had been propped against the wall facing the elevators on Rains' floor by these same men. A cardboard sign written in sharpie and hanging round the dead man's neck read: "Do NOT Enter or You will be SHOT."

Trenton and Elspeth were escorted into a guest bedroom.

"I will see you shortly," Rains said as they stepped into the room. "Hector, see to it that they have food and drinks."

Then he left. The door closed with a click. Trenton waited a minute before testing the handle.

"Locked."

"Can we trust him?" said Elspeth.

"We don't have much choice right now. Besides, of all the people he chose to save from that shitshow in the White House, you were the only one. I just tagged along. God knows what happened to his own men."

"We have a TV," said Elspeth, immediately reaching for the remote. Trenton was already calling Darkman when a message flashed up on his screen. Amber alert.

"Holy shit," he said.

Elspeth looked up from where she was already sitting on a twin bed. She did not have a phone, so Trenton showed her the Twitter account that the whole city had just been ordered to follow.

Wow, I only had three followers this morning now I have more than 87,000!!!#Goodtobeking #alienqueen

"He's clearly a narcissistic psychopath," she said, for once ignoring her own rule not to diagnose people who were not her patients.

"No shit, Sherlock," said Trenton, returning to his call to Darkman. He muttered into the mouthpiece, aware the place was probably bugged. "Listen up. We're at the Watergate with Rains. We were at the White House for that crazy alien gender reveal, but he got us out, just in the nick. I don't think he means us harm right now, but that could change any minute. Says he has a plan to get us out of here. I need you guys to stay put for the time being. If you don't hear from us in the next twenty-four hours, come looking for us. But be very cautious. His guys are well armed and trained."

As soon as he hung up, he was back on Twitter. @MajorDomoWH was already livestreaming from his new domain, walking through the corridors and rooms of the White House as if he owned it. Which, of course, he effectively did.

"Not nearly as grand as I'd expected, I have to say," Dalrymple said. "I've worked in far more impressive places in my time, But I have to say, you can sort of feel the… I don't know, the history, the *majesty* of the place."

"And talking of majesty," he grinned. "Here is the East Room, which is the largest room in this place. That's where the Queen has taken up residence. And look, coming down the hall now, here comes President Bradley..." He pointed and whoever was operating the camera turned around to show a small flotilla of gurneys being wheeled down the hallway by Rains' goons. As they passed, the camera showed the people strapped on to them. The president, struggling like a madman to break free, rolled his eyes wildly at the camera, his screams muffled by a gag.

"And his chief of staff Mr. Dan Razaq..." the Major Domo went on as the second gurney was wheeled by. "And the speaker of the house... oh, and of course, the lovely Ms. Diane King of CBS news. Loved your interview with Li'l Doll, by the way, Ms. Keane," he gushed as the struggling media star was pushed past.

"Now, they're headed off to the State Dining Room, just over there, where they will enjoy their time transforming into the queen's new generation of swarm masters," he said. "I know, all sounds a bit crazy, doesn't it? But you know, the queen is an incredibly powerful being who was unjustly forced from her own home planet in a coup, and has come here to regroup and build a new swarm so she can eventually go back and reclaim her throne. So hurrah, right? Once the president and the others have fully absorbed the DNA bomb, they will have all the powers that her species enjoys, *plus* the genetic health of having been cross-pollinated with an entirely separate species, which is good for the health of everyone. Win-win!"

"Anyway, she's had a very long journey to get here, so she's just taking a nap in the East Room here, I don't know, shedding some skin or something, but then she's going to be very hungry. So when she gets up again, we're all going to pop out and hunt her down something to eat. She eats just about anything, so we'll see what we can pick up. See you all in a bit then. Bye."

The major domo waved at the camera, smiled, then made a "cut' gesture with his hand. Transmission ended.

"Not only is he a total psychopath, he's not nearly as posh as he makes out," said Elspeth. "You can hear his real accent slipping out beneath the polished voice he must have learned at butler school. Strong hint of south London. What our snobby English cousins would call 'common.'"

"I wondered what that was," said Trenton. "Guess he's good at adapting to new environments. And of course, now he's probably the most powerful human in the world."

"What do you think she eats, by the way?" she said.

"I don't know," said Trenton. "But I wouldn't go outside until that sick fuck says she's back in her nest."

PART VI

That same day, as the residents of the alien queen's freshly minted realm were watching in sheer horror as her bloody reign began, the Japanese whaling ship Nisshin Maru No.4 was steaming south into the waters of Antarctica.

Her captain, Hideki Takahashi, had sailed these waters as a young man, before the ban on whaling in the Antarctic. His mission when the ship left Shimonoseki Harbor ten days earlier had been to carry out the annual "research hunt" in Japan's territorial waters, harpooning up to 200 Minke, Wright and Sei whales. When the news came through of the alien landing, Captain Takahashi had considered turning back to port: many of his crew favored the idea, either to look after their families or, in the case of several of them, to join the spaceships and leave this world for good. Whaling was, they argued, an honorable way to earn a living but not an easy one, and the Russians had promised a new world of plenty.

But the captain had other ideas.

For years, the Japanese whalers had been forced by bleeding heart liberals to stay close to Japan's shores, going through the motions of hunting without ever engaging in the real thing. Whaling was in the blood of the Japanese, it was part of their culture: what had seemed like a temporary moratorium had become a permanent ban. Now the waters of the southern ocean were teeming with cetaceans again, and the eyes of the world were focused on these alien ships. They should sail south to the Antarctic, the captain believed, just as their forebears had kept whaling even during the war, braving the American subs that sank their ships.

Captain Takahashi assembled his entire crew in the messroom. He argued that most sensible Japanese people would refuse to join the alien ships, but warned that the exodus of so many people around the world would mess up supply chains for years to come. If they returned to Japan in a few weeks with a hold full of fresh whale meat, they would be welcomed as heroes. And their haul would make them rich men.

That swayed most of his men. As thousands of cargo ships, container giants and fishing fleets around the world plowed full steam ahead for the nearest port, the Nisshin Maru No.4 headed for the pristine waters of the Antarctic.

Captain and crew kept up with developments back home via their satellite comms. They watched with a mixture of awe and envy as the Russians made their orderly departure by the million on to the ships, followed by city after city around the world. The news that China had marched its entire urban population out into the countryside disturbed them: Beijing was already a superpower on their doorstep and would only be more dominant if even half of the rest of the world decided to leave.

But the news they heard from Tokyo was the most shocking. Millions upon millions of people turned out in the city to join the exodus, many of them reassured by what they had seen in Russia. Crew members frantically tried to contact their family members back home and urge them not to go: scuffles broke out over who would get to use the satellite phone first. When the captain intervened, one of the cooks screamed at him: "You did this! My wife and kids are joining the ships without me, just so you could go hunt your fucking whales!"

Captain Takahashi stepped up and slapped the man.

"The next man who talks to me like that will go in the brig!" he snarled.

Two days later, he was sitting in his cabin, writing an email to his wife. She had been way too canny to get on that alien craft, unlike that fool of a cook's wife. There was a knock at the door.

"What is it?" he barked through the door.

"Captain, you'd better come to the bridge quick," said the first mate. "There's something strange up ahead."

Takahashi folded his laptop and followed his subordinate back to the bridge.

The ECDIS, or electronic chart display and information system, showed the Nisshin Maru's current position on the southern ocean, as well as the topography of the seabed, the ocean temperature and currents. Normally, it would show any other vessels within a hundred-mile range, but today the whaling factory seemed to be the only ship on the surface of the ocean. As soon as he looked at the chart, Takahashi saw what had caused the consternation on the morning watch.

"That can't be ice," he said. "We're still too far north for ice sheets."

"We can't figure out what it is," the watch officer said. "But it seems to cover the whole surface of the ocean about twenty miles south of us. Maybe an ice shelf broke off?"

It certainly looked like ice: a solid mass picked up by radar floating on the surface of the ocean. It was too big to be an ice shelf though: drifting this far north, such a vast shelf would surely have been broken up in the swell and by the strong current into smaller components. There were gaps, it was true, fissures that seemed to run through it. But if it were solid ice, that would spell trouble: the ship was not fitted out as a breaker.

"Send out the drone," said the captain. "Let's get a closer look."

Twenty minutes later, the Mantis UAV launched from the upper deck of the ship, skimming south towards the mystery obstacle. It only took the rotary wing drone half an hour to close in on the object, by which time all the senior officers were gathered around the monitor to see what it might be.

The first images were blurry: the shelf seemed ragged and half submerged. It was white, but not as white as an ice shelf should have been.

"Zoom in closer," Takahashi ordered.

The drone swooped in, skimming at about 100 feet above the phenomenon. It seemed far less solid at this close range, with sea water clearly visible in the frequent gaps between the mosaic of pieces that made up the whole.

"Down further," the captain ordered, squinting and leaning in.

As the drone hit an altitude of fifty feet, there was a sharp collective intake of breath.

"Is that... are those bodies?" said the first mate, his hand coming up to his mouth.

Takahashi nodded slowly. "I think they are." He caught his own hand shaking and put it behind his back, afraid of showing his shock to his subordinates.

The drone was moving slowly now, almost hovering at a standstill as the operator's grip loosened on the joystick.

"They don't have any heads," the operator said, staring at the screen. "Do you see any heads? Is that just the angle?"

"No," growled the captain. "They don't have heads. None of them. Bring it down closer."

The operator brought the drone down to 20 feet above the ocean's surface. The bodies were clearly visible now: headless, limbs entangled, covered in hoar-frost and half frozen to each other in patterns that resembled giant ice crystals. They were all pale, no doubt bled out by the decapitations. The crew sat in stunned silence, unable to find the words to describe what they were thinking.

"Pull up!" the captain suddenly commanded. "Up!"

The drone operator pulled the joystick back and the small craft ascended. The captain was breathing heavily, and the color had drained from his own face. He had seen blood and viscera on a huge scale on this very ship, but this was something entirely different. He reached for his water bottle with both shaking hands.

Now that the drone was back at five hundred feet, the observers could take in the sheer scale of this raft of human bodies.

"That must be twenty miles across," said the first mate.

"More," said the chief engineer.

"How many people would that take..."

"Millions."

"Where did they all come from?" said the first mate, but even as he said it, he knew the answer.

"The aliens," said Takahashi. "The aliens did this. Took the heads and threw away everything else that they didn't need."

· | ·

Joe had quickly become obsessed with what was now being promoted as Mayor Domo Television Inc, or MDTV. Within a few hours of that first tweet, a YouTube channel had sprung into life, while all the social media platforms that the citizens of the new realm had been ordered to subscribe to were filling up with news flashes, photos and video clips from the White House. Almost instantly, the English butler had become the internet's greatest-ever online influencer. The alien queen's freshly minted subjects, holed up in their homes, swiftly resorted to their old habit of endlessly swiping their screens for the latest updates.

OMG!!! Up to 3 million followers now! Some as far away as Singapore and Australia. Shows there's still life at least—and Internet—out there!!!

Five minutes later:

Stay tuned! Interview with Her Maj coming up tonight, after she's fed!! Gonna tell us what she knows about other alien species that landed round the world! How cool is that?!

"You getting any idea what's actually going on in the rest of the world?" said Ed. He had seen messages posted from different countries, even more misspelled than usual by panicked people reaching out for any information about what was going on, or what they should be doing.

"Where is everyone?" pleaded one Twitter user in Iceland.

"I'm terrfied can't find my family," said a man in Burkina Faso, together with pictures of his missing relatives. *"I know they didnt go in the ships. Peease pleese help!!"*

"I saw something in the alley," said a girl in Houston. *"It ate the nighbor's dog don't know what it was but it was big"*

There was no response from Darkman. Ed glanced at the lanky figure hunched over his Toughbook, headphones clamped to his head. He walked over to tap him on the shoulder. When he saw the screen of the laptop, he understood why Darkman was silently transfixed.

"What is that? What's the ICR?" he said, reading the Twitter account name.

Darkman slid the headphones back. "Institute for Cetacean Research," he said. "The agency that runs Japan's whaling program."

"Are those... are those *bodies*?" said Ed, screwing up his eyes. Joe was standing beside him now, peering closer at the drone video footage.

Darkman nodded. "I guess the ETs took the heads, then when they were off our radar, they just ducked south and dumped the ballast before blasting off into space again."

The three men stood in silence for a long time, as the footage played itself over and again.

"That's gotta be... how many bodies?" said Joe, eventually.

Darkman shook his head. "Hard to say. Millions. Tens, maybe a hundred million. How many went on the ships?"

"And that's just what this one drone saw," whispered Ed. "Oh my god..."

But Darkman had already toggled away, looking for sites that might give updated satellite images of this new human geographical formation that had replaced Antarctica's vanished ice shelves.

Ed and Joe immediately began scrolling through their own phones in search of more images.

"ICR is trending," said Ed. "All seems to be the same footage though."

"Oh shit, look at this," said Joe.

"Something new from the whalers?"

"No," said Joe. "The queen is going out hunting."

• | •

@MajorDomo was livestreaming the event, like it was the Met Gala or some red carpet Hollywood blow-out. Dalrymple was dressed up in traditional British fox-hunting garb: scarlet jacket, beige jodhpurs and black boots with a velveteen-covered helmet, looking every inch the English country gent that he had always served. Rains' bodyguards—who now appeared to have completely switched allegiance to the Queen's man—were dressed in a motley array of uniforms and combat gear, every inch the ruling militia. The camera showed them gathering on the gravel in front of the White House, drinking whiskey served by a flunkey on a silver platter, as several horses were led up for the hunters to ride.

"Look at these mighty beasts," Dalrymple said to the camera. "Donated by a lady in Maryland after I tweeted out that I needed some horseflesh to join the hunt. That lady's not getting eaten by the queen, I can tell you that. So if you people out there want to donate to the cause, come to the White House tomorrow and let me know what you have. We're especially looking for chefs, you know. Desperate need of some good cooking. But look…" he pointed up at the sky. "I've also got my own drone operator. Turn the camera… that's Gary from Frederick, worked on some documentaries about mountaineering, I think. Used to be CIA too—oops, not supposed to say that, am I Gary? C'mon, wave for the camera… oh he can't, might crash his drone…."

There was a shout from the front doors of the White House. "She's coming out! Everyone stand back!"

The camera swung around to the door and caught a couple of the Major Domo's henchmen scuttling for cover. Behind them emerged the ever-surreal figure of the Queen, towering over the humans around her, head darting back and forth as she took in the strange new planet she found herself upon: more agile now, as though recovered from whatever confinement her journey had imposed on her. Her carapace now sported five new heads, the trophies reaped from her encounter with President Bradley's Secret Service detail. The horses whinnied and shied away as she emerged into the sunlight.

Dalrymple went up close to her, the only one apparently unfazed by her presence. The camera caught his face, lingered a minute on the glazed look in his eyes as he and his mistress communicated through whatever device had been implanted in his skull. The exchange was fleeting. His eyes came back into focus and a slight smile played on his lips.

"Okay, everybody, listen up. Saddle up and follow me. We're going to ride down to the Mall and pick up some of the zombies on the way. Can't ride without a pack now, can't we? I know you guys can probably all ride from your days doing Special Ops shit in the Middle East, but I'm afraid it's English style here, not western…"

There were some muttered curses from his huntsman, but they were cut off by a sudden screeching sound. Dalrymple pivoted to see what was happening, and the camera swiveled with him, catching the Queen standing over a pile of thrashing horse legs.

"Oh shit, she's eating one of the fucking horses," Dalrymple said into the camera, giggling and holding his hand over his gaping mouth. He turned to one of the bodyguards, who was staring in disgust. "Looks like you're walking, Boydsy! That one was yours, wasn't it?"

The remaining riders swung into their saddles and set off at a trot across Lafayette Square, then turned right down 15th Street. The cameraman was left standing on the driveway but the coverage instantly switched to the drone operated by Gary, the ex-CIA man from Frederick, who had clearly decided to parlay his talents for a place in the Queen's entourage. He was skilled too: the camera skimmed along next to the hunting party, which stopped outside the eastern gate. Dalrymple bowed his head as though in concentration and a couple of minutes later, around 50 zombies came trotting out of the grounds and settled in around the riders and the Queen. The alien examined them briefly as if they might be food, but then appeared to lose interest.

They trotted down to the Mall. The horses, spooked by the presence of the huge alien, were already tugging at the bit as they came out onto the huge, deserted stretch of lawn, still littered with broken tents and debris from the exodus.

"Look at all this shit," said Dalrymple in disgust. "This has got to be cleared up. Uhelsky, make sure to get some zombies down here and start cleaning up, alright? It's disgusting."

"Roger that," said one of the other riders, his face almost obscured by his military helmet, beard, and aviator shades.

"Now," said Dalrymple. He pulled out a small brass hunting horn and blew into it. A wet, strangled sound came out.

"Fuck it," he said, tossing it into the trash on the ground. "Let's ride!" he shouted, and broke into a canter toward the Monument. The Queen, sensing that the hunt was on, lurched into her own gallop, followed by the horsemen and the pack of zombies, most of them naked but some still wearing shreds of clothing that trailed in the wind as the hunting party barreled down the Mall.

"Nobody goes outside until that *thing* is back in the White House," said BB, staring at her screen.

"As fucking if," muttered Joe.

"And keep away from all the windows and doors. Pull the drapes and keep the lights down. If they're still out there at nightfall, only watch your devices under a blanket. Not the slightest hint that there's anyone in this building."

They spent the next fifteen minutes going through the house, making sure the curtains in every room were not only closed but tucked in tight, held down by chairs or beds. Then, when they were sure no light leakage could betray them, they crept back like fugitives to Darkman's Toshiba, to watch the ultimate in reality TV.

"Where are they?" said BB, leaning in. The hunting party was now galloping over open green fields, the drone expertly zipping between riders: it closed in on Dalrymple, a manic expression on his face and tears running down his cheeks from the wind, then skirted back to the queen, out ahead of the pack. Even watching the monster from this distance was enough to send a shiver down BB's spine.

"East Potomac Golf Links," said Darkman.

"There's a golf course in downtown DC?" said BB.

"Haines Point. Hidden away on a little peninsula just behind the Jefferson Memorial," Darkman said.

"Look at that thing," said Joe. "She must be clocking, what, thirty-five? Forty? Never once slows down. You'd never escape something like that."

Suddenly, the queen seemed to speed up even more. The drone spun a little higher and turned in the direction of whatever had caught her attention.

A group of people were out on the golf course.

"Oh shit," said Joe. "What the fuck are they doing out there?"

"Playing golf, looks like," said Darkman.

It was true: a group of young people, mostly men but with at least one woman, were standing on the green with clubs. A bright red Suburban was parked on the grass, an ice cooler and mini grill perched on its tailgate, like they were at a Sunday football game. One of the men was pulling cold beers from the back. They seemed to have no idea what was approaching them.

"What the fuck are they playing golf for at a time like this?" said Ed.

Darkman shrugged. "People do strange shit in war zones. Once saw a guy gardening in the middle of a full-on street battle."

The people on the screen finally seemed to hear the whine of the drone's motor and looked round to see what it was. That was when they spotted the giant ball of alien limbs hurtling towards them. The drone operator caught the expression of the man closest to it: utter shock and disbelief. The figure at the tailgate dropped his beer.

And then she was on them.

The first guy was tossed high in the air as the queen slammed into him, landing with his back twisted at a sickening angle. He did not move again. The next victim threw up his arms, but the queen crushed him underfoot. She then came to a dead stop in the middle of the remaining golfers. An arm—or was it a leg?—shot out and punched a hole straight through the midriff of the young woman. At the same time, another limb reached out and dragged another of the young men in towards her palpating beak. He had the presence of mind to lash out with his nine iron, but it made no difference. She ripped his head off with one bite.

The last remaining golfer—the one who had been fetching drinks—finally found his feet and started running for the trees. The queen saw him but was already gorging on his golfing partner. Instead of giving chase, she watched as the pack of zombies streamed past and chased down the terrified youth, dragging him back to where she was enjoying her human picnic.

By now, Dalrymple and his riders had reigned in some twenty yards from the queen, watching in fascinated horror as she feasted.

The final survivor, held by the zombies, also stared at the grisly picnic being played out before his eyes. The drone's camera zoomed in his face. All the color had drained from his cheeks, but he couldn't take his eyes off the monster, like a fly caught in a spider's web. When the queen had devoured the first man, one of her arms shot out and dragged over the girl, who was curled in a fetal position, arms over her ruptured midriff. It was not clear whether she was dead already. The alien bit into her thigh and its face was lacquered in arterial spray.

Thankfully, the young man being held by the zombies passed out at that point.

The drone swung over to Dalrymple, who was struggling to control his terrified horse. His face was white as a sheet, but when he saw the drone, he forced a smile for the camera.

"Well, that was fucking mental, wasn't it?" He looked at the rider next to him, as though for reassurance. "Good team building exercise though, wasn't it, Jeff?"

Jeff was staring, his mouth hanging open, and did not answer.

BB turned away from the screen. "Turn that shit off," she ordered Darkman.

Darkman nodded, gently closed the laptop.

"We have got to get the fuck out of here," said BB. "Where the hell is Trenton?"

· | ·

The slight click of the bedroom door being unlocked snapped Trenton out of his sleep. No idea what time it was, but the moon was still up. In the other bed, Elspeth was breathing rapidly in tortured dreams. No lights illuminated the troubled sleepers of the Watergate building, but the moonlight caught the slow turn of the door handle. Trenton reached for a gun that wasn't there.

A figure slipped in and held up its hand in the darkness. "It's me," whispered Rains.

"You're lucky your guys took my Glock," Trenton hissed back.

Rains closed the door behind him and pulled out a small flashlight, a red filter muting its glow.

"We need to talk," said Rains. "Wake her up."

Trenton shook Elspeth. She slowly came to, gasping when she saw the figure standing by the door.

"Lester? What time is it?"

"Just before four. All my men are asleep."

"Don't blame them," Elspeth slurred, her voice drugged with tiredness.

"I need you to wake up now, Elspeth. We don't have much time."

She shook her head, rubbed her face. "Okay, okay. What is it? Are we leaving?"

"No," said Rains. "But we have to get ready. Farmer One will be here soon."

That brought her fully awake.

Rains stepped over and perched on the side of Trenton's bed. "You read the book, didn't you?"

"*My Life Among the Apemen*?" Elspeth said. "Sure. Most of it." Trenton nodded in agreement.

"So you remember your great-great grandmother?" said Rains. "Inali?"

"Wait," Elspeth said, scrambling to get her brain in gear. She'd skim-read the book while drinking complementary champagne on an overnight transatlantic flight. She sincerely hoped her life didn't depend on that knowledge right now. "The Cherokee woman you married?"

"Exactly. Farmer Three and I implanted the next in line into a fetus from the Cherokee nation. I was the one who told her what she really was."

There was a pause, as much for Elspeth to dredge up the details from the book as for Rains to reflect on his lost love. "You guys were... happy together, I seem to remember."

"She was probably the only woman I ever loved, aside from my mother and sisters," said Rains. "She was smart, funny, emotionally honest and... wild. A free spirit. She grieved the loss of her family but embraced all the opportunities that extreme longevity had to offer. The perfect marriage of being a farmer and a human. She was the best of our line."

"So why did they kill her?" said Trenton.

"She had a plan to leave Earth. And that is absolutely forbidden."

Inali had been a bold woman. In her youth, around the time of the American Revolution, she had left the Cherokee lands in the southeast and traveled the continent with Rains, leaving the cities of the east behind and crisscrossing the soon-to-be annihilated nations they encountered. For Rains, that time had been blessed: just her and the wilderness, far from the horrors he had witnessed in the settled world. Inali was at home in this untrammeled world, yet keen to learn from his long experience. For years, they disappeared off any map known to man.

They had two children during these footloose years. The first time, Inali wanted to keep the child, a little boy, but Rains was troubled: he knew that the extraordinary qualities a farmer enjoyed could only be implanted, not inherited. Inali might love their child, but he would wither and die, his germ line simply becoming fodder for the Ma'ut harvest, whenever that came. Throughout her pregnancy, he begged her not to become too attached to the child. In the end, they agreed to leave it with a band of Sioux in an area that would one day become Dakota, but at the time was home to the mighty horse civilizations. The second child, a girl, was left with a French-Canadian trapper living with his native wife in a log cabin in Saskatchewan, together with enough gold to ensure the family never wanted for anything.

When, decades later, Rains introduced Inali to the other farmers at a gathering in Buenos Aires in 1862, she charmed them. Farmer Three, who had suggested the "match" during that meeting in Toulouse, was very taken with her.

"This one is our masterpiece, I do believe," he told Rains at their ceremonial dinner in the sumptuous supper rooms of the Plaza Lavalle. Inali had not blushed: she just stared him in the eye and flashed her teeth in a smile. Perhaps she found him attractive: for sure, Farmer Three exerted the magnetic charm of a psychopath, the first of his lineage to have wrapped the brutal code of the Ma'ut with a veneer of human consciousness. Supple and slender in his build, he had the aristocratic bearing of a prince of the Nile.

"Will there be more of us?" she asked. "Or shall I be the last of our line?"

Three shrugged. "Who knows how long we shall have to wait? At the moment, I believe our numbers are sufficient. Why, do you grow bored of our friend Barbegal here?"

Rains had stiffened at this flirtatious slight, but knew better than to challenge Three. Luckily, Inali just laughed. "Never," she said, reaching out and taking Rains' hand. "We have lived like Adam and Eve in our untrammeled paradise. I could happily turn my back on this world with Lucius by my side."

"How charming," drawled Three. His face was often without affect, making it difficult to read what he might be feeling, if he was feeling anything at all. "I'm afraid I will have to put your idyll on hold, however. I need Barbegal back in Europe. The population is expanding rapidly, and the scientists appear to be making some interesting advances. I want a full report."

"You could come with me," said Rains. "I will show you Rome and Prague. They are really quite charming."

"No," said Three. "I want someone watching the North. And Inali can cross the lines between settlers and natives with ease. This region will become important in the development of the species, after they have finished their war. I feel our mission is going to accelerate in the coming century. Maybe it will even culminate."

That caught the attention of all ten farmers sitting round the table. The harvest was what they had all worked towards, for centuries, but none knew when it would come, or what would become of them afterwards. Farmer One had always insisted he had no knowledge of the Ma'ut's plans for them—if indeed they had bothered to make any for their disposable servants. Every time any of the farmers met, it was always the subject of intense speculation.

"Everyone is to stay in their designated zone until I give orders otherwise," said Three.

Orders, it turned out, were not something that Inali was inclined to heed. Within a year, she had shown up at Rain's elegant townhouse in the Bois de Boulogne. Two months later, she was pregnant again. This time, she was desperate to keep the child: if the harvest was anywhere near at hand, the child itself could be swept up in it. She was no longer the inexperienced young Cherokee girl under Rains' sway. She had seen the world and had grown to envy the bond she saw between mother and child.

Rains insisted. "I fear we have made you too human, my dear," he told her. "This will destroy you if you keep it."

They fought, but in the end, she relented. Rains took the child far to the north, to a small town in Scotland. He promised Inali he would keep track of the child and all her offspring, so she would at least know what became of her bloodline.

"That was my great grandmother?" said Elspeth. Rains nodded, head bowed slightly as if he might feel some slight hint of shame at abandoning his own child.

"I had to do it. For her sake," he said.

Their relationship became strained after that. Inali returned to New York and traveled widely, as Europeans spread out across the plains and wiped out all trace of the world she and Rains had once known together. She spent much of her time at a ranch in Dakota, isolated from the world and close to her own kind, looking for any hint of her features in the young people she met. She lost touch with Rains over the years, until one day in January 1948, when Rains received a telephone call at the villa he was living in on the Amalfi Coast.

After all the years of silence, there was no small talk.

"I have it, Lucius," she said.

"You have what?"

"A way out of here. When the harvest comes. Meet me in London, at our old place."

Rains knew it was unwise to talk further over the telephone. The next day, he flew to London from Rome, and waited three days in a book-lined apartment he kept in Bloomsbury, a place they had stayed during her last trip to Europe almost a century before.

The package arrived on the fourth day. It was postmarked Albuquerque, New Mexico. Inside was a cardboard box containing a small metallic globe: a marvelous object, cerulean blue and with gold buttons on it, each etched with a strange symbol. There was a note attached.

My dear Lucius, please keep this safe. It is our key to leaving this planet when the time comes. I know you have grown tired of the tedious affairs of humans, and don't follow the news. Did you notice the little war they just had? So I'm quite sure the news of the "flying saucer" in New Mexico escaped your attention. I found it quite intriguing, and so I went to investigate. The government here tried to keep it secret, but you know me, when I get something in my head, I cannot let it rest. So I looked into it, and using some of my Maut wiles and my obviously extensive feminine charms, I managed to gain access to the facility where the remains were being guarded. There was a bit of a hullabaloo in the local press, but the Air Force insisted it was just a weather balloon. Guess what, my dear? It wasn't!

It was a space ship. A real space ship! Not the Maut, thank goodness, but a species they had experimented on thousands of years before they ever came to Earth. Like every other experiment, these creatures failed to revive the Goweetha, but their sentience and intelligence were such that they managed to persuade the Maut not to eliminate them.

Instead, they are used by the Maut as ambassadors, to settle disputes between different civilizations and relay messages from their overlords. Seems the Maut are not very good at diplomacy!! Whodathunk? They have also managed to persuade the Maut to spare a small proportion of any species they harvest: they argue that this allows the population to regenerate on the off-chance they may prove useful to the Maut in future. But in reality it is because they themselves almost suffered extermination at the hand of the machines, and were horrified.

They have argued for a safe haven to be established here on Earth, and when the time comes—and they believe it will be soon – humans will be safe on Hawaii. I beg of you, my darling, if you know where any of our children's children might be, let them know where they can shelter. I know it's terribly human of me, but I can't bear the thought of them being processed by this indifferent machine.

Now, for the really interesting part of my little adventure. There were three crew members on the ship that crashed. Two died upon impact but the third survived and was still alive when I managed to infiltrate the top secret facility: thank god we farmers can put humans into a hypnotic state. I'd never really had to use that trick much before, but boy is it ever handy. This creature told me the three crew members had defied the Maut—and their own species — to warn humans of what was in store for them: a pointless slaughter which only a few would survive. Their mission triggered panic among their own kind — they operate under strict rules in order to avoid any backlash from the Maut. They pursued the renegades, and it was they who shot down the craft. It limped to Earth, but only one of them survived the crash.

The survivor told me a whole bunch of fascinating things which I will impart to you as soon as I see you. But the most important was the artifact I have enclosed here. It was concealed under the alien's skin. It is a transponder: if activated, it was meant to lead any rescue party to the distressed space craft. Obviously they couldn't use it in the event because it was their own kind that shot them down. But it told me if we activate it, in principle one of their ships will come to rendezvous with us. It may not work—they were after all renegades from their own species, and anyway, Earth is a designated no-go zone for all life forms until after the harvest. So don't activate it now, even though I have included the activation sequence on the last page of this letter. Also, if you get the sequence wrong it will detonate and level ten city blocks in your immediate vicinity. So keep it safe, dear Lucius, until we are reunited. I am about to leave and make my way to you, but have entrusted this package to a courier I have used before.

I hope to see you soon my love. It has been way too long, and I believe we can rebuild our lives together once we get off this doomed planet and discover all that the universe has to offer! It will be like old times!

All my heart

Inali x

"You have an alien transponder from the Roswell crash," Trenton said, his voice a deadpan. He stared at Rains, still trying to wrap his head around it: not just that the mother of all alien conspiracy theories was actually true, but that it might provide them a way out of this hell.

"*Had*," said Rains.

"What do you mean, *had?*" said Trenton.

"Inali never showed up at the flat in Bloomsbury. I waited three weeks, then had to conclude that something must have happened to her. She had obviously been the first of us to respond to the crash of the spacecraft—otherwise the alien would have warned her that other farmers had already visited—but I doubt Farmer Three was far behind her. It is my belief they caught up with her. Certainly they tracked the package."

"They got it back?" said Elspeth.

"No, but they ransacked the London apartment. Shortly after I left, the woman I employed to look after it let me know the place had been turned over, top to toe. Not a burglary: nothing was gone. They were looking for the transponder."

"But you'd taken it with you?" said Trenton.

"I knew once Inali failed to show up that something had gone wrong. So I hid it at one of my own safe houses."

"You have safe houses?"

"Of course. Dozens of them, all over the world," said Rains. "Some are known to the other farmers, some I have kept from them. I put the transponder in one of the secret ones, in a little village called Clover Mills in Virginia..."

"That's where I was attacked by that man, the harvester!" blurted out Elspeth.

"Exactly," said Rains. "I'd had that place for more than a century. Generation after generation of that family worked for me. I kept them in a mild state of enthrallment — enough that they would never question my presence, but otherwise they could live a perfectly normal lifestyle. I just made sure they never sold the place, and that if anyone should ever come asking for me there, they would contact me immediately. It started out as a blacksmith's and ended up a bicycle shop."

"So that's why they raided it and killed the bike rental guy?" Elspeth said. "They were looking for the transponder?"

Rains nodded. "After I met you that first time, Elspeth, I tracked down the descendant of another of our children. He was living in Toronto, the last in line of the little girl we left with the couple in their cabin in Saskatchewan. I gave him the same coordinates as you. Seems he showed up a couple of days before you. I was very careful...

or at least I thought I'd been. Somehow, they found him through me and followed him to the bike shop...."

"The policeman that day... he said a customer had been killed with the bike shop owner," said Elspeth.

"That was Michel. Michel Valois. Like you, he thought I was a madman when I first showed up. Who wouldn't? But when Moscow happened, he also came looking for me."

"So who exactly has the transponder now?" said Trenton.

"Farmer One," said Rains. "Those were his men who raided the bike shop and staked out any other visitors. You were very lucky to have survived that encounter, Elspeth."

"Where's Farmer One now? Can we get the damn thing back?"

Rains glanced at the window. The first tinge of dawn was rising over the river.

"He'll be back here soon. He would have probably killed me sooner, but he needed me to oversee the arrival of the queen here— her species are an important vassal for the Ma'ut. While the aliens who crashed at Roswell are the A.I.'s diplomats, the queen's species are very effective killers. The credible threat of force, so to speak. So she had to be taken care of. Farmer One had to go manage a rather delicate landing in New York, but he'll be back soon. This business is unfinished, and he is, essentially, a machine that cannot allow any loose ties to remain. Even if the Ma'ut don't officially care anymore."

"So he wants to kill you?" said Elspeth. She could feel her body starting to shake. Just when she thought the situation couldn't get any worse, she realized there was no bottom to this new world she inhabited.

"He does. But your experience with the harvester made me realize we have some small advantage. He will not know you and Trenton cannot be put under his thrall. It's not much of an advantage, but it might help. And I think I may have found another thing he will not be expecting."

• | •

"A'right people, all my little subjects of the realm!"

The Major Domo was standing in front of a large set of double doors somewhere inside the White House, grinning at the livestream camera. Without warning, his expression shifted from excited to solemn with schizoid speed. "Gotta say, I felt a bit bad for those poor people on the golf course yesterday. Nasty business that. Thought about it quite a lot last night when I was sipping a wee dram of the president's excellent Macallen. But I did *try* to warn them. Just goes to show, follow me on Twitter...*or else*! Ha ha!" And he was grinning maniacally again, all memories of the grisly killings dismissed.

"So anyway, as promised, Her Maj is going to grant us a quick audience and answer some of the questions you've been sending me on Insta. So I'm just going to knock and very gently go on in ... " He addressed his cameraman: "Come on Rick, she won't do anything to you if you're with me." He flashed another cheesy gameshow host smile. "*I think!*"

"Ooh look, there she is..." he said quietly into the camera, which was visibly shaking in the hands of the terrified White House cameraman who had been pressganged into Dalrymple's service. After a second, he managed to focus on the massive form slumped in the corner of the room. The queen roused herself slowly, drawing up to her massive full size.

"Fuck me," said Dalrymple. "I'm just never gonna get used to that." He stood stock still facing her, apparently communicating in whatever frequency she used. Then she turned her face to the window and peered out.

"Okay, she's agreed to give us a couple of minutes, so I'd better be quick. He pulled out his phone. "Right, first question from Andrea in Bethesda. She says, 'What has happened to the rest of the world? Has it been taken over by other alien species or what?' Good question, Andrea, I'll put it to Her Maj."

Another minute of silence. The camera stayed focused on the queen, then moved to Dalrymple, who stood there with his eyelids shut, flickering. The cameraman, apparently unable to rip his gaze away, turned back to the monster. Abruptly, Dalrymple was speaking again.

"Right, bit complicated, 'cos it turns out there's a lot of alien lifeforms out there. Most of them are in fact some kind of offshoot of the same experiment we are currently a part of. This A.I. has been trying for millennia to reincarnate its old masters, but so far hasn't got it quite right. *So fingers crossed for humanity, eh?*"

The camera suddenly swung violently to the floor and ceiling. Over the audio feed, Dalrymple could be heard trying to calm the cameraman.

"Steady Rick, she's just moving around to look at me better," he said. The camera settled again. This time, the Major Domo was standing between the cameraman and the beast.

"So anyway," Dalrymple went on, his polished butler's diction fading ever more into his coarser south London accent. "There's been all these experiments and the queen's species was one of them: the Ma'ut tried upgrading the consciousness of her people—well not really people, but you know what I mean... didn't really work in terms of resuscitating the dead master race, but the Ma'ut found that the queen's lot were pretty useful now they could be plugged into its machinery and systems, so they've been using them as mercenaries ever since. You know, 'fuck with us and we'll drop an army full of these things on your planet!' Gotta be pretty convincing."

"So some of the other species were experiments like her and us, and they realized what was coming down the pipe and did a runner, or escaped after the Ma'ut lost interest in them. And some of them— and I thought this bit was quite interesting—are kind of rogue A.I.'s themselves. Seems the Maut ran experiments on its own units of artificial consciousness, but they didn't make the grade either, so they were scrapped. They managed to leg it, but there's this one group of A.I.s that found their consciousness was fading, bit like having Alzheimer's I guess, so they come to the places where the Maut is doing their experiments and they suck up some of the leftovers, to get a hit of organic consciousness. Bit like taking a hit of a drug, apparently. They particularly love kids' consciousness—more joyful than us depressed adults. No surprise there, eh?"

"She said this thing, not sure if it's a poem or what, but it went like this: '*In the dream salons of Exbusqid, the robots pore in fleeting delight over the childhood memories of extinct species.*' Weird, eh, to think something that looks like her could know songs and poems and stuff. Oh well."

He paused, counting off fingers to check he hadn't missed anything. "Yeah, so there was a regional rundown—seems most people in southeast Asia will be used for this kind of "crystal meth" consciousness that the robots get high off of. The Chinese will largely be uploaded into gaming systems and will be lifelike extras in reality video games for all eternity. Most of Europe will just be used as converts to some alien religion."

He frowned. "Is that what she said? Yeah, I'm pretty sure she said 'converts.' Sometimes this thing in my head seems to glitch a bit," he said, tapping the livid pink scar on his shaved cranium, which was already sprouting a dark fuzz.

"Okay then, on to the next question... lots of you asking what happens now..." He slipped into his trance again for a minute.

"Okay, easy one there," he said, his eyes snapping open. "The answer is, not a lot really. You see, we're so used to stuff happening all the time that we've become addicted to it. *But listen up, people!* Your entire civilization has just collapsed, right? What happens now? You try to stay alive, okay, to *not just die.* Because there's a couple of million or so of you out there in the queen's realm: the whole of DC and Virginia, Maryland and bits of ... wait, what's that one above Maryland? Pennsylvania? Yeah, sorry, I'm a bit shit at American states. But *try* to stay alive. I know a lot of you are going to die, it's gonna be rough with no shops and what not, but a lot of people would have just died, anyway. Life can go, and we *want* it to go on. Look, say the queen eats maybe ten people a week, that's not *that* many overall. The spawn will eat maybe one or two a week each once they're on solids, which is after the first month, then about half the number that the queen eats in their first year. I know, there's no hospitals or easy food supplies anymore, so that will raise mortality a bit. But the queen has told me she wants to keep her flock healthy and flourishing, so we'll figure something out, don't worry too much."

He flashed another faux TV commercial-smile at the camera and held both thumbs up in front of his chest.

"You got to stay *positive*, okay, people?"

• | •

Ed felt sick after watching the Major Domo's latest report. It was a bright morning, and he found he wanted nothing more than to feel the sun on his face. He knew he ought to stay inside and watch the rest of the broadcast, if only out of a journalistic duty to bear witness. But he just couldn't bring himself to do it. At least he knew that while the butler was talking to his queen live on TV, the monster wouldn't be out here hunting down humans.

He stepped out on to the churned-up remains of the lawn. The sound of spring birdsong cleared his head. Most of nature wasn't out whack, only the bit where humans were being downgraded to livestock, or extras in an alien video game.

Joe stepped out onto the grass next to him.

"Nice morning," he said, pulling out a packet of Marlboros.

"Didn't know you smoked," said Ed.

"I don't. Used to occasionally dip into Tony's weed, but never tobacco. Found these in the street, though. Figured, why not?"

"Why not indeed?" said Ed. He reached over and Joe held up the crumpled pack. Ed lit one and drew in a long breath.

"Been twenty years since I had one of these. Tastes like shit, but hits the spot," he said, exhaling.

"Don't have to worry about dying of cancer or heart disease anymore," said Joe.

"Nope. The queen's got that covered," said the older man.

"No 401K. No IRS to worry about. Just don't get eaten."

"The streamlined American Dream," said Ed. They both laughed, harder than the joke merited. Ed choked on the smoke from his cigarette and was coughing when Joe raised a hand and stepped down to the sidewalk, straining to hear something.

When Ed stopped coughing, he too could make out a faint electrical whine. In streets devoid of traffic, sound traveled much further, so it was hard to tell where the noise was coming from. He stood next to Joe, peering down the street.

At first, they thought it was some kind of military vehicle, with a handful of people walking next to it. It was round, metallic looking and had a glass dome perched on top. It took a moment for them to realize the thing was *floating*, and the people were attached to it by some kind of hose.

"What *is* that?" whispered Ed.

"I don't know, but we should get back in the house," said Joe, backing up toward the door.

The vehicle was moving down the street at the speed of the people walking all around it. Ever the journalist, Ed pulled out his phone and zoomed the camera in on it: the thing was a dark gunmetal gray and was floating about three feet off the ground. And it was coming their way.

"Ed! *Ed!*" hissed Joe as the other man stood there, staring at the approaching procession. "Get back here now. That's some alien shit."

Slowly, Ed took a few steps back. But the people attached to the machine had already spotted him.

"Mister! Mister! Help us. Get us off this thing," hollered an old white guy in loose-fitting clothes.

"Help us please!" called a young Black woman next to him. "I got a kid, she's only three. She'll be looking for me. I gotta get back to my baby. This thing got me this morning when I was out looking for food."

Ed stopped retreating. Now that the thing was closer, only about thirty yards away, he could see that one of the hoses was connected to a dead body. Or rather, the husk of a dead body: it was more like a skinful of bones being dragged down the street.

"Mister, I gotta get back to my little girl," the woman closest to him was pleading. "This thing, it's sucking the life out of me. I can feel it. Look at these people!"

It was true: the others all looked haggard, their faces shrunken under sagging skin. The old man with the baggy clothes held up his bony hands for Ed to see. "Look at me, man, I'm only 27! I'm younger than you. Get an ax and hack this shit off of me for god's sake!"

He lifted up his flapping shirt to reveal where the hose was attached to the side of his stomach. The intake disappeared cleanly beneath the loose folds of skin, just above his bony ridge of his hip: no blood or ooze, it seemed to have docked with surgical precision.

"How long has it had you?" said Ed. He was filming the scene on his phone as he spoke.

"You gonna post this shit on Insta?" screamed the man. "Stop fucking around and get this thing offa me!"

That raised a chorus of cries from the others—there were seven of them in total, Joe counted, excluding the bag of bones. Ed lowered his phone and backed away. "Okay, wait there, I'll see what I've got."

The machine halted, as if patiently waiting for him to return.

BB and Darkman were at the door too now. Ed pushed past them, but BB grabbed him by the arm.

"Ed, you are *not* going back out there. That thing will grab you just like it did them."

"I can't let them just die like that," said Ed, pushing past her into the house.

BB, Joe, and Darkman stood by the door, looking on in horror at the people attached to the machine, trying to block out their cries for help: the living and the dead, staring back at each other across the abyss.

BB grabbed a rifle from inside the doorway. "All you people, I'm going to need you to duck down," she shouted.

She aimed at the glass dome and fired off a round. The sound of the ricochet twanged down the street. The glass dome appeared unscathed.

"Shit," BB swore. She fired several more shots that glanced off the machine.

Ed came back a minute later, armed with a small hatchet.

"Ed, I am begging you," said BB. "An ax isn't even going to dent that thing."

"She's right Ed, you go near that thing, you'll just be another body attached," said Darkman.

Ed shook his head. "We all gotta die sometime, I guess," he said.

It was the young mother he went up to first. Ed hefted the ax over his shoulder and brought it down as hard as he could on the hose. Behind him, the shrunken old-young man was begging. "Buddy, you gotta do me next, this thing's sucking the life out of me." The young mother was crying. "Whack it harder, please, I can't stand this thing in me anymore!"

The ax bounced off without leaving as much as a scratch. The woman clasped her hands in front of her face and wailed. "Oh mercy god, please..."

Ed raised the ax again, but it clattered from his hands. The woman screamed as he clasped his side and doubled over. A hose had shot out of the machine and embedded itself just below his ribcage. Ed let out a sound like air being forced from a bag. Through the rush of tears he could see Joe running towards him. He started to hold up a shaky hand but BB had already grabbed Joe.

"He's gone Joe! You go near that thing and you'll be hanging off it too. Get back inside."

Joe stood there, frozen in horror. Ed slowly pulled himself upright and shouted out to him.

"Joe!" His voice was trembling from the shock.

"Oh god," Joe whimpered, hands over his mouth.

The machine started slowly moving forwards. Clearly, it had gauged that no more prey were likely to step into its range.

The woman next to Ed had slumped to her knees, but the hose pulled her, stumbling, back to her feet. Ed stepped up and put his arm around her shoulders to help her along.

"Joe, come a bit closer," Ed called. "Not too close though!"

Joe stepped to the edge of the road. The machine and its human appendages were about twenty yards away now.

"Stop right there," hollered Ed. "Joe, you gotta write the story. People have to know what happened."

"What?" Joe called back.

"You have to tell the world what really happened. About Rains and Trenton and all of us. Otherwise, no one will ever know the truth."

Ed bent down and put his phone on the ground. "I made notes on everything. On my phone. Use them. Write it all up and get it out there, Joe. Make a hardcopy in case they shut down the web. Tell them, Joe, the truth matters!"

Joe stood in the street, breathing hard, not daring to get any closer. "Okay Ed," was all he could muster, though he wasn't sure his editor could hear his cracked voice.

"One last thing," shouted Ed as the procession moved farther away.

"What?" Joe said.

"1234," shouted Ed. "The code for the phone."

"That's the worst..." Ed began, almost smiling, but he couldn't finish. He waited until the machine was far enough away that he could retrieve Ed's cell phone. He picked it up and opened it. Ed saw, and waved. Joe held the phone up and started filming as his old editor held the crying young mother. He filmed until the machine turned a corner and headed off through the streets, scouting for more prey.

"Come on," said BB, standing at Joe's side. "There's nothing we can do for him now. And we have to go. That thing clocked us and our location. We can't stay here a minute longer."

• | •

"You moved!" said Trenton, halting the stopwatch on his phone. "One minute and seventeen seconds."

"Bollocks," swore Elspeth. "This is not going to work."

"Keep practicing," said Trenton. "And remember, it's okay to blink, but not as often as normal. Rains said the average person blinks every fifteen to twenty seconds, but only once every forty-five seconds when they're in the thrall of a Farmer."

"And just how in god's name are we supposed to keep track of the time if we can't check our phones or watches?" shot back Elspeth.

"I know, I know," said Trenton. He blew out his cheeks. "It sucks. But it's the only plan we have right now. Farmer One and his goons could literally show up any minute, and if he thinks he's got us hypnotized they won't be expecting us to do anything when crunch time comes."

Crunch time. Trenton's euphemism for the moment Rains expected them to pretend to be hypnotized, when in reality they would be ready to pull out concealed weapons and gun down Farmer One and whatever paramilitary squad he had with him. It was an insane plan, all the more so since Elspeth had never fired a gun in her life.

Rains had given them detailed instructions on how an "enthralled" human looked and responded. Sometimes their eyes would be shut, which would be too dangerous when the showdown with Farmer One came: eyes open, though, and they would have to make sure not to blink too often, or move their eyes to track whatever was happening around them. As Elspeth was discovering, this was extremely difficult.

"Go again," said Trenton. Elspeth sighed, but nodded. "Start off by walking around," Trenton told her.

Elspeth started pacing the small space of the bedroom they were still locked in. She kept her eyes locked on Trenton, waiting for him to make the slight hand gesture that Rains had shown them, the one that the Farmers used to enthrall humans. Barely more than a flick of the wrist, the right hand moving up from the hip to the shoulder, the thumb and forefinger cocked like a kid impersonating a pistol. As she was turning the edge of the bed, Trenton lifted his hand and she froze.

"That wasn't it," said Trenton. "That was just me scratching my nose. So you just froze for no reason. Plus, you were wobbling anyway."

"Crap," said Elspeth. She'd lost count of how many times she'd run through this ridiculous routine already. "Let me try it from just a standing position at the start. Lester said he'd try and get us in position for their arrival."

Trenton sighed. "Okay, but if we're caught on the hop..." He made the hand gesture and Elspeth froze in front of the TV. He set the stopwatch.

A minute passed. Elspeth didn't move a muscle. Trenton nodded, then reached over for the TV remote and turned it on. The screen filled with the latest production from Major Domo TV: this time, Dalrymple was on the White House lawn with a group of his zombies whom he'd dressed up in garish stage outfits looted from some theater or museum. The Major Domo had them all dancing to *Thriller*, following his lead as Michael Jackson and copying the exaggerated zombie shuffle from the video classic. Dalrymple was beaming madly, sweating and making absurd scary-faces at the camera.

"Your eyes moved," said Trenton, stopping the clock. "You're dead."

"Just look at that abomination," said Elspeth, pointing at the television. "That's not fair, turning that on just when I was doing well."

"I hate to sound all Yoda-like, but there's no 'doing well' and 'fair,' in all this Elspeth," Trenton said. "There's staying stock still, and there's dying."

Elspeth slumped on to the bed. "I can't do this," she said, not for the first time.

There was a knock at the door. Rains came in, glancing furtively over his shoulder.

"Okay," he said, closing the door behind him. "I found out where they were keeping your Glock and Sig Sauer. Here, hide them somewhere in here until the time comes."

"Wait, this is it?" said Trenton. "We're supposed to be using handguns in a Mexican stand-off with Farmer One's guys? They'll have AKs and MP5s at the very least."

"I told you, he's clearly given my men orders not to let me have any access to their guns. This is all I could get. Luckily, I saw where Hector hid them."

"Shit Rains, I don't know," said Trenton, looking at the snub-nosed pistol in his hand. "Those are kind of long odds."

Rains said nothing: clearly he knew Trenton was right.

"Can you not just tell them outright to give you rifles?" said Elspeth. "You're still their boss, aren't you?"

"Nominally," said Rains. "I told Hector to give me an AR-15 this morning. He was very polite and respectful, but refused. Said he had orders. That can only mean Farmer One."

Trenton squeezed his eyes with his fingers. "Are you going to at least tell us what your back-up is, Rains? Because I, for one, would like to think there's a little bit more to our plan than the three of us standing there with two pistols facing a firing squad of alien-spawned psychos armed with AR-15s."

Rains looked at him. "No," he said at last. "I want you to remain focused on the part that you can do. But rest assured, that is where I'm going now. To arrange it all."

"Then why can't you just tell us, Lester? For god's sake," said Elspeth.

Rains stepped to the door. "Operational security. Or just chalk it up to almost two thousand years of not telling humans anything of real value. Now, if you'll excuse me. And hide those guns. If my men find them, then we really are done."

He stepped out, locking the door again behind him.

"I don't think he even has a plan," said Trenton. "He just doesn't want us to lose our shit."

"Great," said Elspeth. "Then we're fucked, Cassius."

She took her pistol and hid it in a closet, underneath the bloodied body armor she had worn to the White House. Then she turned back to Trenton and sighed.

"Okay, your turn to play grandmother's footsteps."

• | •

"Hello! And welcome to another day at Her Majesty's White House! Mental, eh?"

The Major Domo threw out his arms like a carnival barker and flashed his trademark cocaine grin. This morning, he was clad in a splendid military uniform: straight white pants and gray nineteenth century tunic, complete with gold brocade and a white sash. The ensemble was topped off with a black cockade in his cap. Darkman quickly identified it as a West Point dress uniform, something the butler must have dug up from a government storeroom. A major's insignia badge had been stitched on to the left breast, next to a military-style name tag reading "Domo."

It was only nine in the morning, but he was clearly hopped up on something.

"Alright, everybody? After that *amazing* interview with the Queen yesterday—twenty-five million views! You see, there's still plenty of people out there!—I thought you all might want to see the rest of the family," he said, making air quotes around the word "family."

"So today, me and Boydsy here"—he gestured to the bearded man at his side, one of Rains' former henchmen—"we are going to take you into the State Dining Room. Or as we now like to call it—the Pupating Zygote Zone!"

He swung open the doors to a large room where once presidents had entertained visiting heads of state at the kind of ceremonies the Major Domo could only have dreamed of serving in his former life.

The giant walnut table had been pushed to the back of the room, and gilt chairs lay strewn across the floor. Eight lumpy forms could be seen on the floor, a couple of them under the vast dining table. Several raised their heads when the Major Domo and his companions stepped in.

"Ta-dah!" he beamed. "Look how big they're getting. That really big one over there..." he started walking over to the largest of the pupae, which reared up slightly as he approached... "I do believe that's President Bradley, though it's a bit hard to tell at this stage. Here, Rick, come get a close up..."

The cameraman came up and showed a hideous maggot-like creature: two arms, still recognizably human, tried to push the creature's body up from the floor to get closer to the visitors. Other stumpy limbs were starting to sprout further down the torso. The human legs had etiolated and lengthened, but were still clad in the stained suit pants the president had been wearing on the day of his final reception. The face was unidentifiable, knobby and distended, the mouth already bulging out into a half-formed beak.

"Pretty gross, eh?" said Dalrymple. "Still, look at this... point the camera at that table there..." The cameraman did as instructed and focused on a small side table with several heavy ornamental candle sticks arranged on top. They were shaking rhythmically.

"That's his *heartbeat*," said Dalrymple. "Ugly as fuck, but strong as an ox. No disrespect, Mr. President. And Mr. Future King."

He turned and led the cameraman over to the next creature, which lay about five feet away. It was a little smaller than the first, but still bigger than a human.

"And this one might be..." Dalrymple clutched his chin, as though thinking. "Hmm, still got a bit of dyed auburn hair, so could be the Speaker of the House. If she still had her gavel I'd know..." He flashed a silent laugh, mouth wide open like a bad mime.

There was a cry of shock from his companion Boyd. The camera swung to him as he backed away from the pupa they had just filmed.

"Fucker bit my foot!" he shouted. "Look, its teeth went right through the leather."

"He's hungry! He's a growing boy!" said Dalrymple. "Which is lucky, because we have timed this little visit to coincide with their feeding time. *What do they eat?* I hear you ask. Well, aside from Boydsy's combat boots, they're still on liquids. You might have seen some strange machines floating round town recently, right? Well, they're gathering what the Queen likes to call the "life force" that this lot need to grow. Not sure what that means exactly, but it does appear to suck the life out of whoever its snags. And I just saw one of them coming up just now..." He walked over to a window and looked out. "Yep, it's coming in right now."

All the creatures suddenly looked up at the windows expectantly. They started dragging themselves with surprising speed over to that side of the room. One of the feeding machines, like the one that had taken Ed, appeared outside: the hoses that had sucked the life out of the former editor and the others snaked in through the open windows. The pupae latched on to them and started sucking greedily.

"And there you have it, folks! Another miracle of intergalactic nature. Don't we live in amazing times? Don't forget to stay tuned to Major Domo TV! Remember, *your life may depend upon it*!"

The camera shut down but the audio feed was still running: the cameraman had forgotten to turn off the sound.

"You gotta get a better tag line," Boydsy could be overheard telling his boss.

"What are you talking about? It's fucking great!" Dalrymple protested. "Snappy and compelling. Come on, let's get a drink. I've gotta meet those engineers and figure out how to keep the lights on. And then I want to know what the fuck happened to my boy Gary and his drones...."

Then the sound cut off too, as the petrified cameraman realized his mistake.

• | •

The new base that BB found was in the abandoned offices of an insurance company, close to downtown. It had clearly been inhabited by a large group of people during the chaos. The nests of blanks among the piles of trash suggested the former occupants had joined the ships, since they hadn't bothered to take their bedding with them. And it had several bathrooms with water still in the cisterns, which was important since the taps had finally run dry that morning.

"Christ," Joe muttered as he dropped the bags full of supplies they had brought from the stockade. "What a dump."

"It's temporary," said BB.

Darkman had been moving some of the cubicles in front of the glass doors, building a barricade. He came and joined them in the main floor space.

"How temporary?" said Joe.

BB glanced over at Darkman. "Few days at most."

"How can you be sure?" said Joe. "What do you think is going to happen in the next few days?"

BB pulled up a couple of swivel chairs. "Listen Joe. I heard from Rains this morning. He has this plan, and he needs me and Darkman to meet him this afternoon downtown. We need to do a little recce with him."

"Wait, you mean you're going to leave me here? *Alone?*"

"It's okay, Joe. One of us will be back here tonight to fetch you. Tomorrow morning at the latest. But this could be a little... well, let's just say we're going to need to escort Rains on a job."

"What kind of a job? What if you get killed? I'll be left here and I won't even know."

She reached out and put a hand on his arm. "It's okay, we'll be back. We're not going to leave you..."

"How can you know that? What is this job? Why do you both need to go?"

"We both need to go. But all you need to do is sit here, guard all our stuff for the night and not let anyone in, okay? And I promise you we'll come back."

"What if you don't? I'll be all alone. There's literally no one else out I know or can trust. And there's the alien..."

"Joe," BB said, holding him by the shoulders with both her hands, feeling the tension in his muscles. "We need to do this. If we pull this off, we will have a way out of this. Away from Earth, but not on some Goweetha slaughterhouse."

Joe swallowed hard, his eyes brimming with unshed tears.

"At least tell me where this job is," he said.

"It's at the White House," said BB.

"The White House?!" Joe almost yelled. "Then there's no way you're coming back. You'll be killed for sure...."

"It's not that bad, Joe. Honestly. Rains has access, it's his men who are guarding the Major Domo. It'll be a quick and in and out. Probably no more than ten minutes. We just have to pick something up."

Joe nodded. He knew BB could not be deterred: he also knew her promise to return meant nothing at the end of the day if she ran into the monster.

"Okay," he said at last. "But listen....if you don't come back..." He took his pistol out of its holster, held it in his hand. The message was clear: he didn't want to live in this brutal world alone.

BB gave him a tight smile, and nodded that she understood.

"Don't worry," she said. "We'll be back alright. And save for those bullets for whoever tries to come through that door."

Darkman held out some notebooks. "I was looking in the storeroom for snacks and found these. Figure you could start writing your story. Like Ed said."

Joe nodded and took them. "Thanks," he whispered. "See you tomorrow?"

"You bet, buddy," said Darkman.

· | ·

Dalrymple was stamping around between the saddled horses, in a foul temper.

"Where the fuck is Gary?" he shouted at one of his henchmen. The man, dressed in an expensive shirt and holding a half-empty bottle of champagne, shrugged and muttered something.

"She wants to go fucking hunting again and I don't want to do it if we can't film it. You, Rick, can you ride a horse?" he barked at the cameraman who dogged his every step.

"No? Well, you'd better learn pretty damn quick if you want to keep your cushy job. Meantime, Mark, Dan, get some GoPros on your helmets and try to keep up with me when we ride. We'll just have to post the footage after the hunt. Ok, Boydsy, Rick, come with me, we're gonna go get the queen."

Dalrymple and his right-hand man headed into the White House, the cameraman jogging to keep up. Running upstairs, the camera caught unsteady shots of the Major Domo's ample behind squeezed into tight riding breeches, before straightening up as they reached the queen's room. Dalrymple, breathing hard, knocked and opened the door.

"Your Majesty, we're here. It's hunty-hunty time. You hungry?"

The huge creature was slumped in a far corner, by a large window overlooking the Ellipse. It made no move as the humans entered the room.

"Your Majesty? Queen of all you survey. Wakey wakey, time to go now."

Still no movement. Dalrymple, clearly more annoyed than ever, stepped right up next to her. The creature lay slumped like a giant rock.

Dalrymple stopped and stared. He looked back at his companions and shrugged.

"Give her a prod," suggested Boydsy.

"I'm not giving her a fucking prod!" he spluttered. "She'll wake up and fucking kill me."

Nevertheless, after a minute more of trying to rouse the monster, her servant did indeed give a tentative tap of his riding boot to her recumbent haunch. There was no reaction.

"She asleep?" said Boydsy.

"I don't know," said Dalrymple. He moved around the creature to get a better look at her face. The camera panned with him, catching the sudden change in the butler's expression.

"Oh my god, I think she's dead."

"*What?*" said Boydsy. He stepped up and gave the creature a heavier kick. Still no movement. He pulled a knife from his belt and offered it to Dalrymple.

"Stab her."

"I'm not stabbing her! You fucking stab her," the butler said.

"If I do it and she's alive, she'll kill me. She won't kill you."

"No fucking way!" Dalrymple pushed away the blade then leaned over the huge body to get a better look at the queen's face. The cameraman had edged round behind him by now and zoomed in. The alien's eyes were glassy and rolled up into its skull. A whitish foam had crusted on her beak.

"Oh god," said Dalrymple. "She really is dead."

"You sure?" said Boydsy.

"Totally."

Boydsy plunged the knife into the queen's leg. No response. "Fuck," he said. "She's dead."

"Told you," said Dalrymple. "What the fuck do we do now?"

Boydsy was still staring at the hilt of his knife protruding from the alien, chewing his lip. He shook his head. "I don't know. All I know is we are in deep shit."

It was almost possible to see the cogs whirring in his brain, clicking into place. He turned to the cameraman, his face suddenly contorted with anger. "Wait, have you been filming all of this?"

"Of course," said Rick. "I was told to always film everything."

"Shit!" screamed Boydsy, stepping up and snatching the camera out of his hands. The screen spun blindly. Boydsy was wearing combat gloves and had trouble finding the "off" button, so instead hurled the camera with all his strength against the wall. The screen went black.

"It's off *now*," he could be heard saying, his breathing hard. Clearly, the microphone was still running.

"What do we do?" said Dalrymple, panic in his voice. "Everyone just saw that the fucking queen is dead. They'll be storming this place inside the hour."

"Let me think a minute, for fuck's sake," replied Boyd. He clicked his radio. "Mike, you read me? We have a situation up here. Lock the gates and get everyone out on the perimeter. We have good reason to believe... what? You saw it? *Fuck*. Okay, just get everyone out at the gates until I say so."

"What do we do now?" Dalrymple whined again like a broken record. "What do you think she died of, anyway? Earth germs, like in that Tom Cruise film?"

"How the fuck should I know?" said Boydsy. "Things die, don't they? Now shut your yap and let me think."

There was a minute's silence, then a sound that might have been gloved fingers snapping. "Okay, this is what we do," said Boyd. "We have to load the pupas into a truck and get them out of here. When they hatch out in a week or so, they'll hopefully recognize you as their interlocutor and we can carry on business as before."

"But we have no idea if..."

"It's the only plan we've got," said Boyd. "Same deal, different aliens. They've seen us, they know us, they know we feed 'em. The queen said it'd be a couple of weeks before they were up and about. We just have to keep them safe until then. Nobody will fuck with us once we have a pack of these things."

He was back on the radio, ordering his men to bring all available trucks up to the front doors. Then another, less familiar voice broke in.

"Er, Mr Boyd, sir?"

It was Rick, the cameraman. "I... I just noticed the red audio light is still on. I think it might still be broad..."

His voice was cut off by a roar of pure rage, followed by several shots. The transmission ended.

• | •

"Holy cow," said Trenton. He and Elspeth were sitting on the bed in front of the TV set in their bedroom/cell at the Watergate, watching the season finale of the Major Domo show.

Elspeth stared at the blank screen. "What do you think killed it?"

Trenton shook his head. "Dalrymple said it was already hundreds of years old. Who knows what its lifespan may have been. For sure it wasn't 'earth germs' like he said – like she'd have flown through space just to have died of a cold. Maybe she was like an octopus, gives birth then just dies."

He stood up and started for the door. "Whatever it was, they've got to be stopped. If we could get enough guns to take out those pupae now..."

Trenton was just about to bang on the locked door when it swung open, causing him to jump back in surprise. Rains stepped in and closed the door behind him.

"Rains," Trenton started to say. "You've got to get a squad over to the White House...."

Rains ignored him. "He's here," he said.

"Who's here?" Elspeth and Trenton said in unison.

"Farmer One."

There was a stunned silence.

"His convoy just pulled up out front. He'll be in here in five minutes. You have to get your game faces on."

"Oh no," gasped Elspeth, starting to hyperventilate. "I can't Lester. I can't do this."

"You have to Elspeth. We have no choice."

She came up to him, pleading. "What if we got your men together and went over to the White House now and shot those creatures? Then we could stay here, couldn't we? We wouldn't have to..."

"The harvesters are here to protect the aliens," said Rains. "That is their main task. Humans are mere fodder."

Elspeth looked like she might collapse. Rains held out a hand to steady her. "Believe me, Elspeth, this is the only way. You can do this. You just have to steel yourself."

"Oh god," she gasped, slumping onto the bed.

"Follow me out into the living room now," said Rains. "Stand by the wall furthest from the front door, behind the kitchen counters, like we practiced. Stay there. He probably won't even notice you. And grab your guns."

Trenton pulled the pistols out from their hiding place, slipping one under the waistband of his pants behind his back, hidden under his shirt. Elspeth just stared at hers.

"I just can't..." she began.

Trenton helped her to her feet. "Come on, I'll put it on the shelf under the counter. You can reach for it there, if we need to. Rains, do you have one?"

Rains nodded and pulled back his jacket to show the grip of a handgun under his waistband. He turned and headed out to the living room.

Trenton half dragged Elspeth out into the living room. She leaned on the marble kitchen counter, trying not to collapse. Rains walked straight to the middle of the room and took up a position beside a large easy-chair.

Less than a minute later, the front door opened and two of Rain's guards came in and took up positions on either side of the entrance. They were followed immediately by three other men—burly, serious-looking, clearly all harvesters—who stood by the walls.

Finally, the small, scruffy figure of Farmer One entered the room. He paused briefly by the door, taking in the scene in a glance, then walked over to the sofa where he sat opposite Rains. A waft of garbage and body odor seeped through the room.

Then another figure appeared at the door. As slight as Rains himself, but darker skinned, with more delicate features. The man was, quite simply, beautiful. His appearance had clearly taken Rains by surprise: he gave him a double take and seemed momentarily at a loss.

"Three? I thought you were in Beijing."

"Change of plans," said Farmer Three. "The Friktha were delayed. Supply chain issues. The people of Zone Twelve get to live another three weeks as human beings, rather than avatars."

Rains nodded. "I see," he said. "There were also some changes here, just now. Did you see the queen died?"

Farmer One evinced zero interest. He just stared at Rains. "It is irrelevant. She was thirteen-point-seven percent past the life expectancy for the species. Her main task was the spawning, which was achieved."

"Did my men get the spawn out of the White House?" said Rains.

"It is not our concern," said One. "The terms of the treaty have been fulfilled. Our work here is done."

Rains nodded. Elspeth, trying not to stare at the men at the far end of the room, felt a faint glimmer of hope at One's pronouncement.

"Except for one thing," the tiny figure added.

Rains nodded. Elspeth could see him tense up.

Farmer One's hand gesture was so fleeting, so casual, that Elspeth almost missed it. It was the same flick of the wrist that Rains had shown her: the move that sent humans into a trance. Elspeth froze.

Her immediate instinct was to turn her head to see if Trenton had also caught the casual hand movement, but she caught herself just in time. Picking a point above Farmer One's head, as Rains had trained her, she forced herself to simply stare. The five harvesters were all—just—in her field of vision.

Satisfied that he had neutralized the humans in the room, Farmer One continued.

"Farmer Twenty-Three was in possession of an unauthorized device. She was eliminated for possessing it. It has recently come to my attention that she had passed it to you, and that you kept it at a safe house. Since you did not report it, I can only conclude you intended to use it."

Elspeth was glad she had been leaning on the countertop when One made his gesture. She pressed down with her hands to stem the shaking in her body. Ahead, she could see all the men in her field of vision staring at Rains, just like a jury.

All except one. With a growing sense of alarm, Elspeth noticed that the one on the far right was staring directly at her.

Her blood froze in her veins. It was all she could do not to stare directly back at the man: it was almost too tempting to flick her eyes between Farmer One and him. Instead, she had to keep staring at the space between them, so she could see just make out both of them.

Rains was standing with his hands folded in front of him. "I have no idea what you are talking about, One. What safehouse? What device?"

"You met one of Twenty Three's descendants in Toronto. We tracked him to a safe house in Virginia. We found this hidden in a strong box there," said One, reaching into an inside pocket and pulling out what looked like a sky-blue golf ball. He held it out in front of him for all to see.

Rains shrugged. "I've never seen that before. What is it?"

"A transponder," said One. "From a trespassing alien ship that crashed in New Mexico."

The man who had been staring at Elspeth suddenly began to move. She desperately tried not to look away from the spot above One's head, but the man was coming slowly toward her now. He looked disturbingly familiar: heavyset, blue eyes, a reddish goatee. *Holy god*, she realized: it was the man who had attacked her at the safe house in Virginia. Her legs seemed to turn to jelly, but she somehow managed to remain immobile, pressing harder onto the countertop. Trying not to breathe too hard.

"Interesting," said Rains, almost nonchalant. "Inali and I didn't see much of each other in the decades before you killed her. How did she come by this?"

Elspeth could barely focus on the kangaroo court in front of her. The man from the safe house was standing right next to her now, staring with unnerving intensity. He leaned in close, his face just inches from hers. Elspeth felt a bead of sweat trickle down her temple: fortunately it was on the other side of her face to where he was standing.

She kept staring dead ahead, pulse racing, trying not to blink.

Farmer Three opened his mouth for the first time. "Why did you meet the human in Toronto, Barbegal?"

Goatee was lifting his hand to Elspeth's face: she saw his extended index finger, cracked fingernail, hovering close to her right eye. *Oh god, I'm going to blink...*

Rains suddenly turned around and barked at the man. "What the hell are you doing with that woman?" he demanded.

The man's finger went down and he turned to address Farmer One.

"Boss, this is the woman I saw in..."

But he didn't get any further. Rains moved with alarming speed and was on him in a second. The man made an "ooof" sound and clutched a small blade sticking from his chest. Rains leapt nimbly over the countertop, yelling out, "Down! Now!"

Elspeth fell to her knees as the first gunshots rang out. Plaster from the bullet impacts sprayed over her head and she clutched her face with her hands. When she glanced up, Rains was beside her, gun hand over the counter and firing blindly at the far end of the room. She was relieved to see Trenton was crouched at the far end of the counter too, holding his own pistol round the edge to fire at the execution squad.

That was when Elspeth remembered that she too had a gun, stashed by Trenton behind the martini glasses. She knocked over a few as she fumbled to find it, then handed it to Rains. He nodded in thanks.

The shooting suddenly stopped. There were assorted groans from the far end of the room, lending Elspeth hoped that at least some of their attackers were seriously wounded. Then that deadpan voice broke through the smoky silence.

"Seventeen, I don't know how you think you will get out of here. I suppose I should congratulate you on your little plan. Quite clever. But you are trapped. There are more of my men on their way up already. If you come out now, I will spare your humans. They clearly mean something to you, since they foolishly risked their lives for you."

Rains looked at Elspeth. She shook her head. "You can't trust him," she hissed. "He'll just kill us all, anyway."

Rains nodded, then reached out and stroked her cheek. When he withdrew his hand, she saw blood on his fingertips. She couldn't tell if it was his or hers. He laid his pistol on the floor next to her and slowly stood up.

"Here I am, One. Are you going to take the shot?"

"Of course," came the monochrome voice. "It is my duty as first of the line."

Elspeth heard a couple of steps on the hardwood floor. She grabbed Rain's gun from the floor and was rising to her feet when an earth-shattering crash blew in the entire balcony window. She was thrown back to the floor in a shower of glass. A sickening screech of metal, mingled with shouts and then a juddering crunch filled the room. Rains had dropped to the floor again, curled into a ball with his hands over his head. Elspeth stared, confused, then did the same.

An ear-splitting boom ripped through the room. Elspeth felt as though the very fabric of the universe was being rent asunder.

Then a crushing silence. Smoke and dust clouded the room. As the ringing in her ears receded, all she could hear was an insistent, mechanical scraping, followed by a feeble groan. Finally, Rains stood up once again and disappeared slowly around the counter. No gunshots or voices this time.

Elspeth clawed her way to her feet.

Through the settling dust, she could make out the wreckage of a large metallic machine. It was a good five feet long and had plowed straight into Farmer One and his men before smashing into the far wall. A pair of legs protruded from the pile of twisted debris.

Rains' phone was ringing. He pulled it out.

"Yes, BB, it worked. Thank you. Tell Gary he's free to go now. Or he can stay with us, if he prefers."

Who's Gary? thought Elspeth. Then it clicked. The Major Domo's ex-CIA drone operator. And the machine that had taken out Farmer One was the drone he'd been filming the queen's hunting trips with.

"How did you get Gary?" Trenton asked, stepping over the twisted metal of the drone.

"We kidnapped him," Rains said, as though it were self-evident. "Dalrymple saw me as an ally, so I was allowed in and out of the White House as I pleased. I took BB and Darkman and we found him in the truck he used as a mobile control command center. I put him under my thrall and we just drove him out of there. Simple, really. Getting the explosives attached to the drone was the hardest part."

A groan came from behind the crushed sofa. Trenton stepped over, holding his pistol in front of him.

"This one's still alive," he said. "Your old buddy Three."

Rains picked his way between the splintered furniture and the congealing pools of blood. Farmer Three was pinned down by the snapped sofa, an oozing gash in his side. He looked up at Rains, eyes slightly unfocused. Then he smiled.

"Looks like I'm about to die after all, Barbegal. Maybe now I'll finally know what it's like to be human."

"Are you afraid?" said Rains.

Three's handsome face crinkled into a frown as he considered the question.

"No," he said at last.

"Then you don't know what it is to be human," said Rains. "You'll die as you've always lived: just an unfeeling machine."

He raised his gun and fired. Elspeth flinched at the report of the shot, grateful that the sofa had shielded her view.

Rains turned to Trenton. "Help me move this wreckage. One had the transponder in his hand when the drone hit. We can only hope it wasn't damaged."

They froze at the sound of running feet. Trenton raised his gun and pointed it at the door as seven men in full combat gear burst into the room. Harvesters, by the looks of them. The men trained their rifles on Trenton and Rains, but Rains stood calmly by, hands hanging at his sides.

"He's under there," he said, nodding at the drone. "He summoned you to kill us, but we killed him instead. It's over."

The men looked confused. Rains spoke to them calmly, matter-of-fact. "The alien queen is dead, too. If you leave now, with all your weapons and vehicles, you may be able to find a place somewhere out there to live quietly for a while. There is nothing for you here."

The men stood there, undecided. They had been summoned by Farmer One to kill these people. Now their leader had to abruptly recalibrate. He was still deciding whether to follow through on his boss' last order when a woman's voice shouted out behind them.

"Freeze! Drop your weapons or we will open fire!"

The men all spun round to see BB, Darkman, Joe and Gary the drone operator pointing automatic rifles at them. Trenton and Rains raised their weapons too.

"You can keep your guns," said Rains. "Just take your magazines out and leave. It's over."

The man at the front, clearly the leader of this small unit, nodded and unclipped the magazine from his submachine gun. The others followed suit. The commander kicked the leg of Farmer One that was protruding from under the twisted metal. He turned to Rains. "You want to come with us? We could use a man like you."

Rains shook his head. "I have some unfinished business here."

"Good luck then," said the squad leader. "Will you bury them?"

Rains shook his head. "No more than we'd bury the drone." The man nodded. Then he turned and led his squad out of the apartment.

"That was close," said Trenton, lowering his gun.

BB stepped up and embraced him. Then she gave Elspeth a long, firm hug, while the men clasped each other and slapped each other's shoulders. Gary, the former CIA drone operator, stood to one side, eyeing the scene with a guarded expression.

"Alright," said Rains. "Let's move the drone."

It was surprisingly light. Gary and Trenton lifted it off Farmer One and his men with relative ease, although one of its bent propellers had embedded itself deep in Farmer One's ribcage. It took longer to find the transponder, which had rolled across the floor and was trapped underneath one of the henchmen's bodies.

Darkman picked it up and gingerly handed it to Rains. The whole group gathered around as Rains took a cloth from the kitchen and gently wiped the blood and dust from the orb, revealing three smooth, gold buttons inset with strange symbols. Rains had long since memorized the activation sequence, but even so, he pulled out the letter from the long-dead Inali to make sure he wasn't about to blow them all to smithereens.

He pressed the first button. Nothing happened. He pressed the second, and smiled.

"Who wants to go for a little ride?" he said.

And he pressed the final button.

THE END

ABOUT THE AUTHOR

James Hider is an author, ghostwriter and former war correspondent who has lived and worked in the Middle East, Latin America, eastern Europe and the United States. He currently lives in Washington DC with his wife, daughter, two dogs and a cat.

NOTE FROM THE AUTHOR

Word-of-mouth is crucial for any author to succeed. If you enjoyed *Ripe*, please leave a review online—anywhere you are able. Even if it's just a sentence or two. It would make all the difference and would be very much appreciated.

Thanks!
James Hider

We hope you enjoyed reading this title from:

www.blackrosewriting.com

Subscribe to our mailing list – *The Rosevine* – and receive **FREE** books, daily
deals, and stay current with news about upcoming
releases and our hottest authors.
Scan the QR code below to sign up.

Already a subscriber? Please accept a sincere thank you for being a fan of
Black Rose Writing authors.

View other Black Rose Writing titles at
www.blackrosewriting.com/books and use promo code
PRINT to receive a **20% discount** when purchasing.

Made in the USA
Las Vegas, NV
12 December 2024

b38933d7-df13-45e6-a4d3-4263623d4b18R01